# TAKES ONE
# TO KNOW ONE

Center Point
Large Print

**This Large Print Book carries the
Seal of Approval of N.A.V.H.**

# TAKES ONE
# TO
# KNOW ONE

## SUSAN ISAACS

CENTER POINT LARGE PRINT
THORNDIKE, MAINE

This Center Point Large Print edition
is published in the year 2020 by arrangement with
Grove Atlantic, Inc.

The text of this Large Print edition is unabridged.
In other aspects, this book may vary
from the original edition.
Printed in the United States of America
on permanent paper.
Set in 16-point Times New Roman type.

ISBN: 978-1-64358-516-1

The Library of Congress has cataloged this record under
Library of Congress Control Number: 2019954785

To my five muses,
Nathan, Molly, Charlie, Edmund, Nicholas,
with love and gratitude

# TAKES ONE
# TO KNOW ONE

# 1

Last night I dreamt I went to Queens Boulevard again. With the stately steps of a bride, I crossed to my parents' apartment house in Forest Hills. Its ten stories of once-red brick had darkened from decades of traffic exhaust, but in the dream it gleamed mahogany. A few doors down from the building, the awning on Perlmutter's Comfort Footwear, bent out of shape in some long-ago hurricane, still groaned. But in my REM sleep, the grinding metal sounded rich and Bach-like, a phrase from a cello suite. Not only that: the orthopedic shoes in Perlmutter's window looked so exquisite to me I thought (or maybe said aloud), *They deserve an exhibit at the Met.* Right next door was Norman's Coffee Shop, where my mother warned me never to eat. But the aroma was irresistible and, as I stood on the median between east- and westbound traffic, I unzipped my backpack and discovered a perfect grilled cheese sandwich.

"I dreamed I was living in Queens again," I told Josh the next morning. We were in the bathroom, at our separate sinks on opposite walls. The countertops were pink-veined marble, as was the floor. Not really garish: his late wife Dawn's style had been safely upscale suburban, which meant excess that never shouted, *Hey look, great taste!* It only whispered it. (Poor Dawn. When she suddenly, shockingly died during a Pilates session from what turned out to be a theretofore undetected congenital coronary artery abnormality, everyone was stunned. Their friends told Josh and each other: *She was the last person in the world you'd think would die young.* Eliza was five years old then.)

Still, a couple of times when I was alone, sitting on the toilet in its own vestibule, I peered out into the huge, polished marble box and saw less a master bath than a family mausoleum. (Dawn herself was in Mount Eden Cemetery in Westchester. She'd grown up in Scarsdale and had once joked she didn't want to be buried with Josh's Grampy Seymour et al. and spend eternity on Long Island.)

As usual, Josh was far ahead of me, already showered, a towel wrapped around about half of why I'd married him. He was shaking aftershave, limey and rummy, into his palm. That sounds like something you'd say meh to at a Virgin Islands happy hour, but this came in a stout English bottle and smelled expensive, which it undoubtedly was.

"What were you doing in Queens again?" he asked. "Was I there?"

I squeezed a squiggle of Crest 3D White onto my brush, which I held aloft like Lady Liberty's torch. "No, just me. I was crossing the boulevard and all of a sudden the world's best grilled cheese sandwich was in my hand."

Tweet-tweet. Outside the arched window over the Jacuzzi, there was a blue sky with cotton-ball clouds. It was a prime May morning. A choir of local birds was serenading us from the branches of a sycamore and a cup-and-saucer magnolia. Or something like that: after three years of marriage and suburban life, I was still working on tree and flower names.

"God," he said. "I don't think I've had a grilled cheese since . . . I was up at Cambridge." That meant Harvard. Simply by his not saying the name, it boomed and echoed off the walls. Not that Josh was consciously boasting. Four years in college there plus three years in law school had given his DNA a crimson tinge. Maybe that Cambridge moniker was an act of charity, to save others the humiliation that they'd gone to some lesser institution. Like Stanford. I was always tempted to come back with: *When I was over in Flushing.*

Josh was no snob. The other half of the reason I married him (once I got over the shock and flattery of his wanting to marry me) was his character: Decency, like treating people up and

11

down the social ladder with equal respect. He was sincere, responsible, and an equal opportunity listener to women and men. It was a given I wanted marriage, a normal life. There was nothing more I thought I wanted than what Josh offered.

When Dawn died suddenly, Josh traded in a partnership at a white-shoe Manhattan firm for a federal judgeship so he wouldn't have to travel and be away from his daughter. It meant a four-mil pay cut, but he was a genuinely good father. True, his lifestyle didn't have to change since both he and Dawn had been born into what I'd only heard about: family money. Not major wealth, like oil gushing from the ground for the Rockefellers, but Tiny Togs (his family) and Cap'n Jake's Cough Drops (hers) were still in business and replenishing third-generation trusts.

His colleagues from the law firm and on the bench routinely said he was brilliant. However, since his brilliance was in jurisprudence, what I saw outside the courtroom was your basic smart person. Josh could fit in with any group, could talk the talk on sports, politics, kids, cars. If an arcane subject arose—such as the time a neighbor explained that she was raising Sussex chickens—he'd ask questions, genuinely curious.

Josh was a touch over six feet, but too honest to call himself six foot one. His body was that male ideal, an inverted isosceles triangle. People constantly went on about his being handsome, as in: *Oh my gawd. your husband is stunning.* Jaws slackened because of Josh's green eyes; they were mesmerizing, like polished jade.

Truthfully? His pedigree, his looks, and his being such a clear winner in life's lottery were definitely alluring. But I also fell for Josh because I fell in love with Eliza. The horror-movie step-daughter I dreaded—a nine-year-old with a Colt semiauto carbine on her shoulder ready to go against any woman moving in on her father, or a bratty, entitled rich kid—never materialized. Blessedly, she was not a precocious child who could navigate a cocktail party. Eliza was just an ordinary brown-eyed, curly-haired girl with a genuine smile and nice enough manners. No star quality, not even best supporting.

Even the youngest child who loses a parent never gets over the loss. But as memories faded, Dawn became less of a real person. She was the sum of all the stories Eliza had been told about her: a distant, benevolent presence. To Eliza's mind, Dawn was more of a tennis-playing guardian angel than an idealized, perfect dead mother who could never be replaced.

Just a few hours after I met Eliza for the first time at the house on Long Island, she said, "My dad told me it was okay if I asked to see your badge." Sure: at that point, I was still with the bureau. My cover was outreach to Arabic-

13

speaking communities: *As-salamu alaykum. I'm Corie, your friend from the FBI.* I taught her my flipping-it-open technique, and she kept practicing saying, "Eliza Geller, special agent." When I caught Josh's beaming smile, the glint of excitement in his eye, I figured he and I were a done deal.

And we were a done deal, though when his eyes caught mine that morning in the bathroom mirror, he wasn't so much beaming as affectionately crinkling up one corner of his mouth. I watched as he ended his daily bathroom routine— squeezing a teensy dab of gel into his left hand, rubbing his palms in circles to heat it, then cautiously running his fingers through his hair so as not to look like one of those mousse men. "What's on your calendar today?" he asked. Then answered: "Right, it's Wednesday. Your group." The suburban self-employed at their weekly lunch. As he walked out of the bathroom into the room behind it—one giant walk-in closet— he couldn't avoid my response, a groan. So he said, "If you say it's boring and you're always dreading it, why don't you quit?"

A judicious question.

Five hours later, I was on the road, early for lunch. Even if I dragged my feet, I'd be on time. True, I could stroll over to Manhasset Bay for a couple of minutes and watch sunbeams exploding on the caps of waves, inhale the aroma of washed-up mussel shells. I'd be a little late to lunch, but at least I'd feel alive. Because right then, I was already numb with pre-boredom, knowing too well what the next hour and a half would bring.

I heard my name shouted across the two lanes of Shorehaven's Main Street: "Corie! Caaaw-reee! Over here." A squawk, as if one of the more clever gulls had mastered English.

Even before I turned, I knew it was Phoebe Melowicz, eBay reseller with a 99.7 percent positive feedback. Ever on the lookout, her head swiveling right-left-right, she waited for a flatulent minivan, a rumbling fish-delivery truck, and then a top-down BMW convertible (its panache diminished by its driver, a guy older than Kaiser Wilhelm). It's not that I couldn't have escaped Phoebe. At my peak, twelve years earlier, when the bureau transferred me from DC to New York to be part of the Joint Terrorism Task Force, I finished the marathon in four hours and forty-two minutes. But she might take offense if I were to cut and run, particularly since we were both headed to the same restaurant—the same table, actually.

"How's things in the pub biz?" she asked when she was beside me. Just as Josh had changed careers for his daughter, so had I. (He did say he didn't see why I couldn't stay with the bureau if that's what I wanted. But sometimes the pressure there left me close to numb, and that hadn't seemed the way to start out with Eliza.) "I read real books are making a comeback," Phoebe screeched. Even up close, she always spoke too loud, as if she suspected all humanity had suffered a hearing loss. At the beginning, I figured she might be somewhat deaf herself and therefore be unable to hear how EARSPLITTING her voice was. Then one Wednesday I discovered she could pick up a whispered, *"Wizard of Oz* collectible plates," across a crowded room.

Phoebe clasped her raffia clutch bag to her narrow chest, apparently ready to be thrilled by whatever I said, and added: "Find any new bestsellers?" I freelanced for three large literary agencies—two in New York, one in London—scouting contemporary Arabic work, mostly fiction, that could succeed in the English-speaking market.

"Well, I'm still looking for the next Ahdaf Soueif," I told her cheerfully, figuring that would buy me thirty seconds of silence during which Phoebe would work on some predictable follow-up question. *Who's Ahdaf Whatsis?* or *What made someone Jewish—you're Jewish, right?—learn Arabic?*

But her follow-up neurons weren't firing. She immediately segued to: "You'll never guess what the trendingest item is on eBay!" I glanced at her shapeless dress, an upmarket potato sack, probably from some season when designers decided to exalt Depression-era farm labor, nicely hemmed, sleeveless of course. We started toward the restaurant.

Phoebe was walking too close to me. I kept edging away, but about ten feet before we reached the front door, I saw I was about to veer from curb into gutter. So I sucked it up, even though I wasn't good with overcloseness. Having to rub up against the chicken-skinned upper-arm flesh of someone who wasn't family or an extremely close friend? Next to a nightmare.

"I give up." I smiled, calling to mind that TED talk that explains even fake smiling will put you in a good mood. It almost always worked, but not this time. "What's trending on eBay?" I asked.

"Girdles from the 1950s!" Of the whole group, I knew Phoebe Melowicz the least, because she dealt mostly in vintage clothes and shoes. Although her business interested me more than data mining or landscape drainage—occupations of two other members—"vintage" is better viewed than inhaled. Phoebe exuded a vague aroma of dead people's closets. Each Wednesday I made a point of breathing in through my mouth while greeting her with an excessively hearty: "Hey, good to see you!"—then sitting anywhere but next to her.

17

"What makes girdles such a hot item?" I asked. "And doesn't the elastic or rubber or whatever was in them disintegrate after all those years?"

She might have answered, but we reached the restaurant. Just as I was about to haul open the wood door, Pete Delaney, packaging designer with a home office, came across Main Street from the parking lot. Pete's own packaging was unremarkable. Though he wore a nice enough long-sleeve blue shirt with a teeny orange polo pony, his pants were strictly old-guy—the baggy kind that makes men look as if penises hadn't yet been invented.

Another lunch person, Iris Kubel, who owned the Movable Garden, once told me she'd been on line for car wash day at the high school and caught sight of Pete, who was serving as one of the volunteer supervisors. "So he'd gotten wet and was wearing this Yankees T-shirt. It's a good thing my windows were up because I probably said, 'Oh my God!' Like his muscles had muscles! Can you believe that?" Actually, I couldn't believe that. Looking at Pete now, you would in no way think *muscles* any more than you would *art* or *design*. You'd think: *Hmm, deputy commissioner of roads in Utica, New York.*

"Afternoon," he greeted us. Pete's accent didn't say much about him, though no one would accuse him of coming from New York. He had those pleasant, middle-aged, out-of-town manners. As always, he pulled open the heavy door and held it for us. However, a nanosecond after we were in, he quickly zigzagged around the tables, ensuring neither of us could get to his favorite seat. Phoebe chose a chair on the opposite side of the round table, so I sat to the right of Pete.

Over the next fifteen minutes, the rest of the suburban seven drifted in: Marcalynn who had cornered the market in writing speeches for Long Island Republicans running for lesser offices; John the landscape drainage guy; Darby the freelance retoucher who had once worked for *People*; Iris the flowerpot garden queen. All nice enough, all out on their own, working from home.

We had already told each other the stories of how we got to where we now were. A Republican congressman lost a primary. A local antique/junque-store owner retired to Delray Beach. Thus, Marcalynn and Phoebe no longer got a paycheck. They no longer had to set their alarms. When you're "let go," that's what happens: nothing.

But for most of the seven, working from home wasn't the result of the perennial vagaries of career wins and losses. They'd been caught up in a global trauma—the Great Recession. All over the world, dreams dropped dead. Careers disintegrated, companies imploded. True, times

19

eventually got better, but some of the people who'd been cast out never found their way back into corporate America. Many in the group hadn't chosen to work from home. That was all they had.

I was probably the only member who'd opted for a downsized life. My job hadn't vanished. I definitely hadn't been fired. I had quit with no plans of getting back to where I'd been. So I really didn't fit in. Also, since I'd married Josh, money wasn't an issue. I'd known when I signed up that the FBI was not the road to gold, but I had never wanted gold. Okay, I had a lottery daydream or two, a wish to fly business class, to stay in hotels in which squeals in the night came from venerable plumbing, not rodents. But since I moved to Long Island, it was as though I'd fulfilled some archaic adage: *Ne'er seek the pot o' gold and ye will find it.*

So in terms of the group, I didn't really belong. I should have realized that truth two years and seven months earlier, after I was spurred to action by a short piece in the *Shorehaven Sentinel* titled "Freelancers Unite over Lunch," about residents with home offices who got together once a week. Had I given it some thought, I should have known that the group might not be the path to friendship. But I was new to the suburbs and lonely. My congenital urban skepticism wasn't functioning at its peak when I read how the six local entrepreneurs who "linked up over salads and sandwiches" would welcome new members. Instead of thinking it would be tedious, I thought: *Cool! Maybe I'll find a soul mate.* Or at least feel a sense of community.

Each Wednesday we followed the same format. Fifteen minutes of free-range chitchat. The ritual passing around of cell phone photos to certify a happy life: pics of the kids with some piece of sports equipment, the new outdoor pizza oven, Posey the kitten inside what I hoped was an empty Cheerios box. Even though I grew up just fifteen miles west of Shorehaven, in Queens, this gotta-be-happy mind-set was foreign to me.

Of course, we of the five boroughs did not pass around snapshots of Aunt Minnie in hospice care. We weren't so concerned about proving to our neighbors that all was well or at least quasi-well. Also, we kept more of a distance. That was probably because we already knew too much about their lives via thin walls and open windows: screaming, pot throwing, headboard humping, TV preferences, Chinese takeout for dinner. I grew up in apartment 5B in Forest Hills, then spent most of my early adult life in a walk-up in Adams Morgan in DC, followed by a studio apartment on a noncool block of Chelsea in Manhattan. In those places, neighborliness was a terse exchange about weather.

Anyway, after about fifteen minutes, the

21

members of the Wednesday group would order. At La Cuisine Délicieuse, everything had a French accent, including the décor. Lots of wood paneling, like a Parisian brasserie. Sconces on the walls, as if to dispel the fog created by existentialists puffing Gauloises. Traditional French food posters, of course, such as Beurre d'Isigny featuring a kitchen maid with creamy boobs like humongous butter balls, holding a large box of the product.

Behind the receptionist's stand near the front door were framed, yellowing reviews from very local food critics—"What's new on Main Street in Shorehaven? *Incroyable* hamburgers and pomme frites at La Cuisine Délicieuse! ★ ★ ★ ½"

We socialized and gave each other support. Like: *You're lucky he didn't sign up with you because he sounds like a total asshole. I know a great mommy marketing consultant.* After we ordered, one of us—we rotated weekly—would speak about what was going on in his/her business life: we called this show-and-tell. That week, it was Lucy Winters's turn. She came prepared with bar graphs and pie charts to illustrate what was going down, data mining–wise. "So I found this amazing sequential pattern for one of my clients," she began. She held up one of her charts, but as her seat was on the other side of me, I would have had to risk leaning forward and dipping my left nipple into the soupe à l'oignon to observe the data. "Consumers who buy motorcycle goggles will buy another pair with polarized lenses within *a month*."

Unless I stuck my fingers into my ears, it was impossible to tune out Lucy completely. But, as in the last couple of weeks, I found myself diverted: I was checking out Pete Delaney, the guy sitting to my other side. Not for any sexual thrill, despite the report about his muscles. But still, a pretty thorough checkout; I had the ability to look at people without seeming to look. My dad had been a New York City cop, a detective, so either it was in my DNA or I picked it up from him as a kid. I put it to good use at the FBI, seeming unaware of or at most indifferent to a conversation while taking in every word.

But this was the first time I got within inches of Pete, seated beside him. There was no immediately riveting finding, unless you counted the liver spots on his right temple, though maybe they were three-dimensional freckles. Weird for a middle-aged guy. Dots and a longer thing. They were arranged like five stars and a crescent, kind of what you'd expect on the flag of some small country bordering on Russia.

"And wait'll you hear this!" Lucy Winters was saying. She tapped her chart with one of her long aqua-polished nails. Each had a different flower painted on it. Her right index finger sported a daisy. "If the consumer's gross income is over fifty thou, he'll buy *another* pair of goggles with interchangeable lenses, the kind for all weather conditions, and within six months!"

I barely heard the group's comments, like whether motorcycle goggles were retro cool or merely retro or whether such buying behavior was a symptom of the decline of Western civilization. To be honest, I didn't want to hear them. Plus, I was wondering why Pete Delaney, packaging designer with brownish things on the side of his head, thinning hair, possibly A+ pecs, and good manners, seemed compelled always to arrive early and sit in that same seat. All right, Pete could be one of those people who believe it's always better to get someplace a little early, especially when he had a need to grab a certain seat at the restaurant's one large round table. I spoke back to that tiny speculating voice in my head: of course it wasn't a Tony Soprano maneuver, facing the door so he could be on the lookout for a goon from a rival family. He couldn't have chosen that place for the water view because there was only the thinnest strip of the bay visible. Nine-tenths of what you saw through the glass was the municipal parking lot diagonally across Main Street.

Pete seemed far more engaged than I in listening to tales of the self-employed, as well as sharing his own experiences. He acted like part of the group. Still, as I watched each week, his eyes always returned to one spot in the parking lot: wherever his car happened to be. Weird.

I then recalled that months earlier I'd walked back to the lot after a Wednesday lunch to discover that I had parked a couple of cars down from Pete's. He'd gotten there first—so quickly I hadn't even noticed him walking ahead of me— and was already inside his SUV. It was a Jeep, very high-end, the kind with a sunroof and fancy wheel covers. Not gaudy at all: a dark gray car so clean I noticed a cloud reflected in the paint of its front hood. Nice enough, definitely the kind of car a packaging designer could comfortably choose: classic styling and, in this parking lot on Long Island, unusual simply because it was American made. Probably top of the line, Jeepwise. I'd seen some of Pete's work when it was his turn for show-and-tell, and he was definitely talented. I remember thinking: *Good for him. Getting canned in 2008 by some big ad agency and now doing well on his own.*

So along with onion soup and a small salad, lunch became me watching Pete Delaney watching his car. I wondered again: *What's with him?* Was he so fearful of somebody backing into his rear bumper? Sure, it was a risk, but it was a risk everybody took. Plus it wasn't a Maserati. Was it apprehension about midday car thievery? Please. Theft of a locked and alarmed SUV from

25

a public parking lot observable from any spot on lower Main Street? Hardly.

Pete didn't seem the nervous type. Not that I knew him—or any of them for that matter—very well. I wouldn't have called him outgoing, though a couple of times I'd overheard him being friendly in that neighborly suburban way: *No problem at all to bring over my snowblower,* he'd once told Marcalynn.

What was he worried about? The thought of a dead body in the back of his Jeep amused me for a minute, but I had to admit it was unlikely there'd be a new body every Wednesday, and the same old corpse would naturally be putrid enough to attract attention. Diamonds? Drugs?

Drugs were conceivable, mainly because (now I was down to the sludge of barely remembered observations) Pete kept getting new cell phones. For a small, supposedly informal gathering, the lunch group had many rules, including one that required us to turn off our mobile phones and put them on the table during show-and-tell. A few years earlier, drug dealers were switching phones—using disposable phones called burners—a lot more often than Pete did. Now, a lot of them had upgraded to burner apps or encryption. Anyway, if Pete were trying to hide the fact that he got new phones, he'd simply bring the same old one to lunch every week.

Besides, anyone stashing drugs in a Jeep was

irreparably dumb, something that Pete Delaney didn't seem to be. Would he hide valuables there, like top secret prototypes of a new line of plastic bags and take-out hot cups he'd designed for some client, like a chain of truck stops? Conceivably, but if that were the case, why would he hide important items in his car on a weekly basis when there were safes and rentable storage units?

Truly, the only intriguing aspect of Pete—a guy so careful, so predictable—was that he was so nothing. The rest of us in the group, me included, openly carried around sacks of our qualities—humor, brains, empathy, pettiness—all those normal human attributes. Big, small, even micro sacks, depending on the individual. But Pete seemed either to have zero baggage or to have put his personality in storage. His friendly neighbor shtick felt like an add-on, as if he recognized that he, too, needed some gear to tote around.

Maybe I was spending too much time these days in make-believe worlds. I covered ten to fifteen novels a month and sent reports to the literary agencies I worked for. An excess of fiction could make reality seem supremely dull with its crappy dialogue and lack of coincidences. It could lead to an unfulfilled longing for scintillation. Compared with the six other suburbanites at the Wednesday table, I was perhaps the only one who was a bit unmoored. Maybe I was creating a story for Pete where none existed.

Unlike the others in the group, I hadn't chosen this turf or been born to it. My husband, though, was born to it. Well, the house we lived in was more his late wife's domain, as she'd fallen in love with it the instant the realtor pulled into the driveway. It was a solid red brick house on three acres. "Georgian revival," my best friend, Wynne, informed me. Wynne was the last word on style. I wouldn't have chosen the place any more than I'd have chosen a yurt in exurban Mongolia.

As I picked crusted cheese off the side of the onion soup crock, I decided my speculating about Pete Delaney's nondiscernible personality, or (on the other hand) his fixation on his Jeep, was not purely a result of Lucy's being tedious. Neither did it come from my reading four or five thousand pages per month. My qualms about him were partly that I indeed sensed something weird. While this *Something's not right* suspicion does occur regularly in crime fiction—and, true, the written-in-Arabic mystery had been enjoying a resurgence recently—I was not simply re-creating the plot of some whodunit set in Algiers that I'd read.

"When something strikes you as weird," one of the instructors at the academy in Quantico told us, "do you say, 'Now isn't that something?' No. Course not."

Before I earned my living on the outskirts of

publishing, I used my Arabic (and good high school Spanish) for the FBI for over ten years. That was why I had a sense of what a drug dealer should look like. I didn't qualify as a narco maven, but when I moved from DC to New York to work in the Joint Terrorism Task Force, some of what I did involved the Tri-Border Area in South America; that's where Argentina, Brazil, and Paraguay come together. Islamic terrorist groups use that territory for drug trafficking and money laundering, mostly to finance activities in the Americas. I got to know some of the DEA, NYPD, and ATF people and interviewed Arabic-speaking suspects or informants.

Pete didn't seem like those drug dealers at all. Unless they were benumbed by their own inventory, even the most seemingly laid-back dealers had a hyperawareness about them, as if they filed down their nerve endings to get a better feel of what was going on around them. Their creepy alertness made regular people uncomfortable. But Pete wasn't like this, even with the intensity of his Jeep focus. He didn't say much, but when he did say something it was guaranteed to be unexciting. I imagined nearly everyone who met him would place him somewhere between "relentlessly bland" and "nice" on the line of human behavior.

"You ask yourself," the instructor said with surprising patience, "*why* is that weird?"

Okay: what was wrong with ordinary? When I married Joshua Geller and adopted Eliza a year later, I had such a bubbly vision of suburban life. *Ah, normality!* I pictured a racially and ethnically diverse group of friends holding Starbucks cups, dressed like a Ralph Lauren ad, each demanding to know if I thought Naguib Mahfouz deserved to win the Nobel Prize.

It's not that I hadn't met perfectly pleasant people, but I hadn't bonded with anyone in Shorehaven except Josh and Eliza. My clique was still composed of my parents in Queens and my best friend since first grade, Wynne, who now lived in Tribeca. My other friends were a couple of classmates from Queens College, the agents and a cop I'd worked with, and a former assistant US attorney who was now in private practice, but they had become people in other universes with whom I occasionally played catch-up. They weren't familiars to keep up last week's conversation on politics or sports or what are you streaming.

"Bread?" Pete asked me. Apparently he'd been holding a basket in front of me and I hadn't noticed.

I looked down, hoping for a *ficelle*, that skinny roll with the delectable outer hardness that puts up a spirited fight when you chew it. But there were only a few slices of blah baguette. "No thanks," I said and set the basket on top of Lucy's plate, as she was still presenting what I prayed was her final bar graph.

Everyone in the group, actually, assumed I'd been in publishing since graduating from college, a belief I never tried to correct. It's not that I was undercover or anything. It's just that when you're in the FBI doing counterterrorism or doing contract work in that field as I sometimes still did, the bureau wanted you under the radar. No questions, no awkward answers.

Since I'd retired from the bureau, it was just easier to tell people: "I freelance for three literary agencies. Publishers are finally starting to take an interest in modern Arabic fiction. No, no translating. I'm not subtle enough and my knowledge of the language isn't all that deep. This is just an excuse for getting paid to read." Around town, only Josh and Eliza knew the truth. (After I retired from the bureau, moved to Shorehaven, and took Josh's name, I was explaining to Eliza the need to keep my FBI connection secret—a big ask for a kid her age. I suppose I went on too long, trying not to scare her and not to sound worried that she'd blab. Once I finished, Josh was more direct: "It's the law, Eliza. Also"—as he paused for emphasis, his face more animated and dramatic than I'd ever seen it, she held her breath—"it's important for all of us that she can feel she fits in, that neighbors don't think she's something out of the ordinary."

Her lips formed a circle and she exhaled slowly. I was expecting a weary *I get it.* Instead she said resolutely: "I understand.")

While I never said anything blatantly false about my having been a special agent for the FBI, I was quasi-covert. Like my dad had (too) often told me: "Where's it written that you got to tell all? What's with women? They have this 'be open' thing. You think it does them any good?"

So, I had a bit of a secret life. I held back. Well, actually I held back from leaving that day. While Pete and the others ambled out the door, I spent a minute with the waiter, ostensibly looking for my car keys under the table. "I thought I heard a metallic sound," I told him. While he and I crawled around, the keys were actually safe and silent in my cleavage. I kept protesting that he didn't have to help me, but he was one of those thin, hyper guys who spend their lives searching for ways to keep moving. I angled away from him and set the keys on the floor. He found them an instant later. "Thank you!" I said. "That was above and beyond." I opened my handbag, but before I could go for my wallet, he shook his head.

"No problem," he said. "Anyway, you tip good."

The act over my keys lasted just long enough for me to go outside and see Pete Delaney on the other side of Main walking to the parking lot. A couple of the others were behind him, chatting or just strolling. He was walking just fast enough not to gather attention. I parallel tailed him on the restaurant side of the street. Twice he turned, once to look in the hardware store window, the other to brush something off the shoulder seam of his shirt. Both standard techniques for checking if there was a tail. Admittedly also standard behavior for a guy not rushing to get anywhere. As he approached the corner, his eyes locked on a runner in a Shorehaven Vikings T-shirt who was holding on to a lamppost while stretching his Achilles tendon. True, the guy was old enough to have seen his last Viking year in the nineties, but did he appear suspicious? No. A Shorehaven High School alum. In tag-team tails there were often one or two joggers, but what could Pete possibly be doing in order to imagine he'd be subject to high-employment tracking?

He reached the corner and was making a right when he turned and looked back—not behind him, but across the street, all the way up to where I was standing. My stomach did its OMG clench for a second, but from training and experience I knew not to play dumb. He'd seen me walking in his direction, way back and across the street. Faking a deep dive into my handbag would only arouse suspicion, if he had any. So I grinned and gave him a friendly wave, as if he hadn't spotted me in a parallel tail. His return wave, like his personality, was pretty bland, but consistent with—gosh darn—his being the ultimate ordinary guy. Something had made him glance across the street and behind him and there was what's-her-name from the group. Corie.

That's why I couldn't stop wondering about Pete Delaney. Why was he perpetually watchful? What was the weird business about him and his car? I was less concerned about the phones, but that was a little odd, too. And why had he put his personality in a storage unit? It could have been that I was creating a Wednesday work of fiction. Except maybe Pete also had a bit of a secret life.

Maybe it takes one to know one.

# 2

"Corie," my mom said. "You know *fahr* better than I whether or not you're crazy." Much of the time, she spoke with a touch of a British accent. A stranger might think she somehow took living in Queens on a literal level, but her speech was more like what the upper-class characters on the soaps use. And in fact, at the peak of her acting career, my mom, Margo Weber (her maiden name), had played the wellborn wife of a nouveau riche billionaire for half a season in 1997 on *Days of Our Lives*. She was killed off when her TV husband, fleeing to his mistress, floored his Lamborghini and ran her over as she was on her knees, inspecting the perennial garden. After *Days*, she did get cast in occasional gigs on TV shows filming in New York, but most of her work was now in commercials, especially the ones you see on local cable, ads filled with anguish: *Is there any way to get the shine back on my porcelain tile?*

"It's just that I worry that maybe I took one quirk this guy has, Pete, and embellished because . . ." The end of my sentence drifted away.

"Sweetheart," she said and paused, making

35

that word an important idea. "Why would you suddenly start embellishing?" She rested an elbow on the table and set her chin on the tip of her thumb. "You're not the one given to over-statement. That's my role."

"True."

We smiled at each other across the table in a tight corner of the kitchen in my parents' apartment. My mom had found it, a small Formica-topped rectangle with chrome legs, on a sidewalk awaiting the garbage truck, schlepped it home, a tour de force for someone who'd weighed around 105 pounds most of her adult life. Anyway, a couple of years before midcentury style became hip, she'd gotten my dad to build diner seats to go with the table. Then, armed with her staple gun, she upholstered the banquettes in some squeaky fabric from the fifties—a design of pink apples on an orange field—cute, albeit sticky in summer. She'd turned a tiny apartment kitchen into something you might see in a *Times* real estate section photo-essay, "Forecast: Getting Cool in Queens."

"So Corie," she went on, "what would be your reason"—she swept her hand outward from her heart, a grand gesture, theaterese for moti-vation—"for thinking this Pete person is con-cealing . . . whatever?"

"Well, you were the one who said I'm not given to fabrication. I guess it's some kind of instinct combined with law enforcement experience."

"Hmm," she said. "Instinct? Well, you've always had a gift for seeing beneath the surface."

"It's not such a gift," I said. "Most surfaces are pretty transparent if you look hard enough."

Her dusty rose–glossed lips edged up into a smile. "Transparent to you, Corie. Give yourself some credit." My mom's eyes and high cheekbones slanted upward at the same angle, so when she smiled, you barely saw the blue of her eyes—just cheeks and a ruffle of lashes.

She leaned against the back of the banquette and folded her slender arms under her teeny breasts. Like so many film and TV actors, she was a scaled-down version of a regular human. Not in height, but so small boned that sitting across the table from her I felt (as I often did) a little like a Macy's Thanksgiving Day balloon: the how-Mom-looked-at-thirty-eight balloon. We had the same hair—blonde brown—same blue eyes, same heart-shaped face. Except I was an inflated version of her. Not fat, though being the sort of balloon I was, I didn't taper in at the waist as she did. At least my boobs blew up nicely.

"Most of the time," she went on, "people fall back on 'I trust my gut' when they have no idea why they do what they do or want to justify some theory. 'My instinct told me such and such.' " She chuckled, her throaty laugh, the one that to me was like a diamond-shaped traffic warning:

REMINISCENCES AHEAD. "I remember one summer I was up in Williamstown. The actor playing Hermia in *A Midsummer Night's Dream*, on the spur of the moment, *during the actual performance,* she got the word from her gut to start staggering." She slid off the banquette to stagger for me, though the kitchen wasn't a very large stage.

Of course I'd heard this one before. I knew my mom's book, *Delightful Show Business Anecdotes*, by heart. That was okay. I could give her a charmed smile here and there, shake my head at the follies of theater folk, yet think about other things. Like Pete Delaney. Or second-guess myself thinking so much about him at all?

I was in Queens that morning because I drove through it into Manhattan once or twice a week to meet with assorted agents at the firms I scouted books for. They claimed they were truly interested in contemporary Arabic fiction. Truthfully? Not most of them. What they really craved was a blockbuster like Khaled Hosseini's *The Kite Runner*: some of the major deal-making agents seemed peeved when I pointed out *Kite* wasn't translated from Arabic and that it had been written in English by an Afghan American whose original language had been Farsi. Aside from the agents, I'd have an occasional meeting with an Arabic-to-English translator or get together with some critic who reviewed books for Arab American websites and publications. Most of the time, I then drove downtown to my best friend Wynne's afterward. We'd case the stores or galleries and then have dinner.

But I hardly ever drove to Manhattan without detouring to my parents' apartment building in Forest Hills. It was less than a mile from Grand Central Parkway, so in addition to their visits to Long Island, I was able to see my parents on my own at least once a week.

My mom, dad, and I had always been a three-some. It surprised us all when, at thirty-five, I married Josh and adopted Eliza. Not that they weren't happy about the marriage, though we were all a little taken aback that at a time other women were settling, I'd come up with such a winner.

They'd become in-laws and grandparents within four months of my telling them: "Hey, I started going out with, believe it or not, a nice guy. A federal judge of all things. Totally not a stiff. Ridiculously good looking. Used to be a major litigator in a big firm. Except then his wife died and he wanted more time to be with his kid, which tells me he's got good instincts."

My mom, of course, was smitten the first time she met Josh. At some point, she took me aside and whispered: "My God! A Barrymore of a profile! And did you know he has a subscription to the Manhattan Theatre Club? *And* he saw the

BAM production of *The Iceman Cometh*, the one I was so mad about!"

My dad, Dan Schottland, retired NYPD detective, got over his suspicions of Josh's smoothness quicker than I thought he would, though maybe that was due to his being insanely relieved I was finally getting married. Or it could have been that he'd called a couple of his former colleagues, a.k.a. drinking buddies, who obliged him by doing a fast background check and told him to stop acting like a fucking lunatic. Joshua Geller might be charming and disturbingly solvent, but not to worry: He was a federal judge with a good reputation. Absolutely legit. "Nice guy," my dad mumbled to me after their third meeting.

"Do you think there's some underlying reason you're . . . I wouldn't call it obsessing," my mom was saying. "But is there something about him that unsettles you? Maybe he reminds you of an old boyfriend?" She slid out of the banquette and for a second I thought she was about to do an improv: her being me wincing at the sight of a man, then recognizing he resembled over-salivating Ricky in tenth grade. Instead, she merely opened the fridge and took out a bowl of plums arranged as if it were ready to pose for a still life. Then she set down small plates, knives, forks, and small cloth napkins. She'd mastered fruit etiquette for her *Days of Our Lives* role. Then she sat back down and waved benignly:

*Have a plum.* I grabbed a dish towel to put over my shirt and took a big red one.

She chose the smallest of the plums, one of the golden kind, and took a bite that was more like a nip.

"No old boyfriends," I said. "It's just when I turned in my badge, I didn't turn in my curiosity about people who seem off." To cover up what I knew she'd take as snarkiness, I told her about a manuscript I was reading, a novel about the widow of a banker in Ammon.

"Sounds good!" she said, then told me at length about Ruby Dee's life after Ossie Davis died: "They were more equals. Partners actually. Do you know their ashes are mingled in an urn"—she blinked to clear her tears—"and it's inscribed: IN THIS THING TOGETHER."

I plucked a plum from the bowl on the table and wandered into my ex-bedroom, now a TV room, where my dad was ensconced in his oxblood-colored leather recliner. He was watching what was probably his third episode of *Luther* that morning. Since his retirement five years earlier, he'd devoted his life to nodding, shaking his head, or smacking his hand on his forehead as he watched cop shows. My mom once confided: "The only thing standing between your father and lunacy is Netflix."

Cautiously, so he wouldn't accidentally hit the Fast-Forward button, he pressed Pause.

41

Reassured, he was able to greet me. "Hey kiddo! How are you doing?"

"Good!" I said with the suburban brightness that was common to all but the moribund in Shorehaven. "How are you doing, Dad?"

"Fair to middling." To my ear, his response was in the nonworrisome range. There were times when the flatness of my dad's voice did scare me, when it sounded like some primitive version of computer-generated speech. "So what's new at the zoo?" he asked.

"Nothing much. Josh has an insider trading trial next week, so he's swamped with pretrial motions."

He shook his head, while managing a small smile. "Amazing what passes for crime in your husband's world," he said. Having been on the homicide, robbery, and sex crimes squads while a cop, he viewed white-collar criminals as arrogant though harmless jerks in Hermès ties who deserved to be charged a thousand dollars an hour by some high-level litigator, get slammed by a guilty verdict, then bashed by the federal sentencing guidelines. "Eliza okay?"

"She hasn't become a teenage pain in the butt yet."

"Good," he said, with as much enthusiasm as he could muster. My dad was six foot two and had once weighed two hundred pounds, so his voice still had some of the resonance some might confuse with heartiness. It wasn't lack of heart; he really did love Eliza. It was just that he had been deflating for years, since 9/11. Every New York cop had his or her story from that time. My dad's was that his partner of seventeen years was killed when the North Tower of the World Trade Center was hit.

Or maybe Dan Schottland had just been an accident waiting to happen, and seeing his city shattered by terrorists along with Mickey Soong's death simply let out the inner melancholic who'd been lurking beneath the sardonic cop's exterior.

"Eliza's volunteering at the town animal shelter," I added. "She fell in love with the place when we adopted Lulu." (Lulu was our lump of a mutt, black with a dashing white mustache. She'd been abandoned, but after twenty-four hours of cowering under a small desk in the kitchen, she emerged, probably to get me to stop lying on the floor close by and singing "Hush Little Baby.")

"Good," he said. "I like when kids get off their ass."

We then had that kind of awkward moment that occurs between two close relatives who can't find anything more to say to each other. But at least I could fall back on shoptalk: ex-FBI to ex-NYPD. Well, not shop exactly, but I gave him all my suspicions, which amounted only to Pete Delaney having what seemed to me an excessive interest in his car and in new cell phones. "Maybe it was a mistake, joining the lunch group," I said. "Except I really didn't know anyone in town. Now I can't get out of it, so with this Pete thing, it could be I'm creating a scenario to keep myself from bolting. Wallowing in faux intrigue."

"What's with the 'faux' crap? And why can't you get out of it?" he asked.

"How?"

"I don't know, Corie." His words came out slowly, as if he didn't quite have the energy for conventional impatience. But he seemed to think he owed me something. Plus he was never comfortable when I was playing what he called the "Boo-hoo, it's my own fault" game. He dragged his feet off the ottoman and motioned for me to sit down. He was realizing this wasn't going to be a simple "Hiya, kiddo" exchange but an actual conversation that might last four or five minutes. "Why not tell the lunch people, 'I don't got the time'?" I shook my head. Josh had suggested I leave, too, though with more upscale grammar.

"Hey, Dad," I said. "Let's be wildly athletic and go for a walk, talk." Now he shook his head, as in: *This is where I draw the line. I got* Luther *on Pause.* "Come on. It'll make Mom happy and, not that I'm going to tell her where we're headed, but we'll go to Schmidt's, have a beer." Not my idea of 11:30 a.m. hydration, but at least he seemed tempted.

"Why don't we drive?" he asked.

It was only a ten-, maybe fifteen-minute walk to the old German bar, just past the outskirts of Forest Hills, so I told him no, I needed to stretch my legs. Reluctantly, he changed to an overly hip pair of sneakers, black with a slash of teal, a Mom online shopping coup. Then off we went.

It was mid-May, and after a cold spring, the world had finally warmed and turned decisively green, though Queens Boulevard—six lanes of buses, trucks, and cars flanked by packed-tight stores, saplings debilitated from carbon monoxide poisoning, looming apartment buildings, and aggressive pedestrians—could not be recommended for its bucolic delights. But to get to Schmidt's Biergarten in middle-class Richmond Hill, we headed south through Forest Hills Gardens, an old-time, upscale enclave of private houses, heavy on the Tudor, old trees, and, even now, some old money.

"Hell of a hike for a glass of fucking Finkbräu," my dad said, not the kind of father who believed in watching his language. I'd always been his pal, not his little princess. "But okay, it's nice out. I'll give you that."

"So tell me about this Delaney character. Is it just the car business with him? You're thinking it's weird because a normal guy wouldn't go to such lengths to keep an eye on a Jeep, even an expensive one?" He ducked to avoid a low branch of some big-ticket tree with gray-green leaves. "It's not *that* weird. Don't you know by now that people who are pretty normal can have a chunk of their lives in which they're crazy? This guy's behavior is just a little kooky. In theory it might get attention from someone in law enforcement but only because it's repetitive. If he was really ape shit but in private, doing God knows what, but otherwise average, you'd never have a clue."

"So you think that's what it is? Just a guy who's maybe wrapped up in Jeeps in a slightly unhealthy way?" I shrugged, even though I remembered it annoyed him. In my teens, he'd say, *Stop with the shrugging, for chrissakes. What've you got a voice for? Talk. Say yes, no, I don't know.*

"Well?" he asked me. "You got something else to offer?" My dad's arms had gotten thinner since his retirement. His biceps, instead of pressing against the short sleeves of whatever sport shirt he wore on his days off, now hung loosely, sallow, growing hairless.

I mumbled, "I don't think so," the way someone under arrest would when being questioned by a tough detective before her lawyer arrived. I turned away from him—though I had nothing to hide—and looked at the houses. So different from the Forest Hills I'd grown up in, which was a nice neighborhood with the occasional sickly tree, but mostly aging apartment houses that looked weary from standing erect decade after decade. Too middle class to be ripe for gentrification, too inoffensively designed to amuse. I hadn't noticed its dullness growing up because all I wanted to do was hang with my friends, and only a couple of them lived in the Gardens. Queens Boulevard or Boulevard Haussmann: who gave a fuck?

But this part of Forest Hills (once "restricted" from Jews, people of color, conspicuous Catholics) still had the atmosphere of a forties movie in which well-to-do Americans talked in that upper-class Franklin Roosevelt way. The houses we passed were definitely as grand as some of the discreetly showy homes in the suburbs: leaded glass, turrets, along with brass knockers so elaborate they could be on the front door of Windsor Castle. WASP heaven.

What they lacked in Queens was the land to go with a grand house. That didn't stop the owners from landscaping as if, instead of a five-thousand-square-foot plot, they had five acres. Ground cover with minuscule pink flowers abutted a silken carpet of lawn shaded by those noble trees. The trees themselves were encircled by large-leafed shade plants and flowers. Clipped bushes spread out to provide the dark green frame for what could almost be botanical prints. Flanking the front doors, giant terra-cotta pots held topiary trees and more ivy than Princeton, though that was just a guess as I'd never been to Princeton. I'd once dated a guy who'd gone there who laughed too loud at movies, which was enough for me to call the whole thing off. I guess that also explains how come I couldn't find someone I wanted to marry till I was thirty-five.

"Corie, kiddo, you into real estate these days?"

"No. Sorry, I got distracted."

"So get undistracted." He seemed to be tiring. His pace slowed and a moment later he was standing still on the narrow strip of grass between sidewalk and street.

"Okay," I said, managing a cooperative smile, hoping that whatever it was that he'd asked me to focus on would pop back into my mind so I could respond in a way that would energize him.

"Oh right! You wanted to know what else I had on Pete Delaney, beyond Jeep watching."

I may have given him a minuscule nudge, but mostly he started walking on his own again. "Yeah."

Maybe neurons abhor a vacuum, which could explain why an image of our lunch meetings popped up. It filled the empty space in my head. "At our lunches, after about five minutes, all of us turn off our phones and put them on the table, facedown. It's a tradition from before I joined the group."

"You turn them off? They don't vibrate or anything?"

"No, because that would mean sneaking peeks

at who was calling or texting. We shut them down. The idea is that one of the things you have to learn to do when you're self-employed is be a decent boss to yourself, allow yourself some time off from constant digital demands. Personally, I think they'd be better off with the phones out of sight, but that's their rule. Anyway, there we are, seven of us around the table, with our phones above the plate. If there's an emergency, a husband or wife or whoever can call the restaurant, ask to speak to so-and-so in the group."

"Okay."

"So even before I noticed him always checking out his car, I had this mental picture of the group as a group. You know how when you go to someplace regularly, you'll notice that all of a sudden the restaurant is folding the napkins into fancy triangles on the plate when before they were rectangles under the fork?"

"Maybe," he said. "I'm not from the big napkin noticers."

"But you would notice that something had changed, wouldn't you? I mean, even if you're not into table settings, you have a cop's sense of 'something's different here.' "

"Right. I'm more geared toward seeing people looking different than they did before or changes in behavior. A guy's drinking Stoli instead of beer, some blabby woman turns quiet."

"So sometime last winter, right around Christmas, because the memory includes those pine tree droopy things, garlands, I realize something's changed. Pete's phone. He'd gone from an ancient flip phone to a smartphone. No big deal. I didn't think, *Ooh a new phone*. Just a tiny detail."

"You didn't notice what kind it was?" my dad asked. He didn't sound exactly intrigued, but at least he wasn't dismissing me out of hand.

"No. It was facedown, plus it might have had some kind of protective cover on it. No distinguishing characteristics. It was probably black. I think all the guys in the group have black phones."

"So? Could it have been a Christmas present?"

"It could have been. He seems to like variety, phone-wise."

"What do you want me to say, kiddo? 'Highly significant!'?"

"Sure. Want to say it?"

"No."

The houses were getting smaller now. Still Tudors and colonials but shrinking to middle-class size. The landscaping was mostly grass and newly planted impatiens—a flower even I could recognize. "I'm really not saying it's highly significant, just that it may have some import. Why does a guy keep changing phones?"

"Corie, you're asking why a guy changes phones. That's climbing up a tree with a hundred branches, and you know and I know that's no way to start an investigation."

Just as I was trying to look cool with criticism, I tripped over a seam in the sidewalk where one piece of pavement had been pushed up by a tree root, then did an awkward line dance to get walking again. "Come on, Dad, I'm not starting an investigation. I'm just curious: talking it out with you."

"What's with you?" he demanded. "Where's your sense of balance?"

"I tripped over a damn tree root."

"You still deal with dangerous people sometimes. If a suspect turns on you—"

"I'm contract now. Ninety percent of the work I do for them, I'm sitting in a monitored room at New York headquarters."

"So fuck the other ten percent?"

When I was fifteen, my dad decided that learning to break someone's nose together would be a great father-daughter bonding experience. So we took classes in krav maga, a self-defense technique with some combative moves developed for the Israeli army. In the nineties my dad had met a crazy guy from Haifa who was training NYPD SWAT team members. There was a sign in the gym that said—in both English and Hebrew—IF YOU FINISH YOUR OPPONENT, YOU FINISH THE FIGHT. We continued going to classes for years, until 9/11.

"I still go to Bazak's place every once in a while," I told him. "Come to think of it, not since I got married. No time. But whenever I went, he always asked for you." He bumped his knuckles against his heart, as in: *I'm touched.* "I still do the balance exercises, believe it or not. And the squats, push-ups, stretches on the days I don't run."

"Some people change phones. Some keep them forever," he said. "The ones who change could be techies, right? There's some stupid saying about boys and toys, so maybe he likes to have some brand-new shiny thing to play with. And couldn't he be a flake who keeps losing his phone? You said Mr. Whosis—"

"Pete."

"Okay, Pete designs things like boxes for takeout and all that. It's also possible one of his clients deals with phones, gives him a big break on price. Or if he's involved in something criminal, he could still be behind the times technologically. Maybe he thinks if you switch phones every once in a while, no one will be able to trace you."

"Conceivable."

"If he has a girlfriend," my dad said, "he could be worried the wife hired a detective who could geolocate him. He tells her he's playing poker with the boys. But it's the Hotbed Motor Inn that pops up on the investigator's screen."

"I don't see Pete having a girlfriend. From what I know about him, which admittedly isn't much, he's a family guy."

"Grow up, kiddo. You think guys with barbecue aprons don't fuck around?"

"I know. Fortunately, Josh wouldn't be caught dead in a barbecue apron. Ergo, proof he's faithful."

"He's not going anywhere. He's crazy about you. He's a one-woman man. Even the first wife—"

"Dawn," I said.

"From the pictures, Dawn looked like a skinny marink who could never let go of her tennis racket, but okay, from everything you say, Josh loved her. And now he loves you. He doesn't cat around. But a lot of guys love their wives and still step out. Means nothing to them: it's like they got phlegm and they clear their throat."

"Love your imagery."

"Thanks. So back to this Pete. He could be switching phones, switching numbers, to keep from being followed. Most likely by a suspicious wife, but who the hell knows. Could he be getting dunned by a collection agency for bills he owes?"

"I have no idea. He has a really nice car. He doesn't seem impoverished or anything. Actually, I think he's doing nicely. At least from what everybody says."

"Maybe he's looking at his Jeep all the

time because he's worried about it getting repossessed?" my dad asked.

"I doubt it. If he was trying to avoid a repo guy, he wouldn't establish a pattern of behavior, coming to the same restaurant every Wednesday at twelve thirty."

"Well, it could be changing phones is a pattern of behavior, too. He likes all the bells and whistles. Maybe he's looking for the best picture quality so he can watch Mets games or porn when he's sitting on the pot. The point of it is, Corie, these hundred branches. You can't climb them all."

"I know. So talking about trees and branches: Do you think I'm barking up the wrong tree with this Pete thing?"

"Kiddo, all you've got is one case of slightly unusual behavior: him choosing the same seat to keep his eye on the car. But I gotta tell you, even that's questionable. He could just be a creature of habit. Come early, stick to the same chair he had the first time he came to the restaurant." My dad made a lip-smacking sound, but then I realized it had nothing to do with Pete Delaney; we were less than two blocks from Schmidt's and he was thinking about a stein of Finkbräu.

"So you think I should drop it?" I asked. "Get a life?"

"Or own it. You know how to investigate."

"Not the way you do. Once I became a special

agent, mostly all I did was documents and emails for senior agents. Then I got moved to the burqa detail, interrogating women who couldn't be alone with a guy, but that was mostly interviews. Same in New York when I was on the Joint Terrorism Task Force, except there I did men, too. My boss said I could make anyone talk."

"Want to know what I think?" my dad asked, not that he waited for an answer. "Look, you can read your fiction and regular books in Arabic. Let that be your business. Enjoy your family. Have a baby, not that I'm pushing or anything. But if you want to find out about this Pete guy, no reason you can't do that, too. You got the chops for it. Get off your ass."

# 3

I thought it would probably be healthier to get Pete Delaney out of my head—and while I was at it, forget the suburbs, too. So instead of taking my usual direct route from my parents' apartment in Forest Hills to Wynne's in Tribeca on the expressway, I took the local streets: Queens Boulevard west toward Manhattan. A bleak stretch of chain stores hawking LUXURY SOFAS AND MATCHING ARMCHAIRS! FREE OTTOMAN! gave way to homier convenience stores with signs in Korean, Chinese, Greek, or Spanish. On the side streets, I discovered residential neighborhoods that had transformed themselves, blocks of walk-ups now so cool that all the residents appeared to be wearing bike shorts and sleeveless T-shirts from esoteric protests.

I would have prolonged the drive, except I'd skipped lunch only twice in my life, when I felt my choice was survival or a turkey sandwich. So a couple of miles from the bridge, I took an illegal right on red. Some inner GPS navigated me to a fried chicken wing place in Long Island City I knew from driving to my parents' when I worked in Manhattan. It was one of those anonymous-looking, decent food joints favored by Feds, cops, and a well-mannered class of drug dealers.

It was around one o'clock, so I had to wait a few minutes for a table. I chatted with the cashier/receptionist about her manicure: eight long lavender nails and two coated with silver glitter. The lives I'd chosen—special agent followed by literary scout with home office—pretty much precluded sparkling metallic middle fingers. She said the key to maintaining any manicure was to learn to sleep on your back with your hands over the blanket. Also, not to roll around too much when fucking, which we agreed was kind of sad. I asked her if she'd ever heard John F. Kennedy's quote, "Life is unfair," and she said yeah, though she thought it was something her grandma had said, not a president.

A table opened up. After a few minutes a waitress tried to hand me a plastic-coated menu with the splotches of many lunches, but I told her I knew what I wanted: a salad with blue cheese dressing on the side and a small order of wings, no sauce. Each came only one way: salad was cut-up iceberg lettuce, wings were deep-fried with "our famous krispy crust," an alliteration I'd always loved for its capricious spelling.

The salad came first. I dumped about half the dressing on it, then used my knife and fork to toss it. Crunch, crunch, and the blue cheese was good, too, but after the second bite my nostalgia for Queens diminished: Pete Delaney returned. Well, my dad had reminded me that an investigation was not a ninety-minute event held on Wednesdays.

While I was eating, I searched to check Pete's social media. His name was annoyingly common, and I had to look at several Peter Delaneys across the country before confirming what my initial poking around had showed: he had no personal social media presence—not Facebook, not Twitter, not Instagram. Not even LinkedIn, which was a bit strange for a guy who had sup-posedly been looking for a job a few years back. He had a business Instagram account, which was solely pictures of pretty packages with hashtags like #packaging #branddesign #packagingdesign #brandidentity. But what guy his age didn't have even a Facebook account to post pictures of his kids and ill-considered political diatribes? Even Josh, who had a sensitive (and public) job and never posted, had an account. Who, in this day and age, was simply off the social media grid?

I considered the Wednesday group. Who among them might have some insight or info on Pete? Darby and John, the two other guys, probably knew more about him than the women. That was mainly because if Pete was going to chat with someone, it would more likely be a guy. Not that I detected any evident misogyny about him. He was simply a man of a certain age used to the common ground of safe suburban subjects—sports, travel shortcuts—the sort who felt uneasy with sentences that began: "What are your feelings about . . . ?"

I noticed the same chunk of lettuce poised on my fork had not yet made it to my mouth as I'd been so busy thinking. Okay, so the guys would know more about him. But I couldn't think of a pretext to call John Grillo since I had no credible questions to ask about landscape drainage. Darby Penn, the photo retoucher, was out since the eight thousand framed pictures of Dawn around the house probably had anti-UV glass: sadly, they hadn't faded, so I had no conversation openers. Also, pulling aside or phoning any I-know-you-slightly guy would seem peculiar and evoke lots of *What the hell does she really want?* musings.

With women, though, it wouldn't be peculiar at all. Ideally, I needed a natural blabber. A flashing, LED bright arrow was now pointing directly at Phoebe, the eBay reseller. I must have had a sudden smile because the waitress beamed at me and said, "Your chicken's almost ready. Each batch we fry fresh."

I had to think of a reason to call her instead of texting. Business: I considered what eBay-friendly stuff I had that might excite Phoebe. The pair of Rollerblades that had moved with me from DC to NYC to Shorehaven wouldn't do it, but I tried to remember what else we had in our basement. It had a wine room we never used. About two years earlier, I'd looked inside and come across a bunch of Dawn's stuff. Clothes in luscious fabrics, wildly expensive shoes. I felt sad for them, consigned to that underground room before their time. I kind of wished I could bring them upstairs, let them dance under the stars. Naturally, two seconds later I realized they were a metaphor for Dawn, so I closed the door.

About a month after her death, Josh explained, he had asked her mother to take whatever she wanted, which turned out to be all her jewelry (except for diamond stud earrings, her engagement ring, and a Cartier watch he'd already put in a safe-deposit box for Eliza). After his mother-in-law came Dawn's two closest friends. They took handbags and shawls and scarves, but neither wore a size 2 dress or a 10A shoe. To their credit, it in no way sounded like a grab. They packed up cartons to go to Goodwill, but they set aside her designer clothes and shoes and advised Josh to take them to a consignment shop or an auction house—a task that would never make his to-do list. I guessed that besides bringing back the misery of losing her, it would offend him to turn Dawn's possessions into cash.

I, on the other hand, could live with that anguish. Wynne had offered to photograph the items she thought were worth something and send the pics to museums with costume collections, but we never got around to it. So what would lure Phoebe Melowicz? I wasn't about to let her loose in the wine room. However, Josh had said to do whatever I wanted with Dawn's things (including tossing them if their presence bothered me). It wasn't that he had no feelings for Dawn; it was only that he had no feelings for stuff. He had loved her. Not only had he told me that, but I could see the delight on his face in the photos of them as a couple. How deeply? Josh wasn't a man who turned his insides out. Besides, he wasn't the guy he'd been with her. After she died, his life turned more somber. He quit his exhilarating law practice and became a judge, a career that might have prestige, but was seriously short on glam. Otherwise, he would have risen from a hotshot litigator to a superstar, with Dawn—who probably wouldn't have minded having her hand kissed by international bigwigs—by his side.

Anyway, I decided to sacrifice a purple Dolce & Gabbana dress on the altar of inquiry: Wynne had said it was probably worth a few thousand and I had muttered, "Insane." At that time, I was just starting to get used to the idea that I was now a person who lived in the world of money, who could either spend or bypass two or three thousand dollars without much thought.

So before the chicken wings, I took out my phone and called Phoebe. "Oh my God!" she shrilled, though then her voice dropped to a warier octave: "You're sure it's not DG? You know, their cheaper label. Not that I would say no to that either."

"This is their high end. I don't know anyone who's a size two, so I can't give it away. I told Josh it was probably worth something. If we sell it, we could let Eliza, our daughter, pick a charity to donate the money to, a way of honoring her mom's memory."

"That is totally wonderful!" she yelled. I'd forgotten how loud her voice could be, and my phone amplified it; I clicked down the volume a notch. We made a date for her to pick it up on Saturday morning.

"I would have asked you about it on Wednesday," I said, "but I thought you might not want to talk business in front of the group."

"Not during lunch, I guess," Phoebe said. "But I sold Marcalynn Schechter's mom's Cuisinart Gridler and electric deep fryer when they got a restaurant stove. I remember one day, right after we paid the check, Marcalynn walked around the table and asked me if I thought there was a market and I told her, 'Cuisinart Gridlers SELL LIKE CRAZY because you can put their parts in the dishwasher SO THEY ALWAYS LOOK CLEAN IN THE CLOSE-UPS!"

"That's great! Did you ever work with anyone else in the group?"

"Iris is always looking for old pots for planting

her things, and if one of them has a chip IT'S NOT A DEALBREAKER."

"That shabby chic business?" I asked.

"Totally, because someone gave me a cachepot, except with a small crack, and I wasn't sure but I asked Iris and she bought it for WHITE GERANIUMS and you know what her client told her? That it made her feel like landed gentry!"

She was on a roll, and unless I wanted to hear about a coup in the auction of a 1995 Photoshop CD, I needed to press on. "Ever deal with any of the men in the group?" I asked.

"No," Phoebe said, which would for anyone else be a perfectly normal answer. But coming from her, a such a rapid one-word response was surprising, almost startling. There should have been a break, just so she could gather some memories about how John threw out a Ferragamo tie—its pattern would be described with numbing intricacy—and he didn't even think of offering it to her just because it had a gravy stain HE WRONGLY THOUGHT was permanent.

The waitress set down a small, paper-lined, plastic basket of chicken wings. Not wanting to interrupt my phone call, she leaned over and tapped the napkin dispenser on my table. I responded with a thumb-up and what I hoped was a lettuce-free smile. Then I asked Phoebe: "Not even from Pete? You'd think with him being a packaging guy, he'd wind up having, I don't know, all sorts of pretty papers or plastic thingies."

"No," she said, even quicker this time. True, "no" means "no." But with talky people like Phoebe, who have no filter between mind and mouth, it did not necessarily mean an end to the conversation. I decided to consider her "no" an invitation that included *RSVP as fast as you can* written on the bottom.

"Pete doesn't seem like the world's most approachable guy," I prompted her. When she didn't answer, I pressed a little harder: "I can't imagine going up to him and asking him something business related. He seems nice enough. Actually, I've heard he can be really thoughtful. But one time . . ."

"WHAT?" Phoebe sounded almost desperate, like the Persian king pleading with Scheherazade: *Go on with the story. I need to know.* I couldn't figure out if she was mad for gossip in general or supremely curious about Pete Delaney.

"Last year for Father's Day," I began, "I got my dad six Mets tickets. Great seats, field level, near the Mets dugout. I figured he could take five of his poker buddies out for a day."

"Right! I hear you," she said.

I was making up this Pete vignette as I went along, so I took a hesitant breath to stall. Unfortunately, it made me think maybe this wasn't a terrific idea, considering how Phoebe was given to random chatter. "Phoebe, this is just between us."

"Of course!"

Was she sounding too eager? "Because if it gets out, even if it never gets back to Pete, it could affect the tone of the lunches."

"Oh, I know, I know. Because there are stories I could tell about people in town who tried to screw me fifteen ways till Sunday. Isn't that an expression? But I never mention a name because . . . Actually, I forget the exact reason why, but the eBay group for sellers says it's sound business policy not to name names."

"So I was thinking about wrapping the tickets somehow, so it didn't look like I was just handing him an envelope. Anyway, a Wednesday or two before Father's Day, I told him about what I'd gotten my dad and asked if he had any thoughts about how I could wrap them."

"WHAT DID HE SAY?"

"Nothing. That was the thing that got me. He just kind of stared, like I'd made some shocking proposition." Phoebe laughed—not softly—sounding slightly unhinged. "And then he shrugged. Obviously it was an I-don't-know shrug. Except he didn't say one single word! He didn't do anything wrong, but it was just really weird, you know?" I made a mental note to ask Josh about the difference between slander and defamation. However, I didn't have to say any more: all I'd wanted to do was get Phoebe talking.

And she did talk. The beginning was rapid but so soft it sounded like the voice of someone I'd never met. "Okay, so what I'm going to say is just between us, too." She paused. "You and me," she added, in case I didn't understand.

"Absolutely," I assured her.

Even over the noise of other chicken eaters, I could hear her swallow. "Corie, can you keep a secret?"

Does the sun rise in the east? "Of course I can," I told her. "And didn't I just put my faith in you?"

"Yes. But this is really upsetting."

Knowing Phoebe, I thought it might be about a mummified mink stole she found in someone's armoire and not at all about Pete. "I can take it, Phoebe," I said.

"All right. Just between us?"

"Yes."

"Okay, so my brother-in-law's sister was getting married. I needed dyed-to-match shoes. This wasn't on a Wednesday." I tilted the phone away from my mouth and started on a wing. I could probably get through an entire flock of chickens if Phoebe launched into one of her digressions. "So I went to Jildor in Great Neck. You know it? The shoe store."

"Yes, sure."

"Then you know the parking. It was crazy to

66

look for street parking. Anyway, it turned out there was a space, like two stores down. But the car in front of me put on a signal, so she was going to take it. It was a Tesla. That's like over a hundred thousand dollars. And she goes for street parking? Fine, you live your life. I'll live mine. I decided to go to the lot where they have the meters, not the garage. But all of a sudden, I see there's a car in front of the Tesla that was already starting to back into the space. So what does she do, the car in front of me? She sneaks into the space SO FAST and the other car has to slam on his brakes so he doesn't rear-end her, and PS, SHE GETS THE SPACE!"

A fluted paper cup of coleslaw came with the chicken wings, but I decided to wait to avoid the crunch—and because I sensed who the guy who lost his parking space was. "What happened then?"

"Well, the guy just doesn't drive away. He gets out of his car and it's PETE DELANEY! And her window was closed, but his voice was really loud." Even Phoebe's pause felt earsplitting. "He didn't yell like someone totally furious, but you could so hear him. He called out to her: 'You're a C-word! That's what he called her on Middle Neck Road! And I'm one hundred percent sure she heard it."

"You've got to be kidding! I don't think I've ever even heard him say 'damn.' "

"Then he took his fist and banged the side of it on her window two or three times, like a hammer. *Boom. Boom.* Maybe another *boom.*"

"It sounds as if he was furious," I said.

"No. That's what was weird. He seemed regular, calm, and it was more like letting her know he was there. That made it creepier, in a way. Like 'I'm banging in case you didn't hear the C-word,' which you know she must have. 'I am making a point.' Beyond scary."

"He doesn't seem given to emotional displays," I remarked.

"You're telling me! So, like, you think she would start her car and pull out. I mean, if someone's that weird, you know not to deal with him. Except she didn't care. She opened the door, got out, and there she was, standing right next to him. White leather pants, stiletto heels. A little chunky in the thighs. I mean, the whole scene made me so nervous and I wasn't even part of it. And what does she do? Just walks around him, like he was a traffic cone. I sold one once on eBay. Thirteen dollars. Normally I don't handle stuff like that, but it was to accommodate one of my regulars. Anyway, Pete just stands there, staring at her. And then he gets in his car and drives away."

"Wow," I said. I had to admit it wasn't much. It was oddly comforting to know that Pete had enough of a temper to shout *Cunt!* It was so at odds with his holding-doors-open midwestern behavior always on display at lunch.

"But that's not all!" Phoebe added. "He gets into his car. The Jeep that's always clean. And he drives off. Fine, finished. So I go to a parking lot, leave my car, and walk back. I'm turning the corner and I'm almost at Jildor and I see Pete's car again. It's parked at a hydrant. The blinkers were on."

"Was he in it?"

"No, but I saw him, like a couple of feet away, walking toward Jildor. And I'm thinking if they have men's shoes there, or did he go around the block and now is checking the stores to see which one she went into? Do I have to tell you? I was a basket case!"

"But so vigilant," I told her. "You must have been a detective in your last life."

"I love those raincoats they used to wear. You know, knockoffs of Burberry."

"Right. So Pete is walking toward Jildor . . ."

"Yes, except all of a sudden, he isn't going there. He steps off the sidewalk and is walking on the street. He went right past a couple of cars parked behind that Tesla. So I kind of went behind an SUV and peeked out a little. I couldn't figure what was going on. I thought maybe she'd gone back to her car or something and he was going to call her the C-word again. Except she wasn't there. He had his keys out and like I can't even call it keyed. HE GOUGED A DEEP LINE FROM THE BACK OF HER TESLA all the way to the front. THE WHOLE SIDE! He must have pressed so hard because it looked like he dented the metal. He walks a little more and puts the key in his other hand. Then he casually turns around and does it again, lower down on the door!"

"Holy shit!" I put down the chicken wing. "Listen, Phoebe, do you think there's a chance he saw you?"

"No, because you know what I did? The minute he started walking back and I saw he was making another key mark, I got back on the sidewalk and went straight back to my car. So my back was always toward him. I was, don't call me crazy, frightened. Or at least very, very upset."

"I don't blame you," I told her. "I mean, even if he didn't seem angry, it's such aggressive behavior. You wouldn't want to get near anyone in that frame of mind. And you definitely wouldn't want someone who's supposed to be an okay guy to know that you saw that ugly side of him."

"Corie, I am so glad you think that. It's weird, coming to lunch every Wednesday and having to look at him like he's a normal, quietish guy."

"I can imagine! With me it was just a strange reaction when I asked him about how to wrap some Mets tickets. No big deal. But with you, seeing that kind of revenge. Most people, even if they were boiling inside, would drive away and eventually cool down. Right?"

"Right."

"But he cooled down only to the extent that he figured out a way to give payback."

"Yes! Sooo destructive." Phoebe said. "He did plan. You know how I know?"

She was waiting, and I wasn't acting when I gave her a breathless: "How?"

"Because when he called her the C-word, he was just wearing a zip-up jacket. But the second time with the key? HE HAD PUT ON A BASEBALL CAP AND PULLED IT DOWN, so like you couldn't see his eyes. A disguise, but not a disguise. A different look, if you know what I mean."

So I told her: "I do know what you mean."

# 4

My best friend appeared dubious. "That's it with the sleuthing? A guy loses his shit and keys a Tesla?" Winifred Finkelstein had been my BFF since day one of first grade. Eleven years later, in high school, a month before she took the SATs, she changed her name to Wynne ("the *e* is silent") Fairclough. Not that she was trying to be anyone but herself. It was just that her essence had a different name.

Wynne's mouth often preceded her internal censor by several seconds, so it was no surprise when she added: "Not that I'm questioning your investigative instincts, but it seems more hostile adolescent behavior than a sign he has a grotesque secret life."

"But he's not an adolescent. He's in his late forties. I'm not saying he shouldn't have been angry. But at that age, when something mildly shitty happens, anger is the normal response, not rage. And even if he felt rage . . ."

Wynne nodded, and the tiny diamonds embedded in the platinum balls that were her most recent pair of overpriced, understated earrings reflected a hundred minuscule spears of light. "Gotcha. You're saying that a guy his

72

age should have the self-control not to act out."

What drew us together when we were six seemed to be the same glue that still kept us together. Nothing escaped her vision and judgment, from the quality of the chalk we used to make pictures on the sidewalk to going shopping with me and my mom so she could signal me which denim overalls were the ones to buy. And I was the psychology maven, deciphering behavior, advising her on how to deal with her perpetually battling parents.

Friendships often fade after high school, but we stayed close both emotionally and geographically. Except we not only loved each other; we also loved learning about each other's worlds. Wynne, not Win, knew she was meant for Manhattan and so went off to Hunter College. Like Queens College, Hunter was a commuter school, meaning she had to take the subway home to Chez Finkelstein in Forest Hills every night.

After our graduations, as I was leaving for Quantico with a BA in Middle Eastern studies, Wynne's BA in art history scored her a job as an editorial assistant at *Glamour* magazine. After three years she rose to assistant editor but was still writing copy under headings like "What (Not) to Wear with a Sheer Dress." She moved on to *Vogue*, which soon recognized her *sans défaut* taste and made her a photo stylist. A year later, she was promoted to associate fashion editor.

While I slept with guys from Agricultural Research to the National Nuclear Security Administration, the sort who'd mutter brief apologies for still sleeping on futons before we went at it. (Later, when I met Bashir—the only former boyfriend I could think of without a yawn or a shudder—I was awed that he'd built a Murphy bed in his studio apartment with bookshelves on each side and also that his sheets were clean.)

Anyway, while I was still in DC, Wynne became engaged to Clive Cohen, an investment banker. Wynne redesigned his library and sent him for removal of the hair on his knuckles. She redid his entire Village mews house and his wardrobe. He had her choose his car and then a weekend palace in East Hampton. When he decided that finally he'd become a patrician, he went rogue with a nineteen-year-old NYU philosophy major. Wynne ditched him, relieved. She'd clearly overestimated his capacity for personal growth. He still let his toenails grow to disgusting lengths and remained rude to waiters.

Just before I transferred from DC to New York, she quit *Vogue* and opened Wynne Fairclough, Design. Her first client was the wife of the guy who was to have been best man at her wedding: "If you can make Clive look classy, just picture how you can redo me and Ryan!" Ryan was a challenge, a man who resembled Jabba the Hutt; Wynne kindly envisioned "rich and rotund" and drew on Holbein's painting of Henry VIII. A newly bearded Ryan in a coat with sable collar made *GQ*.

Wynne Fairclough's taste was touted to be—and was—superb and expensive. She had no single "look" but suited each job to the individual client. An article in *W* called her the style whisperer and one blogger of Euro-chic explained her job as "life designer." She looked as if she could come from anywhere: Paris, Cape Town, the Bronx. She was of average height, a touch below average weight. Chocolate chip–color brown eyes and dark brown hair that she always wore in a ponytail. "Wynne Fairclough's iconic ponytail," the *New York Times* called it. Her only makeup was a touch of eyeliner and false eyelashes, the latter obviously a better quality than the millipedes she'd worn in eighth grade.

"This Pete," I told her. "He deliberately gets there early to grab the same seat every time, so he can keep constant watch."

"So your dad agreed you should investigate him?" She pressed the upper part of her chopsticks against her forehead as if to nudge her mind into comprehension. "That was before he went to war against the Tesla, right?"

"Right."

"I sort of get it."

"No you don't," I told her.

She smiled. "I get that you and your dad have the same deductive gene, so investigating is probably the smart thing to do."

We were having take-out Szechuan at the new dining room table in her loft. The table was a hugely long, dark wood thing that looked as if it had been lifted from dinner hour at Hogwarts. I muttered the word "refectory," and Wynne offered a single chuckle, as if I'd made an ironic comment on furniture styles. I hadn't; I'd just been pleased with knowing the word "refectory." She told me it had been handcrafted by a brilliant young artisan in northern Thailand who was famous for the beauty of his chisel marks. Wynne sometimes drank her own Kool-Aid.

"When my dad used the word 'investigate,' he might have been humoring me," I told her.

"I don't see him as the humoring type. He's always been more like: 'What are you, some kinda dipshit?' "

"Exactly. But he and my mom . . . They seem to think I'm having trouble adjusting to suburban life. Which I'm really not. It's just that it takes time."

"Of course it takes time." She furrowed her brows so deeply that a ridge formed between her eyes—that best friend intense gaze signaling concern, one step before worry, two before pity. "To be honest, I think they may be right. It's not just suburbs. It's aesthetics, too." Maybe she picked up my exhalation of impatience. "Don't get your knickers in a knot. I genuinely think your environment is so important for reinforcing your sense of self. You know your house isn't typically suburban. If it was ordinary, simple, I wouldn't say anything."

"Of course you would."

"But there's an institutional quality about it. I'm sorry to say it looks like Tara—reimagined as a reform temple."

"You're not at all sorry to say it."

"It's not as if you chose it. Maybe that's one of the reasons you can't settle in. Face it, Corie. It's not you. I don't even see how Josh could have let Dawn buy it. An entire driveway of stone blocks with a double border."

"Stop digressing," I said, though our friendship itself was a thirty-two-year digression. I hadn't a clue what our original subject had been.

"It's not just about whether your house is attractive to whoever is visiting," Wynne said. "It's that it's not *you*." Then she went on, not even pretending to throw it off as a casual question: "Are you worried that he still daydreams of Dawn?"

I paused before answering. "No. Well, I'm sure he thinks of her on their anniversary, maybe other times. But I don't sense any profound sadness in him. There must be times he misses the liveliness of the life he had with her. Being a litigator, he was an action guy. She was very social, loved getting dressed up, going to events. She was a throwback to her mother's generation, a glam wife for a high-powered husband. Not a genius, but she was animated, hospitable, had ten outfits for any occasion. He hadn't had that with his family."

"The dress his mother wore to your wedding looked like it was made from infested mattress ticking. And his father keeps saying, 'How duh yuh do?' to people, like he's in the House of Lords."

"They're not going to open a charm school," I agreed. "Anyway, Dawn went like that." I snapped my fingers. "What choice did Josh have? He had to make changes. He saw that after a few months."

"What about the housekeeper, nanny, whatever she was?"

"He could lie to himself that Wanda was an ideal mother surrogate and then keep flying off to Paris and Stuttgart. But she wasn't the ideal anything, just a nice employee. So he left his stimulating law firm world. And Dawn probably isn't on his mind a lot, because she wouldn't belong in the life he has now. Being a federal judge can be very cerebral, and you don't get invited to clients' weddings in Sardinia. So besides time healing all wounds and all that, he's living in a different universe now."

When Josh and I were becoming an item, I had

worried that Dawn would be an unseen presence in our relationship. Whenever I visited the house in Shorehaven, there was no place I could turn without seeing her framed image. All over: Dawn, Dawn, and more Dawn. As Josh later told me, some grief counselor had suggested it nine years earlier so that Dawn could still be a part of his and Eliza's lives. Nice idea, I supposed, though he and Eliza didn't seem even to glance at those snapshots anymore. Early in our relationship, when Eliza was spending the weekend with Dawn's parents, we headed up to Josh's bedroom for the first time. Again, there on his nightstand: Dawn. This time she was in tennis garb with a teeny skirt, framed in silver bamboo. Long legs, not shapely, though not toothpicks. Slightly elongated nose. She came across as profoundly slender and pretty: Keira Knightley crossbred with a whippet.

So I suggested we find someplace other than their bedroom: I understood he might want to keep his wife's picture, but I couldn't make love with her checking out my moves. "Sorry," he muttered. "Such a part of the landscape, you don't even notice it." The photo vanished in under thirty seconds. The ones in other rooms stayed. No one ever bothered to take them away. They appeared to be what Josh had said, part of the landscape—like doorknobs, always in the same place and never noticed.

"I wouldn't call Josh's taste cutting edge, but for a conventional guy, he's got a decent sense of style. Except the house is so overdesigned. So it's not him, it's not you. Ergo . . ."

"Josh let her do what she wanted. His parents had money but the house he grew up in, where they still live, I wish you could see it. It looks like they bought it from Miss Havisham and then added indoor plumbing. Whenever he grew out of his clothes they sent him and the housekeeper to his father's salesman at Brooks Brothers. He never gave appearance another thought." (The Geller family's only fashionisto had been Great-grandpa Irving who'd founded the still lucrative Tiny Togs a century before Josh.)

I took up a piece of lamb dotted with Szechuan peppers and, with a small prayer, popped it into my mouth. Naturally, Wynne had her own sets of chopsticks, elegant and enameled in darkest red. Our years of eating takeout from white boxes and drinking beer from bottles were done. She now had antique porcelain bowls she'd bought on her most recent trip to Shanghai. Also, we'd gone from Sam Adams to Puligny-Montrachet.

"Okay, Dawn had her chance to choose a house. Now it's your turn. It's not fair to you to have to live in Temple B'nai Tara." It was so like Wynne to see style symbolizing a marriage, though maybe the idea had merit. A master bedroom so large it felt as though it should have tiered seating for an audience wasn't—to me—loving. The downstairs half-bathroom was totally black and white. The silvery faucets had onyx handles and the toilet was black; it looked like a horror movie's entrance to hell.

I knew Wynne was hoping for me to live the way I'd always wanted to, assisted by her design gifts and Josh's money. But I said, "You don't marry someone and adopt his kid and right away try to erase the past. I was enough of a change in their lives."

"Not first thing. That would be selfish, to say nothing of tasteless. But you're totally a unit now. If you're going to stay on Long Island, you should have a fun project and a house that's you. It might keep you from fixating on guys keying Teslas and staring at parking lots." She adjusted her watch, a hefty gold oblong that looked as if it should be worn by a rich arms dealer. She insisted it was a classic.

"I don't need a project," I said. "I have a job—"

"Sitting around reading books all day—" Wynne interrupted.

"But I like reading books."

"What I'm attempting to point out," Wynne said slowly, "is that after all your years of action and badge flashing and hot guys who pack heat, you've moved to another country. Look, I'm not one of those snotty shits who mock suburbia. Some of my best clients live in Greenwich. But

81

you may not have enough to occupy you. I didn't tell you, Corie—you told me—that you haven't exactly made a ton of friends there."

"It's so awkward. The women go around in threes, fours, and they're so involved in their conversations that, you know, one of them might smile. But if you're walking the dog and they're out for a run, no one stops and says: *Hello, I'm Daphne Teitelbaum.* And wherever you could normally start up a conversation, they're already in the midst of one, on their phones. I joined the temple, Citizens for a More Beautiful Shorehaven, the Wednesday lunch group. I was always part of something: fifth grade, the FBI. For the first time now, I'm alone."

"It sucks. Look, I'm sure you will meet some cool people there and probably soon. But meanwhile, you've got to deal. Your biological clock is ticking louder and louder. Every day you're worrying whether to have a baby because it'll get in the way of your relationship with Eliza, which is certifiably insane. And Dawn's last act on earth was buying those electrified candelabra sconces with fake wax drippings. What the fuck? Is that any way to live?"

"I couldn't stay on the task force and be married, have a new kid, not with the hours I was working. Especially when I was totally wiped from years of exhaustion."

"You could have taken family leave. Okay,

that's over, done. But you've got to know if Josh wanted another Dawn, another chic, aspiring suburban mom, he would have married one. He chose you."

I sighed and rubbed my temples. I was weary after my parents, the conversation with Phoebe, and walking with Wynne around a gallery that looked like the Museum of Stripes. I just wanted a cup of strong tea and the brilliant strawberry gelato Wynne had been touting.

"I'm going to be honest with you," she said.

"Whenever a suspect said that, I knew a shit storm was about to begin." She grinned wryly at me. She knew and I knew her life wasn't exactly too perfect to question—love affairs with twenty-six-year-old social media tycoons; convincing an oligarch in exile that a chair modeled on Tsar Nicholas II's throne was not considered elegant in Manhattan; serial feuds that got started when she tried to enforce peace terms on her warring parents and siblings. It did not evidence what Socrates would have called wisdom. But I could see she was compelled to dive in anyway.

"I am not a terrorist," Wynne said. "I'm your dearest friend and I am telling you that when one begins to obsess about a random man going crazy in Great Neck and decides something about him is deeply wrong, it might be a signal that one is not content with one's life. Maybe you never really got over Sami. Maybe you're subconsciously thinking 'Someday' and that's why you're not committing to this house, this life."

That hit home and probably more forcefully than Wynne had intended. I poured some more wine into a glass that was so delicate that it looked as if it would crack if I sipped too hard. Never having been the sort who understood the phrase "comfortable silence" (unless it was some mutually agreed-upon period of quiet for reading or contemplating a Scrabble move), I guzzled the whole glass of wine I'd just poured, then tried without success to find the famous chisel marks.

I could see Wynne wasn't going to talk first. She had an ability to move to someplace else mentally and deliberate whether to assemble a collection of vintage oyster plates for a client or simply get a hugely expensive matching set.

"First of all, Sami's a nonissue. Or damn close to it," I told her. "We were coworkers and—whatever—lovers. Both those ties are cut." I made a snipping gesture with two fingers. "And second, I don't live an undercover life. But except for Josh and Eliza, no one in Shorehaven knows that I was with the FBI. They all think I spent my entire career in the lit biz pushing stuff in Arabic. Mostly their response is: 'Eeew, their writing is really gorgeous, but how do you read it?' Plus, lowlife prejudiced remarks. I'm not living a lie, but there are times it's better to be vague because of my contract work for the bureau.

"And here's the thing: I don't know when it started, but I started getting similar concealment vibes from Pete Delaney. I sense he's hiding something, too. Either he's not all he appears to be, or something else is going on. Unless it's all in my head."

"Unless," Wynne repeated, which was more politic than: *Of course it's in your head, asshole.*

"And I'll concede that his verbal tells are almost imperceptible, that the other group members wouldn't pick up on how he uses the same phrases about himself every time. Oh, and another thing I just remembered: that he seems to have an unvarying story, phrase-for-phrase if not word-for-word, about getting fired from his ad agency and how rough it was, looking for other work during the recession and having to open an office at home."

"Isn't that the truth?"

"Probably, but it's as if he's reading it from a teleprompter. Unvarying and unengaged."

"But we all have stories about our lives that we tell over and over again," Wynne said. "Like after I broke the engagement to Clive and *Vogue* was downsizing and wanted to send me on a photo shoot to the Everglades not just as editor, but to double as stylist, and how I took a hike and opened my own shop without a single client." I nodded, having read or watched interviews with her. "The more you tell a story, the more polished it becomes. I'm sure I use the same phrases time after time."

I breathed quietly for a minute. "But here's the difference," I said at last. "There was a video on how to keep a low profile for yourself that they had me watch before my exit interview. Keep your story short, light. Have a few vignettes of what your life was so you don't sound like you've memorized your past. People do use the same phrases, okay? But it shouldn't come out fluidly each time. Even my mom, who could memorize Shakespeare's history cycle in a week, might stumble or hesitate. But it would wind up sounding authentic because it's human. Not with Pete. It's always smooth. Smoother than he appears to be, actually."

Wynne didn't say yes or no. She just offered an italianate shrug, complete with raised palms.

"One more thing. He has this combo of risk avoidance and risk seeking that just struck me as odd."

"Like what?" she asked.

"Funny, like this would occasionally happen to me for weeks before I started thinking something was up with him, but it's just bubbling to the surface. When Hurricane Sandy hit, that was pre-Josh. But someone in the group mentioned to me how much he admired Pete. Pete was 'awesomely prepared for any emergency.' He had a backup of food, water, flashlights with good batteries, a sump pump. Oh, and a generator that was hooked up to his computer, so supposedly he could keep in touch with his clients in case of any disaster."

"So? He read an article on emergency preparedness and followed every bullet point," Wynne said. "Or he's a control freak."

"But he's a risk seeker, too. He never looks before he crosses the street. One of the other guys in the group saw a car screech to a stop and said something to him like, 'Don't you look where you're going?' He said that Pete shrugged it off: 'I'm not going to stop for them. They'll stop for me.' "

"That is so arrogant."

"I know, and so crazy. And another thing. This doesn't fit into the crazy category, but he always pays cash. I've never once seen him with a credit card, and I mean that literally. He opens his wallet, and there are no cards in there. Not a one. Just a driver's license and a Shorehaven Library card. And a couple of pictures of his wife and kids."

"Do you want me to give you a list of reasons people use cash?"

"I know the reasons."

That wasn't stopping Wynne. "Okay, some have a cash business, which can be anything from selling drugs or stolen antiquities. Admittedly this

Pete person is a product designer so his clients aren't going to mail him, whatever, five thou in cash. But maybe at some point, like after he was fired, maybe he had to max out on credit cards and he's scared about that happening again. He could have a spending issue and his wife doles out cash to him to keep control. He could have a political objection to consumer credit card debt. You can't always tell from the outside what's going on in someone's life. You of all people, a trained snoop, should know that."

"Of course I know that," I said, as warmly as I could. I did not add: *Everyone fucking knows that.*

She paused, then gently asked, "What's he like overall?" My guess was that Wynne wasn't asking to get more info on Pete; she wanted to gain insight into why I was so intrigued.

"What's he like?" It was less a repetition than my own query to myself. "Low-key, polite. Solid citizen type. He doesn't talk all that much, but when he does, he's all right. And in some ways, like being part of the community, volunteering at the soup kitchen at a church, and offering to teach one of the guys how to put new wire mesh in his window screens, he seems downright decent."

"But you're seeing some kind of similarity between you and him?" Wynne asked. "That there's something he's hiding, or at least not making public?"

"Yes. And you can see, it's obviously a strong feeling."

"So how about this? You feel some weird kinship or similarity. Hiding something. But does it have to be something bad? Maybe he's like you, a retired FBI agent."

"What?" I was thrown by what she said and couldn't answer.

Wynne kept going. "Or a cop or who knows? Maybe he was a spy for the CIA. Hey! A product designer. He could have been like that guy in the James Bond movies who made all those cool weapons. Remember that gorgeous Aston Martin that sprayed an oil slick from the rear so the bad guy behind James Bond would skid off La Grande Corniche? There you have it! In the UK he was called . . . I think Q. But here? Pete Delaney."

# 5

I suppose I still had Wynne's voice in my head
as I observed that my office, like most of the
house, was still decorated in Dawn's taste. It
had been her workout room. The wallpaper was
the palest shade between pink and lilac, a faux
suede that felt vaguely like human skin. It was
as if Dawn's spirit had fused itself to the room's
structure to guard against my fucking with her
design concept. I'd pretty much left it as it was
except to remove a rowing machine, a floor-to-
ceiling mirror, and a ballet barre and to buy a
leather recliner.

When there was a freezing spell that turned the
pavement to a sheet of black ice, I ran on Dawn's
treadmill, though I was half convinced it was
haunted. It would speed up of its own volition,
from a five to a killer eight, or, conversely, stop
suddenly, as if someone had pulled the plug.

After just minutes at the keyboard, my neck
got stiff, maybe payback for recommending a
novel I barely liked (though one that could sell
in English-speaking countries). It was tolerable
if you liked "a tendril of black hair escaped the
embroidered green band of Karima's shambar."
Except my own take didn't really matter. I needed

to come up with enough books worth translating into English to justify my fee. As a vice president of one of the agencies told me, "Hey, literary merit is terrific, but not, like, a requirement. The book's got to move." This one, as my dad would have said, would go nowhere fast.

My mind didn't drift from what I'd read; it shot back to Pete. Wynne had suggested that he could be one of the good guys: law enforcement. That hadn't occurred to me, but it wasn't totally bananas. However, I couldn't buy into her James Bond analogy in which Pete was the American equivalent of Q, retrofitting Corvettes with giant cans of Pam to spritz out from beneath rear bumpers. There was nothing about him that said cop, and not DEA, ATF, or ICE. I'd met only a couple of guys from NSA. They tended to be cerebral, though like the Secret Service in their humorlessness; that was the only way Pete would fit in with them. Basically, he was too concerned with himself to have the awareness of others or the bent for puzzle solving common to investigators.

Still, CIA was possible. It was filled with people who were sure they had superior smarts and license to strut their stuff. Eccentricity wasn't a prerequisite for employment, though the agency definitely condoned it, along with occasional sociopathy. But I couldn't fathom why someone engaged in espionage would operate from a home office on Long Island. If he'd retired from government work, as I had, I could come up with dozens of reasons why he'd want his past blurred, if not invisible. Except he really did have that skill—packaging design—and that was a subset of Madison Avenue, not espionage.

I considered the possibility, which had nagged at me even before Wynne articulated it, that the problem wasn't Pete at all, but me. The world I was now living in was not a perfect fit. I had a limited ability to tune in to conversations about little Harper's tribulations with common core math, or the marble/quartz/granite/polished concrete countertop contretemps. I'd met a couple of women close to my age at a Women in the Bible class at temple, but the nicer one worked in the city and the other had an intermittent southern accent—"Whan Ah wuzz at Duke we would lay-uph"—and then she'd demonstrate, yukking it up as if Daddy had been R. J. Reynolds and not Mitchell Kolodny, DDS.

I felt the urge to move, to get out of the house, though not far. I went into the backyard to see if any of my gardening—half an hour's worth—had come to figurative or literal fruition. I had begun the previous spring, though I calculated the cost of the few tomatoes Eliza and I harvested in August that were actually edible probably was around five dollars each. I was giving it one more year. The most basic planting: impatiens, begonias, some blue things that smelled like cheap weed, along with the grown-from-seed infant vegetables that came in little dissolvable pots you just stuck into the ground.

I was no expert on lettuce growth rates, but I was slowly realizing I hadn't planted enough to make an evening appetizer for a dinner party or even lunch for myself. I pulled off the largest leaf, figuring at least it might look nice sitting under a glob of tuna, but ate it on the way back to the house. Not a very satisfying snack, but as it turned out, in its own crisp way, it offered a Proustian moment.

A lettuce leaf: I recalled sitting across from Jillian King in the New York FBI's Human Resources as she took a break from the Caesar salad she'd been eating when I had arrived a few minutes early for my bureau exit interview. She'd pushed the salad away from her. I said I could come back later, but she shook her head, though the fork holding half a leaf of romaine and crouton stayed aloft until she had to pick up her pen.

For some reason, she had an enormous fondness for me. The "for some reason" was because the few times I'd met with her after my transfer from DC to New York had been pleasant but businesslike. At one annual evaluation, though, Jillian told me I not only read people well but also treated them well without sacrificing any authority. "Excellent qualities," she'd said. I couldn't wait to get back to my desk to call my parents and tell them.

I guessed she was somewhere in her fifties, African American with an auburn pixie haircut. She was big breasted, big shouldered, and her wobbly double chin was the only part of her that didn't look powerful. She'd been the one who had urged me to accept my boss's offer to work on a contract basis. Her advice was: "Never slam a door unless there's something you've got to lock out forever."

Jillian King excelled at all kinds of HR wisdom, like telling me not to preface my opinion on any subject with: *I think*. "Don't be the kind of woman who softens whatever she's going to say. Spit it out. 'I think' implies other people think differently from you. That's ceding authority. Got it? Ditch your mealymouthed"—she pushed up her alto voice into a quavering soprano—" 'I think.' "

Swallowing my lettuce, I decided what I needed to do was call Jillian.

I spent a few minutes trying to come up with a story to explain my interest in Pete, but in the end, mostly because I couldn't think of one that Jillian wouldn't see through, I called and went with something just short of the truth.

"There's a guy in my town I'm wondering

about," I told her. "Seems pleasant, works at home as a freelance packaging designer, probably makes a decent living."

"How old?" she asked.

I'd always been lousy at judging age. He appeared to be older than Josh but not that much, so I said, "Maybe late forties? Anyway, he seems to imply, though never directly, that at some point he did some sort of hush-hush work for the government." This was the untrue part, but it was plausible enough and I was pleased with it. "Nothing to do with his design business."

"If I had a dollar for every basic guy who hints he was CIA," Jillian said, "I could buy my own Caribbean island. They never insinuate the bureau, which would be insulting if they weren't such losers."

"This is the thing," I said. "He's not a loser. Not a winner either. Just incredibly bland. But I'm wondering because I was on the task force and was told to keep a lowish profile because I'm still doing contract work on terrorism cases."

"You think I don't know that?"

"I just want to make sure he's just a basic guy looking for a little glam. Not somebody who might recognize what I'm doing. I'm not Corie Schottland in my day-to-day life. I'm using my husband's name, Geller."

"I know that, too."

I smiled. "What don't you know?"

"Very little," she said, and I had no reason not to believe her.

"This guy and I are in a group of freelancers. Seven of us. We meet for lunch once a week, talk about marketing ourselves, inkjet versus laser printers. Gets us out of the house."

"And you want?" Jillian asked, though she knew the answer.

"I want to know if he actually worked for the government and is being indiscreet about it or, frankly, if he's just pulling it out of his ass. I'd appreciate it if you could check him out. Is he anyone I should be extra careful with or steer clear of? I'm not looking for any detailed info about him, just whether he ever did any government work."

"Military, too?"

I found myself smiling in gratitude, as if I were sitting across from her. "That would be great!" I gave her Pete's name, phone number, and address, and Jillian said that while she couldn't make it a priority, she'd get back to me as soon as she could.

I felt so much better; but then, late afternoons and nights were the good part of the day for me. Eliza was home. After school she'd drop her backpack in the mudroom, come into the kitchen, and hug me for a few seconds, resting her head on my shoulder. Her exhalation of comfort warmed my neck. Maybe it was because she'd gone so long without a mother that she needed physical reassurance; she needed to prove I was still there. She soon ran up to her room, two stairs at a time. Even in a different room, I felt comforted simply because my daughter was in the house. She reminded me why I belonged in this place.

I set the table. I smoothed the allegedly no-iron napkins as flat as I could get them. I had no idea why, after getting married, I chose to follow so many rules from my mom's unwritten book, *Margo's Bizarre, Antiquated Housekeeping Decrees and Passé Upper-Class Lingo*. My dad told me it started early in their marriage when she had a nonspeaking role as a housemaid in a stage revival of *The Philadelphia Story*. Like paper napkins are an abomination. Among all mothers' Ten Commandments, how many listed: *Never, under any circumstances, call a couch a "sofa"?*

The evenings were best of all because Josh was there. Except when he kept a jury late to keep it from hanging or if he was out of town (I hated those nights), he'd be home by seven. I'd always thought of myself as much less sentimental than other women I knew, so it surprised me how important it was to me to have my husband coming home for dinner, to have that routine of intimacy, to be a family. Cognitive dissonance– wise, I had to concede that because I'd spent my entire working life with other people, my pleasure at having him home could have been simple relief at having another adult in the house.

This was an ordinary night, and Josh was home for dinner. As always, I was slightly dumbfounded for the first few seconds when he walked through the door from the garage. His hotness demanded that I stop and look. The following sixty seconds were devoted to turmoil: *He's decent, brilliant, stunning, wealthy, devoted, and what the hell made him choose me?* Which wrestled with: *Definitely a brilliant catch for almost any woman . . . except maybe me.* Then, abruptly, my disquiet ceased because I was famished and dinner was ready.

I'd almost missed meeting Josh. My chance came via an invitation to the retirement party for the assistant director in charge of the FBI's New York office. Though I'd been in meetings with the assistant DIC and had even gotten a letter of commendation for an interview he'd observed (in which I got a suspected terrorist's landlady to speak volumes), I was nowhere near his inner circle. I assumed that whoever had organized the event wanted a few young'uns to lighten up the middle-aged suits or realized there weren't enough women to show how enlightened the honoree's views on gender had been. I deeply didn't want to go. I tried a hoarse voice at work that day, but nobody noticed. I was about to complain about a sore throat but then realized that if someone higher up had singled me out as a bright young thing, I really had to show.

The party was in a bar downtown, near bureau headquarters. The only way to circulate was to move back and forth through the long, narrow room packed with people in itchy winter clothes. I'd had too much white wine because the only way to escape a bore was: *Just going to get a refill.*

I switched to ginger ale. As a bartender handed me a glass, I spotted what was easily the best-looking man in the bar standing beside me. He looked as if he'd dropped in from a superior universe and was neither delighted nor repelled by ours—just observant. He wore a dark navy suit of such quality it seemed made from a finer fabric than existed on earth. I practically had an orgasm from the sound of his smooth, deep voice as he asked the bartender: "Do you have Grey Goose?"

Bottom line: he bordered on incredible. Older than I was, early to mid-forties, handsome in the way of Mediterranean men: golden skin, pure green eyes instead of the predictable brown, hair so dark it looked almost comic book black, and the broad shoulders/slim hips combo. Clichéd good looks, only better: I was ashamed to be so spellbound by the sort of guy women got silly about: *OMG, isn't he gaw-geous?!*

Also, he gave off success vibes. Truthfully? I

was totally egalitarian, usually self-confident, but he seemed too high up the ladder for me. Not snobbish, though. Even in that first glance, he seemed relatively benevolent. Intelligent, too, and self-assured. A tad sad, though maybe it was simply that he felt down at being stuck in a bar that smelled like beer, not Dom Pérignon.

So here I was, taking sidelong peeks at this incredible guy. Recently, my phone battery had died in my gynecologist's waiting room and I wound up skimming a *Cosmopolitan* article about how to act when you're thrown into an awkward situation—like walking up to a stone-faced maître d' or this actual situation, meeting a guy so fabulous you can't bring yourself to actually look straight at him. What do you do?

You smile at him. And by smiling, you appear self-confident enough to realize he's not a divine presence, just another human being. Also, your smile signifies you're happy with your place in the world. So I smiled, and Gorgeous Guy gave me half a smile back, which I interpreted as either shyness—I am courteous but not interested—or that he had been on the verge of taking his vodka and walking toward the back of the bar to find someone he'd prearranged to meet. To this day, I still can't believe that article maybe changed the whole course of my life.

But then that *ding!* of innate comprehension went off in my head. It signaled to me that he did think I was attractive. Hot actually. He took a deep breath (an emotional cue you didn't have to be a special agent to recognize). His eyes stayed on me but without staring creepily.

Much of the time, like about 75 percent, men's reactions to me were more in the *semiattractive* or *good boobs* or *ethnicity?* category. I was fine enough for routine interest if no one beautiful was in the vicinity, though not sufficient to make a much-desired man elbow his way through a crowd at a party. But with a couple of forward body shifts and a step, Glorious Guy came into conversation range. He spoke first, a plus because so many trite openings were swirling around my head that none could emerge.

We got through "Josh" and "Corie." He: "Had a few cases with Bob when I was in the US attorney's office." Me: "Worked with Bob on the Joint Terrorism Task Force." I thought his attention might wander when he heard I wasn't a high-powered attorney, but on the contrary: Josh's eyes seemed to brighten when I told him I was FBI. We moved on to Harvard and Queens College but just that second, Ashleigh Verdon, a special agent, clopped up to me in thick-heeled, black platform shoes that made her look as if she'd borrowed a giraffe's front feet, though for all I knew, they could have been a new style. She cooed, "Corie, you look amazing! Blonder, right? Did you highlight it yourself or have it done?"

Then she spotted Josh. Obviously she hadn't read the smile article. Her eyes went vacant, not so much stupid looking but lifeless. Having experienced the shock of him just three minutes earlier, I understood that on glimpsing someone so terrific, not only are you at a loss for words but also your personality momentarily disintegrates. Josh nodded politely at us both and walked back to the knot of people gathered around Bob.

"Oh my God, do you know who that is?" Ashleigh demanded. I was so bummed at losing my 10 percent chance of maybe making an impression on Josh that I shook my head too hard and maybe made a sour face—not that she noticed. "He's a judge!" she went on. "Judge Geller! Federal, Eastern District. He was, like, one of the top litigating partners at Shannon Little. Then. His wife died. Suddenly. He had a kid. So"—she rested her hand on her chest and took a deep, calming breath—"there was an opening for a judgeship and he got appointed. I mean, he couldn't stay a major, major litigator flying all over the world, having two-month trials and leaving the kid. Well, he could've but he didn't. Everyone says that just goes to show you what a caring . . ."

I let Ashleigh blather hoping that Josh would extricate himself and make his way back to me. He'd want to take up where we left off: to tell me where he went to law school and how his wife died. Perhaps he'd want to hear how I joined the FBI. Maybe there'd be dinner in Chinatown afterward. But he never came back.

So I found my coat on a hook beneath four others. I hoped he was watching out of the corner of his eye and noticing I'd ditched Ashleigh and was on my way out. But he either hadn't seen or didn't care. I went out into a sleety, cold night feeling that the brilliant relationship that was about to enfold us had been yanked away.

At eleven the next morning, Josh called. Asked me out for dinner that night. Said, "You have a great smile."

So I, who thought that I would inevitably have to settle or stay single, got the ideal package. Looks, self-confidence, intelligence, sex, decency—even money, since he had made a pile during his litigator life and had what in his circle was known as "family money," which did not mean an NYPD pension. Okay, not copper mines or banks, but people kept producing tots and the Geller Company's toddler clothes were still considered classics in the twenty-first century. To this day, I'm still not sure how this happened. By waiting until my thirties, I was supposed to settle. Not to find someone, who (I couldn't stop myself from thinking) was out of my league.

Josh was also great in bed. Admittedly, when out of bed, I often felt I was married to the *New*

*York Times*, all the sections. Often insightful, usually informative, sometimes stultifying. Never outrageous.

Josh said he loved me partly because "you are so adventurous." I never actually got what he meant, unless it was some Jewish-girl-with-gun thing. Anyway, once he saw how Eliza and I fell for each other, he was ready for marriage. So now I had a place in the world. And a husband excited about my "spirit" and "intelligence."

The weird thing was that later, judging from his late wife Dawn's insipid collection of books, plus meeting her parents and a few of her Long Island friends, I realized she hadn't exactly lived the life of the mind. When she thought *creative,* it was Jason Wu, not Rebecca Solnit. I had trouble picturing them spending actual time together. And while I could easily see Dawn as a litigator's wife—probably a better one than me—I had trouble seeing her fit into the space Josh now occupied as a judge.

Dinner at a foodie heaven in Brooklyn with, over a dish of raw fish cubes, a long, spirited debate on a study of recidivism in the Eighth Circuit? The chief judge's wife passing around her iPhone so all us spouses could see her photos of illuminated medieval letters she'd taken on her travels: "I don't know if any of you are familiar with the iconography of *The Neville of Hornby Hours*, but . . ."?

To Josh's delight, I chatted her up on Arabic calligraphy.

I was never a fan of mushy love poems: no "I love thee to the depth and breadth and height/My soul can reach"—even when I was fifteen. But an Egyptian poet, Farouk Gouida, wrote something I could buy: "And if I were to choose a home/I would say, my home is your Love." That seemed true, that first year of marriage—even with Dawn's rose marble fireplace mantel casting a pink glow over our bed.

Our first year *did* have that pink glow, which is not to say the rest of the marriage was dulled by brown smog. But being in love filled me with such euphoria that some of my other qualities got pushed to the side—like street smarts. So I didn't pause to think, *Hey, maybe a guy raised by parents so serious-minded they wouldn't listen to NPR because it was too shallow might not always be a ton of laughs.*

Even on our honeymoon Josh didn't totally rebel against his upbringing; he didn't turn giddy with love. Still, he let himself be lighthearted, wanting to join the world outside our house and the courthouse—to have fun. With Eliza and me, he hiked in the Catskills (while his mom and dad's preference would have been to stay home reading monographs about the geological formation of Kaaterskill Falls). The three of us checked out museums from El Museo del Barrio to the New York City Fire Museum, ate our way through the Feast of San Gennaro in Little Italy, took a course in Thai cooking. Such a great time!

Since I wasn't thinking straight, I didn't consider that he'd married dopey (but soignée) Dawn to rebel against the family solemnity. Or I didn't stop to think that maybe he loved it that Dawn looked like the coolest of modern women but, in spite of whatever strength she had, was willing to be that gold standard of conventionality: the devoted wife. Penelope to Odysseus, Carmela Soprano to Tony.

But that's what happens when you get so blissed out that your street smarts take a leave of absence. They can't speak up and remind you: *Yo, he didn't become an editor of* Harvard Law Review *by making merry.* Or: *He had to leave his law firm because there was no Dawn around to take care of the kid while he spent three weeks in Liechtenstein negotiating with its government not to extradite his client.* I never thought to look to a future where his congenital gravity and ambition would bounce back.

"I got a great invitation today," Josh said. When he got excited, as he was then, his voice got deeper, filling the room like a baritone singing a key line in an opera. Even if you were nodding off, you sat up and listened. Which I did, because, unusually, he hadn't gone off to his study that night to review some book for a learned journal. We were sitting side by side, our feet companionably sharing an ottoman, for a TV news night. It had been one of those days with six major breaking news stories, and we needed to catch up with the latest miscarriages of justice and international outrages.

"Tell me," I said enthusiastically. A great invitation? It was probably for some event that to me would be a snore, like a panel at the American Society of Comparative Law, but the setting could be Santiago. (Actually, in the second before he spoke, I'd already switched the setting to La Paz.)

"I was asked to be a visiting judge in the district court in New Orleans."

"New Orleans?" I repeated, cautiously. I was one of the twenty-seven people in America who didn't adore the city, though naturally I'd felt horrible about Hurricane Katrina. "So when would this be?"

"August, September." Probably he saw my head tilt as I waited to hear which one. He turned his full attention to me. "I may not be gone the whole eight weeks," he said. "But I can't give you a guarantee. They have an extremely complex case about offshore natural gas drilling rigs that involves companies in Canada and Germany. I would go down for the last week of August to hear motions, and then the trial."

"They can't send a couple of their cases up to district court in Brooklyn?" I asked. He gazed intently at the remote, as if trying to memorize its face.

I took the remote out of his hand and turned off a former solicitor general who was making an important point; Josh jerked his head back, offended at my rudeness.

"But you just got back from that voting rights discrimination case in Atlanta three weeks ago."

"I realize I've been asking a lot of you," he replied.

"So if the New Orleans trial starts in September, there isn't any way this gig will be part of a fun family vacation."

"No, but we can all go away the first and second weeks of August. We could do something . . . fun. It's too hot to go to Morocco, which I know you've been wanting to do, but instead of hiking in Idaho, we could go to—"

"Morocco is not too hot. They have fabulous beach resorts," I interrupted. "But that's not what we're talking about."

Josh uncrossed his legs. He put his feet on the floor and I thought, *Nothing is wrong with him. Even his toes are handsome.* I was suddenly aware I hadn't gotten a pedicure for at least a month. "I told you I received a great invitation," he said. "And suddenly you get all out of sorts."

"You just told me you may be gone for up to

eight weeks. That was exactly what you told me before Atlanta. But it took six weeks, and I missed out on a really juicy FBI contract job because someone needed to stay home with Eliza. And you're going for what? Natural gas? New Orleans in fucking August isn't April in Paris. What do you need it for?"

"It's very prestigious to be asked."

"Why do you need prestige? You're a federal judge. You have a lifetime appointment."

"I'm thinking I might like to be considered for the court of appeals."

If my throat had been working, I would have gulped, but I'm pretty sure all I did was blink a couple of times. We'd talked about this a couple of years earlier, when one of his colleagues ascended. If that sounds vaguely religious, it kind of was—in the view of some. The purity of the position: reviewing the record of a case in trial court, sometimes hearing oral arguments from attorneys. But no lying witnesses, no unjustly accused defendants—just the written word. A vital process, but work of the intellect, not the heart. I think I scrunched up my nose and probably said, "Blech" as we discussed it. Josh had conceded, "It can be pretty dry, but any district court judge knows it's an honor to even be considered." I think I agreed with that, though at that point, I still believed his striving days had ended when he left Shannon Little, that whitest of white-shoe firms, to go on the bench.

"And the only way to be a visiting judge and add gold stars to your reputation is to leave me and Eliza again for a couple of months? You'll have been gone more than you're here."

"We could see each other on"—he paused— "on some of the weekends."

"What if the bureau calls me for another contract job? They say there's someone in LA who won't talk and we need you, Corie Schottland, to give it one last try?"

"Your parents could help out for however long that would take." Being married to a lawyer meant getting not only an instant answer but also one that sounded so reasonable it would take half an hour to figure what was wrong with it. Josh sounded as if he'd drafted some Equal Opportunity and Unending Fairness in Marriage Act.

"What about our deal that we're going to have a normal life?"

"Corie, plenty of people travel for their careers. This is not abnormal."

"Also, don't forget a couple of months ago you flew off to Boulder for a week for . . . what was it? A complex federal litigation seminar. Okay fine. And then some American Bar Association thing on bail reform for a few days. Was that also for the honor?" I took his nonanswer as a yes. "You didn't even mention wanting to be appointed to the court of appeals."

"It's a vague desire," Josh snapped. "Not even a serious contemplation."

"Leaving us, again, for two months is pretty serious to me. I thought the whole reason you left the law firm for a judgeship was to avoid being apart from Eliza."

"But we're married now."

"True. But you're married to me, not Dawn."

"For God's sake!" It was a quiet outburst. I could see him imploding, lips pushing tight against each other, eyes contracting. This was Josh's alternative to an explosion. "What do you even mean by that?" he finally said.

"You seem to want me to give you what she did." Even though Josh wasn't one to offer glimpses of what he was thinking, he couldn't help it this time. His arms could hardly wait to cross over his chest, and his shoulders bulked up and moved forward. He was defending himself against whatever mush-minded idea I had that was coming his way. "Your deal with her was that you could follow your career wherever it took you. That was her. Not me. We had an understanding that your career was taking you to the Eastern District court in Brooklyn and then home again. That's it. You said you made that decision and you had no reason to go back on it, especially with me in the picture. Equal opportunity: my law enforcement career would be doing the occasional contract job, but I'd find a job with regular hours so we could have a normal life."

"I was perfectly fine with your staying at the bureau," Josh said. "I actually urged you to keep at it. I never said to go into publishing. And I never insinuated that I wanted you to be a full-time housewife."

"I knew that, but I also knew becoming a mother to Eliza would take time. Working anti-terrorism was incredibly draining because I stink at compartmentalization." I never really felt up to the job, yet they kept piling on the responsibility. As one guy who clearly never read his Dostoyevsky assignment remarked to me, "Corie, we think of you as the Grand Inquisitor." I had no idea why he was even saying that, because I tended to recall the mistakes I made much more vividly than my successes. "Maybe I should have stayed on and just switched to a job pushing papers," I continued. "But I couldn't think clearly at that point. I was burned out, so far away from the ordinary life I always wanted that I wasn't sure I'd ever find my way back. And then you came along wanting what I wanted. Normality. A family."

As I was speaking, Josh's constricted face loosened into something between neutrality and benevolence. "I hear you," he said.

"Good." The bureau had been big into

mirroring emotions, so I became a reflection of his neutral benevolence. Instead of saying: *You hear me? With my voice, how the fuck could you not hear me?* I told him: "I understand you miss the action you had when you were a litigator. The competitiveness, confrontation, whatever. But I assumed that for a judge there wasn't any career ladder left. That you'd just be a judge. You seemed so content with that."

He smoothed down his shirtsleeve and started refolding it. In a second he would say something well reasoned, so I didn't give him a chance. "I don't even get why you'd want to do this," I told him. "In district court you're dealing with people: emotion, surprises, meting out justice to the perpetrators and ultimately the victims. On the court of appeals, you don't get any of that. Just a bunch of lawyers talking about arcane parts of law."

He shrugged defensively. "I find it interesting."

I exhaled. "We agreed to be fifty-fifty parents. Look, in four years, Eliza will be in college. Assuming we didn't have a baby . . ." He leaned forward, wanting to hear if I had an announcement. But I just kept going. "You could quit the bench, go back to a law firm, join a think tank. I could go back to the bureau or some big international investigative firm and get paid scads of money. But for now, a deal is a deal." I turned the TV back on and handed the remote back to him. Then I added, "Simple justice."

"Simplistic justice," he shot back, though his tone was quiet, almost kindly. "The law says marriage is a legal union of a couple as spouses and defines its basic terms. But even in the best of marriages, it's an incredibly adaptable contract that's constantly being renegotiated as life changes: economic realities, childcare, household responsibilities."

"Right. There's always room for change." Josh nodded a single time: Glad to see you finally get it. So then I added: "Except any changes in the contract have to be agreed to by both parties."

That's when he left the room.

# 6

Around one o'clock the next day, I made myself a tuna melt, put on a Mets cap, and grabbed a can of lime-flavored seltzer. I stuck my phone into my back pocket, a book—*Quantum Physics for Poets*—under my arm, and went outside. Reading mostly fiction for a living overburdened me with imagined worlds and lives. For pleasure, I found myself reading more and more nonfiction. History, politics, biographies, and intelligently written, dumbed-down science. Knowledge for knowledge's sake.

I liked trying on other lives in my imagination. Maybe I got that from my mom. While I read *Charles Dickens: A Life*, I was teaching Victorian literature in my head. I became an archaeologist digging up ancient China while reading *The Eternal Army: The Terracotta Soldiers of the First Emperor*. I'd always been drawn to these temporary jobs since I'd never had any one single grand passion of my own.

Like I hadn't chosen Arabic; it had chosen me.

I was pretty good with languages. No one mistook me for a native speaker, but I was good enough so that from my Spanish I could often get the gist of an overheard conversation in

Portuguese, sometimes even Italian. But another romance language? The idea of two semesters of *Je m'appelle Corie Schottland* at Queens College didn't exactly give me a *frisson*.

I decided on Russian: I wanted to read Gogol, watch depressing movies without having to read the subtitles, go to all those vodka-soaked nightclubs in Brighton Beach. Except Elementary Russian was filled and I needed a three- or four-credit course, though who knew back then that Russian would once again turn into such a marketable skill? Since I was already primed to try a non-Latin alphabet, I chose Arabic 101 almost arbitrarily, figuring (wrongly) that my bat mitzvah Hebrew would help me master all those curlicues.

Despite its difficulty, I did fall in love with the language—its golden age literature, especially— so I wound up majoring in it. I got a travel grant and spent a summer living with a family in Jordan. Later, I spent the second semester of my junior year at the American University of Beirut studying *maqāma*, a form of rhymed prose— mostly on scholarship, but partially funded by my entire bank account, plus help from my parents. So I could definitely manage a meaningful conversation in Arabic. Of course, by that point, I'd already started and dropped majors in theater and political science. Who knew if I'd stick with it beyond college?

But then came 9/11. Overnight, I put aside all thoughts of role-playing and became my dad's daughter. I would serve my country. Get the bad guys. The only question became whether I could be good enough to be truly useful.

Now, here I was in yet another life. My big dreams of marriage and a family had never been this grand. They'd been more on the split-level level: spending nights in a queen size with a pleasant, relatively solvent, and intelligent husband who didn't fart in his sleep. Along with all his other pluses, Josh's gastrointestinal tract was serene.

Sitting in the backyard, I had to admit real fresh air smelled better than a clothes-dryer sheet. Our dog, Lulu, kept me company while I had lunch on the bench beside Dawn's rose garden. It was late May, but the bushes were already filling out with pink and red blooms. A few yellow ones had opened, but though they were beautiful, their heads hung low. Probably missing Dawn. I'd given them some rose food, but they weren't responding well. Still, nature was nice.

I took a big glug of soda, which was when Jillian King called back. Lulu leaped off my lap. "Found your guy," Jillian said. I covered the mic so she wouldn't hear me choking on sparkling water. "But there was nothing to find. Never worked for any government, federal or local. Never in the military. No arrests, no nothing.

A blessed bore." I thanked her profusely and promised that when I was downtown, I'd stop in and say hi.

So now I knew that all Pete's quirks—from his sitting where he could always watch his car to his switching cell phones—weren't the behaviors of a former feeb or postal inspector. He appeared to be just a blah suburbanite. Okay, not quite blah since he had an ugly streak of vindictiveness and odd behavior that was worth investigating.

Well, that's what my dad had suggested. Like a lot of cops, he was a major mystery fan. I assumed he'd read some Sherlock Holmes (even though Arthur Conan Doyle was on his lengthy list of anti-Semites who didn't kill Jews but they should go fuck themselves anyway). My guess was he'd read the Sherlockian maxim: "When you have eliminated the impossible, whatever remains, *however improbable,* must be the truth." Except his version was: "Once you exclude everything else, what you got is probably the truth, but just in case, don't toss your notes."

Trailed by Lulu, I went up to my office to type up my many random thoughts about Pete. Between that and looking at images of the Google results for "good packaging design," I almost forgot to pick up Eliza after her dance lesson.

Chance t' Dance was annoying not only for its ridiculous apostrophe, but because classes could run anywhere from five minutes to twenty minutes late, leaving parents in their cars to call their friends who were a quarter mile away waiting for their kids to emerge from the music school, Bach & Roll. Or they could stare through their windshields at the rear entrances of a bakery, a bicycle store, a real estate office; there was also a shop catering to late elementary and lower middle schoolers where Eliza had bought her collection of tiny tubs of lip gloss in revoltingly sweet scents, like decomposing watermelon or fetid peach.

Suddenly I realized I hadn't been paying attention to whether Eliza had emerged from the studio. The longer I lived in Shorehaven, the more susceptible I became to helicopter parent syndrome and all its terrors: if not constantly monitored, a child could be abducted or bitten by a Global South mosquito.

Eliza wasn't naturally aggressive, but she was strong enough. She'd learned some smart self-defense maneuvers from the Shorehaven Academy of Martial Arts. Plus I'd coached her to become an effective screamer: it was so inbred in women to avoid causing offense that most barely raised their voices when met with some objectionable or even appalling act. I didn't want her being the sort of girl who would genteelly murmur: *Please don't do that.* I wanted her to be capable of roaring *No!* Eliza, after much encouragement, developed a sonic boom of a voice, almost as loud as mine.

I had my head down pondering in what era cuticle maintenance became a thing women were supposed to do when someone said, "Hey, Corie." An instant later, she added, "Ooh," as if she thought she'd wakened me.

Iris Kubel, owner of the Movable Garden and Wednesday lunch group regular, took an apologetic step back from my car window. "It's okay," I assured her. "I was here, but my mind took a hike and my eyes closed." I got out of the car. "What class is . . . ?" Naturally, I couldn't remember her kid's name.

Before I could say "your daughter," she said "Annie." Then she added, "Jazz. Whatever that is. They throw their arms up into the air a lot, then walk and wiggle, then change direction and do the same thing. And your . . . ?" Her hesitation was over not only the name, but whether Eliza was my daughter or stepdaughter.

"Daughter. I adopted Eliza the year after I married Josh. She's in hip-hop. Every week after class, she insists on teaching me the moves and humoring me, like: 'Hey, you're killing it!' "

Iris shook her head like: *No hip-hop moves for me, ever.* Well, she didn't look any more like a dancer than I did. She wasn't a beach ball, but she was more spherical than not. It worked for her. Roundness is childlike and lovable, like the creatures in cartoons, R2-D2 and BB-8 in *Star Wars*. Even her broad and freckled upturned nose appeared plump. Her adorableness, however, was slightly at odds with her personality: pleasantly direct but definitely uncute.

We were at that awkward moment of deciding whether to keep chatting or do the hyperanimated *Great seeing you* business, when it occurred to me that Iris had been the one who told me about having seen Pete in a T-shirt at the school car wash fund-raiser: "Like his muscles had muscles," she'd said one Wednesday as we spotted Pete across the street while we waited for the light to change. "And you'd never know it to look at him on a regular day." I figured it would be weird if I launched into Pete Delaney's pecs right away, so I asked, "How's the sowing and reaping business this week?"

"Really amazing," she said. I noticed then that she was wearing English gardener clothes, that messy gentry style I remembered from old BBC sagas I used to watch with my mom when my dad had the night shift. Iris had on a washed-out black T-shirt, an old multipocketed khaki vest, jeans, and those high green rubber boots that had yellowed from years of sun and mud. "In fact, I just came from my wholesaler with a ton of heuchera," she continued. "Oh my God, May is always a killer month for me. Everyone is still totally in love with heuchera now. It does great in shade so I'm mixing it in a lot of pots." Obviously I blinked because she added: "They're perennials, an evergreen genus. The leaves come in a gazillion colors. I'll show you. You should see what I've got in the back of my van."

Iris may have looked as if she'd plod slowly across the parking lot, but she was definitely jet propelled. She got to her van before I did. As she opened the back doors, I was prepped to ooh and aah at her plants politely, but it turned out they really were gorgeous. All sorts of reds, oranges, greens, and purples from mauve to the darkest shade of wine.

"Wow!" I said. "Too bad it's not Wednesday. After lunch you could take us outside and use these for your show-and-tell." She smiled—not just good manners but genuinely pleased I was so enthusiastic.

Chance t' Dance classes were blessedly still in session, so before the kids started pouring out, gyrating or pliéing, I said, "You were the one who really got the Wednesday group started, weren't you?"

"I was. During the recession."

"What an awful time," I said. "One day you're rushing to get to work, you belong in some hierarchy with workplace relationships you look forward to, or not. But the next day, you're suddenly on your own."

She nodded. A strand of light brown hair

escaped from the giant tortoiseshell clip on top of her head and hung down on her cheek. "Absolutely. And with no one to talk to. I mean, out of the blue, I would have company when I was potting lantana because people were working from home, and they were so glad to be with someone else. So I came up with the idea of a lunch group. Network, exchange ideas for running a business from home, a little gossip about what's going on around town."

"How did you choose who was in the group?"

"It just kind of happened. I knew John Grillo because I volunteered at Old Westbury Gardens and he'd worked there as a landscape architect. But by the end of 2008, he had his own business. Terrain and drainage."

"Such a nice guy," I said. "Don't you love his voice?" I figured I should make some chitchat before I jumped on the Pete wagon. "Soothing, but not the super-soothing manly hum that puts you to sleep."

"Yes!" Iris said. "And even though he's so dressed down, he reminds me of those guys in dinner jackets in black-and-white movies, with his white sideburns. So suave. And next came Phoebe. She was always texting me when she got anything that looked like it could hold a flower."

"And Pete?" Curious but casual. I kept myself from looking at my watch, though I worried that the kids would come flying out any minute.

"I think . . . oh, John brought him in. Their wives got friendly volunteering at North Shore Hospital, feeding people who couldn't feed themselves. I've got to give them credit. I don't know that I could do that. Anyway, John heard about Pete losing his job at an ad agency and starting his own business at home."

"Right. These guys who stay at home? It's a plus for the community. Weren't you telling me Pete was working at some car wash fund-raiser at the high school? He looked like a Marvel muscleman?"

"Right!" Iris said. "I cannot get out of my mind that he was in a T-shirt and I was shocked that, you know, like he had a body. Not Marvel quality but ripped."

"So why does he dress like he does? I can't get my mind around that he makes a living as a packaging designer."

"Neither can I. Maybe he's conservative life-wise or stylewise. But pants belted halfway between his waist and nipples? Ewww! Just plain ugly. Because his designs are good."

"Right," I said. A couple of fingers of a gardening glove stuck out of one of her vest pockets in a perky fashion, like a man's pocket square. I checked her hands. They were manicured, the nails a pearlescent rose. She seemed to need to have everything pretty.

"Remember when it was his turn to talk one

week and he brought in that bag of coffee beans that looked like a take-out cup?" Iris asked. "That was cool. Imaginative." I nodded.

I didn't have time to go through Pete's oeuvre: "So he's doing well with his own business?"

"He must be. I asked if he'd be willing to make up a logo for me. I made it totally, totally clear that I'd insist on paying his usual fee. Okay, it wasn't the biggest job, but I wanted something better than what I had on the truck and my website: an old Tuscan pot with calibrachoa, coleus, petunias, lantana, and—" She broke off. "You're not a gardener."

"No, though I know the word 'petunia.' "

"That's a start. Anyway, my sister photo-shopped this big pot for me. It looked okay, not too amateurish. But it wasn't sophisticated enough for the client base I wanted to attract. Anyway, Pete was polite, but weirdly . . . stiff. He said something like: 'I appreciate your thinking highly of my work, but I make it a point not to mix business and social relationships.' Not 'I'm sorry.' Not 'I'd be glad to recommend someone to you or tell you what you should be looking for in a designer.' " Iris shrugged, then suddenly seemed to notice the strand of hair that had escaped from her clip. She caught it and put it back.

"When you say, 'weirdly stiff,' was there anything really off about the way he was acting?"

Iris shook her head. "No. Not really off. Just not going along with the usual interpersonal stuff."

"That's how he strikes me, too," I offered encouragingly. "Just a little off. You know, there's an Islamic proverb. Well, there's always an Islamic proverb, but this one is so perfect: 'Feed the poor and pat the head of the orphan.' It really means to show compassion to people in all sorts of need, whether it's a physical need or an emotional one."

I must have missed the door of Chance t' Dance opening because the girls—and the three boys who had their own hip-hop class—came pouring out. The girls were practically in uniform: black leggings and white shirts, their ponytails dancing up and down as if to the beat of some song they could still hear.

One of the interview techniques I used was getting inquiries to sound like conversation. At least I hoped so, so I quickly asked: "So if he was so definite in his 'no,' could you take that as a sign that his business is doing well?"

"I guess so. Actually? Really good, now that I think about it. He doesn't beat his own drum, does he? But I have a client right around the corner on Greensward and the last time I drove by the Delaneys' house, I saw they'd put in a new driveway, Belgian block, and did a major landscape overhaul. The landscape design wasn't up my alley. The kind that's in such good taste it looks bland. But hey, life has lots of different alleys." Iris stopped for an instant to wave at her daughter. From twenty feet away, the kid looked pretty, slightly rounded, with petunia-pink bangs. "They did put in a copper beech that I thought was a gorgeous specimen. Must have cost him close to the national debt! So I guess he's raking it in."

# 7

On the rare occasion when my dad was denied a favor, he resorted to the con. In every other way he was as ethical as the best of cops, except for that willingness to announce to anyone who said no to him—from the super in our building to a captain in the NYPD—"Hey, you owe me one." He mixed a little disappointment, some anger, and a sprinkle of disgust with the sorrow of a humanitarian whose benevolence has meant nothing.

So when he came over the next morning, it took him just two calls to get Pete's last known addresses. The most recent was from the early 2000s, when he'd been a Madison Avenue top packaging star—or best supporting—and, if Google Earth could be trusted, he'd lived in what looked like a Norman château. The house was a mere nine miles from mine, in an affluent hamlet sandwiched, like a tasty country pâté, between Old Brookville and Upper Brookville. It had been just him and his wife Jenny then. I assumed they must have been planning a family since the house had five bedrooms. They'd sold the house in 2009 and moved first to a garden apartment in Shorehaven. Two years later, they bought their house on Amberley Road.

We hopped into the car, and I drove east on Northern Boulevard, past a zoning mishmash of fast-food restaurants and high-end shopping malls. My dad seemed slightly bummed that he didn't have to play his "you owe me" card since he was almost immediately able to reach a Nassau County PD homicide cop he'd worked with on two cases. "Hey, Bernice, kiddo!" he boomed into the phone. Detective-Sergeant Wollman had no problem with professional courtesy. He told her what he needed, and added, "I'd appreciate it, and for fast you get extra credit."

We were still in Nassau County, but suburbs had turned to country. Old Gold Coast estates and potato farms had been subdivided into mini-estates. There was a barn here, a paddock there. The side roads looked torn up, but in an English village way, like a setting for a *Father Brown* episode, that would play to an Anglophile's aesthetic.

The local cops worked out of an intensely sweet white cottage with black shutters. Letters in an old-fashioned font spelled out OLD BROOKVILLE POLICE and arched over the door. But we didn't have to stop there and make friends, because Bernice Wollman called back my dad in less than five minutes. He put her on speaker so I heard her say, "Okay, Dan. None of the locals on duty ever heard a word about Pete Delaney. So assume model citizen until you learn elsewise."

"Will do," he said. I prayed he wouldn't tell her she was a real sweetheart for helping him out. "You're a pal, Bern. Thanks."

Most of the houses were traditional—Tudors, Georgians, and a couple of Dutch colonials. But there was one that didn't fit: a single-story built on high pilings that was mostly glass and rough grade wood. It looked as if the original owners had come to the neighborhood after winning a full set of architectural drawings for a beach house at a charity raffle. But since it lay directly across the street from the château the Delaneys had owned, I decided to go there first. However, my dad eyed the long path leading to the house and the staircase leading to the entrance and said, "You go. I just came along for the ride." I felt myself swallowing. Nerves. I hadn't done door-to-door in ages. "It'll look like overkill if two investigators come for a background check. You can handle it."

The woman in the beachy house looked at me as if she saw something that made her want to throw up. But then I realized it was ordinary caution. Her lips were pressed tight together, except some doctor had so overdone the filler that a closed mouth gave the impression of imminent spew. Actually, she was pleasant, and told me: Sorry, they'd only moved in a year before and really didn't know much about the neighbors. No, she hadn't heard a word about any people who had moved away.

I walked across the street—a healthy stroll—and knocked at the door of what had been Maison Delaney. A voice said over a speaker, "In a minute!" but it was more than that. I started thinking how for so many years on the Joint Terrorism Task Force, I hadn't had to conduct routine investigations—no knocking on doors to ask the kind of questions that were the bread and butter of detection. No ninety-second Q and A's. People were brought to me. I got to question them in one of several examination rooms. I had access to my own tea bags and honey. Sometimes I'd go to one of the triply secure spaces in the Metropolitan Correctional Center. At either place, whenever I finished (for better or worse), I had something resembling a connection with the person I'd been interrogating.

Still, I liked this—going in cold, being outdoors, going from house to house. Of course, federal agents and cops more often found themselves in piss-scented buildings, climbing creaking stairs to the fifth floor of a walk-up, listening for trouble but often just hearing the crunch of insects' exoskeletons under their shoes.

The house was owned by a couple named Tuccio, both dermatologists. Neither was home, though. The housekeeper, whose name was Martina, was easygoing and probably lonely.

She gave me a guided tour of the house that for a second made me recall Wynne once saying that the color of grout should not be chosen lightly. Anyway, Martina mentioned that the kitchen was going to be redone, so I got a view of what had probably been the Delaney kitchen, with turn-of-the-century stainless steel appliances, a glass cooktop, and dark wood cabinets with windows. One member of those silently seething couples you see on *House Hunters Reno* would shake his/her head and proclaim, "I cannot live with that," but it looked okay to me. Upscale but not fancy. Martina, who wore a half-apron she tied with a big bow in the back, said she was sure she had never heard the name Delaney mentioned. But she gave me the name of a friend around the corner who'd been working at her employers' house for more than thirty years.

My dad waved at me as I passed him and said he was dandy, watching an episode of *Death in Paradise* he'd downloaded on his cell phone.

I finished up the rest of that block, which was three houses on one side and two on the other. Only one person was home, a guy in his late teens who looked as if he was still stoned from the night before, but he mumbled that they had moved into the area just four years earlier. No, never heard of a Delaney.

Neither had Martina's friend around the corner, Olga, though she had begun working for the family she took care of when they moved in twenty-eight years earlier. She thought she might have heard the name Delaney, but only in the context of the youngish couple who didn't have any children yet. No, never heard anything negative about them. She didn't think they were an important part of the community but gave me two peanut butter cookies and the name of a woman farther down her street who had been around forever, one of the few original owners left. Olga opened the door and pointed at the house, which might have been the largest log cabin ever built. I slipped the cookies into the pockets of the lightweight blazer I was wearing.

Mrs. Lena Rattray, the owner, told me not to call her Ms. Then she asked for ID. I pulled a Bulldog Investigators business card from my cross-body bag. One of my dad's fellow retirees had sent it to him when he and a New Jersey cop started their own business. This particular card was more useful than most because the name on the lower left was E.J. Lyons; it was perfect for me to flash.

She went and got her glasses to examine the card. At length: it was as if she were studying for a final. The she held it aloft so that light from the antler chandelier in her hallway illuminated it further. She didn't seem suspicious, just intrigued by it, as if she had some arcane specialty like business card paper stock. Finally, she handed it back to me: "What's the E and the J for, Mrs. Lyons?" she asked.

"Emma Jane," I said.

"You have a background?" she inquired, taking off her glasses and hooking an earpiece over the scoop neck of her long-sleeve mustard yellow T-shirt. I guessed she was in her late sixties, with that slightly coarse salt-and-pepper hair and mottled skin that signified an unfortunate lack of vanity (which bothered me to be thinking because I knew it was antifeminist, but a little argan oil never killed anybody). She did look fit, though, or maybe "strapping" would be a better word, with big shoulders, long arms, and large feet. They were firmly planted, in part because she was wearing some leather equivalent of white sneakers with ultrathick soles.

"A background as an investigator? Yes," I lied pleasantly. "I was with the NYPD for twenty years." I went into the story about investigating someone for a big job in a private equity firm—someone who had lived in the neighborhood about ten years earlier. "Peter Delaney. His wife's name is Jenny—Jennifer. They lived in that house on Rolling Hills Road that looks like a French château. It's a light pink now, but it may have been . . ."

"I know the house. Delaney. I thought he was in advertising."

I had a few seconds of dizziness, the way you

do when you realize you hadn't thought something out well enough and you expect to hear your supervisor say: You're a goddamn shithead, Schottland! I nodded enthusiastically at her superb memory. "That's right! He had been a packaging designer with one of the major agencies. But he lost his job in 2008." Mrs. Rattray nodded back. "Then he went back to school for a master's in finance." She nodded again, which signaled that she had accepted not only me, but the entirety of my C-minus narrative.

"Want some coffee or Coke?" she asked. She didn't seem a natural in the hospitality department, but I was at least a break in her day.

I told her I was overcaffeinated that morning but could do with some water. I followed her sensible footsteps through the massive log house into the kitchen. It looked like one of those Adirondack lodges you see in movies where guests gather around a fire at night, tell ghost stories, and then someone lets out a blood-curdling shriek. But it was, after all, Long Island, and the only sound she let out was *Oops!* when the morning coffee she was pouring over ice cubes overflowed her glass. I took a sip of my water and listened as she told me what she knew about Jenny Delaney, which wasn't much. She'd heard from one of the neighbors that Jenny Delaney was expert at knitting and crocheting, a woman of many afghans. She also seemed very sweet and friendly, but not overly friendly, not like in the pushy sense. For me, "pushy" was one of those warning words, but happily nothing else followed

"She sounds nice," I said neutrally. "What about Mr. Delaney?"

"I hardly ever saw him. Just at a couple of community get-togethers."

"Did he ever act as if he'd had too much to drink?"

Mrs. Rattray shook her head. "No. And he certainly didn't seem like one of those quiet drunks either, the ones who walk back to the bar and the next thing you know they're on the floor and blaming the rug." I gave the first *Huh* of a laugh before realizing she hadn't meant her remark to be humorous.

"Drugs?" I asked. "Did he ever seem over-talkative? Laughing more than a situation called for." I took one more sip of the water she'd given me. I did not tell her that it's a good idea to dump your ice cube bin every month because ice picks up freezer odors. Hers had a vague taste of frozen hot dogs.

"No. Nothing like that."

"Did he ever act . . . blissed out, as if he were seeing the face of God?"

"That's a good way to put it," she said. "I know what you mean, but not from him. Bliss didn't seem part of his makeup. Not from drugs. Not from anything as far as I could tell."

"I see you're very observant," I told her. Her head went down, probably a nonconscious nod of agreement.

"I'll tell you the truth," she said; "there was nothing about him that I ever saw that would make him unfit for an equity job, not that I know exactly what that is." Well, neither did I. "So as far as your investigation goes, I don't think there was any problem when he lived here."

"No loud music? Any fights with neighbors? Any sign of abusive behavior on his part? Not just physical: could have been verbal." She shook her head again. "Did he spend a lot of money? Expensive cars, remodeling the house?"

"Not that I ever saw."

"Is there anything else about him you have observed? Positive or negative."

Mrs. Rattray got busy aligning the hem on the sleeves of her T-shirt. "You know I hate to say something that could ruin his chances . . ."

"Please—unless there's some blatantly bad behavior, there's nothing that would stop him from going where he's headed."

"He was hard to talk to. Not shy. Some men are shy." She licked her dry lips. "Some men are just awkward in social situations. Probably more me than him, anyway."

Her stopping, I sensed, had to do with not

wanting to be seen as a gossip rather than not wanting to talk. Still, I had always been skilled at encouraging witnesses to talk but not to over-state (which could be a disaster with a grand jury or in a courtroom). "It may not be you, Mrs. Rattray. Not all gut reactions are correct, but a lot of them are." I tilted my head slightly, as if to better pick up not just her words, but her vibes.

"I always felt inhibited talking to him," she finally said. "Not because he couldn't give me a sentence or two back. I just couldn't tell what he was thinking. I was sure it was nothing positive, which is okay. But was I boring him or saying something he didn't like? I remember telling my husband that even if I was clever or beautiful, it wouldn't have mattered to Mr. Delaney. Nothing would have."

"How did your husband respond?"

"That's what was so odd. He told me, 'I find myself avoiding him, too! Not that there's any-thing wrong with him . . . Except maybe there is.' "

Wednesday came around again, and it was my turn for show-and-tell at the group's lunch. I held up the English translation of Ahmed Mourad's thriller, *Vertigo*. Its jacket was predict-ably dizzying but also sophisticated. It was drawn from a low, cinematic angle. Blood from a Francis Bacon decapitated corpse was echoed in the typography. A few members of the lunch group offered such appreciative *Mmm*s and *Ooh*s that I quickly did the disclaimer business: I had zero to do with bringing that novel to the English-speaking world (and by the way, the novel had no connection to the Hitchcock movie).

"I picked this book because it's a good illustration of the differences between English- and Arabic-language book-jacket design," I began. "Now, considering that I work in publishing, you know I'd never say a picture is worth a thousand words. But it is worth something. And later, I'd be interested to hear what you think the book covers have to say about how different cultures view the same story." Actually, I wouldn't be interested, but asking for input was probably number three on the group's unwritten rules of etiquette. Every presenter could go home thinking: *Wow, all those comments. I get them so involved.*

That day, I'd planned to set a trap: hit the visual during my show-and-tell. Usually I'd talk about a particular book or different agents' reactions to the same work of fiction or speak about a genre, anything from romance to graphic novels. But that day, I thought maybe an eyeful of heartrending or violent book art could evoke some response from packaging-sensitive Pete Delaney that a mouthful of words couldn't. Worth a shot. I saw myself asking him casually: *So Pete, what do you think of this package?* Whatever his answer, it would be revealing.

Okay, so maybe it was an emaciated little fantasy, but I was enjoying it, especially since it ended with me triumphant: *He disclosed the truth without knowing it.* At the least, I'd have the chance to observe him looking at artwork—some of it violent or at least icky. And who knew what clues I'd find in his reaction? *Damnably clever of you,* as my mom would say, mimicking some BBC via PBS detective.

Except maybe it wasn't so clever of me this time, because Pete wasn't at the lunch. When we had all arrived at the table, Iris told us not to hold Pete's usual seat because he was in Kansas City. He'd emailed her the day before that he wouldn't get back until late afternoon.

Still, my show had to go on, so I held up *Vertigo.* Hmm: I noticed a couple of queasy expressions. Then, Phoebe Melowicz shrilled *Eeew,* and added, "Caaaw-reee! We're in the middle of lunch."

Oops. Even though the illustration was stylized, I had to admit it probably wasn't a picture to accompany quiche aux légumes on Long Island.

"Sorry." I put the book facedown on the table. "It is disturbing. Crime fiction is a way for writers to challenge the powers that be. It talks about injustice. Don't forget. This is set in Egypt. In recent years, what with Mubarak, Morsi, el-Sisi, violence by the state . . ." I mumbled on for a few minutes.

Years of working on terrorism cases had almost paralyzed my gag reflex. It was like when my dad worked homicide and the detectives passed gruesome crime scene photos across the pizza box. It's not that you don't get appalled by the awful things people do to people. It's not that you're untouched by death and pain. You just stop getting shocked. However the brain worked, it trained itself to go straight from sickening observation directly into analytic mode, skipping emotion—or maybe just stomping it down.

After a few more moments, most of the group wound up engaged in my discussion. Fortunately and unfortunately, they segued into a predictable, relatively uninformed discussion of the Middle East. (Not Darby, the photo retoucher. He got busy examining all the books in the tote bag I'd brought. He had a magnifying light on his cell phone and was totally immersed in the details of the jackets.) Meanwhile, Marcalynn began praising Netanyahu. Maybe I was snappish when I said, "We're talking Arabic books here," which caused Lucy the data miner to mutter: "A plague on all their houses." I corrected her: "A plague o' both your houses!" Iris, who seemed to sense I was overly irritated at the misquote, cut me off to remind the group of our no-politics rule and how excellent it was that the group had gotten through

141

the 2016 election unscathed. Then John Grillo asked if I'd go halfsies on a crème caramel with him, as we sometimes did, and I said sure.

The following morning on my way to the Italian deli, I kept hearing a moan from my car. Low and husky: erotic in a guy, distressing in the rear axle of a Subaru. So I abandoned my goal of fresh mozzarella and drove to the Subaru dealership. I negotiated a loaner car, one of those gray sedans that mean-spirited corporations give salespeople.

The sky that morning was grayer than the loaner. Backlit by an unseen sun, it sucked the color from the already murky pavement and cast a shadow over the storefronts and medical buildings of Northern Boulevard. The air felt thick. I wished I could be anyplace else.

Anyplace else except home, that is, because the next item on my to-do list was finally writing my DON'T RECOMMEND report on a collection of seven short stories. They were all set in a souk in Tangier during one week: a great concept, except the stories were more like vignettes. A widow looks for a serving tagine and as she bargains, recognizes that the seller used to live in the town she came from. That was it. A meticulous description of the tagines, of a remembered lamb dish: no plot, no resolution except the Arabic equivalent of: *Say hi to the folks for me.*

So I wasn't in any rush. Yet another DON'T

RECOMMEND could wait till after lunch. I drove back to Main Street in Shorehaven with a vague idea of checking out a spy novel or a mystery. I was tired of screens. I pulled into the library's parking lot and took out my phone to get a note with a list of "you've got to read it" books, but I got to the picture of Josh on my home screen. We'd gone fly-fishing in Idaho and I caught him with two days of beard and (slightly) messy hair: East Coast legal guy as rugged western dude. I smiled at him. It was from when we'd had more than intermittent fun.

Most couples with a fourteen-year-old kid have familiar relationships that range anywhere from loving to near death. What I'd noticed living among them is they had no new stories for each other, only reruns. Josh and I were still in that "surprise" stage where—presto!—untold anecdotes still popped up, hidden qualities might burst out. Like Josh going to the bottom drawer of his desk in chambers, pulling out a harmonica, and serenading me with "Swing Low, Sweet Chariot." Me telling him how I'd tripped a woman trying to run out of her apartment so she could escape an interview. Her arm broke and I felt zero guilt about her screams, though I spent a couple of weeks feeling guilty that I was heartless enough not to feel anything.

These occasional revelations were a definite plus. They added zing. Which I needed because night after night of listening to Josh at dinner could be less than transfixing.

Sure, he'd been out in the world, but he wasn't worldly in any bon vivant way. His was very smart. Cerebral, even. And considerate, responsible. But sparkling? Only his eyes.

Dinner could be a heavy meal if Josh chose the subject. His idea of fun table conversation was *How was your day?* over the arugula salad and cross-examining Eliza on what she learned about friendship and isolation in *Of Mice and Men*. He'd ask me about Palestinian writers living in Jordan through the grilled chicken and roasted corn, and give us his day in court until sorbet and cookies were downed.

Other people didn't find him dull. At any gathering, he was congenial company. Or at least his looks and manners conveyed charm. But at home, he seemed to feel that if he didn't guide the conversation, it could go anywhere. I saw his mouth inch into an upside-down U when Eliza and I became enthusiastic about the Cylons in *Battlestar Galactica*. He definitely didn't buy my "They're really about the nature of consciousness" explanation or Eliza's "They were monotheists, probably, and the humans believed in *gods!*" It could have been his upbringing; in his family, the F-word was frivolity.

I put down my phone. My hands, on their own volition, sought the steering wheel; I couldn't

144

reach for the door handle and get out, go into the library. Instead, I took out my phone and googled "copper beech"—as in the high-priced tree Iris had spotted on Pete's lawn. After scrolling through enough images to establish an I-Thou, I drove to the Greensward, the street Iris had mentioned her client lived on, around the corner from Pete. From there, I then made a few rights and lefts. At last, on a three-block-long street called Amberley Road, there was a house with a copper beech tree shading the front lawn. I stopped.

What had I learned at Quantico about stakeouts? I couldn't remember anything useful other than common sense: *Don't park directly across the street from the subject.* Not that I was staking out the place. I was just parking diagonally across the street and a couple of houses back. Well, why not? Casa Delaney was a really nice house, on the small side but dignified, set back from the sidewalk on a rise of lawn. It was two stories high, made of some white material that wasn't stucco, brick, or shingle. However, on the roof, two window things protruded, as if 9 Amberley Road were undergoing some form of asexual reproduction that could ultimately mature into a full third floor.

From the sidewalk, five brick steps led up to a straight brick path that was perpendicular to the front door. On either side of those entry steps was an iron railing flanked by thigh-high evergreen bushes with buzz cuts. Even in the day's gloom, the house seemed bright and cared for. The copper beech stood on a pristine lawn. It looked as if it could be as high priced as Iris described it. Purple leaves nearly obscured widespread branches. The gray trunk was so understated it seemed designed like architecture. On the front of the driveway, two black garbage cans and an orange recycling pail were precisely lined up, equidistant from one another.

Scrunching down in the driver's seat just in case (though I felt safe in the anonymity of the loaner car), I took a picture, then pulled away and parked around the corner. There, I texted the shot to Wynne and wrote: *Impt: tell me abt ts house. $$? In gd taste? Anything notable abt it?* I hoped she wasn't with a client because then she turned off her phone completely.

I gave her a few minutes and blessedly, heard the *choo-choo* text tone on my phone. *WTF? Colonial revival style DK $$ depends on acreage & hood lks well-kept gd taste tho too symmet & safe no notable Garage added later Waiting for funeral to start client's mom he hated her but will inherit Yay TTYL*

Wynne's response left me discontented, though I didn't know what she could have told me about Pete's house to make me shout hosanna. I guess what I was yearning for was collaboration. A partner. But abbreviated input from a style queen (who had strong opinions on everything) would have to do, plus she concurred with my judgment. Since Pete was a packaging designer, I expected he had a reasonable grasp of aesthetics: and in fact, there was no mailbox shaped like a golden retriever.

The buzz-cut bushes and groomed lawn could be expensive to keep up and raised unanswered questions about his finances, but maybe he did the maintenance himself. I drove around the block again and parked across the street and a fair distance back. I could watch his house through the windshield.

Nothing much was happening, which I suppose was to be expected at ten thirty on a Tuesday morning. A car pulled out of one driveway and a North Shore Flooring and Carpet truck backed into another. A woman in jeggings racewalked with a tiny, black sheared poodle running to keep up with her; the poor thing looked like a cockroach on a leash. Then a local sanitation truck, the same company that worked my neighborhood, turned the corner and started on Pete's side of the street, blocking my view of his house.

Part of me was thinking what a total waste this was. Even with my window opened, the loaner was getting hot; added to that it smelled slightly sweet, as if it had been sprayed with some new, odor-absorbing product that had its own smell.

I understood staking out took patience and discipline. I remembered my dad saying that after about a half hour, when you have nothing more to say to your partner, it was like going into a Zen state. Now and then your consciousness tapped you on the shoulder to enumerate Mets pitchers who had been on the injured list that season. He added that he'd kind of liked it and that when his mind was someplace else or nowhere, he was at his most alert.

Some movement caught my attention. The sanitation truck stopped at Pete's house. The driver, short but broad, jumped down from his high seat and hurried to the curb. He wore a blue bandana around his neck, and I wondered whether it was for fashion or for lifting up as a filter over his nose.

Which was just when I saw Pete Delaney come around from the far side of his house carrying a big pruner, a kind of Edward Scissorhands thing. (I hadn't seen the movie, but the pictures of it creeped me out when I was a kid and I'd avoided anything with Johnny Depp for years.) I started chewing on my knuckles, which may have blocked about a third of my face. Not that I was trying to hide. Just nerves.

Then Pete sauntered over to the garbage truck, and my heart began to beat so hard I could have been a soldier about to go into battle—which was somewhat pathetic considering that what I was facing was a sanitation guy lifting off the lid of the first can and Pete going over to say hello. All looked perfectly amiable: the guy dumping, nodding, moving on to the second can, saying something, Pete responding.

The sanitation guy pressed a button to turn on the rotary that shoveled in the trash, then drove on to the next house, giving Pete a final wave. Pete waved back. He was wearing those chamois gardening gloves, except they were a little large and made his hands look like Mickey Mouse's.

I would have moved on if the giant blades of his pruner hadn't suddenly started snapping the air. Pete was warming up as he surveyed the bushes on either side of steps to his house. Except they were perfectly even. Still, he snipped from the right side, then backed up to check out the symmetry. So I waited and waited some more. Finally, after five minutes of what seemed obsessive-compulsive twig clipping, he wandered around the side of the house.

Whether it was my bureau training or my dad's "Detective Dan Is on the Case" shoptalk at dinner, I knew not to leave once Pete was out of sight. Instead, I waited for seventeen minutes— fifteen being too predictable. Finally, when an attention-getting red Escalade cruised down the street, I pulled out in my gray loaner and drove past the house and copper beech.

Did I realize how unbalanced my behavior

would have appeared to any rational observer? Sure, plus I felt elated when, after a series of meaningless left, right, left turns, I spotted the sanitation truck.

When the driver stopped, I pulled in front of his truck and trotted over as he was dumping a can of trash. I used the benevolent but not suspiciously friendly smile I used with witnesses and said hi.

Fortunately, he was a good-natured sort, with a weathered and pockmarked face along with a couple of bottom teeth missing, the kind of person who's had a tough life but doesn't want to tell you about it. "Hi. How are you?" the guy asked. He had a Latino accent.

"Fine thanks. You?"

"Good."

"Didn't I see you on Amberley Road about ten, fifteen minutes ago?" I asked. "Talking to a guy cutting his bushes?"

"Yeah. His place, it's very neat."

"The reason I came over to see you is my husband and I are thinking of moving to that street. I was just wondering how often your pickups are?"

"Tuesdays, Saturdays."

"That sounds good," I said, while he looked into the depths of someone's orange recycling pail and saw a single can of Dr. Brown's Diet Cream Soda. He exhaled wearily.

"Nice people on Amberley?" He gave a single

nod that indicated: *Definitely.* "The guy with the perfect bushes?" I asked lightly.

"Yeah. Nice." He lowered his voice. "Good tip at Christmas."

"That makes him wonderful."

"Yeah. He's fussy though. That's probably the right word. Always comes out to say hello, but always watches me. Maybe the last guy who worked my route left a mess, and Mr.—I forget his name—don't like messes." He pushed out a breath that came close to a snort. "Like I do?"

"You think he'd learn by this time that you know how to do your job."

"Yeah, but he's not bad," the guy said. He even offered a smile. "Works at home. Not much happening, I guess." I thanked him, wishing that someone nice like him worked my street instead of the guy I always thought of as Sullen Dennis. Then I drove away in the loaner car.

A couple of minutes later I pulled into the parking lot of a dry cleaner because I needed to think. Why would Pete watch his trash being collected so closely? It could be about neatness. He might just as likely be checking to make sure all his stuff was not only dumped but also pulled into the innards of the truck. He'd had some white garbage bags, the tied kind you use in a kitchen. The other bags were black. So I had no way of knowing if he shredded his personal papers or had anything incriminating—from used syringes to chemicals to aging counterfeit stock certificates. Which drove home the point that despite my fixation, I had no concept of what Pete could be guilty of.

The next day, Wednesday, was the lunch—what I'd gone from thinking of as a dreaded commitment to now seeing as the most exciting event of the week. Just before I left the house, I glimpsed myself in the downstairs bathroom mirror and realized I'd gone uncharacteristically neutral. A taupe T-shirt, taupe-and-black cotton scarf, and black jeans. My makeup was minimal; my eyes, normally blue enough to rank number two in most guys' Corie's Top Ten Assets list, were faded to a shade between the palest blue and white. Also, I'd put on that lip-color gloss that brightened every woman's complexion except mine. My face looked like a yearbook shot at some Catholic girls' school that didn't allow makeup.

I arrived at La Cuisine Délicieuse and immediately became rattled because it struck me that I had zero recollection of having driven there. Zero. The bureau had been big on mindfulness, though they called it something more butch back then: staying in the alert zone. Shortly before I left the job, we had to watch a video about what happens when an agent isn't in the zone. Someone missed a piece of fabric on a branch of a bush because she got distracted by a tweeting bird, which struck me as sexist since no male agent would ever be fingered for being stirred by a skylark. Another genius, while executing a search warrant, failed to open the third of five drawers in a file cabinet because he was disrupted by a great manly sneeze; he went from drawer two directly to drawer four.

I had surpassed the group's unwritten acceptable unpunctuality rule of four minutes. Scurrying into the restaurant, I saw everyone else seated—Pete in his usual chair. I wound up between Darby Penn, the photo retoucher, and Iris.

"Sorry I'm late," I said to the group and got that brief hum of phrases like *no problem*. In a bow to the month of May, the restaurant's air-conditioning was off, though it was seventy-six degrees outside. Immediately, the humid, motionless air enveloped me. The restaurant also smelled fishy, probably from the previous day's special, bouillabaisse.

For the first time, I realized how uncomfortable the chairs there were: plastic versions of the woven rattan French kind, easily movable, so that a Parisian having a *café filtre* could effortlessly move from one scintillating conversation to another.

Not only was I stuck where I was, but one of the rear legs on my chair had lost its rubber tip; it was shorter than the other three. Every time I shifted, the chair seemed to overreact—so it was hard to stay mindful. Every jerk seemed a major interruption of my chat with Darby. He had once worked at *People* magazine, and after I asked him how much retouching had been done on the handsomest men pics, I wobbled a bit wildly and didn't hear his answer.

I was reduced to sweat-dribble-in-cleavage state. I moved closer to the table and sat back. An instant later, the chair lurched. Suddenly I was heading backward, madly flapping my arms to prevent embarrassment and a skull fracture. Darby and Iris simultaneously grabbed the back of the chair and helped right it. When I was upright again, I thanked them a bit too profusely. "I'm fine!" I announced at least three times. The members of the group smiled at me with the reassuring warmth of people who don't regard sangfroid as a cardinal virtue.

But seconds later, when the waiter came over to take our orders, my mouth got so dry and my throat so tight that first I gulped, then got out "Caesar salad," in a too-loud froggy voice. I couldn't decide if Pete tilted his head for a second to look at me oddly just as Iris was asking, "You okay?"

"Absolutely," I said, taking a mindful sip of water, a small sip, swallowing carefully so I wouldn't start coughing. God knows I'd been in far tenser situations—a couple of life-threatening situations actually—and hadn't been anywhere near so rattled.

I glanced at the little plate of foil-wrapped pats of butter on our table, but my eye immediately caught Iris Kubel breaking off a piece of her roll. As usual, her hands were perfectly manicured, without even a teeny chip in the nail polish. Their pale skin, dotted with freckles, seemed like that of a fragile aristocrat rather than someone who schlepped fifty-pound bags of compost. Then my other eye took in Darby's hand. He was African American, a couple of shades darker than Josh. I knew he used computers almost exclusively in his work these days, but I could picture him in his early years at the magazine, his lean, long-fingered light brown hand holding steady the thinnest brush to delete some flaw in a photo.

I peered around the table as Marcalynn Schechter opened her computer with a flourish so we could be delighted by her presentation on how she created a speech for her latest client, a state assemblyman from Suffolk County. She had the Alice-in-Wonderland hair that Fox News females, no matter what their ethnicity, seemed to have. There was a winning cheerleader smile, complete with dimples, to go with her flippy blonde style. Though she looked chatty, she didn't say a lot either to the group or one-on-one, except at show-and-tell. Marcalynn's need to communicate seemed to be satisfied mostly through the speeches she crafted for her clients. Admittedly, there were the ever-changing but politically consistent bumper stickers on her dark red Honda Odyssey whose messages she slipped into conversation, but mostly she was quiet.

As Marcalynn clicked a few too many times trying to retrieve her PowerPoint document, Iris Kubel leaned toward pasty-faced Pete and said, "I forgot to ask. How did your trip go? Indiana, right?"

"Same as always. Left last Thursday afternoon for a Friday morning meeting. Just a quick trip to show my designs for a new packaging line."

"Oh, work related," John Grillo piped up. "I assumed it was just to see your mother."

"Both. I combine PrimoTech with visiting her." Marcalynn held up her index finger to indicate *Just another moment.* Pete realized he had to fill the silence: "Power strips, the thing for plugs. They added a couple of USB ports. They're in South Bend. I rented a car at the airport, then drove to Fort Wayne. That's where the nursing home is."

"How's she doing?" John asked.

"Kind of sad. She can remember I'm Pete but not that I'm her son. I stayed at my brother Brad's, so I saw her the next day, too."

Finally Marcalynn triumphed. She came to a page that read: "What is there to say about the capital budget?" with clip art of a woman, arms out in a *Huh?* Unfortunately, her next click did nothing, leaving the clip art lady still asking, *Huh?*

Lucy, the data miner, asked Pete: "What does Brad do?" He peered at her closely for just a second too long, then answered: "He's a painter. A house painter." That could have been it, but maybe because Lucy was still looking at him, he added: "Brad's got a really good eye for color."

Brad might be a color genius. Both brothers might have inherited artistic talent or visual acuity. On the other hand, Pete could be doing what the pros do: offering down-to-earth details to humanize a nonexistent person: Brad. What the bureau called creating a legend. The FBI subscribed to that method by concocting detailed cover stories for undercover agents and protected witnesses and came up with crazy uncle Norman in Chillicothe or not being able to find a split pea soup as good as mom used to make.

Of course Wynne would mutter: *Maybe Brad is real. And happens to be a house painter.* Maybe.

I wondered about PrimoTech. Presumably, it had a conference room or just a large office where several people could meet. Pete wouldn't be demonstrating a power strip wrapper on a picnic blanket out in the sun.

So how come the backs of his hands were so tanned? A rich tan, not a Midwest-in-May tan.

Something was wrong about that. His hands looked so much healthier than his pallid face. Why? I couldn't swear to it, but I was 95 percent positive his hands hadn't been so burnished at the previous week's meeting. Surely, I would have picked that up.

Even though it was becoming more and more plausible that there was something a bit off about Pete, I reconsidered my fixation. He was a guy who went outside. He was obviously interested enough in landscaping to buy tools for it (plus a big-bucks tree). So the back of his hands would tan. Big deal. Except then a quiver ran up my arms: He'd been wearing chamois gardening gloves the day before. If anything, his hands should have been paler than his face.

Marcalynn was digressing, that much I could tell, saying that her assemblyman had to walk a fine line between being pro education and anti local school tax hikes. His photo came up, generic assemblyman, benevolent smile, loosened tie, in a classroom surrounded by adorable elementary school kids, primarily white, as he was.

*Snap out of it,* I ordered myself. Listen to Marcalynn, because she was saying something I hadn't heard before—that a picture like the one she was showing was useless because it was now so commonplace in our culture. Stay mindful. She was talking about the tough work of pushing voters out of their partisanship and moving them away from campaign cliché torpor and social media mania.

Later, when I got home, I made myself go upstairs to outline my report on the book of short stories. Fine. My tension eased a little, even though I didn't like writing negative coverage. I calmed down even more when Eliza got home back from her friend Chloë's house and Josh arrived for dinner. He had been reading a law journal article about Virginia, which once had the death penalty for sodomy. So we talked about what it must have been like for gay people in the eighteenth century. It was a refreshing conversation of substance and actually interesting.

Later, he and I decided no TV. We read quietly and companionably in the room I called the den and that Dawn had called the library, probably because it had a brass table lamp.

But after excellent lovemaking, in the quiet of the night, I turned my back on Josh to better concentrate on what really mattered to me: ashen-faced Pete Delaney and his suntanned hands.

# 8

I'd been to the Middle East, Europe, South America, and Asia, but central New Jersey was new territory. I was on my way to visit the one professor from Queens College with whom I still stayed in touch. A few months ago she'd posted on Facebook that she was hit by a delivery guy on a bike. Both her knees were shattered and she was stuck in a distant rehab facility. At least a bed and good care were available, but it was fifty miles from her home. So that Saturday I left Josh to give Eliza the tennis lesson he'd been promising her. Relying on my GPS, I found my way through a state that seemed to frown on streets with names; everything was Route 47 or 583, which was not only confusing but also disheartening to the verbally oriented.

After an hour and a half of trees, industrial parks, towns, and, finally, intensely cute villages, I stopped at a supermarket to buy a pint of Nadira Jaffri's beloved Cherry Garcia. I also picked up a prepaid phone. Then I drove the last three miles to the rehab place. It was a low stone building with long, horizontal windows. An overlarge, thick slab was laid on top, probably a misguided homage to Frank Lloyd Wright.

Part of my mission to New Jersey was legit. I really did want to visit with Professor Jaffri. Having taken her Women, Gender, and Sexuality in Islam class and getting together with her once or twice a year since, I knew how miserable she'd be at her loss of independence and mobility.

I was glad to see her face brighten when she saw me at the door. I had worried she'd be too down for engaged conversation but within two minutes we were talking politics. I brought her up to date on the Arabic-speaking world's science fiction, much of it currently dystopian. Filling her in took time since the only work close to the genre she'd ever read was the classic *One Thousand and One Nights*, which I guessed could be called proto–science fiction. It was written in the ninth century.

Instead of heading back to Long Island after happily savoring Ben and Jerry's, I headed south for another fifteen minutes. I was in the mood for intrigue for part two of my mission: getting far enough from metropolitan New York so I could check out Pete's story about his brother, Brad Delaney.

Did I contemplate how crazy this was, my concern about getting distance from Long Island in case Pete had access to geolocation technology? Yes, for about two or three minutes I understood some might call me delusional.

Mostly, I soared on that high that comes with a

new case. The elation can even happen when I'm sitting at a desktop computer. But a road trip? Glimpsing real life recede in my rearview mirror? Wow! My single responsibility was working on the Pete Delaney matter.

Right after the Wednesday lunch, I had checked out brother Brad. He did have a basic website: Brad's Painting and Wallpapering, with a stock photo of a paint can, a rainbow arching up from it. The site had a phone number but no address. The exchange really was a landline in the Fort Wayne, Indiana, area. Brad lived! Or maybe not. There was no gallery of his work on the website, just generic photography of pretty rooms in what I sensed were different parts of the country, as if they'd been lifted from a Benjamin Moore brochure. The store had no Yelp or Google reviews, which further pushed me toward believing Brad could be a cover story for Pete's having family in Indiana.

But what the hell was Pete actually doing in Indiana? Or in not-Indiana, what with that dark tan on the backs of his hands. At the very least he was using that state as a setting for his background story, part of which meant paying five or ten bucks a month for Brad's website.

I felt for the prepaid phone in my purse. Maybe some drug dealers were still using prepaids as burner phones like those on *The Wire*, but technology had gotten more sophisticated.

Most agents I knew used bureau phones with apps that generated alternative numbers. With a single cell phone, you could have one number on which a suspected terrorist's wife can reach you in case she decides to rat him out, another number for the owner of a beauty supply warehouse suspected of selling him peroxide and acetone, and so on. There was even this kind of app for civilians, but since I had only one call to make, a prepaid was cheaper and had no learning curve.

I pulled into the parking lot of a three-store strip mall, bought an iced coffee at Dunkin' Donuts, and drove another ten minutes to a wooded area. I opened my window partway and inhaled the pine trees. Being in Nowhere, New Jersey, off the road, inside the requisite locked car brought on a wave of nostalgia for going to obscure places all over the world that almost knocked me over. Ah, the good old days in the early aughts, when I would fly home to DC from London and be told I had to leave for Krakow in three hours to witness an interrogation. (I was conveniently forgetting the few occasions when my life was on the line, and I'd needed to repress the thought, *Why the fuck did I join the FBI?*)

I glanced at the prepaid; there were two bars, enough reception to make the call. "Hi," a man's voice said. Recorded. "This is Brad from Brad's Painting and Wallpapering. I'm out on a job or else I'm spinning my color wheel to help you find the perfect shade!"

He didn't sound like Pete. Besides his pitch being lower, he had a more pronounced mid-western accent. Well, of course I knew it could be Pete using voice-changing equipment and flattening his *a*'s a little more. Then the voice went on to say, "Please leave your name and number so I can get back to you soon. I check my messages pretty often. It won't be long before we can talk about your painting needs! Have a great day!"

Once back on the turnpike, I pulled into the first rest stop I came to. There, I dumped the prepaid in a garbage can filled with fast-food accoutrements. The sound of a cell phone landing on a can of Monster Energy should have had the clink of finality. But it was like a piece of music lacking a consonant final chord.

In the ladies' room, I logged in to an FBI data-base from an app on my phone. It had been in the back of my mind to try to get access. The only way I could think of was by using the alphanumeric code for the last case I'd worked on as a contract op about a month before.

In the front of my mind, I was aware this was risky, to say nothing of stupid. But there was also some small reason for optimism: the bureau's cybertech had improved vastly since 9/11. Still, it never got five stars. The worst that could happen?

The case would be marked closed. No access. Okay, I admit there was a teeny chance I could lose my security clearance or even get arrested. But as my dad would say to my mom when he strapped on his Kevlar vest and noticed the color drain from her face: "Remote possibility, Margo. I can't do my job thinking 'possibility.' I've gotta think 'remote.'"

So I thought "remote" as to my chances of getting in trouble. Leaning against a monolith of a vending machine that dispensed condoms, Benadryl, Advil, and Dentyne, I got entry to the site. Within ten seconds after I input Brad's number, up popped the address associated with it—a number on Fairfield Avenue in Fort Wayne.

Except there was no Brad's Painting at the address. Actually, not counting the website with its phone number, there wasn't any evidence that a store existed. On Google Earth, the address appeared to be a small office building. While that wasn't enough for a rush of joy, I felt a tingle of satisfaction.

Two days later, I got more than a tingle. That was because I'd set up a meeting with Sami Bashir. An objective observer might tell me: *Once you are married, there is no justification, ever, for calling an old boyfriend. Any information he possesses can be found elsewhere. And that other thing he possesses can only lead to lifelong regret.*

So if not that, what did I need Sami for? He was smart, as well as street-smart, but not an intellect like Josh. His looks were simply okay. Average height, medium brown skin, dark brown eyes neither oversize nor sparkling. Black hair, longish but cool, apparently his only concession to style, though it might have been due to infrequent trips to the barbershop. His generous nose had been broken a couple of times, so it was now more wide than protuberant. He was so broad that the nickname given to him by one of the other DEA agents, Mono—"ape" in Spanish—had stuck. But right after meeting him, a few days after I'd moved up to New York to be part of the Joint Terrorism Task Force, I was drawn to him. I came to find his looks irresistible.

Sami came across as tough in a way 99 percent of semishaven guys could only dream about. The reason? He was a genuine hard-ass. The terrorists who dealt in drugs to finance their operations, congenitally suspicious, required less convincing than they might have that he was one of their own. His appearance, his fearlessness, his fluency in four languages—including Arabic—seemed to seal most deals.

"You're looking good," he said. It was a Monday afternoon. I'd spent the weekend putting together a teak garden bench with Eliza, the upscale version of yard work. It had been one of those online temptations, ideal for the sophisticated sucker who might not believe "easy to assemble" but succumbed to "no tools necessary," which would have been true only if you had fingers that could turn a bolt with wrench-like power. By the end of the weekend I'd developed the beginnings of the deep bronze color that construction workers have. Just a little less intense than Pete's hands.

"Seriously," Sami said. "I've never seen you so not pale."

"Is that part of the previous compliment?" I asked.

"No, it's a new one. In Rio, you could pass for a Carioca, and that's a compliment, too."

"I know. Thanks."

"You're welcome." Sami had to be wily and deceptive to stay alive, but when it came to personal relationships, he was guileless—generous with praise ("That was really terrific, how you helped that old man down the subway stairs and made it seem that it was truly your pleasure"); open to a fault with disapproval ("Is that new makeup or something? Jesus, it makes your eyes look like you're going into rigor mortis").

The table we were sitting at was so small that our knees kept brushing, and we kept shifting in our chairs to avoid any hint that we wanted to touch each other. It was four o'clock and the little bubble tea place in Chinatown was nearly empty.

You wouldn't find task force or bureau peeps hanging there. Sami was Muslim enough that he didn't drink alcohol, though his looks made it feel as if he were in a dive in São Paulo slinging back cachaça instead of sipping grapefruit tea through a turquoise straw. "You look good, too," I added.

"Same old," he said. "But you look good in a new way. Rich."

"Stop it, Sami." I was suddenly self-conscious. I was only wearing jeans, retro high-tops, and a loose, white cotton sweater, but they were of better quality than what I'd worn in the old days. Since fourth grade and the occurrence of the great purple pants/pink shirt debacle, I'd been following Wynne's advice: *Keep it simple if you don't know what you're doing, and you don't.*

"Blonder," he said. "Your hair wasn't dark, but it didn't have those streak things in it."

"How come I haven't seen you in, whatever, three years and you're talking about my hair and not—"

He cut me off. "You know exactly how long it's been, Corie, so cut the 'whatever.' And don't give me pop psych, like: 'You're avoiding intimacy.' "

"Intimacy isn't on the menu anymore," I snapped back. I can't say I saw hurt on Sami's face, because if you spend your adult life subduing emotion in order to stay alive, your lower lip doesn't quiver when a former lover gets snarky. So it was either intuition or wishful thinking that made me sense this wasn't an easy meeting for him, either. "Anyway," I exhaled. "I did get highlights in my hair."

"And you called this meeting so I could admire your high-class hair streaks?"

"Yeah, and it worked, didn't it? No, I called because I needed your savvy. But I do miss you sometimes." That was an attempt at casual honesty. Except just then I felt the sort of pressure along my cheekbones that can precede a horrible, weepy episode. Such humiliation in a bubble tea shop bordered on the ridiculous. Luckily I had the law enforcement/self-control gene from my dad along with the performance gene from my mom, so instead of blurting out an awkward cover-up sentence or—nightmare scenario—bawling, I played the pro and added, "And also . . ."

"I wondered when you'd get to it," Sami said. I loved that he never tried to be Agent Cool, the kind of guy who never offered more than a half smile. His grin showed relief that the subject had been changed, though I doubted that he'd been on the verge of blubbering.

"I need you to do a background check for me."

He rubbed his cheek with the flat of his hand. I'd always been a fool for that macho sandpaper sound. No doubt he'd picked that up in the almost two years we'd been together. "Political? Someone on the no-fly list?"

"Of course not. I wouldn't ask you anything that might compromise—"

"Pack the speech, Corie. Is it some financial thing you're involved with? Or your husband?"

"No! It's a guy—" He smiled, though this time it was not an expression that demanded heavy effort from his facial muscles. "Don't be an asshole," I told him. "There's less than zero about this person when it comes to anything sexual or emotional. He's someone who lives in the same town on Long Island as I do."

"Hey, exciting!"

"Oh shut up Sami. You grew up in New Jersey. You're not exactly Mr. Cosmopolite. Anyway, you know that gut feeling you get when there's something wrong about somebody?"

"Of course I know it." He paused. "But that's mostly because I'm dealing with actual psychopaths."

"You're saying the FBI doesn't deal with psychos? 'Practice limited to CPAs'? Good to see you're still basking in interagency harmony." I overcame an urge to reach across the little table and touch his hand, which was gripping his bubble tea glass, now empty. His big knuckles had always been a draw. "And maintaining your affection for the bureau."

"It's not like when I deal with CIA people on the task force. I mean, they're fucked up because they can't approach any problem without asking

170

themselves, like: 'Are the geopolitical ramifications of delimiting an inequitable supremacy of bilateral sovereignty . . . Blah blah blah.' But at least they have some interest in how the world works. Your feebs keep vetoing most of the action in the Tri-Border Area because they truly believe the farthest point south in this hemisphere is Cuba."

"Wrong!" While I didn't shout it, no one in my life had ever told me, *Sorry, I didn't hear you.* "Did you ever think a veto was a response to your agency's half-assed strategic planning and political naïveté?"

Sami, however, behaved as if he hadn't heard a thing, as if I had in fact accepted his criticism of the bureau. This wasn't some new routine, ignoring objections to what he said or did. If it sounds like standard machismo, with which a man disregards a woman's opinion simply because she's female, it wasn't. He did the same with men. Sami discounted whatever Sami wanted to discount. Contrary opinions and consequences didn't seem matter.

That might make him sound like some TV antihero who seduces death. True, at times he could be a magnet for violence, though he'd chalk it up as a fringe benefit of the job. Yet unlike noir guys, he wasn't dark all the time. That was a quality electrifying in a two-hour movie but tedious in life.

"Hey," he said. "Remember that day we walked right around here, somewhere in Chinatown? That little boy, maybe two years old or something? He was standing on the edge of the sidewalk trying to start up a conversation with a pigeon."

I nodded a few times too many, until I knew my voice would sound composed. "He was so adorable!" I said. "When the pigeon wouldn't look at him, he switched from Chinese to English and kept saying, 'Hi!' "

" 'Hi,' " Sami repeated, though his attempt to sound childlike didn't come off. Every once in a while, when we met someplace, we'd start repeating "Hi," to each other, our own greeting: maybe we kept holding on to that boy, our kid, the one we'd never have together.

"Hi," I said back, but I wanted to get off the subject. "You know what I think of so fondly?"

" 'Fondly'? Is that your new favorite adverb? I'll miss 'quintessentially.' "

"Shut the fuck up, Sami. Maybe I said 'quintessentially' twice in my life."

It delighted me how he enjoyed language. Soon after he came to New York to join the task force, we were sitting in Columbus Park behind the courthouses, just two colleagues brown-bagging it. He pulled out from the back pocket of his pants a paper that he'd printed. It was "Give Me the Splendid, Silent Sun," Whitman's paean to Manhattan; he got up from the bench both to recite it and (I thought) to honor the poet. "Give me faces and streets! give me these phantoms incessant and endless along the trottoirs!/ Give me interminable eyes! give me women! give me comrades and lovers by the thousand!/ Let me see new ones every day! let me hold new ones by the hand every day!/ Give me such shows! give me the streets of Manhattan!" Sami was reading it so fervently that Walt himself would have applauded.

I got a too-big mouthful of tea down in a series of small sips and said, "Let me give you the story on this guy. His name is Pete Delaney and he's a packaging designer—"

"Already sounds like a threat to national security." I waited. "All right, tell me about him."

I did, and by then I was so well acquainted with the details that I practically had an outline in my head, presenting each point in sequential order: from Pete's same-chair-positioned-for-optimal-Jeep-watching; to his tan hands; to his going berserk over a stolen parking space; to my chat with his sanitation guy; to my inability to confirm a genuine Brad's Painting and Wallpapering.

At first Sami shrugged, that gesture that means whatever the shrugger wants it to mean: sounds dubious; could be; have to think about it. Then he massaged his eyebrows until they looked like black caterpillars. "If it was me?" he asked. "Yeah, I'd think what you're thinking. Something could be funny about the guy. Of course, there might be some simple explanation."

"Like what?"

"That he's one of those right-wing privacy nuts. Or an apolitical type who has a slight streak of paranoia." Then it was my turn to shrug.

"That doesn't account for a fake brother. Or that the backs of his hands are so much darker than his face—and it happened in what I'm 90 percent sure is a few days. Did he go out in the sun in a shroud with hand slits? Come on, Sami. How does that happen?" I demanded.

"I give up." He waited, just in case I had a theory. When I didn't say anything, he went on: "You think he's on something? Prescription, non? Does he have dilated pupils or clench his teeth?"

"No."

"Sweats?"

"No, none of the signs that I know of. The opposite, if anything. He's consistent: no behavioral changes, kind of a flat personality. Not like if he's tranked. Just a dull dude."

"So you want me to check out this Pete Delaney?"

"Please," I said and followed it with a smile. He gave me a look that said: *Don't overplay your hand.* But I could see that despite himself he'd melted a little. He'd once told me that I had a killer smile.

"And you have no idea what he could be doing, if he's actually doing something?"

"Not a clue," I admitted. "Though I don't think . . . I'm pretty positive that he's not ex–law enforcement. I don't think I'm looking at another version of me, retired, silent on my past, maybe overly cautious." I wasn't going to tell him that Jillian King from HR at the FBI had already checked that out for me.

"How did you get pretty positive?" Sami asked.

"Rampant self-confidence."

"Right. Okay, but I'll still give that a fast check."

"You know I still have my clearance."

"Corie, do you think I'm worried about that?"

"No. Actually, that's why I'm bothering you with this, instead of somebody else."

I thought he was going to say no, he knew that the real reason I had asked to see him was that I was still lusting for him or at least still in love. But he didn't bring up our past again, which showed me that in the years since I'd last seen him, he'd grown less in-your-face, or at least less in mine. Probably religious constraints entered into keeping our past off-limits. Aside from not drinking alcohol or eating pork, Sami was a pretty secular Muslim, but he'd probably hold back sexual banter with a married woman. Without doubt he knew that infidelity was con-demned in the Qur'an. Or maybe he understood that although I was glad for a reason to see him, I wouldn't be unfaithful to Josh.

"I wouldn't want you to compromise yourself," I went on. "But you're the only one I can trust to do this."

"Compromise myself? Don't get dramatic. It's a small favor," Sami said. "So write down whatever you have on him. I'll let you know what I dig up. Whenever."

# 9

It's one thing for Sami to criticize the"—Wynne lowered her voice to a whisper as if the small East Village art gallery had state-of-the-art audio surveillance—"FBI. Though you do it, too! You went from pride in your shield or badge thing to calling the bureau the dumbest fucks in government."

"I never called them the dumbest," I said. "That's a tie between the postal inspectors and the Secret Service. No, most of my problems with the bureau were about its inflexibility." I spoke in a normal voice since there was only one other person in the gallery, a twentysomething at the front desk. Clearly she'd recognized Wynne when we'd come in, but now we were at a more than safe distance. Also, she was now engrossed in cleaning under her fingernails with her lower left canine tooth.

I stared at the young woman, intrigued, but Wynne wasn't mesmerized by her grooming. Her eyes stayed on me, narrowed, as if she had to squint to better perceive my flaws. Something was on her agenda. Sure enough, she made a *tsk* right before she spoke, that single click of tongue on hard palate, a Brooklyn-Queens sound that translates to *I really hate having to say this.* "For God's sakes, what possessed you to call Sami?"

"I was getting nowhere fast. I needed someone who'd be willing to bend a few rules and do some background on Pete Delaney. Not that bureau agents don't bend rules, but they do it mainly for their own careers. Or revenge. Sami's more generous. He'd fuck over authority for any of his friends in the law enforcement community."

I was trying to keep my eyes on a picture from the gallery's exhibition. It was a mosaic comprised of marsupial, human, and insect faces, each less than an inch across. They were slightly convex, cut from some pliable metal, and painted. It was hard to overcome the urge to push in a face and see if it made that satisfying, tinny pop-out sound. However, when you stood back, the faces disappeared; what you saw was a patchwork of harmonious colors. At least, I supposed they were harmonious. Anyway, colors that looked good together.

"Those little human faces look like individuals. And I love the juxtaposition of, like, a praying mantis face and a koala bear, even though I don't understand why the artist picked marsupials and insects. Do you?"

"No." She was wearing a short dress the color of undyed Play-Doh. It was fitted on top, flaring below the waist. She tugged at the hem on each side for reasons I couldn't fathom because it was perfectly even. "But while we're talking juxtaposition," she went on, "how about Muslim and Jew?"

"How about it?"

"I'm not talking prejudice. I'm talking that you are married. And not to him, because religion turned out to be an issue."

"I know I'm married. And marriage was never on the table with Sami and me. Religion was the least of it. All right, not the least, but it was not the deciding factor. There was no decision to make. He chose to live a life that ruled out marriage. Service: like a priest, except to the United States instead of the Church. And without the celibacy, of course. I couldn't have a husband who'd be saying, 'I'm leaving tomorrow,' so even if you're working with him and know where he's going, you have no idea how long he'll be gone. It could be a long weekend or five months. Not for me. All my life I wanted a family. Including the husband part. I wanted precisely what I've got now."

"Then why see Sami again? I'm not only reeling about your actually seeing him again, but that you initiated it."

"What's to reel about? I saw him, visually. I'm not *seeing* him, like going to an Indian restaurant and discovering we both love the cauliflower and potato thing."

"Aloo gobi."

My phone started vibrating. During my bureau days, I had kept it tucked in the side of my bra, under my arm, which precluded a clingy shirt but ensured I wouldn't be interrupted by the cutesy ringtones that I tended to favor or, more important, wouldn't miss a call. I kept it up when I first became a mother and Eliza was calling me four or five times a day. I understood she was checking if I was still alive, so I kept her as close to my heart as possible.

By now she was reassured, but the phone placement habit stuck. I pulled it out: Sami. " 'Scuse," I mumbled to Wynne, though I was halfway to the door. I walked outside. The street outside the gallery area had been partly gentrified, so when I said hi to him, I was on a narrow area of polished paving stones in front of another gallery. Its windows displayed things that looked like small meteors—the kind that might hurtle to earth and crush an Alfa Romeo yet not obliterate civilization. Right beside it, set back from the crumbling sidewalk, was an old-fashioned pharmacy whose sign said KAPLAN'S DRUGS.

"So I did your bidding," Sami said.

I laughed and said, "That's so like you, the obsequiousness."

"I live to serve. You know, your Pete really is boring. But not the kind of boring that makes you think 'cover-up.' "

I could feel the air going out of me. "So you think he's okay?"

"Corie." He always said my name as if it were a separate sentence. "You didn't say, 'Clear him or put him on a shit list.' How the hell do I know if he is okay? Do you want to know what I found?"

"Please, go ahead."

"No criminal record. No record of any court action, including bankruptcy. Birth certificate, of course." Birth certificates meant nothing, which we both knew. They could be found or bought, the best ones being those of people who died in early childhood, in a different venue from the one in which they'd actually been born—ideally a place where record keeping was lax. Still, unless Pete had been planning a criminal career sometime between kindergarten and when he worked for the ad agency, chances were his name truly was Peter Delaney. "Born in Fort Wayne City Hospital, October 19, 1969."

I'd switched screens and was typing in his information. "Parents' names?"

"Joseph Delaney and Margaret Spencer Delaney."

Sami spent his first ten years in Brasília; his grandparents had emigrated to South America from Egypt. Years later, his chemist father was offered a job in New Jersey, and the entire family—grandparents included—wound up in New Brunswick. Though Sami's speech was

181

accentless, I sometimes heard the music of Portuguese more than the words. "Joseph Delaney and Margaret Spencer Delaney" sounded a little like a dance song, though admittedly not a samba.

"Okay," I said brightly, not that I felt it. "Thanks for doing this."

"Two more things," Sami said. It was so easy to picture him talking. His upper and lower lips were of nearly equal size and shape; with his mouth closed, they looked like an ellipse with a fold down the middle. "One: you didn't ask, but I checked and he's not in any witness protection program I could access. Listen, he could be ex-CIA who's gone to ground, but I also looked into the packaging designer thing, whether he'd worked for an ad agency. There is a record of him at JWT, which used to be J. Walter Thompson."

"Yes! I knew he worked at a big place, but I totally forgot the name. Thank you. This is super helpful."

"I'm not done being helpful," he said. "I got a photo placing him at JWT. I'm emailing it to you. Are you using the same address for your bureau-related email?"

I gave him my new alternative email address I used for contract work. As I talked, I noticed Wynne standing in front of the door of the gallery we'd been in, too far away to eavesdrop but still able to witness my überfemme stance, which she was kind enough to mimic. By the time I realized

I had been smiling as I spoke to Sami, it was too late to change my expression.

"Am I off the hook now?" he asked.

"Yes, totally. I'm so grateful. Just one more thing."

"Hey, I've got a job."

"I know. It's not a huge favor. Well it is, but not timewise. Can you see if you can find a birth certificate for Pete's brother, Brad or Bradley Delaney?"

By the time I opened Sami's email displaying a picture of a woman and three men, Wynne was hovering overly close to me. I could smell the flower scent of the pomade she used so no wayward strand could detract from her pony-tail; every hair was in place and shiny. The pomade was from England and had a sweet but subtle bluebell scent.

"Who are they?" she asked, looking at the picture on my phone.

"It's from some advertising industry magazine." I spread out the photo so that the man second from the left took up most of my device screen. "That's Pete Delaney."

"Looks . . ." Wynne paused for a second. "Late nineties. That other guy in the red-and-black-striped sweater. So Kurt Cobain. Ugh, that girl in the culottes. Dreadful! You cannot name one person who was ever enhanced by culottes."

I brought the photo back to size so we could

read a couple of lines beneath the pic: THE TEAM THAT CREATED COOKIE CRUMBLES: L TO R, ELWYN PORTER, PETER DELANEY, JESSICA SCHWARTZ, NICK FALCONE.

Wynne took my phone, again enlarged Pete, and shrugged. "The faces are kind of fuzzy, but you can tell he's not a looker. Though you wouldn't pass him on the street and vomit," she said. Pete had had much more hair then, light brown, and it was combed back and full, as if his entire head were one large pompadour. I didn't know enough to deem his clothes late nineties or really put them in any decade. Gray pants, not tight but definitely not the old-guy baggy ones he now wore. White shirt in the style of a conservative business shirt but made of some more relaxed fabric like linen. "What's the point of the picture?" she asked.

"It verifies his identity. Like you see in all those cop shows, how some perp gets hold of a birth certificate, almost always of someone who died young, and then bases his entire bio on a fiction created around the name on the certificate." She nodded and tilted her head, waiting. "This photo of Pete means something. People with nonglam jobs often don't have pictures of themselves in magazines. Well, now they do, or they have the equivalent on social media. But this places Pete Delaney in the job he claims to have had: an employee of a big advertising firm. Honestly?

It's disappointing. He isn't using some newish fake identity. It's either his actual name or a false one he's been using for years and years. He was a packaging designer . . ."

I let out a big, silent sigh, so Wynne finished my sentence: "Who's still a packaging designer. So you're what? Discouraged that he is what he says he is, and was?"

"Yes, though come to think of it, that's really not the hugest deal. Whatever is wrong with him, I don't see it as an offshoot of packaging design. He's not creating darling little zip bags for methamphetamines."

"But you did say 'meth.' In your mind, is whatever he's doing criminal?"

"Well, I know enough from my blessed human resources person and from Sami that I can be ninety-nine percent sure Pete had no government connection. Not like a perv, but yeah, criminal. There was something wrong about him that made me leery."

"Well, you are a trained investigator, so that's something." I felt relieved that Wynne now seemed to be taking me more seriously after having been dismissive.

We walked back to the gallery and sat on a metal bench in front of another of the artist's mosaics. We were too far from the work for me to see what the individual pieces were, if they had changed from marsupials to cats. From this distance, the tones of the pieces of this mosaic created tall and short rectangles. Almost a city. Not a big one. More like Fort Wayne. "Trained investigator or not," I went on. "Am I back at the beginning? Still asking myself how to distinguish between a gut feeling and my personal conspiracy theory?"

Wynne put her palms together and rested the area between her brows on top of her index fingers, that devout gesture you see in the Christian section of bookstores. It was one of her deep-in-thought postures, like when she was agonizing between Frette and Porthault bedsheets for a client. "At first I thought you're doing this because you need some excitement."

"But you don't think that anymore?" I asked hopefully. An insight was just around the corner.

"No, I still do, but I also think there's more. I've pretty much stuck to one thing all my life. Call what I do aesthetics, call it design. Aesthetic assessments change, and certainly design preferences do. But I've stuck with my passion through a million different permutations. I wound up making a business out of it. But you were never like that. Don't give me that sideways look, Corie. It's not a criticism. It's an observation. You just change interests. And with the change, you view yourself as a whole new person. You went from actor, lawyer, political strategist, Middle Eastern scholar. And that was just in college."

186

"But one thing was always consistent: to settle down and have a family."

Wynne stood and walked over to one of the smaller collages. Unlike me, she wasn't a sitter in galleries and museums. She was so visually acute she could take in an artwork in less than a minute. I got up and joined her. "I know you always wanted a picket fence life, though you certainly never seemed unhappy being single," she said.

"What about you?" I asked.

"We're not talking about me. You. You took Arabic because registration for Chinese 101—"

"Russian."

"—whatever you wanted had closed. And you hated it. You said it was incredibly hard. Then all of a sudden you fell in *love* with it." She hugged herself on "love." To outsiders it might seem a mean gesture, but it had been one of our shticks since middle school. "You'd be a diplomat in the Mideast and peace would reign. After that, it was no, not a diplomat, which was astute because your diplomacy quotient is close to nonexistent."

"And you're secretary of state?" I demanded.

"No. The only way I could be diplomatic would be to take a lifetime vow of silence."

I went back to the metal bench and sat more gingerly than I had the first time. Finally, Wynne joined me. "But 9/11 changed everything," I told her. "You know that. I applied to the bureau right after winter break of my senior year. I wanted to serve my country. So what if I tried on lots of future selves before that? Most people do it when they're twelve or even twenty because they have no one clear vision of who they are. They're just a bundle of interests. All I know is that when I joined the FBI, I had no idea what I was getting into. It wasn't naïveté as much as the world had changed. I came to be passionate about the work, but there was hardly a night I didn't feel sick with exhaustion."

"Except now you're out of that loop, living the life you supposedly dreamed of. But you seem to be searching out a high level of pressure. That's what I'm having trouble understanding. Maybe I do, because you're way understimulated. Except for Eliza, and Josh on occasion, you don't love your life. Not the way I do or your mom does or your dad used to. Sometimes you look so not there, like you're in cardiac arrest. You need a jolt to keep going."

I shook my head slowly. "I'm not looking to go back. There were things I saw that will always haunt me." Wynne jerked back her head. She looked startled. "And no, I won't talk about them even now, even to you, and not only because they're classified. There are things I did, too."

"Like what?" she asked quietly. Her tone was placating, as if the tiniest bit more pressure could send me over the edge and I'd never come back. "You, personally, did something?"

"Not killing or torturing or anything like that. But it's not like I long for the old days. It's more complicated than that. I'm not really at home in either world, to be honest." I stepped forward to take a closer look at a bluish-green mosaic. "I mean, it is true that Josh can be less than a thrill a minute. Sometimes less than a thrill a day."

I'd heard how legions of women were after Josh starting after Dawn's funeral, bringing him brisket, homemade cookies/brownies/madeleines, notes of solace, sympathy poems, and, several weeks later, erotica. Women pursued him for months, years. I'd met some of them around Shorehaven, at the courthouse, at legal events in Manhattan and Brooklyn; a fair number were both prettier and smarter than I was.

Yet I got him. I still wasn't sure why. I gathered he viewed my work for the bureau as exotic. He was definitely hot for me. Now and then he even called me Nike, as in the *Winged Victory* statue, with her sinewy legs and powerful torso. Many nights, more asleep than not, he'd run a hand over my quads or hamstrings. Hot for me though I quickly realized I wasn't his usual type. Sometimes I had worries—not exactly fleeting— that he'd revert to pattern and fall for someone who was not only excessively svelte, but in his estimation substantive: an expert on aleatoric music who was also teaching herself Sumerian. Yet, I was pretty sure that he'd been faithful to Dawn, and he seemed congenitally monogamous. On the other hand, she'd been a five-foot-ten size 2.

I continued: "Josh is everything I've always wanted."

"I get paid extra for agreeing with your self-deception." She paused. "Okay, that was too direct. Except you've told me that he's not perpetually scintillating."

"I know. And more and more, he doesn't take time to have fun with us, or me, anymore. I thought he was happy where he was. But now he's trying to get on the court of appeals. Which would be a huge honor, but . . ."

Wynne nodded with understanding. "It's so important to him to be taken seriously," she said.

"Right. It was easier to prove himself in a law firm, because the cases you brought in and how you performed were objective measures. It's different when you're a judge, and even when you're great, how many people really care? Other judges and a few academics?"

"It seems to me Josh needs to be admired and not just by you," Wynne said. "I don't mean that in a sexual way or anything. Don't you think he wants his wonderfulness announced, like: 'Hey, the court of appeals thinks I'm boring enough to get a seat'?"

"I think so."

"Is that it?"

"No. And I probably am sick of reading so much Arabic literature, and some of it really sucks, that most of the time all I want to do is sit in front of a huge screen and watch three episodes in a row of some second-rate British mystery series. And never again look at a book in any language."

We went to the gallery next door to check out the meteor things. Wynne called them turds of the gods. I pointed out that several had red SOLD stickers on their bases. Wynne checked, and even she was shocked that they cost between forty-five and seventy thousand dollars per turd.

After two more days, I caught myself fondling my cell phone and realized I was like Aladdin's mother rubbing the lamp he'd brought home. A jinn would appear. I'd be so startled I'd waste a wish asking for a call from Sami, who'd give me new and startling information.

Or maybe it wasn't the information that I was wishing for. Maybe it was Sami.

# 10

The local hardware store bore a sign that said EST 1911, though it looked as if it had been in Shorehaven since the town's founding in 1643. In contrast to the hardness of the fluorescent-lit big-box stores, this place had a reassuring, can-do atmosphere that was welcoming—causing suburbanites to pull back their shoulders and stand taller as they came through the door. Even if they'd bought their split-level only five months earlier, they moved confidently toward a wall near the entrance, covered with a timeless collection of bolts, nails, and screws: *Gotta get my materials*. It gave them the sensation of knowing their houses deeply, and of having roots in Shorehaven's equivalent of a trading post: *Just pickin' up some round-head nails*.

The locals could still buy modern items like ceramic outdoor cookers and gizmos that turned toilets into multitaskers. But the homey cedar barrels filled with flashlights that got wheeled out during hurricane season and the tiered pine bins of power-tool accessories warmed up any coldness of clamshell packaging. Rough wood, a much-used bristle broom leaning informally against a display of rakes, Doris smiling behind the counter adding up purchases—these charms turned customers into the kind of neighbors who, in an earlier era, would call out on leaving: *See ya at Fred's barn raising.*

I was studying sandpaper when I heard: "Hi, Corie." It was John Grillo, landscape drainage expert and, today, my answered prayer. John was not only a member of the Wednesday lunch group; he was also the guy who brought Pete Delaney into the mix.

"How are you, John?" I asked. His full head of dark hair, contrasting with white, brushed-back sideburns and his outdoorsy bronzed skin, could have made him swoonworthy, the type of man whom women would confess: *OMG, isn't he hot for a guy his age?* Except his equal opportunity directness—no dancing eyebrow, no glance up and down a woman's body—diminished the crooner sizzle my mom would have adored.

"I'm good, except I ran out of extra-fine sand-paper." It was chore day, Saturday morning just moments before nine.

"Painting something?" I asked. Being the only child of a DIY dad had at least given me experience and vocabulary, if not skill.

"The damn dog finally got old enough to stop chewing the legs on the dining room chairs," he said. "So I'm in the ninety-ninth step of sanding and varnishing. You?"

"Talk about sanding . . . I'm thinking of getting

my dad a random orbital sander for Father's Day."

"Good gift," he said, nodding a little like a bobble head.

"Oh, while you're here, I've been meaning to ask you forever. It was you and Iris who got the lunch group going, right?"

"Right. Well, it was really Iris's idea."

"And she brought in Phoebe?"

"She did," he nodded, recognizing a fond but hazy detail from a decade earlier. "I just rounded up . . ." If John's consciousness were visible, I could have seen Pete Delaney teetering on its edge. But I gave him a minute to see if he could retrieve it himself. "Pete Delaney," he said finally. "That big *Mad Men* ad agency he was working at? Gave him the ax. Relatively small severance package, from what he said."

"He must have been devastated," I said.

"I guess," John said. The tip of the collar of his three-button sport shirt turned up and he smoothed it down. The shirt was rich people's dark green, like racing cars and walls hung with paintings of game birds. Instead of a polo pony insignia above the left pec, there was an arc, like a small hill, with LANDSCAPE & DRAINAGE above and J. GRILLO, BLA, MLA below. "With Pete, kind of hard to tell what he's feeling." I nodded, not too vehemently. "He isn't a big talker. You know, midwesterner."

"Well, I've met midwesterners who won't shut up. It could be more personality than geography."

"He's not your typical guy," John replied.

"Why do you say that?" I picked up a small sand block and checked it out, just so I wouldn't appear to be hanging on his answer.

"Because. Because it's not like he's antisocial." But he seemed to hesitate after that point. I nodded again: *Keep talking.* "Actually, he does stuff that people do when they're trying to come out of their shells. Coaches softball, volunteers at the soup kitchen over at the Lutheran church."

Being religious didn't mean you weren't a criminal, I knew. People killed in God's name; clergy abused children. The greatest traitor in FBI history, Special Agent Robert Hanssen of Counterintelligence, was famed for his devout Catholicism. But I asked anyway: "He goes to the Lutheran church?"

"I don't think he's a member. We went out for dinner a couple of times. Our wives do volunteer work together. He was saying he likes helping out at the soup kitchen there, but he OD'd on religion growing up."

"A rough childhood?" I asked.

"No clue. Guys like him don't talk about themselves."

"Right," I agreed. "You know, the thing you said before, about Pete trying to come out of his shell. That's a really good insight." During

195

my time at the bureau, I found that when I was interviewing people, telling them they had good insight made them want to keep on showing how perceptive they were.

John did just that, mentioning that Pete didn't seem to have any real friends in town, but his life seemed to revolve around his wife's large family. "I guess that's enough for him." He hesitated again. I waited, sensing in his total lack of movement that he had more to say. "This one time, we went out to dinner—the two couples. His wife was joking and laughing about how much he was out of town. And he said—quietly, but ice cold—'That's enough, Jen.' My wife told me later that his wife went white as a sheet. And I've got to admit, his wife was quiet for the rest of the dinner. It was just weird, you know?" He bit the side of his lip, as if worrying that he'd said too much. "Anyway, he's good at doing you a favor, like I said I needed a really hard drill bit and he lent me one. Cobalt. But that doesn't mean he wants to play poker with you. And come to think of it, I wouldn't want to play with him."

Now I needed to get John Grillo's mind off Pete. On the off chance that he ran into him in the next day or two, I didn't want John saying: *Just was talking about you with Corie Geller.* So I got John to walk me over to the orbital sanders where he got emotional about their workings.

"Don't even think of getting one without a dust bag," he warned. After I vowed I would never do such a thing, I kept him busy recounting the activities and college choices of his three kids. At last, as John finished recounting how his daughter switched from psychology to mechanical engineering at the University of Vermont, I sensed Pete Delaney had been erased from his consciousness.

"Sounds as if she made a really thoughtful choice," I said.

"That's the perfect word for her, 'thoughtful,'" he replied.

I pondered what he'd said: It was understandable that like many people Pete could be shy, try to be part of the community, but still focus mostly on family. Perfectly ordinary, totally normal. But it also made sense that a person engaged in a criminal enterprise would want a tranquil, even mind-numbing life. Middle-class felons want the security of being conventional. Pete could be dealing drugs, counterfeiting, engaging in human trafficking: all those required a distribution network, but theoretically he could remain hidden behind his facade of normality, enjoying a restful life when not doing his thing, whatever his thing was.

Back when I'd been working with Sami and the group, we hadn't dealt exclusively with Islamic terrorists in the Tri-Border Area. We ran into middle-class and high-net-worth Americans as well. A dermatologist owned a lab in Rockland County, New York, that tested for skin and toenail fungus. You could not get more blech or more boring. And that was the perfect prescription for a cover-up for what he was doing—purifying inositol in his lab. He used it to cut cocaine, which he also did very efficiently.

Just as I got home with a gift-wrapped orbital sander, I got a text from Josh: *In study on phone. Lunch at 1? LY*—the last standing for "love you," what we wrote at the end of notes. He started that when we first got married and I asked Josh how come it wasn't *ILY,* considering *I* was a single stroke and he didn't exactly have carpal tunnel syndrome from banging his gavel. "I don't know," he'd said. "It's kind of relaxed, familiar. Don't you like it?" I smiled and told him it was fine, which is what you do in the first year of your marriage. Or at least it was what I did.

I trotted into Josh's study. He was in his leather chair reading a gray-covered document and saying, "No" and "Ax that" into his phone. Then he listened with lips pursed, as if he had yet to be persuaded by an argument but at least was contemplating it. I wondered why he didn't go out and sit under a sycamore; it was gorgeous outside.

A minute later he ended the call and stood to

kiss me, more a prelude to lunch than passion. I announced: "I want an herb garden with lots of pots."

He nodded, then realized more was required. "Sounds great," he said. While he didn't become breathlessly animated, he wasn't dismissive.

"One of the women in my lunch group has a business with flowerpots. Really nice stuff. I have no idea what it costs. Maybe a bundle, maybe not. I texted her and she said it was fine for me to come over."

"Good. I mean great—your wanting to do something around the house. Other than your redoing the bedroom. But I can't recall you doing anything else." He said this with some reservation, just in case I'd added a wing to the house and he hadn't noticed it.

"The bedroom was pretty much it. Hey, I'm a cheap date."

"Cheap date but a class act," my husband said. I did love it when he was gallant.

"Thanks."

"Do what you want, Corie. Hire Wynne if you want."

"The reason I brought it up is we agreed that if either of us wants to change anything, we had to discuss it first. Remember?"

"Right." He didn't remember. "I suppose I was thinking a major project, ripping out a kitchen, replacing it with a sauna. But this is fine." He swallowed, took a breath, manned up, and asked: "Would you like me to go with you?"

If I'd said yes, he probably would have done it without complaint. But I caught the slightest lowering of Josh's shoulders as he expelled a breath of relief when I said, "No, I'm fine. Eliza's over at Chloë's doing some secret Father's Day project. So I'll see you at one or thereabouts. I'll pick up a tomato or two. Can you do tuna or egg salad?"

"Deal," he said smiling, then lowered his head to become a person of substance again.

Iris Kubel's house was not grand, but to me it was pretty near perfect, a family-size cottage made of chubby, roundish stones, with wood trim. At some point it must have been the caretaker's house on one of those grand Long Island estates. Wide-spreading trees with the still-mellow green leaves of late spring shaded the front. We strolled around to the sunny backyard, though the light seemed softer there than in the rest of Shorehaven, as if it were filtered to shine on the fairies and sprites whose spirits animated the cottage. It was the house I would have chosen for myself.

Both Dawn and Josh had some deep-rooted belief in the necessity of "entertainment space," as if they held weekly balls instead of the annual Thanksgiving dinner and seder. Our conservatory, the glassed-in room where we served drinks and hors d'oeuvres, was more suitably sized for the court of King George IV than for three Long Island Jews. Though I loved Josh, our need for space didn't jibe. He was not a stone cottage kind of guy.

Iris guided me around her garden filled with receptacles, from clay urns with cherubs on the handles to stone saucers to reclaimed wood boxes that I nixed since they reminded me of coffins without lids. I showed her some shots of the back of the house and she suggested old, mossy terra-cotta pots flanking the kitchen door.

"If you have to walk sixty feet to get a few sprigs of thyme when you're making beef stew, trust me, it's not going to have thyme. Or you'll use some dried stuff that's been in a drawer since 2009. Ick." Instead of the usual giant clip Iris used to keep her light brown hair in place, she had three large, randomly placed barrettes. Since she was wearing short gardening gloves, she scratched the top of her head with her wrist bone. "You're sure there's all-day sun there?" she asked. I said yes, and she dictated a list of the herbs I wanted into her phone, then suggested several different colors of basil, hyssop, and lavender. And definitely edible flowers. "During World War II, when the French couldn't get pepper, you know what they did? Used nasturtiums!"

We went into Iris's office, which doubled as a dining room. Her desk looked out on her garden through French doors—not the white formal kind, but the kind with glass set in old wood frames. It didn't surprise me to find that Iris's desk was beyond neat, with just a keyboard and a huge flat-screen monitor; any other tech equipment was hidden. All the papers and catalogs were stacked in alignment in a single rectangular basket according to size, the largest catalog on the bottom, a blue packet of forget-me-not seeds on top.

She punched some figures into her calculator app, humming as if to animate the numbers with music, and gave me two nonshocking estimates for the project—one using a version of terracotta made from recycled plastic that she said looked "reasonably decent" and the real thing, vintage and mossy and chipped here and there. I chose the real thing, which pleased her. We spent nearly an hour planning my herb garden, though Iris said she'd have to come and take precise measurements before it was finalized.

"No wonder they put you in charge of keeping attendance and dealing with La Cuisine Délicieuse," I told her. "You're so thorough."

"My husband calls it OCD," she said, smiling. "But actually, he likes it. He knows that if left to his own devices, he'd be living on top of a garbage dump and eating banana peels for breakfast. And the funny thing is both his parents are originally Swiss. They're supposed to be a neat people. Who knows? Maybe that's why they left."

"I really admire order," I said. "I wish I were better at it. By the way, do you keep some kind of calendar for your gardening?"

"I keep one for every client that pops up as a link, plus my own. I grow a lot from seed, so it's not just when to plant things on the ground or in their final pots." Iris smiled a lot, and with her entire face, eyes crinkling, happy mouth pushing up full cheeks. Even her wide, freckled nose scrunched upward. "Even though I'm outdoors so much, I have the soul of an accountant. I love calendars, spreadsheets, all sorts of organization."

"No kidding. I wouldn't have guessed."

"A good spreadsheet gives me so much comfort."

"Do you keep any records for the lunch group?" I asked casually.

"Oh sure. Who's there, who's not there, whose turn it is for show-and-tell. I mean, not that they really need me to do it, but that way I can remind people whose turn it is the following week. Or like, if they forgot their wallet or something and someone else puts their lunch on their own credit card, I can say, 'Phoebe, you owe Darby seventeen seventy-five.' "

"That's great! Do you make any other notes?"

"Well, to tell you the truth, it's not as if my left brain is at war with my right brain. They get on fine. So even though part of me is a CPA, the other part is sentimental. Like even though they are a cliché, I love using bleeding hearts or weeping lantana. And I love my spreadsheets because they're also a diary."

"A diary?" I asked, wanting to hug her or at least pinch her plump cheek.

"For instance, if Phoebe has some big item on eBay I'll put it down. Remember she had that vintage bicycle with the giant front wheel? She got over two thousand dollars for it! Sometimes, when I'm scrolling through, it brings back stuff I've forgotten."

Iris went into her kitchen to make me a cup of mint tea and came back with flowered cups and saucers that looked very much at home in the cottage. I took my tea from a small china tray and asked: "Would it be possible for you to lend me your records for the group? Or email them? I'm trying to learn how to use a spreadsheet. A couple of the literary agencies I work with are pressuring me to use one to keep track of the books I'm reading for them, and I'm sure the others will be following soon. It's a little confusing for me, even though the purpose is clarity. Maybe if I could look at a sample of something that's not all numbers, with names I'm familiar with, it could help."

"Which spreadsheet do they use?" Iris asked. I gave what I hoped was a look of: *Help me out here,* and she said, "I use Excel."

"I think that's it! Would you mind?"

"Of course, it isn't top secret," she said in her smiley way. "Sure. I'll email it to you as an attachment."

Which she did. By the time I got home with two tomatoes and ciabatta bread, it was in my inbox. Iris really did love those details. What I especially admired was her noting all the cities Pete Delaney told the group he was visiting.

# 11

I began the day at seven a.m. with a plan to stay mindful. Several minutes later I noticed I'd squeezed tinted moisturizer onto my toothbrush. Living in the moment might become an issue that day.

The cleaning service arrived at nine, so Lulu and I holed up in my office to escape their vacuum cleaner, which roared through all the rooms on the second floor. As usual, Lulu had wedged in beside me on my recliner. I kept trying to focus on an Egyptian crime novel. I could tune out the noise, but the dog kept switching from trembling that broke my heart to crazed barking, so I wound up alternating between the tenderest consolation to a madwoman's "Shut the fuck up!"

Was brother Brad Delaney a fiction? I'd asked Sami to look into it, but either he hadn't found anything or he'd taken off for Ciudad del Este to play a Brazilian terrorist aligned with Hezbollah.

I managed to brush off Sami (and Brad) by saying "mindfulness" out loud. I worked at calming Lulu again, to say nothing of myself, and mindfully looked for the point where I'd left off reading. As I was skimming I caught the Arabic word for burglar, *sariq*. Immediately, questions popped into mind: If Pete is involved in a criminal enterprise, what would it be? Burglary? Was there such a thing as methamphetamine packaging design? I waited for a gut reaction, but none came.

It took me a couple of minutes to realize Lulu had fallen asleep and that the cleaning service guys had gone downstairs. The same two usually showed up to clean the house: Tomás, short and beefy, with a neck that descended straight from behind his ears to his shoulders. His knowledge of cleaning hacks was awesome. Frodo, whose real name I couldn't remember, resembled the wide-eyed actor in *The Lord of the Rings*. Just his eyes, though, because this Frodo probably weighed 250. His huge blues blinked with abnormal infrequency. Despite his size, he wasn't at all threatening. He spoke about two words a year but always brought a Milk-Bone for Lulu, which he presented to her as if it were an engagement ring.

I cherished these guys in the vague way I had great affection for some people I saw regularly but didn't know personally. They were micro relationships of pleasant hellos, a smile, and a couple of words, then convivial good-byes. I felt similarly tender toward the cheese slicer at Stop and Shop and the health insurance assistant at my doctor's.

I went downstairs, followed by Lulu. Frodo was in the kitchen, climbing a ladder to clean from the ceiling what seemed to be—as I peered up—several Halloweens' worth of cobwebs, which I'd never noticed. Tomás was wiping the inside of the plastic garbage can, one of my mom's fantastically helpful household hints that she'd offered him when she had been at the house one cleaning day: "Dear," she said to him, crooking her finger and giving him a come-here gesture. "Let me show you something you just might have overlooked." Recalling that moment was always good for a cringe and a blush.

Tomás glanced up at me and said, "So you got a new safe." Every few months, he lifted the hangers and dusted the rods in Dawn's closet— an area large enough that a couple of laps around it could qualify as aerobic activity. "You're going high tech, Mrs. G."

"The insurance company said they'd give us a five percent discount if we got a fireproof safe with a fingerprint scanner," I told him. "We needed a bigger safe anyway. Too many papers."

"A lot of people around here are getting them. Gun safes."

"Who has guns in this neighborhood?"

"You'd be surprised."

I was surprised. Ubiquitous alarm systems, check. Cameras at every entry point except the cat door, check. But Nassau County's gun and

Taser laws were stringent enough to make all but the most determined settle for a canister of pepper spray, and even that was no picnic to obtain if you lived downstate.

"You think I'm the armed and dangerous type?" I asked.

"You gotta be kidding. No, no way was I saying *your* safe is for guns."

Of course it was a gun safe. I kept up my skills by going to a shooting range every few months. Technically I still met bureau standards, though if a suspect rushed toward me and suddenly pulled a weapon, it was fifty-fifty if I'd be the one to get off the first shot.

I made up for that with martial arts during my time at Quantico. Back then, it was mostly DT—defensive tactics—like weapons retention and arrest strategies. My advantage over some of my colleagues was that I had some background in martial arts: the krav maga I'd done with my dad. By mid-2002, trainees were being taught more belligerent skills, offensive and defensive. But by then I was out of Quantico and working in DC's ugliest building, fittingly named for J. Edgar Hoover.

"Mrs. G.," Tomás added. "I didn't mean to be nosy about the safe."

"I know that. Listen, I was the one who was nosy, asking about who has a gun safe around here."

"That's not being nosy. Your husband's a judge." I nodded, assuming he meant that if Josh received threats, he might want a weapon in the house. "Some of the people could keep a gun around because, you know, they have *so* much cash."

"Which I'm sure they report on their taxes," I said, and we both smiled. "So who are the others? People you wouldn't think would want a gun in their house?"

Tomás nodded. I understood that, like lawyers and doctors, cleaning people had a code of ethics. You don't blab about one client in front of another. It's disloyal and also bad for business. Yet I'd worked with enough witnesses to be able to recognize the signs of an internal debate. So I used my *I understand* expression, which was to convey some interest but not rampant curiosity. And in part because we had a pleasant relationship—businesslike but a little jokey—and also because he'd once told me he appreciated that Josh always wrote him a note with his Christmas tip, his internal debate ended. "Just between us?" he asked.

"Yes. Just between us."

"Like I'm not mentioning people who live alone, especially ladies and old people, though some of them shouldn't be having a gun. But at least they keep it in a safe. But you know Dr. Warren? The foot doctor? Not a real doctor, she just does feet." I thought I'd heard the name so I gave him a nod and a look of surprise with it. Like: *How could Dr. Warren possibly need to be armed?* "Even if she's got prescription pads or wads of cash, does she need that kind of a safe? It's not even a finger safe. It's an eyeball safe."

"That's pretty hard to understand," I said in what I hoped was an encouraging manner.

"And there's a guy who works at home." I inhaled, but if I exhaled I wasn't aware of it. "I was just there a couple of times, when someone in another crew got sick. Like he's got a stick up his you-know-where. Don't go here, go there, be careful with the printer, don't open any of the magic markers. Like we're going to draw on his walls? The first time I was there he took his water bottle with him when he went to the bathroom. Was he thinking we would take sips when he's out of the room?"

"I don't like him, whoever he is," I said. I quickly swallowed because I was sounding a little croaky. "What kind of a safe does he have?"

"Not too big," Tomás said. "Bigger than yours, though." I had lots of questions, but I didn't want to make him aware of my interest, a.k.a. obsession.

"Weird," I said. My heart was beating even though my head said, *Big deal. What did you discover? The guy has a safe in his house?*

I knew who it was, but confirmation was always

welcome. "I remember!" he said just then. "His name. Mr. Delaney. You know him?"

"Actually, yes. I met him at some business group here in town." I paused. "Your description of him? Perfect."

Fortunately, Lulu had a great sense of timing. She went into Doberman mode, growling with a fierceness that was laughable coming from a dog ten inches tall. "Shush!" I snapped. Then I glanced out the kitchen window and saw she was being a proper guard dog, warning me of a stranger in a black T-shirt. He was walking across our terrace pulling a red wagon. It was filled with clay pots.

Seconds later, Iris Kubel came into view. She was wearing an outfit I'd seen once at lunch, a red gingham jumpsuit, though the large red banana clip keeping her hair off her face appeared to be a new accessory. The red theme was completed by sun-bleached red gardening clogs. I excused myself and went outside.

"This is Alex," she said. I said *Hi* and he said *Ullo*, in what sounded like a Russian or Slavic accent. Sadly, not only was he lacking the Slavic cheekbones, but his elongated face so lacked structure and color that it resembled a peeled potato. "I just want to get some measurements. You told me it was okay to come around the back anytime."

"Absolutely! That's fine."

"I bought these pots along, hoping you'd be around, to see how you felt about them." Not deeply.

But stone and terra-cotta meant much to Iris, so I told her, "Lovely!" The vessels had a mossy patina and zero cherubs. What was there to object to? I helped her and Alex haul the pots around. Of course I knew the taller ones should go in the back, but Iris arranged them so they appeared to have been set in their places over generations in an English garden.

I offered them coffee or iced tea. Iris went for the tea. Alex passed and asked if he could walk around and check my shade plants—he called them something that wasn't "hostas"—that bordered the wooded area way back in the yard.

I suppressed the urge to tell him they weren't mine; I often had to control my impulse to disavow Dawn's many decorating choices. I recognized it would come off as unseemly, for example, to whisper to the plumber that it had been my husband's first wife who'd chosen faucet taps with FROID and CHAUD on them. So I just said sure.

"I took a glance at those spreadsheets," I told Iris. "I think they're going to be really helpful. I was amazed how much information you can get in them."

"The more you get to use them, the more you'll

love them!" Maybe she sensed her fervor was weirding me out, because she unclipped her hair, nervously retwisted it, and secured it again.

"I saw an example online where you can track projects," I said. "That could be major for me when I'm pitching agents on a bunch of different books. Fiction, nonfiction, genre, title, author, setting . . . Who knew that spreadsheets were a lot more than numbers?"

"Exactly! People just don't know." Iris took a sip of tea and smiled benevolently as if she'd made a convert to her religion. "I keep track of what's been planted, what's in the greenhouse space I rent, or what I still have to get. Hey, by the way, just think: this weekend, you'll have your choice of four kinds of mint for your iced drinks. Oh, quick tip, if you like sangria, adding a little mint, a little basil takes it to a whole other level." She seemed pleased at the thought. "I love it when people really start getting Excel!" And she clapped her hand over the red gingham that covered her heart.

My dentist's office had so much leather-and-chrome Bauhaus furniture that I knew I was over-paying for my annual cleaning. I stared down at my iPad, at a blog I was reading on Arabic feminist fiction. As usual, my thoughts strayed and I found myself recollecting Pete Delaney's show-and-tell talks at lunches over the last two-plus years: take-out cups; too-adorable underwear for the recently potty trained; organic shredded coconut; tiny tools for computer maintenance. Fortunately, the woman who had said, "Excuse me" as she took the chair beside me was leaning away, so I wasn't distracted by overcloseness or shoulder bunking with her. A couple of times I glanced up and saw her smiling with intense toothiness. Having noticed I was reading Arabic, she was being extra sweet—as if to make up for all the hurts inflicted on Muslims.

I smiled back and who knew why, but up popped a memory of Pete's telling us about Cupcake in a Tube, a startup on the verge of going bust because its packaging couldn't stop its icing from turning to ooze in hot weather. He'd saved the owner with new materials and a clear cylinder with a push-up bottom rather than a squeezy container and had her reconfigure the product so the icing on top spiraled through the cake, so the total cupcake experience kept going right to the bottom. As Pete was demonstrating with a garish pink-and-white strawberry shortcake cupcake, Darby Penn had muttered to me, "Who the hell would buy their kids that crap?" I nodded but still thought it was pretty clever.

I had driven straight home and looked up Cupcake in a Tube, which turned out to be in Pittsburgh. I called its owner, C. Collins. All along I'd bought the story that Pete was talented enough to make a go of it alone. But what if he just pulled some nicely packaged items off the shelf at Rite Aid or Home Depot and claimed credit for the design in show-and-tell? True, I'd seen the photo of him in the ad agency, and his having worked there checked out, but that was then. Was he doing packaging design in his home office now or something else?

I gave the cupcake lady a cover story of my plans to launch a new company, Biggy.com, which would sell athletic wear for XXXL men. One of the first things I learned at Quantico was constructing whatever narrative you might need before beginning an interview; you could embellish on the fly, but it was hard to create. I told her Biggy was capitalized and ready to go. But I wanted to check out her packaging designer, Pete. I didn't offer her his last name hoping that she would either fill in the blank or say: "Pete?"

"Pete Delaney, you mean," Chrissy Collins said, sounding as perky as her name. It was easy to imagine her as the entrepreneur who deeply believed that a cupcake in a plastic cylinder would make the world better. "He is just so great at what he does!"

My heart sank at the thought that he really could be legit, though I said, "Excellent! Is he a fast worker? I mean . . ."

I had no idea what I meant, but Chrissy knew. "Medium fast. Like a week or two, maybe three, for drawings and your basic mock-up."

"The mock-up's done in person?"

"Totally. He insists, but at least he doesn't ask for business-class travel. You sign a contract with him for the job, and he brings his stuff to you. No way he's going to email drawings or send out the mock-up. Then, assuming you like what he's done, you move on to step two. I thought he was unbelievably good. Not just design. Knowing what different materials could do, patient at explaining."

"Pleasant to deal with?" I asked. Chrissy made a humming sound, the nonverbal equivalent of so-so or not terrible. "Unpleasant?"

"No. Just very, very businesslike. Like I started gushing a little about how much I loved his work. He wasn't embarrassed about me going on, but he didn't seem like it made him happy. He's just like in some neutral gear all the time. Which is all right as far as I'm concerned."

"That would be fine with me, too!" I told her, sensing I was beginning to mirror her cheerleader brightness. "So after you accept the drawings—"

"You don't have to accept them right off. I mean, if there's something you want changed, there's a revision step built into the contract. And then when you agree on everything, the second part of the contract goes into effect."

"Do you happen to know where he lives?" I asked.

"New York. Long Island. Where are you?"

"Actually, not that far from there. New Jersey."

"Great! Then you wouldn't be running up big travel expenses."

"Right," I said, suppressing an exclamation point. "By the way, do you get to keep the drawings and mock-up? I mean, that way you can give your web designer an idea of what you're doing and literally take the package to the bank."

"No. But I see it this way. He's someone I found online and he turned what could have been a total life disaster into the basis of a successful business. My theory? As head of a company, you're looking for someone who's good at what they do and not looking to make a killing at any one job. If you want personality—"

"Hire a stand-up comic."

"That is so cute!" she said. "And totally true."

In an ideal investigatory universe, I would have remained untouched. But I was disappointed that Chrissy hadn't said, *Pete who? I used Adorable Packaging Concepts, Inc.*

I was so deep into my reverie that the dental hygienist had to call my name twice before I recognized it. So with a theatrical sigh (that explained why I had to stop majoring in Drama, Theatre, and Dance after only six credits), I stood to face her.

# 12

ate that afternoon, I went through Iris's
spreadsheets. I couldn't find any pattern in
the dates on which Pete took his trips, although
someone else who'd gotten further than I with
the basics of calculus might have been able to
come up with an algorithm that would lead to an
answer. But I was confident enough to keep at
it. I noticed that sometimes only the cities Pete
had talked about were listed, and not the precise
dates of his trip. Still, from all I could glean, his
average trip seemed to take three days.

I swiveled from side to side in my office chair
musing about how almost everybody, informed
or uninformed, had an opinion about almost
everything. I was sure that universally accepted
restaurant behavior was the only thing restraining
the people at the table next to us and the waiter
from chiming in on the two-state solution and
whether the jacket art on the Arabic translation
of *Huckleberry Finn* (which I'd showed the
group) captured the nineteenth-century American
zeitgeist.

In spite of Pete's not being there, I felt less
alienated than usual from the Wednesday group,
probably because I'd been speaking. Also,

over dessert, John, Iris, and I started discussing wireless mesh networks; I'd been contemplating replacing our emotionally fragile routers. They frequently needed to be unplugged and given time to compose themselves.

But also, I'd grown fond of Iris. For a woman given to plastic hair clips, she had a nobility about her. She reminded me of a pioneer woman who made the trek west with a wagon train; I could imagine her in a bonnet, holding a rifle. It wasn't just her freckles and deep smarts about people and plants that gave the impression of grit. Iris was astute enough to recognize her own strength yet not to be enamored of it. She was tolerant of foibles. Through her mojo, I found myself accepting the others more—of course with the exception of Mr. Delaney.

I decided my newfound benevolence was a good thing. I was always at my best being part of a group. Despite being an only child, I didn't have a do-it-alone mentality. From being a trio with my mom and dad to playing on Forest Hills High School's softball team to working on the Joint Terrorism Task Force, I liked belonging. I recalled how comforted I'd felt when I met Wynne in first grade. We melded almost immediately. Kindergarten had been so lonely, but with Wynne, I was half of a duo.

That night at dinner, I told Josh and Eliza that I was going to invite my parents over for barbecue on Sunday: would they take charge of my mom (who was at her happiest with an audience)? No subtle shudders on their parts, no whining. Actually, they got along great with her. She and Eliza were good for at least an hour with makeup and hair. Then, when Eliza would meander off to the side porch with her device, my mom could have quality time with Josh. She'd go slack jawed in awe as he prepared his barbecue sauce for the dry-rubbed brisket: *Apple cider vinegar!* Afterward, he could revel in her discourse ("Your mother is so much more substantive than I ever thought an actress could be!") on some Shakespearean history play. She'd pick ones that were pretty obscure that she was mad for—*Henry VIII* or *King John*—though few other people had seen or even read them.

"My dad seems a little down lately," I said for Eliza's benefit, since Josh knew I was worried about his continuing depression and his reluctance to push himself out of his chair to walk even two blocks down Queens Boulevard for fresh bagels. Who knew: maybe even chewing a bagel took too much energy for him. Then I turned directly to Josh: "I heard about a cold case at the bureau, from 2004, and I'm going to try to rope him in on it. I'm not on it officially. But I'll mention that if I get anywhere with it, it could put me in a good light with the new head of the task force, maybe get me something more interesting than the last couple of gigs I've done for them."

Josh and I lingered at the table nibbling on a biscotti we'd split while Eliza went to open the back door for Lulu. He lowered his voice to ask: "Would you mind if I brought up antidepressants with your dad?"

"Of course not. That would be great. You know how far my mom and I've gotten."

"Maybe he's hesitant to give it a shot because he thinks you want the old Dan Schottland back. He senses he can never be that same guy. He doesn't want to disappoint you."

"Well, that's the best theory I've heard so far because he's so dead set against pills or a shrink. My God, every other cop in the department had therapy after 9/11. But before you know it, it will be coming up on two decades, and he's still mourning Mickey Soong. Not just missing him, which is totally understandable: grieving for him. But he won't even go in the vicinity of the shrink."

"Well, I'll call it 'counseling,' not 'therapy,' " Josh said. "I've been thinking about an analogy with some other illness, asking him if he would take medication if he had diabetes. Presumably he'll say yes, and then I'll ask if he could recognize he doesn't have enough insulin, why can't he recognize that he's not getting the right amount of some neurotransmitter. It has nothing to do with moral fiber. It's biochemistry."

Eliza's back was framed in the door as she waited for Lulu to do her business at her spot in the backyard, then spend ten minutes sniffing for intriguing scents in the grass. Like my mom, my dog performed best before an audience. I took Josh's hands in mine. "I love how you think about things I don't know you're thinking about," I told him.

A few days later, the week before Father's Day, my parents were over. My mom was teaching Eliza to make noodles from scratch. I asked my dad up to my office, ostensibly because the door was rubbing against the wood hump on the floor; I was pretty sure it was called a threshold. Once we got there, I told him, "Forget the door. I was using that as an excuse."

"Not a very good one," my father said. "Though maybe you put one over on Lulu. You still thinking about your lunch guy, Pete?"

"Yes."

"You get anywhere beyond some quirks, like watching his car? Jeep, right?"

I smiled and nodded, acknowledging his memory and, frankly, grateful that his mind had not turned to mush from years of watching cop shows and snacking. If anything devastating happened to him, Utz sourdough hard pretzels/Budweiser could be written beside "cause of death." Often there were granules of salt on his shirt and chest hair, though it appeared my mother had brushed him before they left Queens.

While I let my computer sit waiting, I brought him up to date on what I discovered about Pete Delaney. "One of the lunch people, Iris, organizes the whole thing, to the extent that Wednesday lunches at a restaurant need organizing. Like on someone's birthday, the rest of the group pays for his or her lunch. She sends out an email—"

"I've gotta tell you, I'm all for women, right? You know that. But Christ, why can't people stop with the 'his and her' shit?" He shook his head wearily, but the rest of his body didn't move. I noticed that the XL polo shirt my mom had gotten him a few years earlier, a darkish, close-to-NYPD blue, was now so big on him that the shoulder seams hung down an inch on his arms. Somehow he'd lost weight on a pretzel and beer diet.

"Fine. We'll do 'her' for two, three millennia. That'll start to even things up."

I'd pulled in a chair from the guest room that morning and switched it with my desk chair so my dad would be able to swivel and rock while I showed him Iris's spreadsheet. I typed in a password and it materialized onscreen. My dad leaned forward, then backward, then stood and motioned me to switch seats with him so he could be in front of the monitor.

He said: "I got a prescription from the eye

doctor for glasses for the computer, like between reading glasses and watching TV glasses, but what the hell am I going to do? Spend a hundred and fifty bucks when I can squint for free? What's all this? The cities he's gone to?"

"Yes, I looked it over, but I can't come up with any pattern in the timing of the trips."

"Your Iris does this with everybody, keeps all this info on everybody in the group? Is she nuts?"

"No, though maybe she's a teeny bit OCD. That stands for—"

"Give me a break. I watched every episode of *Monk*. Does she have that germ fear?"

"No. Actually, it's probably more of a passion for order, for cataloging, than OCD." I would have told him about her gardening and how I hired her for a potted herb garden, but he was studying the spreadsheet. Otherwise he would have demanded: *Why can't you stick some parsley in a pot yourself and call it a day?*

It took him about five minutes, but finally he said, "I don't see any pattern either, though sometimes she doesn't fill in the dates of the trip, just the cities."

"Well, he's not always specific. No 'on or about the sixth, seventh, and eighth of December.' He'll just say, 'I'm going to Roanoke to show them the chicken wing packaging mock-up, but I'll be back for the weekend.' "

"There should be a capital punishment for

whoever invented Buffalo chicken wings," he said.

"A law for one person would be a bill of attainder," I told him, dredging up some distant memory of a either a conversation I'd had with Josh or a question from the AP exam in US Gov. "That's unconstitutional."

"You *like* Buffalo chicken wings?"

"No, I hate them, though not enough to suspend the rule of law."

"Okay, let's focus. From the dates your lunch lady did mark down, it looks like his average trip lasts"—he crossed his arms over his chest and tried to swivel, then realized he wasn't sitting in the office chair—"what? Three days?"

We both did some breathing and thinking for about ten seconds. Then I said, "That's the number I came up with. Doesn't three days seem a little long to show a client some packaging? Even if you show it one day, and you wait around for them to approve or make some changes, that would make it a two-day trip. If he's near Indiana, maybe he'd see his mother. But nobody would hang around town waiting for a client's decision. They'd get back to you by email, phone call, whatever."

"Maybe Mr. Pete takes an extra day to go on a bender, find some companionship—girl, boy, whatever he goes for."

"So I'm going to tell you what my gut says.

And you're going to say, 'If you rely on your own instincts to solve a case, you'll mess up. Your gut isn't as good as your brain.' " I used "mess" because over the years, I'd discovered I could never say "fuck" in front of my dad, even when we were both in law enforcement mode. "But my gut says Pete's not a particularly sexual person, unless he has some peculiar preference."

"We got a guy once who shoplifted small shit like gloves or socks and would go into the men's room to get, you know, his jollies with it. Mickey said, 'Why can't he buy a pair of Fruit of the Loom socks and save himself a petty larceny charge?' But I said it was the stealing that made it a thrill, not the socks."

"Maybe Pete travels to commit a felony."

"Like what?"

"Dealing in arms and ammunition. Running a sex slavery ring."

"Endless possibilities," my dad said.

"Not endless, because with him it's not a full-time job. He actually does packaging design. And he lives a seemingly normal suburban life. He reminds me a little of me. He's got a narrative he sticks to. With me, it's my bureau affiliation. Not just in the past: I'm still a contractor and have a knowledge of active terrorist networks, especially in the western hemisphere. But both he and I present as living ordinary lives. Except I'm always vigilant, and I think he is, too. There's a cloak over something. I hope I'm better at hiding it than he is."

"You're normal," Dad said. "Maybe he's not and that's what you sense."

"Maybe," I said. "Anyway, other than his wife's family and making some effort to be part of the community, which might be for show, he's pretty much a loner. But he might go to a local museum or something in whatever city he's in."

"A museum?" my dad said.

"Or something," I repeated. "The point is, three days."

"Okay, for the time being, let's go with no pattern to his trips, and he stays for an average of three days, which seems a little long to discuss the chicken wing box. So remind me what else you got on him."

"Okay, keep in mind that he's a pallid guy. He's so white you think, Jesus, he's the only member of *Homo sapiens* who didn't originate in Africa. Anyway, he was going to miss one of our meetings, said he was going to South Bend to see a client. He's from Indiana, so he said he'd probably rent a car to visit his mother who's in a nursing home in Fort Wayne. He's got a brother who lives there, too, so he'd stay with him. He said. But that was before the weather got warmer. When he came to lunch the next Wednesday, I picked up, almost subliminally, that something was off. I took your advice, used my brain time instead of my gut. I started analyzing what was off about him on that day, and suddenly I realized: his hands were tan."

My dad slapped down his palms on either side of the keyboard in frustration. "I'm not hearing anything potentially unlawful from you."

"I'm not talking felony now. I'm talking lying. A visit to Indiana where a pallid guy goes for three days and comes home looking as washed out as ever. Except for his hands! They're dark tan. I checked and the weather in Indiana then was mostly in the fifties and cloudy. And before you ask, the answer is no: I can't give you a guarantee that his hands weren't tan from the summer before. But they would have called attention to themselves back then and I'm pretty positive I'd have noticed. And by the way, it wasn't as if he came back to New York and got a semisunburn. The overcast weather must have moved east because it was in the low sixties here and cloudy."

I paused, ruminating. "I keep trying to think of a situation where people's hands are exposed but their faces are hidden. If it was only one hand, maybe he was driving with his window open and his arm hanging out. But it's both hands, and that's just bizarre."

I thought he might get dismissive, which with my dad could mean anything from smacking his forehead to a brusque: *You're talking through your hat.* "Okay," he said. "Let's go with your instincts on this. You're saying on that particular weekend he wasn't in South Bend showing off a package or going to that other city, Fort Wayne, to see his family?"

"Well, I think I'm saying more than that." I leaned forward, resting the heels of my hands right above my knees. "Yes, it could have been Phoenix and not Fort Wayne for those particular three days. But what about all these other places he's gone to?"

"You're saying he makes them up? Says Detroit, except it's not Detroit. It's Salt Lake City?"

"No, I'm just saying that some of them are open to question. I did check on a project he did, designing new packaging for a company called Cupcake in a Tube."

"Why the hell would you put a cupcake in a tube?"

"A woman in Pittsburgh named Chrissy got inspired. I'd remembered him bringing in the product to show it to us. At every lunch, one of us talks about what we've been working on, so the others can get a broader vision of the wonderful world of home-office entrepreneurship. Anyway, I called this Chrissy and pretended I was checking Pete's credentials. She vouched for him in terms of the quality of his work, which she really liked. Basically indicated that he wasn't a lovable soul, but she didn't care because he was good at what he did and also very businesslike. And yes, I checked her out. She exists, her cupcake company exists, and many, many people want to push up the bottom of a tube to eat a cupcake."

" 'No one ever went broke underestimating the intelligence of the American public.' You know who said that? H. L. Mencken, that fucking anti-Semite. He should only drop dead."

"He is dead," I said.

"I know." My dad seemed gratified. "So you're saying Mrs. Cupcake is alive and living in Pittsburgh."

"Right. And you can look at the spreadsheet and see lots of cities, though not the company he visited and not the product."

My dad scrolled to the right to look at the column of cities Pete went to. "So first thing, you've got to remember the packages he designed, see if you can correlate them with any of these places."

"That's a good place to begin. The problem is more than half the time I'm there, I tune out. And I'm thinking it might not be good to start asking this or that member about what kind of packaging Pete brought in to show us. I've already chatted about him with two, no, three of the group, and if I ask any more pointed questions, it will scream out for attention."

The ploy I used to get Iris's spreadsheet was

not brilliant in its subtlety. Phoebe had something on her mind, and all I had to do was go on about Mets tickets/Pete's weird behavior and she spilled the episode of the keys, and I got John Grillo to do his version of character analysis in the hardware store. In his case, I'd had to keep talking to him about other stuff to cut any Corie-Pete link that might have formed in his mind.

"You're thinking one might say something to the other and out of the clear blue sky they'll wonder why this woman who's married to a rich, good-looking judge is so curious about a midwesterner with tan hands?" He stopped for a second, then shook his head. "Stop with the sour puss. Since when is 'rich' a dirty word? Everybody knows Josh made big bucks practicing law, plus his family is loaded. And then the wife left him a bundle."

"He did some legal thing, bypassing Dawn's inheritance. It all goes to Eliza."

"It's a rich guy that can afford to turn his nose up at a giant inheritance. Anyway, I agree. You can't go around acting like you've got Pete on the brain."

"Right. If the opportunity came along, someone talking about Pete, I could theoretically push it a little, but not too far."

We passed into silence. Maybe it was something in our genome, a dot on a strand of DNA that caused soundless cogitation while we were gazing up toward ceiling or sky. I had no doubt that he was worried that I was unbalanced over the Pete business, but he also seemed to be getting more engaged by my questions. I was also relieved that he wasn't making any moves to go to the bathroom—where he could narcotize himself by sneaking in earbuds to stream five minutes of some ancient episode of *NYPD Blue.*

Being with my dad was a plus for me. I could collaborate, at least a little. He'd been in the business; he knew not only what was relevant but also that some leads were worth following simply because they were intriguing.

Sure, I did have Josh. But though he was my partner in life, in no way did I want him as a partner in this. I needed a snoop more than a logician. An airtight case was one thing, but I was also after the living, breathing truth. And the truth could be that Pete might be guilty as hell of . . . something or even several somethings. On the other hand, I might turn out to be crazy as a shithouse rat, and maybe Josh didn't need to know that.

"Okay," my dad said. "Can you print out a map of each of the cities he says he went to?"

I found myself smiling. "You want to see if there were any major crimes or incidents committed on the days he claims he was there?"

"What are you doing? Trying to give me positive feedback by looking all thrilled by the most elementary investigation maneuver?"

"No, it's just what I was thinking to do, so I was smiling at us being on the same page. And stop looking at me and interpreting everything I do or say into my trying to make you feel better. I need your expertise. Trust me, if you were a chemist or worked at a Starbucks, I wouldn't be asking you for help." I got up and we switched seats so I was at the monitor. "What do you think? A fifty-mile radius?"

"You know what my motto used to be? 'Whatever it is, double it.' Radiuses, I'm talking about. Okay, you risk spreading yourself too thin. But if you do make it a hundred and work your way out from the center and it turns out to be fifty-one miles away, you'll give yourself a great big kiss." He lifted his chin and chirped a big, fat kiss into the air.

"Fine. How do you want to do this? You take half the cities and I take the other half?"

"Hmm," he said, corkscrewing the side of his mouth.

"Translation?"

"It means print out what you have on him and I'll look it over tonight. But then tomorrow we should work together. That way, one of us can ask questions or tell the other one: 'Hey, you got your head up your ass.'"

"An offer I can't refuse," I told him.

"The offer I can't refuse is downstairs. Can you smell your husband's brisket, you should pardon the expression?"

# 13

I called my dad at nine the next morning to check if he was on his way. His first words were: "Why do I have to drive to Long Island?"

"Because we'll be working together and it's better if you're here." My response came out like a monotone, but it was propelled by a long exhalation of impatience. "Even if I send you the spreadsheet as an attachment, it may have different pagination on your computer." I was making this up as I went along. "Why should we have to go through: 'Go to the middle of the page, third column from the right, just below where it says Tulsa'?"

"Bullshit," he said. "You're just worried that if you can't see me, I'll be muting *Bosch* and watching it with subtitles."

He could have more intuition than I gave him credit for. "Actually, I was thinking a six-pack of Bud during a two-hour conference call wouldn't encourage cognitive clarity."

My dad arrived an hour later, with the spiraled top of a cop's small notebook sticking up from his pocket. He was hugging a plastic barrel of pretzels, in a size suitable for a Super Bowl party. The printout of Iris's spreadsheet on Pete

Delaney was in a folder tucked under his arm. When he climbed the stairs to my office, his head and neck seemed a bit more aligned with his spine than they had been lately. He gripped the banister not so much to pull himself up as to steady himself so his dearly beloved snack food wouldn't tumble to the floor. He even moved at a slightly faster clip than his usual trudge.

I motioned him to my recliner while I took the desk chair. My dad pushed himself three-quarters of the way back. I wheeled my chair over the wood floor so I could share the footrest. The first time Josh took me through the house he had pointed to the floor and told me that it was maple and that Dawn had it installed by a company that specialized in gym floors: "She researched it. Maple is the ideal wood for athletics because it can take a beating." I wondered how a 110-pound woman doing side lunges could be considered a beating, though I just said oh.

My dad opened the spreadsheet folder and held up a finger—*Give me a minute*—while he looked over the printout I'd given him the day before. I saw a lot of yellow highlighting and bright blue underlining and slanting red lines going between items in different columns— handwritten, not computer generated. I wheeled my desk chair over to my monitor.

Earlier that morning, before my dad arrived, I had been able to associate a trip Pete took to

Boston on March 19 with an unsolved robbery that went down on the following day. An armored truck was in front of the bank in Manchester, New Hampshire, a city about an hour from Boston; the bank was trading old fifty- and hundred-dollar bills for new ones. The guard from the truck passed through the ATM lobby. There were a few people getting cash or depositing checks, including the local cop—or at least a guy dressed like one.

After the new bills were safely in the bank, the guard lugged out the old bills. As he passed the ATMs, the "cop" drew his service weapon and, with the butt of it, hit the guard on the head. It happened so fast that a couple of customers who didn't see the cop hit the guard in the head ran over to him thinking he'd had a heart attack or stroke, not a concussion.

As the fake cop exited the bank, a Toyota Camry pulled up and he hopped in. The getaway driver floored it, and they and $350,000 in dirty money—with nonsequential serial numbers—were gone for good.

My dad glanced up and I asked, "Do you think we should consider crimes committed by more than one person? I found a bank robbery in Manchester." I gave him the details. "The Justice Department has that region as a high-intensity drug-trafficking area. Heroin, opioids."

He shrugged. "Three hundred and fifty thou

could buy a shitload of opioids. Or even be seed money for a new drug distribution network. But I don't know, Corie, we're flying blind here. Where did you find this?"

"Just tooling around the internet this morning before you got here."

He seemed pleased by that. The right side of his mouth rose up into a quarter smile, the way it did when I was in high school and brought home an A in physics or took down a two-hundred-pound guy in a krav maga demo. "Okay, let me think," he said. "Bank robbery would be federal. Can you call somebody at the FBI up there, get the details?"

I wasn't so sure about that. They'd probably check me out. Impersonating a federal agent could get me three years. And I was no longer a special agent, just a contractor. Not that I couldn't find a way, but it was a high-risk prop- osition. Three years in the slammer was not doable in terms of the biological clock. And it probably wouldn't look great for Josh to have to answer questions about his felon wife during the Senate confirmation hearings for the court of appeals.

"So?" he asked.

I admit I smiled to myself imagining the Honorable Joshua Geller applying for conjugal privileges in a federal correctional institution. Still, having roped my dad into this mission,

I could hardly say no to his first request: my making a call.

But then he himself said, "Nah!"

" 'Nah' what?"

"Nah, unless he hooks up with the same confederate for every job, assuming there's more than one, doesn't it feel like he'd be a one-man show? Because listen, kiddo, if he's such a neat freak or control freak and living a life on Long Island that's protective coloration, he's not likely to trust a partner."

"I agree." I felt stiff. I stood and linked my fingers together and bent forward till they grazed the floor. Then I did a pull-head-down-to-shoulder stretch for a minute. "He's not going to trust a confederate. He is such a perfectionist. Unless he has someone who's not just submissive but close-mouthed. No. He just wouldn't."

"Okay," my dad said. "There's all that plus we have limited resources. We can't go chasing after every felony committed in the areas he's been to. Or not been to, since we don't know if he actually wound up at the places he said he was visiting."

"Another thing," I said. "You know how I told you that an average trip for him takes three days?"

"Yeah."

"Okay, say Pete goes to a client for one day, shows the packaging, lets the client and the staff, if there is a staff, play with the mock-ups, ask questions, make suggestions. That's one day. Possibly a follow-up the next morning for an hour or two. After that, there's nothing more to do because he's all business. So at the very least, he's got thirty-six hours more."

Shockingly, my dad stopped cradling his pretzels and lowered the container to the floor beside the recliner. He clasped his hands behind his head and stared at the ceiling. When I was a kid, I'd always felt as I watched him waiting for an idea, it would not simply pop into his head but actually materialize in some dramatic fashion. Lightning would singe his hair as it zigzagged into his head delivering a theory; a carrier pigeon would hurtle down from the light fixture and land on his lap so he could grab a message from its teeny claw.

But as always, no visible drama. His raised feet simply rotated back and forth, like antennae searching for signal, and after a couple of minutes of being otherwise motionless, he blinked and announced, "You're saying his way with a client is strictly business. No 'Let's have dinner and schmooze.' No golf. No 'I hope you've got time to show me the sights of Toledo.' "

"Wouldn't happen. From everything I've seen or heard, he's not discourteous. But not warm, either."

"So he uses a trip to an actual client as a cover for something else?"

"That's what I'm thinking," I said.

He engaged in a few seconds of chin rubbing before he spoke: "Your Pete would say he was going to Minneapolis. He'd stay for a day, day and a half, do his business, and then he's off to, whatever, some city: Louisville. Okay, say he goes to Louisville." He glanced up at the ceiling for help. "Maybe he drives, maybe he flies: doesn't matter. He'd use fake ID. Even if it turns out that all your unemotional lunch guy is doing is picking some random city, like Louisville, to connect with some hottie, he's not gonna leave a trail with scans of his driver's license and credit card."

"He always pays cash for lunch."

"But you know and I know," my dad said, "that paying for a plane ticket or a car rental with cash just rings those bells. The protocol is the same whether it's a get-together for a day of God knows what in a motel or a bank robbery. The idea with both is not to be traceable to the PI your wife hired, or to the Feds. So obviously you don't use your own credit card. And these days, cash is suspect."

"Well, I don't know how sophisticated he is, what kind of fraudulent ID he could get. And with counterfeit credit cards? It's getting harder, what with the embedded chips, and algorithms for spending patterns."

"There's always the just-stolen card, which

does mean big risk," my dad said. "Except big risks aren't going to stop some people, especially if a guy is going for a major crime. Stealing a card just so he can get to wherever he's gotta go? That's not major: there are pros who do it. In for a penny, in for a pound."

To concentrate, I pressed those points at the top of my nose, right beside my eye sockets. "Okay," I said. "Our assumption should be that what he's doing is something criminal. Not cheating on his wife. If he wanted to spend the day in a motel with a dominatrix, he could have his pick on Long Island, pay cash, and get home without having to eat airport food."

"All right. I'll go along with you on that for the time being, except Auntie Anne's pretzels are good. Okay, so he's going to some city and he tells your lunch group about it. It's probably legit, in that he either has a real client there or a fictitious client he's created a story for. He's not going to commit a crime in that city just on the odd chance there could be some kind of publicity. He doesn't want to say he's going to Cleveland and then have someone from your lunch group or his church soup kitchen listening to CNN on a slow news day and hear about a kidnapping in Cleveland, the day he was there. Not that it's likely any of you would think that, but a guy like Pete wouldn't give anything away."

We agreed that instead of me calling the FBI

about the bank robbery in Manchester, my dad would track down the local police detective who'd first been assigned to the case and see if he could get any usable information. We were both a little dubious about it because with our single-player theory, someone like Pete would work alone. In Manchester, there'd been a getaway driver. Possibly he'd hire local talent, then kill the guy once he was a safe distance from the bank.

After he left, I spent a couple of hours on the internet and phone just to continue to correlate intriguing felonies—ones worth traveling to commit—with the dates Pete was away. I'd stuck with offenses that appeared to be committed by just one person.

I applied my dad's standard of a one-hundred-mile radius around a city. Pete had been in Buffalo for three days in late May the previous year. Looking at a map, I saw that part of the circle included Canada. The day after his arrival in Buffalo, there had been a major fire in Toronto—ninety-nine miles from Buffalo—where a carpet warehouse, Mister Rugg, burned almost to the ground. Clearly, arson.

The bottoms of my feet began to tingle, my sign of excitement, as I read the fire inspector's report. One person could pull this off: it was effective arson, though definitely not sophisticated. Fires tend to move upward, and with arson, the worst burn marks would likely be on the floor of the warehouse, not the ceiling. A local TV report I found on YouTube said that gas chromatography from the crime scene showed gasoline had been poured on the floor. *Excellent!* I said to myself as the tingle nearly reached my ankles. Gasoline was easy to buy. There was the added plus of not having to worry about taking black powder or ANFO explosives across the border into Canada.

Still, I knew how I often got swept up by the first juicy prospect. Actually, not so juicy, since it had been an inelegant job. Why call in an out-of-town arsonist to pour some ExxonMobil on a cement floor? I only spent one more minute on the internet to discover that sure enough, two and a half months after the fire, the owner had been arrested.

That night, my mom called and said, "A leben ahf dein kepele, dahling!" She sounded as if Queen Elizabeth had just learned Yiddish. The words were an affectionate blessing, *a long life on your head.* "Your father was on the phone all afternoon, taking notes, using that mahvelous NYPD voice he uses with out-of-towners. So sonorous! You didn't just give him something to do. You got him out of the house."

"I just hope this turns out to be something. I mean, that I'm not pulling him into what turns out to be my own delusion."

"Don't think like that!" Mothers. With Eliza, I tried not to edit her thoughts unless I thought she was headed off the rails. Clearly, this was a reaction to my mom's perpetual boosterism with me: *Be positive, Corie. Learn to love yourself. When you get into negativity, tell yourself: Stop!*

"Trust your gut!" she added.

"Okay, I will." I didn't give her a chance to clear her throat and ask: *Did I just hear a smidgen of sarcasm?* Instead, I said: "I'll text him in a few minutes and ask him to drive over tomorrow, tell him I work so much better with a partner. Oh, and let him know I bought his pretzels so he doesn't have to bring his own."

She said, "Splendid!" And for the rest of the conversation we discussed cucumber gazpacho and her friend Lily's failure to get a callback for a Centrum Silver commercial.

The next morning fluctuated between drizzle and downpour. From my office, my dad and I could hear the soothing racket of rain on the copper roof of the portico just outside my window. We exchanged printouts, our timelines of felonies committed on the days Pete was out of town. As we read through them, we asked each other for more information every minute or so. Since my dad had the recliner, I gave him a coffee table book to lean on. (I didn't have a coffee table, so I kept the book *Design and Texture: The Magnificent Art of Moroccan Furniture* on the floor. Wynne had given it to me, yet another unspoken nudge to either redecorate my office or move.)

My dad and I combined our two lists, then created a master list from that. It didn't have a title, though it could have been "Felonies That Could Have Been Committed by Pete Delaney." We agreed that for the moment we should assume Pete wasn't the batty sort of criminal, like the one we came across who repeatedly sneaked into stables and cut off horses' tails (Denver area) or another who specialized in knocking over portable toilets at construction sites (Buffalo).

Instead, we created groups of felony crimes that could be committed in just a few days: burglary, robbery, homicide, kidnapping, sexual assault. After fifteen minutes in the kitchen for elevenses—in our case, coffee, pretzels, and staring out the windows as the hard rain blew sideways—we returned to my office. We worked up a blended list of all crimes ranked (somewhat idiosyncratically, I had to admit) according to my dad's instinct. I figured it this way: not only did he have seniority, but he was the realer deal in the detection biz.

My specialty was people—figuring out what they needed emotionally, financially, and culturally. How could I—as a special agent—fulfill those needs in order to get the subject to cooperate with an investigation? I knew some veterans in the bureau referred to it as "girl stuff," but one of my bosses in DC had called me a master manipulator. Obviously I preferred the latter description not only because it was less sexist but also because it was more accurate. Whether being interrogated or conned, the subject should never feel played. Nor should he or she believe the interrogator is clever. That's not easy. A lot of investigators can't resist their egos. They have to demonstrate: *I'm so fucking clever.* That can work on the stupid, the weak, and the fearful. But the savvy and the strong get taken in when they're comfortable enough to believe they have the upper hand.

My dad and I talked back and forth all morning. He made a few phone calls, tapping old pals to get info while I searched media accounts of incidents where someone like Pete could be the perp. None of the homicides we checked out on the days he was out of town pointed to a serial killer. But just to be sure, I tracked down the names of some midlevel shrinks and scientists at the National Center for the Analysis of Violent Crime.

I reached a psychologist and told her I was retired from the bureau but wanted to do an article debunking internet reports of ISIS-inspired homicides of individuals—a project that had zero basis in reality. We chatted for a couple of minutes, and I assumed she probed enough to believe that I was authentic because when I gave her three possible time periods, she looked them up while I held on.

Nothing, she reported, though sometimes reports come in months or years later, when a victim's body is discovered. She'd promised to make a document with the dates and, if anything popped up, she'd get back to me. "Good luck with your article," she said. "Gosh, it sounds interesting!"

For lunch, I made my dad's favorite—panini with mozzarella, tomato, and basil. Then he went for a "ten-minute nap" on the couch under the portico, with the rain on the roof as a lullaby. He looked so comfortable there, covered by a light throw blanket, that I figured he was good for at least an hour. As I headed back to my office, I was tempted to go into my bedroom for a nap of my own. But the prospect of an hour alone on the computer with Lulu sharing my chair snapped me out of that.

I'd never learned to work efficiently as long as I had an internet connection. If a paragraph or even a phrase in a manuscript I was considering rang the déjà vu gong, I suspected plagiarism, so I'd search around for a bit. Maybe I'd find something, maybe not, but then I'd meander, unaware I was meandering. When I came back to reality, I'd discover I was watching a Lauryn Hill video or ordering a lilac-scented candle. Once I found myself studying a topographic map of Wyoming with no clue how I got there.

But by myself that early afternoon, I was incredibly focused, as if I were working on some time-sensitive investigation—which, with available minutes ticking away, I guess I was. So along with the bank in New Hampshire, I discovered that on that same day there was a nearly $2 million heist from a jewelry store in Wilmington, Delaware. (One of the items snatched from its vault was a diamond-and-emerald tiara that had belonged to a Romanov. That city had never struck me as a center of grand style, though maybe some dumb-ass Du Pont had wanted to wow the locals.) Wilmington was far beyond the hundred-mile investigatory radius from Boston, where Pete Delaney was supposedly meeting with a client. Still, it was reachable by plane, train, car, and bus in less than half a day.

I discovered my favorite gnawable knuckle, the ring finger of the right hand, was ensconced in my mouth. Ergo, something was bothering me. It didn't take me long to realize that if Wilmington was a possibility, at a five-and-a-half-hour drive from Boston, so was almost any other city in the country. Well, the far West was unlikely because, in addition to actual hours in the air, there would have to be the added trips to airports and flight delays. Still, widening the field gave me all sorts of possibilities. To keep things manageable,

I kept with March twentieth, the day after Pete arrived in Boston. See what felonies went down that day across the country.

There was a homicide on Galveston Island in Texas, a resort community on the Gulf. A rich guy from Houston had bought an expensive second home on the water and spent his long weekends and vacations blasting music, days and nights. (One report mentioned neighbors were aghast at songs like "Smack My Bitch Up.") Cops, court dates, and fines, along with lawsuits by the local community association, ensued for more than a year, but to no avail.

Late on that day in March, when the Houston guy was leaning on the railing of his porch looking out on the canal that led to the Gulf, he was shot twice with a hunting rifle. The autopsy results showed the angle of the bullet was somewhere near 60 degrees, so it came not from his across-the-canal neighbor driven mad by "Smack My Bitch Up" but from a person on the water. Both bullets hit, and that ended the guy's Spotify Premium subscription for eternity.

There was a kidnapping in Birmingham, Alabama. The owner of a building supply company was kidnapped on the twentieth and found the following day in a neighbor's driveway, still drugged, his hands and feet bound with duct tape. His eyes and mouth were covered with duct tape also, and he didn't remember hearing any voices, so he could not be sure whether he'd been taken by one person or more than one. No ransom was demanded, and no one realized he'd been snatched until after he'd been discovered. He lived alone, having just been divorced from his third wife, and he was known to come into work late; no police had been called about his disappearance until he was found, not even at two in the afternoon.

Since the victim vanished and reappeared without anyone but the perpetrator knowing, the FBI hadn't been called in. The Birmingham PD had handled it, and the kidnap victim was suing the police: In addition to his eyes and mouth being covered, he had a thick paper shopping bag over his head that was tied around his neck with more duct tape. The perp had thoughtfully cut a few airholes in it. The cops who found him as well as the EMS people who came to the scene did cut the binding on his wrists and ankles. However, they were unwilling to take off the bag and the tape around his neck until forensics got there. Unfortunately, their van had a transmission glitch, so that took over an hour, during which the victim became so hysterical he had to be restrained.

I could have stayed online for hours searching for felonies, checking my hunches, reading whatever police reports I could access using the code number for my most recent contract case.

There was a magic immediacy (and sporadic incomprehensibility) in reports written by crime fighter types who think prose is a foreign language.

I hadn't been so engaged since I left the bureau. I'd given up trying to deny that my new life was as exhilarating as my old one—only quietly exhilarating. Instead, I explained to myself that I'd traded the thrill of being part of a team doing something important for a realer life filled with family. I'd quit because I wanted to be committed. To a star-quality husband, to a wonderful child. To—maybe—future children. Understood, commitment was a wee bit boring. Commitment meant a life where I couldn't just say: *Ta-ta! Tired of New York. I'm off to Djibouti for a couple of years.* Sometimes, on bad nights, my new life seemed the end of possibility.

Glancing at the bottom of my monitor, I realized my dad had been napping for nearly an hour and a half. He'd been on hold for so long that being back on the chase once again had knocked him out.

I called the Birmingham PD and got the number two guy on the kidnapping case, Sergeant Wiley Wilson; he talked so slowly it gave my mind time to meander. (I wondered if other than Woodrow Wilson and Walter White in *Breaking Bad*, I could come up with any alliterative W names. Walt Whitman. Wendy Wasserstein.) Anyway,

Sergeant WW didn't question my intro, that I was a former special agent who was now a contractor for the FBI, which admittedly did have the benefit of being true. The victim, LeMayne Atkinson, had been found in a neighbor's driveway in his own gated community. Sergeant Wilson and I agreed it was a good thing the neighbor's car had a rearview camera and a bad thing that Atkinson was suing the department. Having established camaraderie, the sergeant said it looked like a one-man job to him "as long as the perpetrator had some strength, because LeMayne had a gut like the old Phillips 76 ball. You know, like from the gas stations."

"Right."

"But he had enough Rohypnol in him to knock out an elephant. That's a big date rape drug."

"Right."

"He was awake but was still having tremors when they found him. Bad stuff."

"What about the shopping bag over his head?" I asked. "If his eyes and mouth were duct-taped, why would anyone use a bag, and a paper one?"

"I've been asking myself that," Sergeant Wilson said. I waited. "Weird is what it was."

"Right. Was there any marking on the bag, any design or print?"

"No. Just a plain old bag."

"Brown paper?"

"White. Just plain though."

"Was it a strong kind of paper? Like if you had a load of heavy groceries, or a couple of twenty-pound barbells, would it hold up?"

"Sure. I mean, unless you were holding it up off the ground and you dropped a barbell from ten feet up. Then? I don't know."

"Have you ever seen anything like that before?" I asked.

"No, ma'am. Never."

"Could it have been some kind of imitation Ku Klux Klan hood? Was the victim African American or some other minority or, on the other hand, someone who might be involved with the Klan or a militia, where a white hood could be a kind of payback?"

"No, Atkinson was white. Owns three building supply places and more the golf club type than thinking about hate crimes, far as we can tell."

So the shopping bag made no sense to me. Well, other than Pete might have a stack of plain white bags to use for prototypes. Still, for someone so dedicated to maintaining a facade—if that indeed was the case—it seemed unlikely he would add such unattractive packaging to his MO.

When my dad came back upstairs, I was filled with so much information that when I tried to report it, he kept saying, "Slow down, kiddo."

"This is the problem: I have too much to choose from. Listen, you know I'm more an interrogator than an investigator. Give me a tutorial. Where do I go from here?"

"Stop with the tutorial business. You know what to do."

I was about to say, *No, I have no idea where to go from here,* when "Narrow it down" popped out of my mouth. Before he could say anything, I responded by pointing out the flaw of that method. "How the hell do I narrow it down? Go back to a one-hundred-mile radius? Set a floor for profit, like if some crime—robbery, drugs, whatever—doesn't bring in at least a hundred thou, forget it? Since he's so much of a loner, don't go near anything that smacks of an accomplice?"

"Look, anytime you narrow you run a risk of missing what's just beyond whatever perimeter you set. That's the minus. The plus is, you can focus. You can talk to a small number of people and you, because you are a good interrogator, can get more out than witnesses and law enforcement think they know." I nodded. "But listen, Corie, you need something to jog their memory." He turned and started walking out of the room. "Be back in a sec. I saw you got that expensive vanilla ice cream in the freezer, like what you put out with the brownies Eliza made. How old is it?"

"Dad!"

"I hate when it gets those icy dots all over the top. But a good vanilla ice cream? God's gift to the world."

"Fine. Listen, Dad, you said to jog their memory. Are you talking about a photo of him?"

"Yeah, of course. I could probably get someone I know who has an in with motor vehicles. A retired guy, like me. But the pictures on licenses are lousy. When you blow them up, it looks like eyes and a mouth wearing a wig. Unless your guy's bald. So you need to get a decent picture without calling out, 'Hey Pete, say cheese.'"

"I know. There's a teeny picture in a magazine from years ago, but it's too low resolution to print. Hey, that vanilla ice cream? I got it last week. It's not even open. Consider it all yours."

# 14

It was Darby Penn's turn for show-and-tell. He carried in his new laptop, so huge and seemingly so light that there were several *ooh*s of envy, and Iris said, "Thou shalt not covet thy neighbor's computer." We'd slid our chairs so all of us could view the screen to watch his slide show: his retouching of the photo that dominated a Tommy Hilfiger underwear ad. My chair was almost behind Marcalynn, mostly because she was seated beside Pete.

I watched Pete watching the screen. Whenever there was a visual demonstration of any kind, his head jutted forward and back, over and over, the way a pigeon's does. Odd, since Pete wasn't a bird compensating for having eyes on separate sides of his head. As he momentarily shifted forward, I managed to peer down a gap in the back of his shirt. Any tats near the nape of his neck that could be leads, like a Celtic tree of life or a navy anchor? None I could spot, though the restaurant's light was dim and my pupils were still recovering from Darby's brilliant laptop screen. So I studied the shine on Marcalynn's blonde hair and made a mental note to ask her after lunch whether it was product or natural sheen.

As we paid the check, Marcalynn thanked me for thinking it was natural and said it was something by Redken but couldn't remember the name. She'd take a picture of the bottle when she got home and text it to me. Iris and John had already gotten up and were beside Darby, telling him how terrific his show-and-tell was. Just as I was about to add my praise, Pete, still seated, called out to Iris: "I'm driving down to Philadelphia. I'll leave there Wednesday after rush hour, so most likely I'll be back for the lunch. If not, I'll email you. Okay?"

"Fine," Iris said.

John Grillo turned to Pete. "*The* most boring drive. Wouldn't the company you're working for pay for a train?"

"No. It's a startup. Money's tight."

"What do they do?" John asked.

"It's called WAW! It stands for What a Waist! The thing they make is supposed to make men look like they don't have a gut." Pete appeared somewhere between neutral and weary when it came to WAW, but with the two other men in the group wildly attentive, he got as animated as I'd ever seen him, which was somewhere between lackluster and bland. "It's Lycra and nylon lined with cotton, goes from under the pecs down to midhip. Essentially they tiptoed around patent infringement and copied that Spanx thing."

I noted that Pete was doing what I'd learned

at the bureau. Not with Spanx—with creating a legend. A legend wasn't just DOB and job, family. It was all the details about what you're doing that become part of someone's daily routine. If you're living a life not quite your own, you need a narrative and to offer some specifics—just not too many, because that arouses suspicion: *Why is this person going on and on?*

Pete continued: "I don't mind driving. I listen to audiobooks. On plane rides, too. I'll probably leave Sunday night. We're having a barbecue for Jenny's dad's birthday late that afternoon." The barbecue was a nice touch, I thought. So visual, so homey.

"What kind of audiobooks?" I asked, which I figured was safe since he knew I worked for literary agencies.

"Usually sports bios. Once in a while something about history. The first time I bought one, I made the mistake of picking a book about John Adams. It took me almost a year because it was unabridged."

Like all skilled dissemblers, including me, when faced with a never-before-asked question, Pete went with the truth—unless it would be a giveaway. For me, it was second nature not to mention the decade-plus at the bureau and just answer: *I wasn't up for graduate school. Someone at the placement office had a job listing that said, "Must be familiar with contemporary*

*Arabic fiction."* Okay, lite lie: The placement office was not Queens College's. It was HR at the FBI, which had contacts for when it wanted to place agents or former agents in a credible job.

I quashed a flare-up of the fear that Pete really was just a freelance designer driving down to Philly, listening to an audiobook on LeBron James. Good thinking that was underscored by a call early on Sunday.

Very early, at 5:38 a.m. My phone gave its nighttime ring: two notes from some slice of silicon that yearned to be a flute. Josh had trained himself to ignore the sound, which was easy because (a) it wasn't loud, (b) he had a will of steel, and (c) it rarely rang. The bureau had called precisely twice in the middle of the night since I'd resigned. This call was from my dad.

He'd just left Pete Delaney's house. Or, to be more precise, Pete's garage. "Fucking thing's alarmed," he said.

"The car?" Then I got clearheaded enough to ask: "You went to Pete's house?"

"No, the garage. The house, too, without a doubt, but I didn't get near it. Listen, it's an old house, right? Built in the nineteen twenties or thirties." This wasn't going to be a one-minute chat. I got out of bed and slipped into the bathroom. "A one-car garage," my dad went on, "because who had two cars back then?" I remembered what it looked like, white, squarish, and unobtrusive, its roof pitched at the same angle as the house's. "But it's alarmed up the wazoo like he had a million bucks' worth of power tools in there. I borrowed infrared binoculars from Joe Calabro. Remember him? After he retired, he set himself up as a PI. Nice little operation he has now. You once said he looked like what's his name in the CIA."

"Leon Panetta," I said. My dad was obviously driving back to Queens from Pete's home. Once he got a hands-free phone holder, he'd discovered calling me or my mom was way better than CBS on AM, though we didn't give traffic updates. I sat on the edge of the bathtub and put the waterproof pillow between my neck and the wall. "Right, so Joe lent you his infrareds."

"Yeah. What got me was how subtle Pete's wiring was, like hardly thicker than a couple of hairs. Okay, a little thicker. But I would never have seen it in a million years without the binocs, and it was *above* the windows, not underneath. The windows of a *garage*. Wires ran the same length as the window casing, then they disappeared. Threaded into a hole made with the thinnest drill bit."

"But you saw it from . . . where? Your car? How was that higher than the top thing above the windows? You didn't go onto the property, did you?"

"Of course I went onto the property. Couldn't

have seen it from ground level. They had an old tree. Went up the first branch and—before you have a shit fit—okay, the second branch, too, but it was steady. Sturdy. Whatever. Perfectly safe." I suppressed a vision of my dad's lifeless body sprawled on Pete's exquisitely tended lawn, revealed as night turned into dawn. While I was at it, I also suppressed the sound of my mom's shriek on hearing the news. "I just got that feeling of wrongness about him," my dad continued. "Contagious from you. But it was a weird setup. I mean, he doesn't have a two-hundred-thousand-dollar Lamborghini in there. But because the alarm wiring was so—what's the word?—meticulous, I figured there might be motion sensors, too. Better I didn't go up to it, touch it. His system may not be totally up-to-date, because it wasn't wireless or Bluetooth or whatever they call it. I looked on my phone, under the Settings thing. Nothing showed up."

"But it was good enough to do the job if someone tried to get in."

"Oh yeah. More than good enough."

"Does his wife have a car?" I asked. "The times I've passed I haven't seen any other vehicles in the driveway."

"A Buick," he said. "Pretty new, not top-of-the-line. A Verano. Probably gray or light blue. It was parked in a little bump-out of the driveway, toward the garage." I remembered seeing that area. "Anyway, I tried to make out exactly what he's got inside the garage, but there wasn't enough light. All I could see was that whatever extra space he had, he used for storage. Storing what, you're going to ask. Can't tell you, because he had cabinets, some like school lockers and the others regular. There were drawers and a counter for workspace. And get this. His car. The top of the steering wheel of the goddamn fancy Jeep? It covers the mileage readout on the bottom of the odometer. Too many cars like that these days."

I really wanted to spit out, *Oh fuck it!* but held back because he was my dad and also because I didn't want to make him feel as if he'd failed me, so I said, "Bad luck, especially after you climbed a tree."

He sounded weirdly cheerful. "All is not lost," he announced.

I stood because my pajama bottoms were thin and my butt was starting to numb out from the tub's cold porcelain. "What do you mean?"

"Joe gave me some gizmo that reads mileage. Does it by calculation, the rotations of the wheel. He told me to stick it under the front fender on the passenger side. For some reason, even if a suspect is the paranoid type, they don't check as closely around that particular wheel. I was kind of hoping Joe would lend me one of those geolocation devices, like you see on TV shows, where they can follow a car and get a readout of

264

where it is. He has one, says it doesn't work all that great, but he's using it on a case."

"But the garage was alarmed," I said. "How did you get in there to put—"

"I didn't get in. Do you think I'm nuts? I got there at two thirty. Did the tree-binoculars business. Then staked him out from around the corner with my car windows open, so I could hear any ambient noise. Probably dozed off a couple of times. But I sure as hell heard a garage door open. At five on the nose. And what do you know, it was him, going past the street I was on. It wasn't quite sunrise, but the sky was lightening a little. No cars on the road yet. I followed him from a good distance with my lights off, until we got close to Shorehaven Avenue. Then I turned on my lights and kept going. Only for about fifteen minutes, even though I had a full tank. I could have tailed him to Philly if necessary. But he pulled in at that diner on Northern Boulevard, just over the border in Queens.

"So the second he's inside, I parked, got out of the car, and headed toward the diner in case he looked out, which he didn't because he's at the counter, checking a menu. Probably ordering something to go. So I get Joe's gizmo out of my pocket. It's not much bigger than a half dollar, and I go around the passenger side of his Jeep, quick as a bunny, and stick it where Joe said to, high up under the fender. Before Petey boy looks

265

up, I'd already scooted around the Jeep to the driver side, to see if I could read the odometer. No luck. In two seconds, I'm three cars away from his. When he does look out to check his Jeep, I'm on my way into the diner, at least twenty feet from his car. It was a cop's dream: when I walk in, he's looking at his car. I got a table toward the back, ordered one of those giant fried dough things with powdered sugar your mother would kill me for eating so I better dust myself off. Anyhow, a minute later they were handing him a paper bag at the cashier."

"You are terrific!" I told him, probably a little too loud because I heard a sleepy gripe of protest from Josh but then silence. I lowered my voice, but my dad said he couldn't hear what the hell I was saying, so I spoke a little louder. "This is so great!"

"It may be great, but only if you can signal me next Wednesday at your lunch when he stops looking at the street. Even if it's just for a few seconds. I've got to retrieve that damn thing, get it back to Joe."

That next Wednesday, as I was crossing the street from the parking lot to the lunch meeting, my heart fluttered a great deal, then settled into an ominous kettledrum beat. Could Pete's guard over his car get cut off for the necessary minute so my dad could take back the mileage detector?

I took a seat almost across from him, between John and Lucy Winters, the data miner. I was waiting for the usual slackening in Pete's attentiveness, which came when the waiter went through the specials. While the written menu at La Cuisine Délicieuse never had anything new, Pete did focus on the day's specials. They were mostly some variation on a chicken theme: fricassée de poulet à l'ancienne or coq au vin. They weren't all that special, though the chef was given to occasional mutinous moments when stuffed squid would be announced. Half our group would wince and Iris might murmur: "Poor Squidward." Pete was in the daring half. The only time he ever called attention to himself was the time he said he'd try the tripe. Many were aghast.

So as Pete glanced from his menu to the waiter, who was describing the cold soup of the day, I asked John to order me a hamburger, medium, and took the long route to the ladies' room. I was wearing one of those ruffle-necked muscle minis made out of lightweight sweatshirt fabric, not to show off my triceps (at least not that day) but because it was the only article of clothing I owned that screamed out loud. Vibrant scarlet! Me, walking through La Cuisine in a red dress, was the signal to my dad: *Now!*

It felt like forever hanging out in the ladies' room, but I used my timer app: just three minutes.

I examined a jar with dried lavender that must have been picked in the late nineties. It was set beside paper hand towels on one of those small, unstable tables that seemed manufactured solely for bathrooms in restaurants. With over a minute to go, I got a text from my dad: *46 mi. not enuf to get to Phil & back. Maybe good for round trip JFK or LGA. Plane to Phil??*

Walking back to the table, I thought that certainly there were planes that went from New York to Philadelphia. However, I never heard of anyone who took one that wasn't a stop on the way to somewhere else. Either you drove or you took the LIRR to Penn Station and went by Amtrak. So it was possible Pete tossed his plan for an audiobook festival. Or he had gone somewhere else before Philly, if he'd gone there at all?

When I got back to the table, we took turns talking about what we were working on. Pete said his Philadelphia client, who owned a chain of truck stops in Pennsylvania and West Virginia, loved the new carryout bags and hot and cold cups. However, he nixed the napkins, claiming they were too girly. "They were white, one-ply paper napkins with part of his logo: a blue eighteen-wheeler," Pete said. "I don't know whether he just didn't want to spend the money or if he thinks real men don't use napkins."

It didn't sound like a business meeting that

had required Pete to leave at dawn on Monday and not to return until Wednesday close to noon. Unfortunately, nobody asked him anything more about his trip and I couldn't be the one who did. When my turn came, I spoke about planning for the Frankfurt Book Fair, which didn't take place until October. But I told the group about needing to line up meetings with some new publishers of Arabic literature I hadn't met, hoping they'd give the agencies I worked for a shot. Two sentences weren't enough, so I offered up a scintillating three-minute discourse on the wonderful world of international book fairs, then went back to my burger.

That night, Josh took Eliza and Chloë, her BFF, to a Mets game while I met Wynne at the Whitney to see a Calder exhibition where the sculptures had room to move around, as they'd been designed to do. Then we went to a restaurant on the roof of a nearby hotel with great views of downtown. To Wynne's annoyance, the restaurant was no longer cool, though it had been the week before. Now it was mainly tourists and a lot of old guys with women younger than we were. "Must be father-daughter night," she observed sourly.

I'd had only one drink since I'd be driving home, but I felt myself getting a little maudlin. I realized I had one hand on the stem of an almost empty martini glass. The other rested on my stomach, right around where my ovaries would be: both of them were probably shriveling into the size of desiccated peanuts at that very moment.

However, I perked up at the thought of the list of felonies I'd compiled on the days Pete was supposedly in Philadelphia and told Wynne about how I had recruited my father. "My only worry is that if it turns out to be a big fat nothing, he'll be so depressed."

"My only worry," Wynne said, "is that you'll be the one depressed. But maybe that's good. You know that old song Ella Fitzgerald sang? Now the Swing Ninjas are covering it: 'When I Get Low I Get High'? Deep down you think you're tough, but deeper down you're afraid you're a sensitive petunia. But you're not, you know."

"I don't know. Sometimes I worry that I made the wrong move, going into my dad's business, so to speak."

"It was after 9/11!" Wynne said. "You wanted to serve your country. You knew Arabic. You never gave it a second thought."

"What I mean is, maybe I'm really my mother's daughter. I got the acting gene, not the cop gene, and when I was in the bureau, I was just deep into a role: special agent."

"And you're really fragile? Which was why in sixth grade you punched Matt Blumenthal in the mouth and knocked out his tooth?"

"He squeezed my boob. What should I have let him do, squeeze the other one? But I've never been truly tested."

"Fine, so join the marines. 'Truly tested.' What the fuck does that mean anyway? Running with a grenade between your teeth? Being a Gandhi or a Rosa Parks?"

"Normality may not be all it's cracked up to be."

"What in life lives up to its billing?" Wynne asked. "Anyway, what's next for you? With the Pete business, I mean."

"I need to start looking at something beyond a computer monitor. But first, I have to get my hands on the picture of him. Interesting how, with practically everyone in the world having a camera on their phone, he's avoided being photographed."

"Maybe he thinks he's unattractive," Wynne said.

"There are forces in the universe beyond aesthetics. But it's so hard to avoid being in a shot. Like there are days when I look like a Gorgon and I tell people: 'Please don't get me in this picture.' And someone says 'Oh stop it. You look great.' So I wind up on somebody's Facebook page looking like a Gorgon. But with Pete, I found only one group photo with him, in an article in some advertising column from years ago. I tried cropping it. But it's really poor quality. Also, it's from the early 2000s, and his hair is thinner now. He's so bland looking he might as well be wallpaper. I've got to find something better."

The next day, Thursday, was without Pete business. I had to finish a manuscript about Mohammed V, the sultan who negotiated the end of French rule in Morocco. It was on a subject about which I knew next to zero but written in a style that made me keep turning the page, wondering what would happen next. I doubted it would shoot to the top (or even the bottom) of any nonfiction bestseller list of English-language books, but I wished it would. So I wrote a report recommending it. Then Eliza came home from school and we went through her drawers to find the perfect frayed shorts; she was starting to pack her trunk for Camp Belasco, a theater camp in the Adirondacks for younger teenagers with turquoise rubber bands on their braces and a song in their hearts.

It was June and the sky was still bright enough at almost nine o'clock that I could walk Lulu without a flashlight. This was one of those magical times of evening, filled with twinkly stars and intoxicating smells from invasive species pushing up through once perfect lawns. I was thinking about getting home and streaming *A Midsummer Night's Dream*, the one with Kevin Kline and Michelle Pfeiffer. One hand held the leash and the other a poop bag. Lulu was sniffing a fallen pine tree branch and seemed to find it irresistible, so instead of tugging her onward, I looked up, wondering whether a particularly luminous star was Venus or a satellite. In the play, Puck asks something like: "Art thou bragging to the stars?" I felt defeated in that instant. Getting swept up in the Pete business, then pulling my dad in, offering him a false hope to be what he was once again.

For whatever reason, that's the instant I remembered a photo of the Lutheran church's soup kitchen volunteers gathered around a stockpot. It had run in the *Shorehaven Sentinel* about a year before, in the Good Neighbors issue.

The *Sentinel*'s office had three desks—two with computers. Also, a staff of one when I got there at ten the next morning, probably a summer intern in his late teens. He was wearing a navy-blue University of Illinois T that still had new-shirt fold lines. I guessed he wouldn't be entering until the fall. He was short on looks, long on muscles, and had no tattoos, probably because his mom wouldn't allow any.

"Hi!" I said, with all the energy I could muster when faced with an eighteen-year-old asshole who didn't say hello and kept eyeing me up and down, unable to decide which half he preferred, if either. Since I needed a favor, I decided on the highly pleasant but take-no-prisoners manner. "You know Prince of Peace Lutheran Church?" I asked, sending up a small prayer that he wasn't the pastor's son. Good, he wasn't, because he nodded in a slow, limited way that indicated he thought he ought to know it. "Well, we've been asked to contribute to an article in the *Lutheran Witness* magazine about our soup kitchen! It's all about how we use fresh ingredients."

He seemed unmoved. He mumbled something that I finally deciphered as the statement: "I'm not the editor."

"Actually, I don't need the editor for this. About a year ago, the *Sentinel* did a really nice article about us. It was about how our soup kitchen is committed to the idea that all God's children deserve the best we can give them." His face softened only slightly but enough to reassure me that he wasn't heartless, just soulless. "You ran some wonderful pictures and we'd love to be able to send them on. We'll be glad to pay for usage or whatever. The one we scanned didn't have a high enough resolution. That's why I am here."

"I really only take ads. If you want to come back—"

"We're under time pressure on this. We'd appreciate it if you could take a look." It was more order than request; I tried to make it sound as if the entire Evangelical Lutheran Church in America was arrayed behind me, arms crossed over chests, waiting for him to show some decency. "Maybe it's filed under 'Prince of Peace Lutheran,' though I don't know. It could be under 'soup kitchen.' "

He just stood there, as if God and the devil were fighting for his soul. I stayed silent, knowing that if I projected any neediness he'd say no. He curled his mouth in annoyance, uncurled it, and finally said, "I'll look." It didn't take long until he came back with a manila envelope.

Five photos of volunteers gathered around a stockpot. Pete Delaney stood behind two people, chin up, seemingly willing to have his photo taken. And while I would not have called the thing on his face a smile, it approximated benevolence. The woman in front of Pete had shifted slightly in one of the pictures, affording the most usable headshot. I took several shots of it. Then, for insurance, I asked the kid if he could please scan it for me. After a put-upon inhale/exhale, he plodded over to the computer.

Naturally, I wished I could text Darby and ask if he could crop the others from the picture and make Pete look, well, the essence of Pete Delaney. My photo-editing attempts were pathetic. Since phoning Darby wasn't a possibility, I called Wynne, who I knew used Photoshop for her business, like to show a client what a wreck of a Mies van der Rohe chair in an antique shop could become after it was restored.

I sent her the scan and got it back hours later, just before she left with some actor boyfriend (who probably wouldn't last long enough for me to meet) for the opening of the Brooklyn Academy of Music's CinemaFest and then a late dinner. Josh was on the patio grilling lamb kebabs.

The headshot of Pete that Wynne photoshopped was perfect—crisp black and white. Not only had she made it look as if he'd gladly posed for a solo photo, but she'd erased his white soup kitchen apron, so he appeared in a plain collared shirt.

I forwarded it to my dad. He responded with some news of his own. He'd called his old sources at AT&T and Verizon early that morning. Since they didn't seem to know he'd retired, they were willing to help. Around 11 p.m., he finally heard from Verizon. Pete's cell phone number, the one listed on Iris's spreadsheet, was still in service. However, for the entire two-plus days when Pete was supposedly in Philadelphia, that phone had remained in Shorehaven. According to information gleaned from geolocation, it had been residing in or around 9 Amberley Road, Shorehaven.

I texted back to my dad that while Pete could have forgotten the phone, he wasn't a forgetting kind of guy. My dad, never a fan of snap judgments, texted: *Didn't need it. Wherever went, prob wasn't traveling as Pete D.*

# 15

I was cleaning out the refrigerator, tossing out an indented lime and cheese that had grown its own sheer white negligée. I also got rid of unidentifiable brown chunks in containers: Stew? The revolting remains of roasted vegetables? Breathing through my mouth helped, as did flouting recycling laws and just tossing swollen plastic containers into a black trash bag.

Since mouth breathing got in the way of my singing along with *Hamilton*, my mind drifted to Pete Delaney. Actually it didn't drift at all but shot into consciousness as if it came from a Glock.

On March 19 he'd been in Boston, and on March 20 there had been that robbery at a bank in Manchester, New Hampshire. The heist with armed robbery in Wilmington, Delaware. That weird kidnapping with the guy with the paper bag on his head in Birmingham, Alabama. In the Birmingham crime, there was no way of knowing if a weapon had been involved, since the guy never saw his attackers. Since Alabama was an open-carry state, like Texas, I chose to lean toward a weapon being involved.

Fantasy, I knew, would offer me zero, as would

reality. I had to get going. So I stuck Wynne's photoshopped picture of Pete into a folder and left in midafternoon for the city. I was planning on meeting Josh in the evening for a judges-gone-wild night, a pretheater Pasta Festa! and then a performance of *The Crucible* starring one of many extremely famous movie actors named Chris. But I had some time before then.

There was only one shooting range in Manhattan, Westside Rifle and Pistol. Even though plenty of women went there, it retained a vague testosterone smell, as if it were patronized solely by guys who did not use deodorant. I left my pistol home in the safe. I wasn't going to take it to the theater since carrying a weapon in a handbag was a mistake made only by low-budget TV shows without a technical adviser, and even the best shoulder holster or carry belt could be seen under silk. And obviously, I didn't want to have to flash my NYC pistol permit at a ticket taker in front of the chief judge's wife, a woman who could be harrowed by a loud sneeze.

Though not exactly a familiar face at Westside, at least I was known. I chatted with the assistant manager, Sergei, a hugely muscular guy whose pointy ears extended almost at right angles from his shaved head, making him look like a bouncer at an elf club. He was the go-to guy for assault weapons, but I'd never been a great fan of shooting. I just did what I had to in order to qualify. However, Sergei and I had bonded over a shared fascination with martial arts.

I detested every other form of athletics except running. I would have said I lacked the competitive gene since even a volleyball game during a day at the beach made me long to sprain an ankle. Except there was something exhilarating about actual hand-to-hand (or foot-to-body) fighting. On the occasions when I'd run out of manuscripts to read/reports to write, I could spend half a day watching Brazilian jujitsu videos on YouTube. Same with aikido and Muay Thai kickboxing. And Eliza and I took two classes in tae kwon do together.

I'd gone to a demonstration of a defensive technique developed by the Russian Special Forces, Systema Spetsnaz, that was supposed to work in real life and didn't require great strength. I'd run into Sergei there. When the demo was over, we said "Wow!" to each other. But that was soon after I'd met Josh, plus I was still at the task force, forever overworked, so I never pursued the system. But Sergei had stuck with it and was now thinking about abandoning the wonderful world of the AK-47, quitting Westside, and opening his own Systema studio.

"It's for you," he told me. "For smart people. Not . . ." He said something in Russian.

"Which means?"

"Street fighters. Animals. You must learn

neurophysiology. Brain. Confuse it. Use opponents' strength against them." He took my handbag and put it on the floor, then motioned for me to take off my shoes.

"This is a silk dress. I'm going to the theater." Instead of inquiring about what I was seeing or saying: *Oh, peach is a good color for you,* Sergei moved to punch me in my solar plexus. I managed to fend off that hit with a swivel. Just as I was going to say: *Ha! You didn't think I'd be able to do that, did you?* he hit me—only hard enough for demo—simultaneously under my arm and on top of my head.

"Confused your brain, Blue Eyes," he said, with a boyish smile, though one that had two gold teeth.

"You did," I agreed, so I decided to be ten minutes late for pasta while he confused my brain several more times in different ways. After I put my shoes back on, I took out the picture of Pete that Wynne had edited for me. I'd printed it out on glossy photographic paper. "Has this guy ever come in?" I asked.

Clearly, this was not the first time he'd been asked to ID someone; cops and Feds routinely checked shooting ranges whenever there was an unsolved case involving a firearm that looked as if it had been used with skill. Sergei squinted, held the photo at a distance, covered the hair and then the mouth and chin with the flat of his hand.

"Not here," he said with depressing finality. "And I pictured him with a mustache. Also not his hair and all that shit. He's not here, ever."

The following day, I drove to check off ranges in Brooklyn and Queens. Of course it was possible that Pete had gotten to be such a crack shot growing up in Indiana that he had no need for practice. And naturally, my following up on firearms could simply be a subfolder of my global Delaney delusion. Whatever, I had to either abandon it or follow up.

There were a fair number of shooting ranges, but I began with only the larger ones, where someone could go for practice occasionally and not be remembered. Queens, borough of my birth, proved to be a bust. Granted I had only one photo of Pete, and he was not someone with a memorable face. But people responded as if I were showing them a featureless outline of a man, the kind of image that says: *person unknown.*

I had better luck in Brooklyn in a place not far from the Verrazano Bridge. I was talking to one of the supervisors there, a guy named Thad Brownell. I knew that because he had a little bar on his shirt with that name. Nevertheless, he introduced himself and pronounced the *th* in his name. I suppressed the urge to ask: *Don't you think it should be Tad?* Probably shutting up was a wise choice since, even though Thad scratched his beard in deep thought but came up with nothing, he was benevolent enough to call over another employee, Rhonda Jaffee.

Like Thad, Rhonda was wearing camouflage pants and a tucked-in white T-shirt with a name bar. But she had some beanie-like thing on her head. It was larger than a yarmulke: more like a taqiyah, the rounded skullcap a lot of Muslim men use at prayers. Except hers was pink, with a pistol design knitted in. I admired it so effusively that she decided I was a soul mate and shared that she had bought it at a craft sportswear store up in Rhinebeck.

"Rhonda's been around," Thad said. "Worked at a bunch of ranges upstate."

Rhonda shook her head patiently, as though this was an old routine they were used to performing. "Westchester," she said. "He calls that upstate, like nobody'd invented Buffalo." She studied the photo closely. I watched her in profile and envied her eyelashes. "Seen him," she said finally. "Hard to tell, but I've seen him. You know, it's like he picked himself a face people wouldn't remember. That's why I remember him! I'm like seventy-five percent sure it was at Hudson. Hudson Rifle and Pistol Range in Yonkers. So if you go up there, save yourself some time and don't talk to Chick. He's a pig. He does everything but oink. Ask for Dennis, but don't call him Denny."

Naturally, I had an overwhelming urge to say *Denny,* or to at least ask him why such a likely nickname could be so emotionally loaded. However, it was clear at first glance that personal questions were verboten with Dennis. His expression was one of perpetual piss, as if he'd been sentenced to life chewing on aluminum foil. He was relatively short and not particularly fit, but he wore a black tank top that showed off marine tattoos on his right upper arm—an eagle clutching a globe with SEMPER FI, a skull that didn't say anything, and a cross with DEATH BEFORE DISHONOR on the crossbar.

I told him Rhonda down at Bridge Range told me I should talk to him.

"You're law enforcement," he told me.

"Ex."

"Let me see your ID." I was prepared with two wallets, two sets of IDs, so I took out my Coral Jane Schottland driver's license; it was not only my name pre-Josh, but the name I still used for bureau business. "Coral?" he asked. If he wanted to smirk, he couldn't because his face was so frozen.

"A family name," I told him (though until I was born, not in my family). Easier than saying I'd been named for an actress my mom had been "mad for" and also for Jane Austen. My dad had wanted to name me after Great-grandma Feygl ("We can call her Faye or something" he tried to assure my mom). Feygl was said to have bitten the leg of a Cossack during a pogrom. But my mom started to cry and my dad gave in because he'd heard of postpartum depression.

"NYPD?" Dennis asked.

"No."

"What then?"

"An agency of the federal government." Since I'd gone that far, there was no reason I couldn't tell him. But he seemed like the kind of guy who required intrigue in his diet.

Since Dennis's face already showed as much revulsion as it was possible to display under the most neutral of circumstances, I couldn't assess how my response went over. But he didn't walk away. In fact, he took a couple of steps closer. Now I could see his left shoulder tat: an octopus with a streamer around it that said FRATERS INFINITAS, which I assumed meant "Brothers Forever." I'd never studied Latin but I was willing to bet there was something deeply wrong with the declension, though I kept the thought to myself.

"Are you carrying?" Dennis asked.

"Not now," I said.

"What do you use?"

"A Glock Gen4."

"You like it?"

"Yeah. You know the saying that someone couldn't hit a barn door? Before I got my Glock, I could hit the barn door, but there was a twenty-five percent chance I'd miss the guy coming out of it. I'm much better now. I like that you can customize the grip."

He nodded, and his expression softened to merely revolted. "More consistent trigger pulls," he told me. I nodded slightly, to the same degree he did.

"I have a picture," I said as I pulled the folder from my handbag and opened it before he could refuse to look. The photo was only minimally crumpled.

Dennis took it and walked over to a showcase that had the kind of high-wattage daylight lighting that stores use to accentuate the features of diamonds or, in this instance, ammo. He put it on the counter, backed up to view it from another perspective, then lifted it and gradually moved it so close that he and photo Pete were practically nose to nose. He was so meticulous in his observation that when he finally said, "He's been here," I got a double shiver of excitement. It was not one of those nebbishy identifications where someone says: *Yeah, maybe, I think so, but* . . . This was a definite ID from a very careful guy.

"Has he been here more than once?" I asked.

"Three or four times," Dennis said.

"Did he make an impression on you?"

He shook his head. "Not him himself. I remember him because it was pretty quiet in here, and at one point I went to the back and as

I passed, I looked at his target and holy Jesus, he was one hell of a shot."

"What was his weapon?"

"Winchester M70. The Alaskan model."

"The M70 is a high-caliber rifle, right?" Listen, there was no point in my pretending to be the reincarnation of Annie Oakley. When it came to firearms, this guy would be able to smell fakery a mile off.

"Right. It's used for defense and hunting. Big game. I talked to him afterward. It was the end of the summer—"

"Last summer?" I interrupted.

"No. Probably a few years ago. He was pre-paring for the start of bear season in New Jersey. Like it was August and bear season doesn't start there till October. Not that he was hepped up or anything. Very flat kind of guy, but he knew his weapons. That Alaskan is a great weapon for bear. He wasn't at all macho. Didn't look ex-military. Not law enforcement. I can usually spot that. Like with you. You're easy."

I got that transitory tornado in my stomach that happens when I'm simultaneously taken aback and disturbed. "What gave me away?" I asked casually, as if I were charmed by his insight.

"You come in and take in the whole room right away. Civilians usually look straight at you first."

"And our friend with the Alaskan?"

"Took in the whole room, which is funny.

Because he sure as hell was never a marine and not any other branch. I can always tell if someone is military. And not a cop either. He was . . ." Dennis was trying to come up with a description.

"He was his own category?"

"That's it. Like I was naturally curious. Did he ever hunt anywhere else? Have a go at grizzlies or brown bears? Normal conversation. But I didn't ask, because he wasn't what you'd call a guy who liked to talk."

"Was he so uncommunicative that he seemed weird or that he was hiding something?"

"No. Not a nut job. You know, within normal. Just low-key as low-key gets."

"The other times he came in," I said, "was it to practice with the Winchester?"

Dennis rubbed the FRATERS INFINITAS octopus on the shoulder thoughtfully. "The next time or two, I recognized the guy, though I've got to admit there was something about him that made me not say, 'Good to see you again.' But while it's interesting to watch the best, I've been around expert shooters too long that I didn't *gotta* see him." He grunted, which I took to be his version of a chuckle. "Not like he was a Metallica concert."

I acknowledged his humor with a small smile. "So you never saw him with any other weapon?"

"I didn't say that. I said the next time or two, not never. Actually, the last time he was in?

287

Probably sometime this year. He had a pistol. Now I didn't see it, but the guy who works with me on weekends clocked him in. Checked his permit, all that, and later, heard from someone in the back that his weapon . . ." My mom would have admired his dramatic pause. "The Springfield Loaded model, laser equipped."

"Laser equipped," I repeated. "Good for low-light sighting." That was about the outer limits of my knowledge on laser-equipped pistols. Well, I did know a laser that is automatically projected toward the target makes the pistol (as they say in gun biz marketing) "an excellent weapon for home defense." And it's no biggie if the target sees the laser. The bullet will close his eyes a second later.

He didn't seem to mind having me around, so I asked if he could check out a name to see whether it matched any of the names on gun licenses of people who'd come in to shoot. When he nodded, I was relieved, but also a little on edge.

I didn't know Dennis. What would happen if he and Pete actually knew each other or had even worked together on God knows what? Wouldn't Dennis call and tell him: "Someone named Coral came looking for you." It wasn't a giant leap from Coral to Corie.

But then why would he ID Pete's photo? All he'd have to do is say, "Never saw him in my life." And interestingly, a guy who'd been around the block as often as Dennis found someone like Pete slightly off-putting. I couldn't see the two of them hooking up for nefarious dealings. Also, I was a trained interrogator, and in Dennis, I didn't see or hear any of the behaviors of a person who is lying.

In fact, Dennis was open. He invited me around the counter so I could look at his computer monitor with him. No Pete or Peter Delaney had been at Hudson Rifle and Pistol. No Delaney from Nassau County, either. So assuming Dennis checked gun licenses as was required by law, Pete must have been using fake ID.

Frustrating. But talk about thrilling! This was progress. A guy doesn't go to the time, trouble, and cost of getting a counterfeit, unrestricted, concealed-carry handgun license unless he has something he wants to keep hidden.

Instead of taking the parkway south, I drove back on US 1, the old Boston Post Road, through quaint and not-so-quaint towns. That gave me the chance to stop at traffic lights and savor my elation. Pete Delaney was a superb shooter! Pete Delaney kept up his skill with firearms—though I had to consider the possibility he was just a guy who loved target practice. But it would be strange for a mere enthusiast to use a fake ID.

But Pete Delaney avoided the customary camaraderie of hunters and gun enthusiasts. Some New Yorkers liked to go into the woods or wetlands and shoot deer, black bears, or wild turkeys over the weekend. Some played Army Ranger. Then there were the antigovernment, racist, anti-Semitic schmucks with automatic and semiautomatic rifles. Whether it was the thrill of the hunt or rehearsing for insurrection, much of the time shooting was a communal activity. However, Pete Delaney was a one-man operation. He might barbecue baby back ribs for the family and volunteer at the high school's car wash day, but when a weapon was in his hand, he was on his own.

I couldn't wait to get home and tell my dad about my day. But in the next cute town, I pulled over in front of a store called Tootsies, yet another salon catering to the suburban foot. This was not a surprise: to me, Westchester was Long Island with hills. I closed my eyes to block the bucolic view of a parking meter in the comforting shade of a leafy tree and called Sami Bashir.

"Obviously you find me irresistible," he said.

"You manage to sound so offhand when you're stating a conclusion you believe in to the depths of your soul," I told him.

"Right. I want to come across as casual so you won't feel humiliated at being unable to control yourself."

"I'm glad you're sensitive enough to protect me from self-loathing. And how you're even kinder to tell me how humane you are—in case I missed your decency. Hey, I need the names of people off the grid who do really good fake IDs. Not necessarily involved in terrorist activity: mostly a source for your average upscale felon. Where the pros would go or a good semipro?"

"Not my turf," Sami said. I knew that, but I also figured he'd know the person on the task force whose turf it was. Before I could ask him for a favor, he volunteered. "I know two people, a cop and someone from Secret Service, concentrates on counterfeiting. I'll get back to you when I get back to you, so don't start asking me when."

"When?"

"Soon, okay? You going away for a vacation or something?"

"Not until my daughter gets back from camp." I heard him breathe. Right from the start, we'd known (though never said aloud) that we'd never marry. So I don't think my having a husband bothered him too much, but he always seemed taken aback that I had a child. "The three of us are going to Idaho. Hiking, fishing. It's supposed to be beautiful. But that's not till August, so I'll be around. Thanks so much for—"

"Okay," he said and hung up without any good-byes.

A half hour later, after I'd stopped thinking about Sami and moved on to whether I should stop at a deli in Great Neck and have the damn pastrami sandwich I'd been obsessing about for at least a week, Sami called back. I pulled off the Long Island Expressway so I could take notes.

"All right, got some places for you. You can get reasonably good stuff, not the crappy ID kids get to drink. They're not superior quality, not like the great freelancers make. But these are good and selective about their clientele. Given enough time, some of them can produce stuff that's pretty foolproof, even with government scanning devices." He gave me the names of printing places: two in Nassau County; one in Suffolk, the easternmost Long Island county; and seven in Queens. He said there were so many places in Manhattan and the Bronx that he didn't even bother taking them down, though he would go back if I needed them. Then Sami added, "For whatever it's worth, I vote for Suffolk County. Unless he's doing some shit in the Hamptons."

"No, at least not that I know of. What's your thinking on it?" I asked.

"Counterintuitive. Manhattan is still the center of the universe, at least for most people in greater New York. Your Pete operates solo, so he's probably given to thinking a lot or overthinking. Instinct might say to do one thing, but he'd think on it and do the opposite."

"Well, for whatever it's worth, I agree with you. Anyway, I have to start somewhere."

"Keep me posted on this. The fact that he can

shoot the balls off a rat from two hundred feet . . . makes him interesting."

I was in the middle of "Thank you, I really appreciate you doing this" when he hung up.

# 16

My mom liked pretty things, but she possessed the lifelong New Yorker's indifference to cars. To her, transportation was subway, bus, or taxi. My dad, then, was free from any demands for good taste and bought a Toyota in a shade of gray so lifeless it seemed to be not an actual automobile, but the ghost of one.

Just as there were good cops and bad cops, there were neat cops and slobs. He was, of course, a good cop, but on the fastidious front he was both. At home he'd be splotched with mustard or dusted with cookie crumbles, but his desk at the precinct had been orderly. With cars he was the sort who'd clean the cup holders with one of the wet wipes he kept in the center console. He pulled into my driveway a little before ten the following morning and used a garden hose to clean off his headlights. Then we headed east, our conversation interrupted occasionally by Google Maps directions. For both of us, Suffolk County, twenty miles and change from the border of Queens, was terra incognita.

"I gotta admit," my dad was saying, "that when you started with the Pete thing, my first thought was you were just looking for a hook to hang your hat on. Your cop hat. Yeah, yeah, I know, special agent hat, but a cop's kid is a cop, whether or not she wears blue." Google got us off the Southern State Parkway and onto a wide road that was home to stores like tire dealerships and hardware wholesalers that distinguished themselves by the relative hideousness of their inflating-deflating balloon people. "Did I ever tell you the story about Rocky Morgenstern?"

Thirty, forty times. "I think so," I said. Even through the khaki of my pants, the car's seat felt on the verge of itchy, like sweaty wool, and kept me from the comfortable small slides passengers do to keep from getting stiff. "Wasn't he the guy who got bored being retired and started—"

"Right. Retired from squad detective in the Sixtieth. Coney Island precinct. Didn't know what to do with himself so he started tailing people out walking the dogs. No pun intended." He sighed: "Tail, dogs. Get it?"

"Right, got it." I smiled and he seemed to pick it up with his peripheral vision, because he seemed encouraged, telling me yet again the saga of Rocky Morgenstern and what he discovered. What had he discovered? Close to nothing— shoplifting, a little geriatric adultery—though he did wind up marrying a woman originally from Minsk who had two Chihuahuas.

"So I thought maybe you were pulling a Rocky, focusing in on this Pete person because maybe, you know, the literary business wasn't exactly gripping. But you know, I did read that mystery you got published about the cop in Cairo and thought it was really good."

I nodded forcefully so he could see I was acknowledging his opinion about the book. It was surprisingly reassuring to hear my dad validate my suspicions about Pete. Auto parts megastores gave way to Home Depots, Buy Buy Babys, and Costcos, and in a couple of minutes we turned onto a street with small houses, Cape Cods, and a model that was half ranch, half two-story, which might sound a little lopsided, but they gave off Mommy and me vibes—tall-short, all dressed in the same shingles, always together. Cared-for homes, the sort that would show up in a montage of a Suffolk County PD recruitment with a voice-over intoning: *We serve and protect all the citizens, while enforcing the law with impartiality, blah, blah, blah.*

"Is the Suffolk PD a good department?" I asked my dad.

"Yeah, from all I heard. I only dealt with one guy. In Homicide. Years and years ago, and he was good. He told me that when you walk into their squad, there's a big sign: THOU SHALT NOT KILL. You don't get more basic than that, and I like basic."

"Be prepared to turn right," the GPS voice interrupted. I looked down on the screen resting on the open ashtray and saw we were a couple of miles from the ocean, though there was nothing to indicate beachiness; the occasional lawn gnome wore a hat and scarf. I felt as if I were in another country, the unchanging good America of our communal fantasy.

After several more turns, we arrived at a strip mall, the sort anchored by a tired supermarket that signaled I wouldn't want to go inside and browse the produce. My dad parked near the shopping carts and got out of the car, stretching each leg then shaking his arms as though he were a long-haul truck driver who'd just driven three hundred miles without a stop. Actually, he looked exactly like what he had been, a plainclothes cop in standard dark gray pants, a darker gray sports jacket that gleamed a bit in sunlight. His rep tie, though, was so jarringly proper it was clear my mom had donated his favorite, which was covered in what looked like amoebas, and replaced it with these navy, red, and yellow stripes. While he went into the store to find a bathroom, I checked my phone and found that except for Amazon, I was in no one's thoughts.

The printing shop, cleverly called We Print 4 U, was a small store that looked as if the two next-door businesses, a dry cleaner and a Subway, were trying to crush it to death. I glanced around the mall and noticed two CCTVs. They seemed focused mainly on the supermarket entrance and the parking lot, though one might take in the facade of the printer.

"Mind if I take the lead?" my dad asked.

"No. Go ahead." He definitely looked senior to me and there was no reason not to go along, especially since he hadn't asked me to take a vow of silence.

He walked in a couple of steps ahead of me. I put on a pair of nineties amber-tinted glasses I'd found the summer before when I was cleaning out the changing room by the pool and stuck them in the mysterious objects drawer in the small desk in the kitchen. Somebody's prescription, but weak enough so I didn't feel nauseated. I followed him in.

The guy behind the counter looked up and instantly made my dad as a cop. The shiny jacket, the gray hair with a side part. He took a step back, did a two-step shuffle, then took me in: khakis, white T, lightweight denim cropped jacket that Wynne had told me I'd love, even though it was stupidly expensive. But she'd assured me: "It's a Helmut Lang and for God sake look at the workmanship." Actually I did love it, and it was cut loose enough to conceal a shoulder holster.

My dad went right up to the red Formica counter as did I, close enough to deduce that the guy had had a poppy seed bagel for breakfast. The guy hooked his finger over the collar of his plaid short-sleeve shirt and pulled it away from his neck, even though the top button was open. "Can I help you with—"

"We met before," my dad lied, and the guy, faced with a generic plainclothes detective, nodded. From the info I had gotten from Sami, this print shop owner had run-ins with the Feds before along with two arrests, no convictions, by the locals. My dad tilted his head toward me and said, "My new partner." Not even a false name. Besides the hideous, overlarge rectangular glasses, I'd pulled my hair back and worn zero makeup, so while I wasn't disguised, I gave the impression of a wan person who'd arbitrarily joined a police department rather than a convent: no one you'd want to look at once, much less twice.

"There's a guy we believe you did some work for," my dad said. "Demanding guy, good eye for detail. Know who I mean?"

The guy shook his head. Then, seeming to feel he had to say something, he spoke to my dad's lapel rather than looking him in the eye: "A lot of people are particular when it comes to business cards, invitations . . ."

"Let's cut the shit." My dad put out his hand and I put the folder I'd been carrying into it. He took out a glossy from among the papers in the folder, all of which were blank but gave the package a nice heft. He put the photo on the counter. I tried that morning to blow it up to an 8×10, but it made Pete look as if he were dematerializing in a *Star Trek* transporter. "When was the last time he was in here?"

The printer guy picked up the photo and though his hand wasn't shaking, it wasn't quite steady, either. He studied the man in the picture, then shrugged and shook his head. "Listen, I swear to you, I never saw him, or even anyone who looked like him." The only distinctive feature in the guy's otherwise bland, round face was his eyebrows. They arched up, then simply stopped rather than descending, giving him a devilish look.

"We're not talking petty larceny here," my dad told him. "This is major. Don't fuck with me." His voice was calm to the point of flatness. I'd never actually seen him at work, and he was good. I felt so proud, and what added to my pleasure was that I'd always believed he was good, but now I could see it. He knew there was little use in shouting at or threatening someone familiar with law enforcement. No doubt the printer had his go-to criminal lawyer, maybe even his own bail bondsman. Except he was nervous enough; at no point had he asked my dad to show his shield. "This is the case with national implications. Understand?"

"Hey, I don't sell to terrorist types." He crossed his heart. "Never, and none of them have ever even walked into the store."

"We're not asking you to make our case for us. We know who and what he is. We just want you to give us whatever information you have. We know you've dealt with him," I said, with a touch of sadness in my voice. I read him as a man who felt put-upon, and a touch of regret in a woman's voice could make him feel understood. Not sympathy: he was too hardened a pro to go for that.

"I swear, I never saw his face before," he tried again, with less conviction but more volume. By now he had turned back to my dad.

"I'm going to give you forty-five seconds," my dad told him. "You can make up your mind to cooperate, give us what we want. Good chance we'll disappear out of your life. Or don't tell us. You know the drill on that one." My dad looked at his watch, a big stainless steel digital number that embarrassed my mom. And me. Even Josh, who seemed to exist in a mortification-free universe, suggested we get him a Rolex for his sixty-fifth birthday.

The guy put the photo back on the counter and swallowed with what would have had great dramatic effect if both of us hadn't witnessed that bobbing Adam's apple business too often.

"Thirty seconds," my dad stated. He sounded so serene.

The guy closed his eyes, then opened them. "He's been in a couple of times," he coughed out. "Maybe three." He cleared his throat. "Four tops."

"How did he come across to you?" I asked. "Give us a sense of his personality."

"He didn't have much of a personality." I waited. "Low-key. Businesslike."

"Businesslike in what way?"

"Not like 'Do this, do that.' More like he just said what he needed and that was it. No chit-chat."

"At any point," I continued, "did you ask how he got to you?"

The guy rubbed his chest where his top button showed off a V of skin so sunburned and dry it looked like beef jerky.

"No," the guy said. "He told me right off the bat. He said Bart had recommended me very highly, that my work was meticulous. He said 'me-tic-u-lous' in this really meticulous way, and he was right. I'm not only good at the details. I see the big picture, too. I'm not one of those photocopying assholes who don't make a good product."

"Who is Bart?" my dad asked.

The printer guy stepped sideways, right and left, like a merengue step in a Zumba class. "Uh," he answered, "like I couldn't really hear him. I thought he said Bart, but maybe it was Art. Or Barr. The way he said it . . . It just sounded right and you can understand that I'm a pretty careful person, but just from looking at him I knew he was legit. Not law enforcement."

"So essentially you trusted him enough just on his appearance and manner," I said. "For your purposes, he didn't seem like a threat."

"No. Listen, I turn a lot of people away because I have a good sense of who's who and what's what. But this was a guy who knew what he wanted."

"What did he want the first time?" my dad asked.

"It was a big ask. Out-of-state driver's license, the farther from New York the better. Also"—he looked at my dad and started rubbing his chest again, harder this time and over a bigger area, as if to keep himself alive, a kind of preresuscitation—"you're not federal, are you?"

"You got eyes?" my dad answered.

"Okay, just checking."

"Are you going to tell me he wanted a passport?"

"No. A NEXUS card. You know, just to go back and forth to Canada, so you can avoid—"

"I know what a NEXUS card is," my dad said. "Did he say he had business up there?"

The guy shook his head. "I got the impression that it was some kind of personal thing. Maybe a woman who thinks she's his wife, except he's already got a wife, so he's got to have a completely new identity."

When people jump to conclusions like this, they usually know more than they're telling. Sometimes they don't even have a conscious reason, but if an investigator can get them to dig a little, there's occasionally pay dirt.

"What made you think it was personal rather than business?"

"Most of the time, someone wants something for a purpose. A driver's license to rent a car or get on a plane. A credit card. Much harder nowadays. Listen, I'm on the up-and-up. I don't deal in stolen shit. I can give references where they can go to get one, but I'm not part of it."

"Right." *Whoever commits an offense against the United States or aids, abets, counsels, commands, induces, or procures its commission is punishable as a principal,* the Justice Department's go-to statute, not as sexy as racketeering, but a prosecutor's faithful old friend. But all I added was: "Let's get back to the woman thing." A firm suggestion that sounded almost sweet, full of wonder: Over the years, I'd learned not to act in a snide or snippy manner, because it didn't produce results. Curiosity, on the other hand, worked because you were asking other people to help you out. It motivated them to think and demonstrate how insightful they were. "What gave you the idea he wanted documentation for another life?"

"Interesting question," the printer said.

"Because someone doing a deal is only going to want basic items. In-state driver's license. Proof of membership in something. Passport, NEXUS card. But he wanted everything in one name. A medical insurance card, library card, BJ's Club card, AAA. Like he wanted a complete, normal-guy wallet. He even said something like, 'I want whoever looks at it to see the same name.' And he wanted to appear as a single guy, so no family pictures, just some images off the web, with an older couple in front of the Christmas tree, and a bunch of middle-age guys like after a touch football game and he had me put his head on one of the bodies. It was like he expected the woman to go through his wallet. He wanted the old couple aged, the photo stock aged I mean, so it would look like he had it in his wallet forever."

"Did he want a permit to carry a concealed weapon?"

"Only one time. I think it was the third."

My dad put his hands on the counter and kind of leaned but not forward or in a threatening manner. He was doing the *I'm interested in what you're saying* routine also. "What name did he use? Did he ask you to come up with something, or did he supply it?"

"He did. Totally. Just wanted printing from me, nothing else. No pointers, no conversation, no suggestions. He had the whole thing figured out."

"And the name?"

"Each time it was a different name."

"Did you get the impression he was getting rid of the old identities?" my dad wanted to know. "Replacing them for, say, a new woman, a new job? Or was he adding to them?"

"Couldn't tell. When a guy like that doesn't talk, you don't push it."

"What were the names he used?"

The printer shrugged a little too hard. "Honestly, I deal with so many people, hundreds of names a year. Most of it legit, you know. You'd be surprised how many people get referred to me for stuff like baby shower invitations. I can't remember."

"Come on," I urged him. "He didn't use Liam or Oliver and ask for his name in blue."

"Try harder," my dad said.

"Listen, my business is based on trust."

This time my dad didn't say anything, just looked at his watch and let the seconds go by in silence. Finally the guy said: "The last time? Because I swear to God"—he crossed his heart—"that's the only one I remember. John Cutler."

"John Cutler," my dad sighed. "For fuck's sake."

"It's a smart choice," I told him. "Not obviously phony like 'John Smith' but in no way memorable. It's not like James or Charles, where there could possibly be a nickname and somebody could ask, 'Are you Charles, Chuck, or

Charlie? Or Chip?' That would make the name stick in your head. A John is a John, and no one renting him a car is going to ask, 'Anyone call you Johnny?' And Cutler isn't uncommon, but it's not Jones or Johnson. It's just some *C* name."

We were having lunch at a place called Fish 'Wich, one of those shacks made of grayed cedar planks you see along the Atlantic coast. It was about a half mile away from the printer's, a genuine stand-alone shack whose specialty was a fried clamwich, which might have been a South Shore of Long Island culinary tradition or just frozen, breaded crap dumped out of a plastic bag into a deep fryer. Both of us went with the filet du jour sandwich, which the waitress said was fried fluke or flounder, she forgot which, but she could ask if we wanted to know, which we didn't.

"So what are you thinking?" I asked him.

"I'm thinking that a guy doesn't need rifle practice if he's fencing emeralds or grabbing sacks of old bills from an armored truck guard."

"True," I said. I took a few seconds to rearrange the packets of ketchup, mayo, and tartar sauce in the chipped cup on the table.

"Very nice straightening," my dad said. "Too bad you didn't learn neatness until you moved out." He smiled at a memory. "It used to drive your mother bat shit."

"Right, and she was so appalled she kept straightening my room." My laundry, too. Balled socks would be lined up in my dresser drawer like chubby soldiers at attention, one after the other.

That led me back to rifle practice and how at better shooting ranges, ammo isn't just dumped into an empty mayonnaise jar; bullets are kept in boxes that are lined up in storage drawers.

I was getting somewhere, but my dad beat me to it. "Listen, Corie, this guy isn't Mr. Crime-o-rama. 'Hey, buddy, need a felony done? Kidnapping, jewel heist, industrial espionage? No need to get your hands dirty. Whatever you want, John Cutler will do it for you!' "

I nodded. "Specialization. Yes! You don't need a rifle to commit a burglary or assault. If you want to be armed, you'd have a handgun."

"Good," my dad said. "So what's a guy going to do with a rifle? Shooting a fucking woodchuck isn't a crime. Shooting a person, a different story."

The words fell out of me: "He's a hit man," I said.

The waitress came over with two bottles of Bud and cold glasses. I was suddenly not just thirsty but also wildly hungry.

"It's gotta be that, assuming he does one thing. Right?"

"Right. Homicide for hire. Because look, Dad, he's still running a freelance packaging design business that I'll bet earns more than enough to support his family and the way he lives. If anyone ever suspected him of anything, they'd probably do a net worth on him and find he's got a nice little business there. Has kids, seems to live on the up-and-up, works in a soup kitchen, for God sakes."

The deep-fried fish sandwich came and I put so much tartar sauce and mayo on it that it had enough fat calories to sustain the average person for a week.

"You want my tomato?" my dad asked.

I nodded, added his tomato slice along with his lettuce, and took a giant bite. "Even though I've got ID from Mr. Tattoo at the shooting range and the printer, when I think of him sitting at the table with us at lunch, all that comes to mind is: *Corie, you're delusional.* Okay, maybe he has a second wife stashed somewhere who goes through his wallet and thinks his name is John Cutler. Maybe they hunt bear together in New Jersey. Maybe they have matching red vests."

"Maybe," my dad said. "But then why does he have his garage so wired up that he would know instantly if anyone touched a door or window? You have long guns, you keep them properly locked up. But not in a fortress, like you're expecting a Navy SEAL team to rappel from a helicopter. Think about it."

I thought about it, while silently amazed that my dad was now the one trying to convince me about Pete. There were lots of small signs and a few big ones that could point in different directions, from nothing to a secret life with another woman to hit man. Jeep watching, many phones, exquisitely fake ID that even pros couldn't spot, and an ability to shoot so close to the bull's-eye that he could get an NRA Distinguished Expert certificate. Possibly a troubled marriage. A lot of coincidences? Or considering the time frame, a trail that at least led to a place like, say, Galveston? Whose hands might get tanned when his face was in the shade? A sniper's.

My dad drove back toward my house, contentedly listening to the mobile police scanner he often took in the car. My mom told me that when they drove through Utah to visit the national parks there, she listened to *Wolf Hall* with noise-reducing earbuds while he checked out how things were going for the local police forces and the park rangers. They'd had a lovely time, both hitting Mute at moments of breathtaking scenery.

I wished for earbuds because after all my dad's help I didn't want to seem like an ingrate by sticking my fingers in my ears. Still, I needed to concentrate. My mind meandered around everything I knew about Pete Delaney. I empathized with his getting fired from the big ad agency. The year 2008 was a miserable time for so many people, including most of our Wednesday lunch group. But he had believed he was one of the pampered artistes at JWT. Then not only was he asked to leave, but he was also convinced he'd gotten a meager severance package. Not what he deserved. And probably without being shown the proper gratitude for his service. I could understand how that happened: Corporations all over the country were on the balls of their asses, having to let so many people go. After witnessing shock, anger, tears, maybe the people doing the firing were less than empathetic. Or maybe Pete had gotten the lousiest of lousy deals.

But he'd gone from a prestige job on Madison Avenue to nothing. Or nothing plus, because he had the added problems of a miserable economy that wasn't making that many new products to package. Yet he had a family dependent on his skills.

Who wouldn't get furious in that situation? But fury was heat. Maybe Pete had instead gone cold inside. What were his skills? Creating eye-catching coverings. And being a brilliant shot, maybe even sniper level. Certainly he decided to freelance, but it takes a while to start making a living at freelance package design. On the other hand, there's always a market for those skilled at getting rid of exasperating neighbors, grasping spouses, undesirable business associates—especially during a great recession.

A cold heart and troubled times can be a tragedy—but they can also be a business opportunity.

# 17

My dad dropped me off at home, and as I walked through the mudroom into the kitchen, I was thinking, *Hmm, a cup of ginger tea.* I even produced a mental video to go with it: me sitting on the big chair on the porch, the mug forgotten on the floor beside me as I methodically made notes on one of Josh's legal pads—narratives and also timelines about every bit of evidence that had led us to consider that Pete Delaney might be a hit man.

Except it didn't happen. Instead of walking over to the pantry to get a tea bag, I discovered myself upstairs, standing in the middle of my office empty-handed. Lulu was making anticipatory woofing sounds waiting for me to sit on the recliner so she could nestle beside me. "Shush!" I snapped. She looked at me aghast, as if asking: *Does this mean we're breaking up?* I picked up a cover letter from some publisher in Cairo that began: "Was the Damascus Spring of 2000 truly a time of possibility or simply of self-delusion? *That Light in Malki* is the story of university student Liliane—"

I lacked the concentration even to finish the sentence. Instead of being energized by the

312

morning, by the positive ID of Pete as "John Cutler," man of a myriad of driver's licenses and possible hit man, I was as exhausted as I'd ever been in my life. The recognition that I might have been right from my first hunch seemed too much to take.

At last I summoned enough mind-foot coordination to make it down the hall into our bedroom. That's where I woke up about forty-five minutes later, covered by a throw my mother had made during the 2015 Margo Weber knitting marathon. It was a soft, white wool—cable stitched like a fisherman's sweater. Either it was really creative, or she had never learned to make sleeves.

Apparently Lulu had forgiven me since, as I opened my eyes, she was lying across Josh's pillow gazing at me benevolently. I picked her up, making sure there were no signs of doggie butt hair on the pillowcase, and did the hug/scratch under the chin business.

I picked up the throw. "Fold it like a fan, but casually, then lay it diagonally," Wynne had explained, "over the foot of the bed." That gave me the idea to call her about the hit. A guy in Texas who played "Smack My Bitch Up" once too often had been shot. Galveston Island was a big place for weekend homes for some of Houston's rich. And if anyone knew where the rich rested from being rich, it was Wynne.

"Of course I have clients in Houston," she said.

"When I designed closets for a couple of them, it wasn't only leaving room for six-inch megaheels on the shoe shelves. There had to be separate shelves for cowboy boots. Two different clients down there who in no way could know each other but both demanded 'cowboy chic.' Blessedly, they were in the minority."

"And the majority?" I asked politely.

"Most down there are just looking for a persona that will come across as chic or refined. Whatever. But not New Yorkish, which for women means—"

I knew she was going to say, "they don't want to wear all black," so I cut her off. "Do any of them have weekend homes on Galveston Island?" I asked.

"I think, yes, one of them does. But she and her husband bought it before she became a client. For some reason she accepted it as part of her divorce settlement."

"Does she go there a lot?"

"No, she bought another house on some other island. Galveston sounds kind of Westhamptonish, except it has the world's largest roller coaster. Or water coaster. She wanted me to redo her place completely, mostly for rental, but when she started talking about fabrics that could stand up to wet, sandy clothes, I passed." Wynne paused for a second, then asked, "Why are we talking about this?"

"Pete Delaney."

"He has a house down there?"

"No, but I was doing a little investigating, on my own and with my dad."

"Oh my God, you pried your dad out of the apartment?" We did a few minutes on whether having a crime to look into was the leverage that got him moving or if he just went along because he was a great father, sensing I needed either his companionship or his help. Then a few more minutes on how Wynne's dad was not a great father, unless you considered the semiannual query *How's my princess today?* a relationship. To my surprise, it was Wynne who steered the conversation back to Pete. "So you think Pete committed some crime on Galveston Island?"

"Yeah," I said. "Some crime. Like homicide."

"No shit!"

"Some Houston guy bought a vacation house on a canal and spent long weekends and also two weeks here, three weeks there totally blasting techno or rave. I'm not up on the genre. Driving the neighbors crazy. They called the cops, took him to court, all that. Nothing worked. Then one weekend the guy was out on his deck, leaning on the railing. The decks are high up because the houses are built on stilts. To keep out the water. Anyway, he's leaning out over the canal looking toward the Gulf and he was shot twice, with a hunting rifle. And check this out: The hit didn't come from some crazed neighbor, or at least it didn't come from another house. It came from the water. Two great shots: got him in the head and chest. Because of the angle of the bullets, the cops think it was someone in a boat."

"So what are you saying?" Wynne asked. "That Pete Delaney from Long Island is, like, an assassin who can shoot a rifle?"

"That's what I'm saying. I tracked down a guy who runs a shooting range up in Westchester who'd seen him. Said Pete was an incredible shot. Expert level."

"I cannot believe you did that!"

"I did."

"But why would people down there call in Pete? Nine-tenths of Texans have guns. Why hire a killer from New York?"

"Mostly because he wasn't local talent, someone who might be known to the cops and could be tracked down and questioned. The Yellow Pages don't have a Hit Man section. So if you're going to hire someone like that, you make inquiries, do super-discreet due diligence, and hire the best person for the job. Ultimately, it doesn't matter if an assassin comes from Dallas or the Bronx."

Wynne exhaled. Then she said, "So what are you going to do now?"

"In an ideal universe? Buy two plane tickets and go with you to Texas."

I never lied to Josh. However, since normal marital exchanges do not occur under oath, there is no obligation to tell husbands the whole truth. So I explained to him that I was going to Houston and then Galveston Island with Wynne for two or three days: She had a client down there. We'd spend a few hours with the client, then ditch her and drive to her vacation house. I'd help Wynne take measurements, then we'd relax, run on the beach, catch up.

Eliza tried not to look overly enthusiastic, but plainly couldn't wait until I wasn't around to stop her from streaming five episodes of *Gossip Girl* a day. Josh nodded and offered a reflexive smile but didn't look thrilled. I hoped he'd realize that it was in fact difficult and annoying to be the spouse left behind—and that he'd rethink his plans to go to New Orleans for three months for that trial. I told him, "Hey, it's two or three days. I'm coming back."

Josh got what I was saying. Good. "Of course," he said, though I wouldn't have called his tone magnanimous. "Relax. Enjoy yourself."

"You'll hate Kaylee's condo," Wynne told me as we hiked through the Houston airport.

"I've never hated anything you've done. Some-times it's just not my taste, but it's always—"

"You'll detest it. She wanted an urbane all-white look. Of course I told her sorry, I couldn't do it. Especially for her, since she's looking to start a new social life. Total white can be off-putting, especially to men. It signals 'No ketchup' or something they're afraid of."

"Uh-huh."

"Also, it screams nineties. So we settled on white and gold . . . beige, really. At least I talked her into wood floors, not fucking marble. Even with that, it still looks like the tomb of the unknown set designer. Whoever did *The Fountainhead*. Except for the art, which I told her had to have color, because if she bought some white-on-white Rauschenbergesque thing, truly urbane people would know in two seconds she wasn't urbane, which is a hugely emotionally loaded word for her. By the way, she only serves white wine or vodka and San Pellegrino, so don't ask for a Diet Coke."

Wynne was right; I didn't like Kaylee Collier's apartment, though the furniture was probably prime deco or midcentury. A humongous crystal urn on a giant table held an acre's' worth of long-stemmed white flowers in the entrance foyer. Elegant stuff, but since her place took up the entire twenty-fourth floor of the building, I couldn't stop thinking: *Too much space, too much money.* A couch was so far from a pair of chairs that, except for its whiteness, the place had the feel of a Ritz-Carlton lobby.

Nevertheless, through the floor-to-ceiling windows, the view of Houston and beyond was beautiful—especially just before dusk. A sapphire sky was painted with such thick pink and gold you could almost see the brushstrokes. Kaylee herself was a teeny woman with a light Texas drawl and the chatter of an intelligent woman who went to New York and London and saw all the Noël Coward revivals.

Wynne had acceded to an all-white wardrobe except for shoes and handbags, so Kaylee was wearing fitted white pants and something that looked like a man's tuxedo shirt, though tailored for her minuscule frame. Her short, seven-tones-of-blonde hairstyle was clipped yet full, as if she'd repurposed the hem of a sable coat. Despite the city's humidity and some pricey spray gloss, it looked dry.

"I can't thank you enough for accommodating me," she said effusively to Wynne. "Agreeing to refurb the cottage." She was drinking gin and something; a cucumber spear was stuck in the glass. I went with white wine and dipped a couple of jicama sticks into a bowl of paleness that I guessed was mayo and white pepper, though the chair was far enough from the coffee table that both the stretch and the dip were barely worth the effort. "My financial planner?" Kaylee was saying. "She says it's not time to sell the Galveston beach house. But renting is a prudent option. So I'm very grateful—"

I was even more grateful to Wynne for taking a job she deeply didn't want solely for my sake. It's one thing to have a friend say, *I'm always there for you.* It's quite another for her to have to face the necessity of using all-weather fabrics.

"No problem," Wynne told her. "I hated leaving you in the lurch, with you not being able to rent the place." Blatant lie. "Anyway, since Corie and I needed a couple of days just to unwind and catch up with each other, I thought, 'Well, why not relax on Galveston Island?' That way I can drop by your house, get the measurements. I never leave that to anyone else. And we can take some nice walks on the beach."

"Can you consider blue and white?" Kaylee asked hopefully. "Even *I* know all white might not be practical for a rental."

I tuned them out for a few minutes and looked outside through the wall of windows. I could have been in a rich person's apartment in so many cities in the world, looking out on the skyline of condos and modern commercial buildings and past that an unvegetated plain that probably kept going until the next city.

"Let me get a feel for Galveston first." Wynne sounded surprisingly mellow, but not only was she well into her second vodka, she also seemed to recognize that Kaylee's fragility went beyond her size, teeny wardrobe, and delicate face. "Blue and white says New England to me, but I'll keep an open mind. For all I know maybe Galveston Island screams blue and white."

"I know you, Wynne! You'll do whatever your heart desires and you'll convince me it's perfect. Of course it'll be wonderful, but just promise me, no orange, not even a touch."

Wynne did her version of a Mona Lisa smile, enigmatic, with . . . could it be a hint of coldness? As in: *If you want warmth you won't question anything I do.* I'd watched her practice then polish that expression during our three years of middle school. Having seen "mysterious smile" as a work in progress, I wasn't disturbed by it. However, Wynne did it with great success on clients and men. Kaylee stopped her chatter for an instant, which was when I jumped in: "Didn't I see some news report about a murder on Galveston Island? Some guy who was playing super-loud hip-hop music?"

"Was there ever!" Kaylee said. She lifted the cucumber spear from her glass, knocked off whatever gin droplets were left, and pointed it at me. "There was this guy from Houston. Now you have got to keep in mind that not counting vacationers and renters more than half the island are Houstonians. Or is it 'is Houstonians'? But not a single one of the people I knew ever talked to him!" I nodded and let my jaw drop as if taken aback at the victim's anonymity. "And when he was looking for a place? He told the broker his business was digging wells, and she thought, *Now isn't that modest of him?* He told her his top was a million five, which she thought was kind of chintzy, but he said he was flexible, kind of hinting money was no object. Turns out the place he bought was around seven hundred thousand. And three guesses what kind of wells he dug?" There was no need to guess because she said, "*Water* wells!"

I knew all this because I'd read about it and watched the TV coverage on YouTube, most of it local stuff. But I gave her a "Wow!" and asked if she'd ever seen the guy.

"No. He lived on a different part of the island. Big boating area. Well, everyplace there is, but he had a canal house and they're pretty much close together. Which is why his music, if you call it music, was like a nightmare having a nightmare." She seemed gratified by that last phrase, and I smiled urbane approval.

Anything I could do to keep her talking. Obviously I had an extreme need to know, but I had also gathered that once Kaylee got started, we were in for a good story. Not in the sense that she would make it up: more like she valued creating a compelling narrative for guests. Especially us, who, being with-it New Yorkers, might expect a raconteur. Wynne, of course, was the real deal, la crème des cosmopolites—stylist to the stylish. Though I was clearly congenitally immune to chic, Wynne had hyped me to Kaylee as her lifelong friend and "*the* go-to authority on modern Arabic literature." That description was as far from the truth as Houston was from Abu Dhabi, but it may have made me seem more intriguing than someone from Long Island with a home office who was wearing flats with a flower print.

Wynne was fine with playing the investigatory role I'd assigned her: curious onlooker. I told her she could ask any question that occurred to her. However, no matter the provocation, I warned her not to display her bored, *I wish I were in Positano* look: "Seem fascinated," I'd instructed her on the plane.

"So what was the victim's name?" Wynne asked Kaylee, fascinated. "How old was he? Come on, give us all the details."

I pressed the button on the mic clipped to my bra. The voice recorders on cell phones were fairly good, but not at a distance. I was far enough away from Kaylee, curled up in a corner of the couch, that we practically needed to yodel to each other. Wynne had told me the condo was "spacious," but that was—a rarity for her—an understatement. Still, I'd come prepared to record, in case Kaylee reeled off a bunch of names or threw in an address or two.

"Let's see," she said. "His name was Trevor Schwarz. Without the *t*. All the media accounts made a major thing about him just having thrown himself a giganto huge thirty-fifth-birthday party in Houston. Kind of strange, you know? Because everybody I know on the Island made the point that he was a loner. No one came by his place ever, according to my friend Lennie."

"Is that girl Lennie or boy Lenny?" I asked. As long as witnesses or locals don't go too far astray, I always let them wander wherever they choose to, with me picking up info along the way. If they get negative feedback when you're interrogating them—blinking eyes, nostrils dilating from stifled yawns—they catch on fast that you think that they are less than scintillating. They feel insulted. But when you question them energetically, it reinforces their belief that their ideas are worthy of attention and they feel comfortable enough to let their guard down.

"Lennie's a girl," she said. "It's really Lenore." I kept my eyes on her, as if eager for more. "Lenore Lynch. She wears two diamond *L*'s on a platinum chain. Different diamond *L*'s, not two of the same kind."

Kaylee turned toward Wynne, who was in good behavior mode. Wynne simply said, "Well, that's her signature." She sounded perfectly pleasant, which I knew took effort.

"Does Lennie live on Trevor's street? Or

canal?" I asked. "I mean, because she knew nobody ever dropped over to his place."

"Yes! Across the canal and down three houses. But it's not like Venice. There are roads in front of the houses."

"So she must have been driven crazy by the guy's music." I really wanted to talk to this Lennie.

"Was she ever!" Kaylee uncurled herself and sat straight on the couch, slipping back into a pair of mustard-colored slides with thick, very high heels. Her feet looked far better moisturized than her hair. "And her husband went stark raving mad from the noise. Not just that. They have two girls, teenagers, and with those lyrics? Beyond filthy! But everybody was in the same boat, so to speak. All the neighbors. You couldn't hear yourself think. If you wanted to rent your place for like a month or two during the summer—that can practically pay for the whole year—people would come to look, get an earful, and of course never come back."

"What did the cops say?" Wynne asked. "I assume she or her husband called the police."

"They came so many times. Told them he could play it only till ten thirty p.m. and only just so long as it couldn't be heard some number of feet beyond his house. They said it was much, much too loud and went into his house and told him to lower it. So he did, right? And they drove away and guess what happened ten minutes later?" Wynne and I nodded: we knew. "Well, this went on for months and months, and getting them to actually enforce the noise ordinance was a huge deal. So there's a community association and they took him to court. They all had to chip in to hire a lawyer from some Houston firm, someone who specializes . . . I guess it's terrible neighbors law. And this Trevor got himself his own lawyer, someone who specializes in, I don't know, individual rights or something."

"So two lawyers fighting what sounds essentially like two different cases," I said. "Did it drag on and on?" I knew it had.

"Months and months, maybe even a year," Kaylee said. "I'm not sure because I was so busy with my divorce and then moving, and I really had no great desire to go back down there even though I got it in the settlement. The minute I open the door of that house? Bad karma. All my ex wanted to do was get up at four in the morning and go fishing and come home late at night. Loneliness vibes."

"I can imagine," I said. "Besides Lennie, did you know anyone else in that community association?"

"Well, lots of folks, but not real well. Oh, wait. Come to think of it, we were friends with Janet and Billy Gregson. An older couple, but lots of fun, full of crazy stories, great bridge players. But after the divorce . . . you know. The ex-wife is like a fifth wheel. Actually, Billy was one of the organizers who got the community association moving on this. If they hadn't . . . ?"

Who knew? Maybe Trevor Schwarz might still be blasting music out over the Gulf of Mexico.

There was no way we could get out of having dinner with Kaylee, though her choice of a sushi restaurant made Wynne and me exchange a glance of the deep concern that New Yorkers feel when eating in a city that is not San Francisco, Paris, Tokyo—or possibly LA (though mostly for salads). While I couldn't speak for Wynne, I envisioned fish marinating for generations, swimming in the petrochemical soup of some Gulf tributary. Kaylee must have picked up our apprehension because, as we went down in the elevator, she mentioned the seafood was flown in every day from Japan.

Actually, the restaurant was fabulous, and I was awed not only by Kaylee's dexterity with chopsticks, but also by her ability to use copious amounts of soy sauce and get none on the pleated front of her white shirt. She was good company, announcing before we even got the menus that she would not be one of those bitter types who consume an evening talking about their divorces.

I gave my usual (brief) response to her inevitable "Tell me about Arabic literature," while Wynne picked up the origins of Roy Lichtenstein's art and graphic novels.

As subtly as I could, I steered the conversation toward Galveston Island. Kaylee offered a keen sense of the sociology and geography of the place, being one of those people who are both socially and visually aware. Also, she had that southern quirk of mentioning names. Not name-dropping—as in: *As I was telling Shonda Rhimes the other night*—but saying, "Aaron Meadows, who's the go-to guy for renting boats." So I got some good leads by telling her I was thinking of going duck hunting while Wynne did her usual house snooping; Kaylee even gave me the phone number of a friend of hers, Lindy Osterman, a woman born and raised on the Island. She was sure Lindy would be "totally thrilled" to take me shooting.

By ten the following morning, I was holding a tape measure in a corner of an egg-yolk-yellow kitchen on Galveston Island, an indication of Kaylee's aesthetic before she'd become "white woman." The blue gingham curtains on the big window over the sink were sagging with the weight of salt air and seawater that had crept into the long-unoccupied house.

"Shooting ducks out of the sky!" Wynne said. She climbed up on the counter near the sink to measure the window. "You are appalling."

"It's not like there's a lineup of blindfolded

ducks with their wings tied behind their back and you go"—I made a plosive sound between a *pop* and a *boom,* the closest I could get to rifle fire— "it's duck *hunting,* not a firing squad."

When I was living in DC, I'd gone with a few people from work to the Eastern Shore of Maryland for a weekend. A couple of them were into hunting. I imagined being good enough at it not to humiliate myself and being complimented with: *Never thought a kid from Queens could get off such a shot.* But when I got a wild duck in the sight, it made me queasy. I couldn't pull the trigger. I had no doubt I could have blown away a terrorist, but this didn't feel like a fair fight. So I hunkered down near the shore in jeans wet from walking through marshes and tried to be one with nature.

"Killing ducks is still killing," Wynne said.

"Then ordering roast duck at Rotisserie Georgette makes you a fucking accomplice."

She rolled her eyes, which was what she always did when temporarily flummoxed.

"Let's get moving on measuring this dining room so I can get started asking questions."

We finished about ten minutes later and Wynne went off to check in at our hotel, abiding by her rule never to stay at a client's house. That was fine with me as the place was permeated with the aroma of incipient mildew. Apparently Kaylee's dehumidifier had given up trying.

My first stop was the marina where Aaron Meadows, boat renter extraordinaire, had his business. I'd imagined a tall Texan, but he was a squat guy with an abundance of red arm hair who looked overheated, as if he were wearing a woolly sweater under his T-shirt. His face was flushed. Thin streams of sweat meandered down his temples and cheeks, but that seemed to be because he was schlepping a giant cooler up the ladder from a boat.

I gave him a business card and told him I was looking for a guy who'd rented a boat that could be easily navigated through the channels without making too much noise. I patted myself on the back for thinking to get business cards printed up before I left, since it was unwise to introduce myself by a name known to Pete Delaney. On the card, I chose a forgettable name: Jane Miller, Investigations. I paid extra for an embossed insignia that looked vaguely law enforcementish.

"What's this about?" he asked.

I didn't need to tell him it was about the murder of Trevor Schwarz, because it could easily get back to the island's police. I didn't want to risk being questioned while still down there since I had zero credentials other than my phony business cards. So as I took out Pete Delaney's picture from my handbag, I let my smile fade and simply said, "He may be involved in some nasty business."

Aaron did a few variations on "Hmmm," scratched his clean-shaven cheek, and said, "Hard to say. Doesn't look like much, does he?"

"No, that's one of his strengths. His forgettable-ness." I went through the "imagine" business: imagine the man in the photo in a mustache, beard, toupee, hat. Aaron Meadows seemed like a naturally nice guy, not just pleasant for business, so he appeared to consider each possible disguise.

"Can't say," he told me. "Don't remember him, but on the other hand, he doesn't look *un*familiar. Sorry, wish I could help you more."

Since he offered, I gave him the date in March when Trevor Schwarz played his last song. We walked into the air-conditioned shack that was his office and he checked the rental records on his computer. Years earlier, when I'd been at Quantico, I learned not to be afraid to push my luck when it came to questioning: the worst someone will do is stop answering and then you push some more. So I asked him to print out his record for that day along with the two days before and after, which he did without a peep. He even stapled the pages together for me.

"How easy is it to steal someone's boat?" I asked. "I mean, do people ever leave their keys inside?"

"Now and then, not often. But you have to get into their house, either break in or have a key, in order to get downstairs for access to the dock where their boat is. Or you need a boat to get to the particular canal."

"And for that he'd need an accomplice. We're not ruling anything out," I said, as if I were working for some great investigative institution. "But he seems to be someone who works alone. Anyway, thanks. If I have any other questions, can I give you a call?"

"No problem," he said.

"And if anything occurs to you—"

"I'll give you a call, Janie," he said.

# 18

Wynne texted: *U ok?* And I sent her the message: *Fine U?* and agreed to meet at the hotel at six. That worked because my new bud Aaron, clearly having a slow day, offered to give me a boat tour. My mom, Margo—"Don't-ever-get-into-a-car-with-a-man-you-don't-know!"—Weber would have blanched, but I sensed his friendliness was just that and it was.

I waited till we passed a second inlet, then said, "Can we go up one of those canals? I heard the houses are really nice." (I'd seen them, too; before I left Long Island I spent an hour on Google Earth and real estate websites looking at the neighborhood, especially the crime scene house, from different angles.)

So while his tour didn't include: *And on the left you have the house where Trevor Schwarz was brutally shot twice,* I got a good feel for the homes and waterways. I asked him to slow down as we passed the one house I was almost positive was it. Sure enough, the sound of a boat's motor churning at that lower speed would not likely be heard over blasting music. If Trevor had been gazing out toward the Gulf, he would not have heard the noise below in the water. From the autopsy report: the bullet entry over his temple and the damage to the muscles of his neck from his head's jolt backward indicated his head had been turned, so he wouldn't have seen or heard the sound of the boat carrying his killer.

All in all, a useful jaunt. I also learned that Aaron was going to propose to his girlfriend, Amber, by putting his gran's diamond ring on top of a coconut cupcake. Also that he'd served in Afghanistan. He asked what my husband did and when I told him he was a computer technician, he laughed and said, "That was a smart move."

Passing on lunch with him, I drove a couple of miles in the car I'd rented at the airport and grabbed a chicken fajita taco and a strawberry milk shake at a fast-food place: my dream lunch, during which I mapped out my strategy for the afternoon.

Would I be running a risk if I dropped by Lennie Lynch's? What if Kaylee, reminded of Lennie's existence, called her to catch up? If she happened to mention the Trevor Schwarz case, might she say: *My designer and her friend from Long Island were just talking about your neighbor's murder?*

It was supremely unlikely, as was the notion that Lennie herself (with her two diamond *L*'s) had chaired the neighborhood association's hit man hiring committee. Still, what might she do, worst-case scenario, if I dropped by to question her? Maybe get word to Pete: *Someone from New York or Long Island was down here asking questions about the Trevor business. In her thirties, blondish-brownish hair, blue eyes.*

However unlikely, I couldn't risk that. I drove to Purple Sage Drive, where Lennie (and once Trevor) lived, but decided against talking to Lennie. Trevor's stilt house, smaller than most on the street, was khaki colored with an excess of white trim; maybe the contractor had fancy brackets and gable ornaments left over from remodeling a Victorian. It didn't shout Texas. The FOR SALE signs flanking the path leading to his front door looked weathered.

I parked down the street in front of a gray house that looked unoccupied. In fact, a fair number of houses looked unoccupied; maybe people came down for weekends and it was so empty because this was only Thursday. (I'd missed lunch at La Cuisine Délicieuse the day before, emailing Iris I'd be in Miami at an Islamic arts festival—which was actually going on down there.) If I returned with the backs of my hands dark, at least it would seem reasonable.

From Purple Sage, I walked along the street side of the canal houses until I turned a corner to Red Yucca Road. Galveston Island wasn't a spot for suburban strolls; besides the heat, the air felt more solid than gaseous: no breezes off the Gulf that day. But the still air did have an appealing perfume, as if a truck came by each week to spray the neighborhood with a blend of manly sweat and salty Gulf mist—included in the homeowners' association fees. I had a brief yet-another-life-choice fantasy, where I lived a few canals over at a marina on a boat with two dogs. Most nights I met my buds at our favorite bar where "This Is How We Roll" always seemed to be playing.

I was the only person out walking. How comforting it would be if, along with a car at Avis, you could rent a dog. That way, I'd look as if I had a purpose. Also, I really missed Lulu.

The houses were more tightly packed on Red Yucca Road than on Purple Sage, separated only by a median grass strip—about as wide as the narrowest driveway in Queens. By strolling up a couple of the strips to orient myself vis-à-vis the backs of the houses right across the canal, I wound up directly across from the rear of Trevor's house. A long white deck ran the length of the second floor. Beneath that level was a porch area enclosed by the stilts, and within the porch, the rear of the house's smaller first story. That was basically an entrance room where visitors could come in from the front door, then head upstairs.

From where I stood in the back, I was just a few feet from a boat slip directly off the canal.

There was some formidable lifting equipment

above the slip, and a boat had been hoisted up from the water. It dwelled there, about six feet overhead, and was wrapped in a blue tarpaulin. Okay, maybe it was eight or ten feet high. I was always bad at judging distances and feared one day another agent would yell to me: *He's right there, twenty yards away and aiming at you!* And I'd have no clue how far twenty yards was.

I could see that if a resident on Trevor's side of the canal had dared to brave the decibels and venture onto her back deck that evening in March, she'd be assaulted not only by the Schwarz sound system, but by the sight of the music man himself, leaning over his railing. If any others had been standing on their decks that night and turned left or right to glower at Casa Schwarz, they might have seen him get blasted into the canal. But more likely, any witnesses would be the residents of the houses across the water, on Red Yucca, which I thought was an unpleasant choice for a name.

I didn't want to hang there too long, even though between my training and my mom's mini demonstrations of the actor's craft, I had a good sense of how not to stick out like a sore thumb. Not quite the female equivalent of Pete's blah forgettableness, but close. I'd worn army-green cropped pants on the drive from Houston to Galveston. After the boat ride with Aaron, I'd taken off my shirt and stuffed it into my bag.

Now my outfit was a white tank top I'd worn under the shirt and a Houston Astros baseball cap that I'd bought at the airport in the hope we'd be able to rent a convertible. We hadn't been.

Trevor Schwarz's neighbors were next on my to-do list. I strolled from a grass median near the canal back to the walk alongside the water. Although it was difficult to see through the dark mesh screens with wire backing—probably some kind of hurricane protection—the boats were hanging high above the slips at the first two houses. There was no sound or light coming from inside. Sure enough, no one was home at either.

Just to be sure, I logged on to a commercial database the bureau used and got the landline numbers for the houses. No answers. Maybe I'd have better luck at the third.

Walking down a median from the canal side to the street side, I could hear a woman's voice. I yanked off the cap, pulled my shirt out of my shoulder bag (which was practically the size of a studio apartment), and fluffed out my hair. The front door was open. Through the screen door, I could peek in. Happily, HGTV had won the builder's heart. The design was open concept. In the kitchen was a woman who looked to be in her early thirties pouring something into a tall glass. According to the database, the owner was Alicia Rendón. Her outfit was shorts and a T, but stylishly dress-down, more lunch on the terrace of a Gulf-view restaurant than washing the car.

Alicia, or whoever she was, had on earbuds and was talking on her phone in Spanish about how Mike never really cared about anyone else's emotional state, though he claimed he did. I rang the doorbell. It just went *Ding-dong,* a disappointment. I'd been half hoping for something Tex or Mex like "The Yellow Rose of Texas" or "Bésame Mucho."

The woman came to the door sipping what looked like iced herbal tea. When I said, "Sorry to disturb you" in Spanish, she immediately switched to English, as most bilingual people did. Sami said that although that seemed an act of generosity, to help me out of my misery, it was a self-defense tactic against my terrible accent. (He pretty much said the same about my Arabic.)

"No problem," she said, though she didn't unlock the screen door. She was short and sort of median, but more toward pudgy than lean. Despite her height, you'd pick her for your softball team.

I explained how I'd been asked to do some background checking on what the neighbors had gone through before what happened to Trevor Schwarz. I didn't say "murder of" since it seemed lacking in politesse. I took out one of my Jane cards and held it up for her to see as I said, "I've been talking to a lot of people on Galveston Island, especially in this area." I found myself gazing longingly at her herbal tea, a pretty pink, with ice cubes of remarkable clarity. This was not Method acting, evoking past dehydration. I was thirsty. I looked back into her eyes and said, "I know it's not the most pleasant conversation, but if you could just give me five minutes, I'd be grateful."

Two minutes later I had my own iced tea— strawberry basil—and was sitting on the modular couch in Ali Rendón's living room. Since it would be expected, I took out a small pad and pen: when you want to keep a potential witness at ease, you don't take notes on a device, as it has a permanence that makes people feel anything from apprehension to panic.

"Are you with the police?" she asked.

"No. I have a law enforcement background, but I'm just looking into the case because there seem to be some issues with Mr. Schwarz's estate."

"He was pretty young," she said.

"Thirty-five," I said. I went through the pre-liminaries. Ali had bought her house two years earlier. It turned out she was a young-looking forty-four, divorced, no kids, and lived in Houston. She'd bought the requisite powerboat and had developed a new social life with local fisherfolk and weekenders. She had a doctorate in health services research from Texas A&M and worked for a large insurance company.

"It's good that I love to get out on the water,"

she said. "Because if I wanted to hang here twenty-four/seven, once that Trevor moved in, I would've gone out of my mind."

"That loud?" I asked.

"Would you believe, louder than that? And his sound equipment had a bass thing. I don't know what you call it, but even if you wore earplugs, your internal organs got to pulsating. Stressful beyond belief."

"Did you ever meet him?"

"No. I lived across the canal, and unless you're into some local social network, you just kind of wave to each other if you happen to walk out on your deck at the same time."

Since I was supposedly inquiring about Trevor Schwarz's estate, I asked a bunch of questions about his source of income, whether there was any conspicuous consumption—even like having a superexpensive boat. She said no, and in fact the only talk about him was the noise his music made. It would start in the late morning and continue well into the night.

"I spoke to an otolaryngologist at Houston Methodist, and he said playing music at that volume can cause noise-induced hearing loss, which is what I suspected. He also said it was possible that Trevor was deaf, or close to it, and we all felt that we were getting there. Anyway, it was an assault. So many of us! We bought these great houses, wanted to have friends visit, and we wound up going other places just to get away."

"And the police? Local governing authorities?" I asked.

"It's not that they didn't try, but let's just say they weren't all that effectual. It was like that old hot-potato game, where one tosses it to the other. Cops, county noise abatement, Galveston powers that be. Sometimes he did stop for a couple of weeks, but then?"

"Did the neighbors get together to make some organized effort to stop him?"

"I mean, I wasn't that involved. I gave them a check for . . . I think it was eight hundred dollars. To hire a lawyer, do whatever to shut him down. We all chipped in the same amount."

"Do you know who was in charge of the effort?"

"Two men. Billy Something. Gregory? Seemed nice enough. In his sixties. From Houston. I heard something about old money and he looks it. You know how they used to talk about women in Dallas having big hair? Well, Billy has this head of white hair that looks six inches deep. Looks like he could play a rich oilman on TV. The other man was much younger, probably around Trevor's age, but with a family. Chester McFarland. Everyone calls him Chet. Seems easygoing, but I noticed his nails bitten down to the quick. That's no wonder: We were all under assault. It was like having someone with a jackhammer move in next door, except worse because jackhammers don't make disgusting misogynistic comments. Trevor's music did."

"Just out of curiosity," I asked, "do you think it's possible that one of the neighbors went over the edge? Shot him?"

"Funny, when I heard about it, that was the first thing I thought," Ali said. "But you see, you probably know more than I do. Because you're looking into his finances and all." She would have made a good special agent. Smart, assertive: most people wouldn't be so direct. Ali went on: "Was there anything going on in the financial area where someone might've had reason to do something like that?" Good investigative instincts, unless, of course, she'd been the one in the boat with a rifle or had hired a hit man and was looking to see what, if anything, I'd detected.

I said, "You've been so nice and helpful. I wish I could tell you."

"Confidentiality," she said. I nodded. "I know I should say I hope he rests in peace, but do you want to know the honest truth?"

"Sure."

"No me importa."

The Billy Gregory whom Ali had referred to as one of the heads of the anti-Trevor movement turned out to be Billy Gregson, half of the older,

343

fun, bridge-playing couple Kaylee had mentioned the night before.

He didn't look like fun to me. He himself was stereotypically Texas size, way over six feet with a major belly that was testing the resilience of his red Henley shirt. His big white hair (with its pompadour) was stiff and oddly glossy. Any normal person (as I considered myself, perhaps erroneously) would not instantly loathe a seventyish guy based on the fact that his hair really looked not like hair at all but rather like a meringue wig. A normal person wouldn't hold it against Billy that before three in the afternoon, he came to the door unsteadily on bare feet (with one big toenail shrieking for fungicide, which didn't add to his appeal), slurping what seemed to be almost a half pint of bourbon on the rocks. It smelled like a quality bourbon. But I detested him the moment he opened the door, exhaled down into my face, looked me up and down, then up again, and demanded, "What can I do for you, honey?" without even a leering smile.

I handed him my Jane card, and began, "Hi. I'm here to—"

He cut me off. "What the hell does that mean," he said, looking from the card to me. "Investigations?" Before I could even get out a word, he demanded, "Who do you work for? Who are you investigating?"

I smiled my pleasant smile that indicated

his question was entirely reasonable. Actually, it was. Whereas Ali Rendón had accepted my explanation that I was looking into some matter concerning Trevor Schwarz's estate, Billy Gregson had many questions, although he seemed intent on not letting me answer.

Finally, I managed to get out some of the details of the narrative I'd constructed: I was a freelance investigator with law enforcement background, hired by the large Houston law firm Norton Rose Fulbright. Some issues with the estate of Trevor Schwarz. "Trevor Schwarz" had a decidedly negative impact on Billy, but "Norton Rose Fulbright" had the effect of a Beethoven violin sonata. His color faded from red outrage to more of a cerise inebriation.

"Houston office?"

"Yes," I said.

"Who do you deal with there?" he asked. I was getting a little edgy thinking that Billy might have an intimate knowledge of the law firm. I had done my own due diligence to create my legend, but I was afraid he might do his and call to check up on me.

"Sean Itzkowitz." I'd picked an actual person from the firm's website. "He's in Trusts and Estates."

Billy nodded once, then did not pick up his head. For a moment it looked as if he either had died standing up or was praying to Itzkowitz.

Finally, he opened the door wider and said, "Come on in, honeybunch."

I followed him upstairs to the main part of the house. After declining his offer of "a little something," by which I hoped he meant a drink, we sat in the living room on some white plastic chairs with turquoise plaid cushions. There was some newish upholstery on the chairs, but the couch, the walls, and even the plantation shutters had the look of an old photo from which the color had seeped out over the years. So while it was possible they were going for a retro-chic style, my guess was the Gregsons had bought their furniture in the seventies.

Before Billy could start interrogating me again, I launched into a series of questions the bureau taught us to use at the start of a net worth investigation. This was definitely not my area of expertise, but every time he answered, I'd say, "Uh-huh" or "I see," conveying a measure of gratitude, as if he was making my inquiry easier.

Still, the more the bourbon level in his glass dropped—and it dropped quickly—the less easy he was to interview. He stopped between my question and his answer. From the floaty appearance of his eyes, he was not being evasive. Just taking a quick trip to another mental state. Switching from the two-syllable "honey" to "hon" was significant only in that it required less effort, and soon he was dropping the *o* and the *n* and I was "hhh." When he started shifting his balls around, I knew I had to move the interview along.

His sense of time was probably more out of whack than his testes, so it didn't occur to him that I'd spent only about five minutes on the Trevor Schwarz estate topic, my ostensible reason for being there. When Billy had opened the door, it was clear he was buzzed. After a couple of moments of obnoxiousness, he'd let me in. But he'd gone from sipping to glugging fast—as I quickly progressed from an annoyance to a possible diversion on a dull afternoon to someone asking the wrong kind of questions to someone female and therefore seducible.

"Let's move on," I said.

He touched his white hair tenderly, as if he were concerned his meringue might be deflating. "Can't we just talk?" he asked.

"Sure," I lied, and with enthusiasm. "Just a couple more items I'm obliged to bring up. You know how it is." He raised his glass to me in a semisalute: *Got it. Go ahead.* "I've heard you're one of the leading citizens in this area. Someone whose judgment people trust." I liked not having to deal with false modesty: Billy nodded vigorously so I quickly moved on: "When all this horrible business with Trevor's so-called music couldn't be stopped by the local authorities, your neighbors came to you solve the matter."

"Legal action," Billy said. "I went with the best and the brightest." He grunted in a way that could best be translated as *bitter irony.* "Fucking loser."

"Did . . . I'm trying to remember his name . . . Chet something. Did he work with you in the lawsuit?" Since he didn't chime in with the last name, I decided to remember it. "Chet McFarland."

"He came in after. He's okay. Corporate troubleshooter type. Troubleshooter, ha-ha-ha. Went from Enron to some other places to Arkema. Doesn't that say something?" Even Billy could tell I looked blank, so he added: "Arkema. The giant chemical fire."

"Right. Of course."

"So after I go through this whole goddamn lawsuit, the association's board tells me, 'Maybe Chet can help.' Like he's a genius and they're just making a suggestion. Truth is, Chet doesn't know his ass from a hole in the ground."

"That can be rough," I said. "Having to work with someone like that."

"Rough doesn't begin to cut it." He said it as if Chet had been not merely difficult but insufferable.

I waited for a few seconds and then asked: "So what did Chet decide to do?" In spite of all the humidity, my throat was dry and my mouth and teeth felt coated with something chalky. No answer. He was thinking: I sensed my question had triggered a degree of sobriety. Though his belly got in the way, Billy bent forward. Suddenly, he banged down his glass. We both looked to see if it had shattered on the stone floor, but it hadn't.

"What the fuck are you getting at?" he boomed. Maybe yelled. At least he was off the "honey" business. I kept quiet, knowing he'd go on. "A little information about some estate issue, you say, but here you are asking me about fucking McFarland." His voice got even louder, as if there were no limits to his personal sound system. "You know what? That don't sit right with me. Know what I mean?"

Billy couldn't make it to the scary dude stage. True, his voice was loud, but not the human equivalent of Trevor's music. And when he tried to get up from his white plastic chair—basically the shape of a flour scoop—he was still drunk and bulky enough that even with his hands braced on its sloping sides, he couldn't rise on the first try. Or the second. Naturally, my being there to witness this only made him angrier. Even when not completely clear minded, he was aware I was some kind of threat. "Where are you going with this, me and Chet? Chet and me?" he barked.

Before he could try rising a third time, I pushed my voice to a deep register and projected. I did not yell, but Billy heard me very clearly: "You and Chet? Let me remind you that the federal murder-for-hire statute makes it illegal to travel or use facilities in interstate or foreign commerce."

Billy Gregson's watery brown eyes scrunched up small, to me a sign of someone desperate to think fast. Also, a tell of anger. He wanted me out, or maybe better, dead. Or just cowed. Whatever worked. But not before he knew what I knew. Yet I also saw that the lower part of his face lacked aggression. His chin flopped and appeared disconnected from the rest of his jaw. The tip of his tongue rested on his lower lip, a nonverbal definition of "dimwitted." Well, when someone aims the word "murder" at you, it can knock you senseless.

The longer we sat facing each other in those 1970s chairs, the more I realized Billy was not swift. Not dumb, because he had the brains to do well enough in business to maintain a second house and a boat. And though all I knew about the game of bridge was that sometimes the word "tournament" was attached to it, it was supposed to require an ability to strategize. But as far as analysis went, a definite nongenius. Also, either he'd forgotten he wanted to stand up and intimidate me or he knew he didn't have the energy to do it without much grunting and strain.

Finally he found some words: "Murder? What the fuck?" I didn't answer him. Another overlong period of silence, and then he said, "What kind of law are you talking about? *Interstate?* If you don't know, we're in Texas, and three guesses where that bastard died. Huh? Can you guess?" Just in case he had anything more, I kept my silence. "So why the fuck are you talking about federal?" I sensed he was looking for something to bang his fist on, but slamming even the most durable plastic doesn't make for a satisfyingly nerve-shattering sound. He'd already pounded his bourbon glass on the floor, so he was left with merely clenching his fists.

"Of course this is Texas," I said soothingly. "Unfortunately, the guy you hired to solve your Trevor Schwarz problem had to travel interstate to get the job done."

This was the part I'd hated most when I'd been at the bureau, watching a person's color grow sickly as he or she gets sick with the knowledge *I may be fucked.* In one minute, going from a normal life to knowing you'll never get back to what you were.

"Are you with the government?" he asked. "Saying you weren't, but you really are."

"I am not with the government."

"Like hell you aren't."

"Calm down, Billy."

"Mr. Gregson!"

"I like to think informality makes for easier conversation, Billy." Payback for *honey.* "Look, you did everything you could to get a satisfactory outcome. You dealt with officials, went to the trouble of hiring a lawyer. You put in maximum effort. I understand how tough it can be, working at your personal best. Your personal best always brings good results. Except this time, you wind up with your neighbors almost as angry at you as they are with Trevor."

He bent over and picked up his glass. His drink had paled and the ice cubes were reduced to chips floating on top. He looked at it sadly. In a perfect world, I would have gone to his refrigerator and discovered a couple of beers from some local brewery; they would turn out to be some perky summer ale that cooled both of us down, and we would talk things out.

I kept going. "And then they foisted Chet McFarland on you."

"Don't try the sympathy shit on me," he snapped.

"It's not sympathy. It's empathy. I'm not pitying you." I left "you dumb schmuck" unuttered. "I'm comprehending the situation you were in. All of a sudden, you're demoted to second in command and this so-called troubleshooter is in charge. Look, I don't know, maybe he did improve an ugly situation for Enron and that other company. But it seems to me that what he brought to the table was big-time trouble for you. You had no choice but to deal with it."

Billy shrugged. That could mean that while he

wasn't yet ready to talk, he might not be averse to my trying to pull it out of him. On the other hand, I had said the word "murder" in his living room; he had no idea who I really was, whom I represented. Ergo, I was a threat.

Threat. He set his feet wide apart, and with elbows out pushed down on the arms of the chair to stand. If he'd wanted to chat about homicide, he would have stayed seated. Besides taking all his energy, getting up made him grunt emphatically with the sound coming from deep in his chest, I suppose it could be best represented by UHHHH. Big deal, a major grunt. But it seemed to mortify him and thus make him even more incensed.

Even before he was up on his feet, I was standing. I moved around so I was facing him. For a second, his eyes darted to a long wooden thing—console or sideboard. I guessed that might be where he had his gun, one of his guns. He didn't look like a pepper spray kind of guy.

On the other hand, maybe he just wanted a chocolate-covered mint as an afternoon pick-me-up or to get rid of the taste of tooth tartar and booze. However, I voted gun.

"Forget about trying to get to your weapon," I said, catching his eyes as they moved back in my direction. "You'd probably miss. And if you didn't, what are you going to do with my dead body? For God's sake, Billy, you're not a killer.

Anyway, you wouldn't get near that console thing."

"Who's going to stop me?"

"Me." I was direct and calm. The edges of his mouth began to creep up, as if he was about to imitate an LOL emoji, but then they slipped back into place. "Okay? Let's de-escalate this thing. I can't imagine you personally killed Trevor. Who in this area didn't wish him dead? But it would take a troubleshooter, maybe someone like Chet, to make that wish come true."

Once again he eyed the console, but with only a longing glance. Then he demanded, "Are you crazy?" Responding to that, even with a no, would be proof of weakness. "Out of here! Now!"

I stayed in place, about three feet away from him. Maybe four. "Who made the call to the guy? Chet? Or did he delegate it—"

Billy didn't leap like a gazelle, but he sprang forward fast enough to grab my right forearm. His hand covered a lot of territory, from just above the wrist to halfway to my elbow. For someone so out of shape and closing in on senior citizen-ship, he still had a killer grip. Then, as if to prove this was not merely an overenthusiastic grab, his other hand clutched the upper part of my arm. He pushed it against my body for leverage as he began bending my lower arm up and backward. "Stupid twat," he said, very hoarsely.

Besides being in pain, I was dizzy—a prelude to the nausea that would come when a bone broke. The normal impulse would be to plead with him to stop or try to pull out of his control. But I'd been trained not to give in to instinct: in fact, in the martial arts I'd studied or simply observed, defying your instinct became second nature.

There wasn't much room to maneuver, but I pivoted so he was more in front of me than at my side. This made the pain shift up to agony. I had a fast but horrid vision of breaking apart a chicken wing. The nausea got worse, but I couldn't rely on vomiting as a weapon.

Now I was close enough to see each individual whisker on his unshaven cheek. I thought, *Blech,* but at least it was a momentary distraction from what was going on with my arm. I was not one for physical closeness (the exceptions being sexually attractive men, cute mammals, and Eliza), and the stink of bourbon breath and hair gel made it unbearable. Plus his croaking "twat" had not been a smart call.

I made a fighting fist with my left hand all in one practiced, fluid move that took less than a second. I was in a perfect position to punch him in the throat, but that could break his windpipe. I wanted him talking, not dead. So I pushed hard against the cavity beneath his windpipe.

That can make a guy cease and desist. Billy's fingers released their grip; he started to crumple but came to enough to stagger around for a minute. One hand on top of the other, he held his throat, making guttural noises. Obviously he was in pain plus. Fortunately he wasn't equipped at that moment to analyze the situation, but I didn't want him anywhere near that console. The pain in my arm and elbow was receding from excruciating to throbbing. I pushed him back to the chair he'd risen from.

Keeping my eyes on him, I backed away to where I'd been sitting but remained standing. I gave him a little time to calm down, but he wasn't into that. His hands remained on his throat. He continued to whimper and pulled his arms so close to his body that they covered his chest.

There was an Arabic saying I remembered: *At the time of a test, a person rises or falls.* The gist of it was that your worth comes out during an ordeal. Not only was Billy losing the fight, he was also flunking Character 101. No conciliatory gestures, no justification, no explanation. Nothing now but nonstop cowering.

"You don't get to almost break someone's arm," I explained, "without expecting consequences." He hung his head in the manner of a naughty boy, which made me want to punch him again, which didn't say much for my character. "Count to five to test your larynx."

"Ug, t, thr, four, five," he said.

"Where did you find the hit man?" I asked.

He took a couple of shaky breaths. "We had nothing to do with his getting killed," he whispered.

"Right. Then did Trevor kill himself? Did he fire two shots from a boat, then levitate up over the stilts and safety rail to stand on his deck, just in time to get whacked by bullets in the chest and head?"

"I swear on my mother's Bible. We only hired someone to threaten him."

"Where did you find the person to hire?" He shook his head. "Billy, I'd really like to leave here." Actually, I was nervous: His wife could walk in at any moment. Maybe she toted a cute little Ruger LCR in the pocket of her culottes. "I told you, I'm not law enforcement. You can talk to me."

"Are you wearing a wire?" he asked.

"No." Technically true: just the teeny mic and transmitter I'd velcroed to a tortoiseshell barrette. Usually I wore it on my bra strap, but that was a no-go with a tank top. He seemed unconvinced, so I lifted the bottom of my tank to show a bare midriff: See? No wire.

"Chet heard of him from someone," he finally muttered. I waited. "From someone he knew at one of the companies. A discreet guy."

"He just called up a person he knew from business and said, 'I need someone to kill my neighbor'?"

"No!" Billy jerked back his head, insulted, as if I was accusing Chet McFarland of lacking class. "He told him the situation and said we needed someone." He caressed his Adam's apple, a genteel reminder he was still in pain and that being forced to talk made it hurt more.

"Come on. Let's get this over with and after I leave, you can have a nice soothing drink with a lot of ice cubes."

"All he said was he needed somebody to come in when Trevor wasn't around and smash all his equipment. To smithereens."

"I assume he had a contingency plan if smithereens didn't work?" There was a lot of leftover adrenaline in my system, and as it subsided I felt more and more exhausted, yearning to get to the hotel, pull a blanket over my head, and sleep. "Like if Trevor took the insurance money and bought a bigger and better system?"

"Then the guy would have to come back, give him a personal warning."

"How personal?"

"Not to kill him. I swear to almighty God. Just rough him up some." I nodded, indicating I thought this was a reasonable explanation. Well, at least he was talking. "So the person Chet called for the referral? He told Chet he hadn't called the guy in about three years, so he wasn't sure if he was still, you know, doing business."

"But he was."

"Yes," Billy said. "My wife is going to wonder why my voice sounds like this."

"Maybe. Tell me the procedure for getting in touch with this guy."

"Frank. His name was Frank."

"Any last name?"

"No."

"Okay, keep going. How did it work?"

"You call the number that Chet got from his friend, former associate, whatever. You leave a message. Your name, number, and say who you got his number from. Then he calls you back within twenty-four hours."

"Did Chet make the call?"

"Why are you asking me that? Chet was the one who got Frank's number. It's not logical to think . . ."

Dodging my question, buying time to think, was not proof positive, just a strong indication that Billy himself had made the call. "Let's walk together on the path of truth," I suggested. He worked up a momentary expression of outrage but couldn't maintain it. "Tell me how come you got the honor of making contact with Frank."

"Chet said we should divvy it up. The responsibility and the risk, not that it was really a risk, because this Frank had come so highly recommended. In a class by himself."

I heard a boat outside. A sputtering engine sound, and when its pitch became deeper, I was terrified it was going to stop and Mrs. Billy would come running up the steps. I pictured her in bubblegum-pink sneakers and baby-blue varicose veins. But thankfully the boat moved on, slowly, along the canal. "And what was Chet's role in this?"

"He'd do the negotiations."

"Face-to-face?"

"No, all on the phone. Frank said, 'You'll never see me and I'll never see you. A perfect relationship.'"

We talked for a while longer, but as we did, more boats seemed to be passing by. Maybe it was Galveston Island rush hour. So my last words to him were: "Give me Frank's number." When he found it in Contacts on his cell, he started reading it off to me. I grabbed the phone and sent it to a onetime-use email address I'd created the night before. And no, I did not say thank you.

# 19

The arm Billy Gregson tried to break was turning more purple than black-and-blue, so Wynne bought me a long-sleeved anti-UV T-shirt on the way back to Houston. It was black with a small, orange Gulf shrimp in the spot where there would normally be an alligator or a mounted polo player. "If Josh sees your arm, he'll think you had more fun than you did," she said. "Fuck with the lights out for the next week."

"I never saw him panting over my forearm." However, by the time I got home, the bruising was more noticeable. Hiding it was for the best, since I'd told him I was off for a couple of days of frolic with Wynne. And Eliza, who could still obsess about the teeny pinprick made by a mosquito sting, would be horror-struck and ask a thousand questions; I really didn't have the energy to construct a narrative to explain the discoloration and swelling. I also had to consider that before going onto the bench, Josh had been the cross-examination king. His exquisitely honed instinct for bullshit could tell him something was off about my story.

I had no regrets about the contretemps with Billy. Part of the job. But it took another day for the adrenaline surge to subside. When I drove Eliza over to her friend's so they could study together for the Regents exam in biology, I was rattled and asked her to turn off her hits station. Not quite an ask: I screeched, "Turn that damn thing off!" though I quickly added, "Sorry. It was distracting." Her thumbs—fast as a humming-bird's wings—flitted across the screen of her phone, to announce to her world how ill used she was.

We pulled up in front of Chloë's house and, mindfully, I put the car into Park so it wouldn't careen down Knoll Street as Eliza exited. Except she stayed put and did the adolescent equivalent of a jailhouse mumble, mouth barely moving: "Chloë's mom likes you to come in and say hi."

My daughter was acting her age, and since she was generally easygoing and mature, I started to seethe. I also was pissed at the thought of Chloë's mom (whose name was something avian, like Dove or Swan or Lark) who was a gentility bully. She demanded that every encounter include chitchat and tea.

"Tell her I sent my regards, but I had to get back home for the electrician."

"That's not true!"

"I know. I'm sorry, but I'm not up for her now."

It took me only a half block to think, Would it be so terrible if I were the one to phone Frank? His contact number, which I'd gotten from Billy, was virtually burning a hole in my cell phone. Even if I deleted it, my memory had grabbed hold after a single glance at the numerals and would never let it go. It was in area code 312, Chicago, though that meant nothing since anyone slightly brighter than my dog, Lulu, could arrange for a call to be rerouted: Frank could be in Baton Rouge or Guam and seem to be phoning in from Chicago.

I figured I had about five free hours, what with the girls' studying and probably sneaking in a couple of episodes of *Riverdale*. In that time, I might either wind up in deep shit or get a humongous payoff by calling "Frank."

Sami, so gifted at undercover, should be the one making the call, I thought. He was better at role-playing than any actor since his cases and his life depended on performance. But he was DEA, not FBI. And we were ex-lovers, not loving friends: I couldn't ask him to take on my case.

Self-deception isn't an option when you're a pro. I knew I couldn't do it alone. Even with a voice-changing app and that first semester of my sophomore year when I was a drama and theater major, I could not totally shake my New York accent. True, I could say the obvious words like coffee and dog and actually sound slightly Minnesotan. But listening to any audio of myself meant picking up on my dentalized *d*'s and *t*'s. I could also hear, like a *plunk,* the occasional *r* dropping out of a word, as when New York became New Yawk, especially when I was talking fast. (It even popped up when I spoke Arabic, where New York— نيويورك —was pronounced pretty much as in standard English or maybe a little more toward New Yurk. But under pressure, I'd still wind up saying New Yawk.)

If Frank indeed was Pete Delaney, he might recognize that if the potential client on the phone said, "I want him dead," with those two *d*'s in the last word sounding a little *t*-ish, he might recall who spoke like that. Okay, he lived on Long Island so there'd be more than two or three, but I'd be among them.

My mom was another story. The quasi upper-class accent she'd made her own didn't even whisper New York. Except even if I could get her to call Frank, give her a script, and rehearse her, she could always get carried away—and start improvising.

My dad? No doubt he could do it. He was a pro. But because he was, he would recognize that calling "Frank" was not family fun time. It was deadly serious and needed to go through proper channels.

Back at the house, I took Lulu into the backyard and let her off the leash. Then I tracked her, vicariously experiencing a dog's life, watching her sniff and trot and now and then race through the woods way in the back as if she were in pursuit of a MOST WANTED. It was fun for about twenty minutes, but then I got to thinking how sad it was for dogs that they couldn't read. They just sat around waiting for you. When we went inside and I got an iced coffee and opened my iPad to Iris's spreadsheet that I'd annotated, all Lulu could do as I scanned down and across the columns of info was lick her privates while keeping an occasional eye on me. "I would if I could," I told her, and she tilted her head in that doggie amalgam of what-the-fuck bewilderment and wisdom.

The house felt overlarge and oversilent with just the two of us, but I was relishing the peace of the kitchen. It was the only room Dawn never got around to renovating, even once. It was empty of her taste and her spirit. Someone else's terracotta tile floor and stone oven for baking bread dominated the space. I sensed that whoever had moved in in the late eighties when the house was first built—the Gerards, I thought their name was—were much more warmhearted than Dawn.

As if to shame me for thinking of him as a workaholic, Josh didn't even try to go to his study that night after dinner. Instead, we watched a couple of episodes of *Rumpole of the Bailey*, an old BBC series about a barrister. It was fun, or sort of, in that British style of drollery, where you don't actually laugh out loud but chortle quite a bit. Josh was chortling at a line that went something like: "I often think knowledge of the law is a bit of a handicap to a barrister." He glanced over at me, checking whether I found it as clever, and I traded my smile for a couple of chortles just to keep him company.

Except my mind was at least 90 percent on where I should go from where I was. Having ruled out partnering with Sami or my parents, I obviously needed to speak with someone in the FBI. Except nearly all the people I knew from the bureau were on the Joint Terrorism Task Force. Though the New York branch of the JTTF was the best of its kind, I didn't need that kind of expertise. I wasn't chasing down a terrorist. Did I have the resources to go after a professional hit man alone? No. But if I brought in all I'd collected on Pete Delaney as a neat package and walked the people at the bureau through it, what would they do? Say: *Hey, thanks.* Or: *We'll have a look.*

And what would I be then? Superfluous. As far as bureaus went, the FBI was as bureaucratic as they came. Okay, if I could interest someone in the case, I might be able to have some role based on all the investigating I'd done. A teeny role. Still, I had to risk letting the bureaucracy take over.

The next couple of days were a washout because we went up to Connecticut for the weekend with one of Josh's former partners at the law firm. The partner and his wife, also a lawyer, were "intelligence is so cool" types. Every activity from hiking to making eggs had a smartness component: a tutorial on moss versus lichen from her; "Two ova over easy," from him. They had a daughter, a Manhattan private school sophisticate, who was Eliza's age. The two of them spent most of two days of sunshine indoors streaming *Outlander* on a cell phone; I took on faith that any explicit sexual content was just a couple of square inches and wouldn't stunt Eliza's emotional growth.

By Monday morning I felt hungover, as if I'd spent the weekend in an unventilated studio apartment drinking shitty bourbon and fighting with people who held stupid political opinions. I took Lulu for a long walk, then popped a couple of Tylenol and drove over to my parents.

It was more living room than kitchen talk. They took the couch while I took the ottoman of the club chair. I brought them up to date on my time on Galveston Island. I was going to edit out my fisticuffs with Billy Gregson, but my need to show my parents my boo-boo, still purple, was greater than my need to protect them. Of course my mom rushed to the linen closet and got some arnica from her rattan basket of ancient, opened tubes and, once it passed her sniff test, gently applied it to my arm. My dad alternated between reacting as a father and reacting as a fellow investigator, so he stayed quiet except to ask, "You okay? I'm not talking about your arm."

"I know," I said. "I'm fine." My mom put away her basket with a "Don't say anything until I get back." She returned with a bowl of cherries and enough cocktail napkins to contain fifty pounds of pits. The next ten minutes or so I explained my decision not to go it on my own, that the case needed investigators who had many more tools than I did, along with legal authority to operate on a national basis. Then I apologized to my dad for giving up and emphasized there was no way I could have gotten this far without him.

"What's with the apologizing?" he demanded. "You're doing the right thing. There's really no other choice, because dollars to doughnuts, this guy Frank is no go-between. Frank *is* Pete Delaney." I nodded. "Has to be, because a guy with his personality, his line of work, he can't afford to trust anyone else."

My mom said, "Agreed. Unless hit men have agents, the way actors do. They'd take ten percent for a two-minute vehicular homicide? Madness."

My dad asked, "Since the Trevor guy was near Houston and your Pete is on Long Island, which FBI office gets jurisdiction?"

"I'm really not sure, though in the long run it ought to go to headquarters because it's not just one hit. It's a case with interstate consequences and they need someone who can put together the grand design."

"Do you still have contacts down in Washington?" my mom asked. She had a small dimple in her chin and when she was in protective parental mode, she'd insert her index finger and press on the area. So right away, I understood that she was worried that I'd hand over all the information I gathered and after a pro forma thank-you, I'd be dismissed. She knew not only that I wanted in but also that if I was forced out, it would be a huge hurt. Working from the cuticle up, I started gnawing off my rose-gold nail polish. "I just brought in all those cherries," she said. "Eat those rather than ravaging your manicure."

"Margo," my dad cautioned her.

"It's a suggestion," she said, "not a command. My God, she's an adult."

I crossed my arms and tucked my hands under my armpits. "All this time I've been thinking about handing over my findings. Deep down I truly believed I could talk my way into being part of any investigatory team. Okay, I worried about getting into big-time trouble for delving so deep and not reporting. But I never seriously considered I'd get booted out, that they'd have no need for me."

They went on being soothing and parental for a few minutes. I'd had vague plans of driving into the city, maybe catching Wynne for lunch, then seeing the Museum of the American Indian, which I'd never been to. Instead I brushed all that aside so I could get home. I needed to wallow in gloom.

But as I was inching out of Queens—the Grand Central Parkway having decided to call an 11:30 a.m. traffic jam—my cell phone rang. Normally, I either ignore a call or pull off somewhere and park, but I saw Galveston, TX, and took the call. A deep, loud "Howdy" came through the car's speaker. "Jane? Aaron Meadows!"

Right! The boat guy. I had given him my Jane Miller, Investigations card. "Hi Aaron. How are you?"

"Real good. Hey, you said to get in touch if I thought of anything?"

"Yes!" I let a Mercedes cut in front of me, which was not my usual style.

"So it probably doesn't mean anything." I could tell he was in a minor snit of embarrassment, something that happens when witnesses contact agents and instantly regret it. "Probably a big, fat old nothing."

"Aaron, sometimes the tiniest observation can have real meaning in an investigation. No matter what, I'm so glad you called. Tell me what you thought of."

"Remember you showed me a picture of some guy, and I didn't remember the face at all?"

"Right."

"Well, I still don't remember anything from his looks. He's like Mr. Potato Head before you stick in the nose and the eyes."

I suppressed a desire to say yup and told him: "So you're saying he's average looking. He doesn't look like anyone at all."

"Nail on the head. It's not like all of a sudden I remembered the face. But one thing I did recall. Right about the time of that shooting—the guy with the loud music? Well, some guy came in looking to rent a boat. I wouldn't have even thought twice about him because he said none of my boats was exactly what he wanted. Except he didn't tell me what he wanted, just said he wanted to look. Fine with me. He looked at a few I showed him and said no thanks."

"But you have lots of boats."

"That's right. I rent more boats than anyone around, so if I don't have it, it probably doesn't exist here. Well, it could, but not likely."

"So what did you think about what he said?" I asked.

"Figured my prices were a little too up there for him. I'm competitive, but there are places where he could've got a better deal, except not with boats in such fine running condition. And clean. Clean is an item for me. So that's why I remember him, because of clean. The next morning, I got to the marina early and just started going from boat to boat. Everything's fine, except on one boat there's a little thing, less than an inch square, not that it was square. A little piece of something brownish right by the helm. Damn, this sounds so dumb."

"Totally not dumb, Aaron. You're a careful guy, good businessman, and you notice things."

"So I pick it up and it looks like a piece from one of those healthy bars. The dry kind. But the thing of it was, I hadn't rented that boat for two days and I was sure either me or one of the boys who work for me had gone over it, and they're as particular as I am. So just out of curiosity, I checked the gas gauge. Then checked that against my records and it was down. Not like kids stole it and took it somewhere far for a big party."

"Did Mr. Potato Head look at that particular boat?"

"He sure did because it's what I would've shown him for what he wanted to drive around the coastline, go in and out of the canals. Kind of the ride I took you on."

"Did you mention it to the police?" I asked.

"I did. They asked me if I'd saved the little brown thing, so I said, 'Hell no.' I can understand they might have been interested in DNA from spit on the healthy bar."

"Did they ask you to describe him, Aaron?"

"They did. And I told 'em, 'He looked like everybody else.' By which I meant, he blended in."

"Right," I said. "Were you able to tell them race, approximate age, height?"

"White guy. Not old, not young, not tall, not short. He looked like he belonged."

"Facial hair?"

"I don't think so. No."

"Birthmarks, tattoos?"

"Not that I remember," Aaron said.

"That's his gift," I told him. "I think he's the kind of person who can look as if he belongs wherever he is. You wouldn't question him walking down Main Street in anybody's home-town. Did he seem at all wrong in any way? Like really nervous? Too smooth?"

"No," Aaron said. "Wouldn't think twice about him. Hardly even thought about him once."

Pete's great packaging. "When he talked, did you get the impression he was from Texas?"

Aaron probably hadn't considered this before, because it took him a few seconds until he answered. "Not from anywhere near here. And I bet you're going to ask if he sounded like he was from anyplace else."

"I bet you're right," I told him. "And?"

"And he didn't sound like he was from anywhere. Not the East Coast, not the Midwest, not Canada. No foreign accent."

I asked about how his plan went to propose to his girlfriend by putting a ring on top of a coconut cupcake. He went on for a few minutes about how she started to cry with happiness and also about their plans, including having a wedding cake made up entirely of coconut and vanilla cupcakes, "because some people don't like coconut." Aaron volunteered to let me know if he heard anything about the investigation around the island.

When I got back to the house, I defrosted some turkey burgers because Josh and Eliza liked them and they weren't exactly work intensive. In the years between Dawn and me, Wanda, the housekeeper, made them so often they went from *Not again* to the beloved old reliable: *Great! Turkey burger night!* I didn't like the way they left a coating on my throat, and I wound up toothbrushing and gargling a great deal after we had them. However, it was thought-free food prep and I needed to handle getting someone with legal authority onto the Pete Delaney matter.

Alas. The person I knew with the most juice in the bureau was the chief of the Joint Terrorism Task Force, Wallace P. Smith. Wally. He'd been around long before the joint task forces were established, a charter member of the old boy network. I wanted to make the point that this wasn't a case for the Houston office but one for headquarters. Except it was hard for me to make any point at all to Wally.

He had never liked me. Even when I was at my peak, establishing close relationships with so many wives of terrorists that I could have formed a sorority as well as getting an amazing amount of actionable info, good old Wally could take a pass on me. I had no idea why he was so eminently disdainful, but that's how it was. Even the times he was forced to compliment me, he did it without ever looking me in the eye. "C'gratulations," he'd say. If others were around, I got a handshake in which his fingers barely gripped mine and his palm stayed a safe inch distant. Working harder, past the point of exhaustion, didn't help with him. Charm was futile. I was stymied on what to try next until my mom said, "Do nothing more, Corie, dahrling, it's simply bad chemistry. Just carry on."

So I texted the second in command, Katherine Nakamura, the woman who called me with occasional contract assignments. CAN WE TALK? SEE POSSIBLE BIG CASE, THO NOT PTA [potential terrorist actions]. NEED ADVICE. I'LL KEEP IT SHORT.

Kath came across as snippy, but that was mostly because she figured out what you were saying before you finished and cut you off with her answer. Not the ideal person to expound a theory to and she'd been with the bureau for only ten years and definitely wasn't part of the old boy network who could mutter a suggestion to a friend at headquarters and have a much better than 50 percent chance of getting a positive response. Still, she had a lot of clout in the task force, since she was fluent in seven languages. Also, having been a diplomatic brat, she could handle herself with police departments and security services in any part of the world.

I'd gotten only to the second bullet point of what I would say to Kath whenever she called—which turned out to be that instant. I went through the Pete Delaney situation in four minutes, from initial suspicion to a seemingly nonexistent brother; Pete's observing every one of his trash bags going into the sanitation truck; his trips coinciding with major crimes; my dad's discovery that Pete's garage had enough security to protect a nuclear facility, plus the fact that his touted trip to Philadelphia put only forty-six miles on his car; his actual packaging design as cover; his firearms expertise; and all about the Galveston case—up to and including "Frank." Without talking points, I was so on edge I figured she'd cut me off with: *Can't help you.*

"I'm thinking headquarters, Criminal Investigative Division," Kath said. She had that clear, no-accent accent of Americans who've been raised abroad. Her keyboard clicked quickly, as if it knew she would find an alternative if it wasn't fast enough. "Hold on," she told me. "I'm looking at their personnel." As with everything else she did, the wait took just seconds. "A couple of people there I could call. Know them vaguely. But that would just be intrabureau query, exchange of information, discussion of murder for hire. Obviously I think well of your abilities, but your unstated point seems to be that you want in on any investigation."

"Yes." Since she didn't say *Impossible,* I kept going. "Look, I've taken this from just an instinct that there was something odd about the guy, secretive. At first I thought he might be ex–law enforcement or CIA, where your time in service is a blank that you fill in with a story. Pretty much what I do. Not inventing a new identity but using my married name and giving the impression that I've been in publishing my entire career. Granted, I had help from the bureau on that. Pete Delaney had no reason to be cagey. He'd had a job at a big advertising agency, got canned during the recession, and started working at home. So his behavior, never letting his car out of his sight, changing phones, keeping watch on how his garbage was disposed of, didn't square with his bio and—"

"So you tracked him. But you don't know for sure that he was in Galveston."

"Correct."

"So this 'Frank' may be someone else entirely," she said.

"Sure," I said. "But his MO, the date of the killing when Pete was out of town, the meticulous planning, the two perfectly placed shots that killed Trevor Schwarz, et cetera. It all sounds like Pete Delaney."

"But—"

This time I interrupted her. "And if it's not Pete Delaney? It's still an interstate case, murder for hire. And the bureau should be investigating it."

"But even though you still have your clearance, even though you still do the occasional job for us, you're not a special agent."

"I know that. But you know what else I know, Kath? I know Pete Delaney, and if it is him, I know his background, some of his habits, how he interacts with his clients . . . the legit ones, I mean. And the one witness who spoke to him, about hiring him to give Schwarz a so-called warning, said pretty much the same thing about his character. Cold, terse, businesslike. Also, I see the guy every week at lunch. I can make judgment calls better than an investigator who's never met him."

"Got it," Kath said. "I'll make some calls. If you're needed, I'll let you know." Then she paused. "Give me this Frank's number."

There were thousands of snarky responses I could give her, but I simply said, "Sure."

# 20

The peeps in the Wednesday home office group met for lunch two days later. I was on high alert from my own adrenaline plus two huge glasses of iced coffee. Pete, naturally, was already in his usual seat at La Cuisine Délicieuse. I just waved at him and Darby as I sprinted to the ladies' room. By the time I got back, the only chair left was the one beside Pete.

Major moment, right? Except it wasn't. Out of the corner of my eye, I could see the dryness of his cheek etched with fine-lined squares and rectangles, like guys with sandblasted skin who'd served a couple of tours of duty in Iraq. Except my blessed contact in the bureau's HR department, Jillian King, had done a background check and said the man I knew as Pete Delaney had no military record. So maybe he had a little vacation cabin in Death Valley.

But other than speculating on the state of his cheek and that he kept his nails short enough to keep them perpetually clean, the only news from the lunch was that Pete ordered the day's special, saumon froid en gelée. When he told that to the waiter, Lucy Winters, the data miner, squished her mouth and nose into a yuck pucker and said:

"*Jelly?* You should text your order with the green puke emoji." Then Pete snapped: "Cut it out."

The following morning, Kath Nakamura, the number two at the Joint Terrorism Task Force, called around eleven to tell me her instincts had been right, that the Pete Delaney matter could not be run from New York. "Let me make a couple of calls, see if I can get headquarters involved and also get you attached to it." My spirit soared until she added, "Don't start packing."

I walked out of my office, followed by Lulu, figuring I'd go for a run with her, but then I saw the pile of manuscripts on my desk. Granted, it wasn't a tower, but I started feeling guilty about some novelist checking her email ten times a day to see if any word had come from the United States or the UK about an English translation. Instead of grabbing one of them, I took my iPad down to the backyard to read an e-edition of a book that was moving toward bestsellerdom in the Arabic-speaking world. Lulu sniffed the grass and finally found a treasure—a crumble of two-week-old hot dog roll.

For the first time in ages I stopped trying to put the jigsaw pieces of Pete Delaney's life into a clear picture. I became absorbed in the universe of the novel. It was based on the life of Huda Sha'arawi, an Egyptian aristocrat and dissident who led women to protest British rule, refused to go around veiled, and wound up being the organizer and guiding force of the country's feminist movement. The writing might not have been exquisite, but Huda was a combo of Carrie Chapman Catt and Eleanor Roosevelt—maybe even more daring—and the narrative had the thrust of a train racing from Alexandria to Cairo.

Just as I was contemplating the amazing turn my own life had taken—choosing Arabic 101 because Intro to Russian was oversubscribed—my phone vibrated in my cleavage. It was Unknown Number, which turned out to be Kath Nakamura. She was halfway through her first sentence before I realized who was talking.

"—and no way through the New York office, as I suspected, though I gave it a shot. Strictly headquarters. This is what I'll do: go through the people I know in the Crim Div, find out who will be handling this, and try to get you inserted."

"Thank you!" I said, probably too effusively because I was still in thrall to Huda Sha'arawi's fervor.

"You're not doing yourself a favor by getting overenthusiastic. You know how it is. You're only a contract worker now, and your field is anti-terrorism. Not the dream pairing for this kind of case. But if you really want it, write a full report with as many bullet points as you can shoot into it. Detail, specifics could weigh in your favor. Listen, since you're the one who is bringing this matter to the bureau, they would expect a complete report anyway. But go all out, with short sentences. Don't get clever, Corie."

"I swear, they'll think I'm from Idaho or wherever—"

"That is exactly what I'd like you to avoid."

"Right," I said. Lulu was rolling on her back in the grass making loud *snrrr, snrrr* growls.

"I hope it's your guy Pete who did the hit in Galveston. Because that could bring part of the case up to New York, and I'd like to be able to sneak out of my office and check out what's happening as the investigation progresses."

Kath was evidently intrigued, which told me that even though she might not like the snark in my reports, she was buying into the reasoning behind my suspicions.

"So you're essentially thinking that this Frank is actually Pete Delaney?" I asked.

"I am not as committed to the Pete Delaney theory as you are. But I know far, far less about the case than you do. What I believe is that who-ever Frank is, he isn't a go-between but the assassin himself."

"I'm not saying that on occasion he might not have a need to bring in someone else," I told her. "But then I can practically guarantee you that the someone else would be dead as soon as his or her part of the job was done."

It was close to five the following day, Friday,

when I heard from headquarters, which at the bureau passed for the speed of light. Could I submit a report on my suspicions and my follow-up by the following Tuesday? Could I? I finished it early Monday, after a weekend of the big reveal of the pets Eliza had created for her new Sims game and also taking her shopping for the perfect sneakers and shirt to wear on the bus up to the Adirondacks for her three-week stint at Camp Belasco, where the kids put on a Broadway musical a week.

Josh and I saw some movie I couldn't recall three minutes after we left the theater. I was too preoccupied thinking about my report, so I took Josh's word that it was thoughtful but could easily have been cut by a half hour. Later, over pizza, I considered for three seconds confessing the truth about the Galveston trip but then unconsidered. Even though I was dying for him to read what I'd written about the Pete Delaney case—and to let me know if anything I did was illegal or ill considered—there was no way I would risk telling him I'd been less than truthful with him. A lot less. And my omission wasn't some marriage-lite secret like: *I spent nine hundred bucks on a pair of Manolos two years ago.* It was: *I'm tracking a guy who lives less than a mile away in a white colonial who seems to be a professional killer.*

Once I sent in the report—a bonanza of bullet

points, conclusions, and several yellow high-lights—I waited. After all my years at the bureau, I understood patience: witnesses didn't cooperate on a timeline; the top people in Counterterrorism and, I assumed, the Crim Div, weren't fans of the snap decision. I understood patience, but I wasn't particularly good at it. I did get a couple of manuscripts read and reports written, but time just slogged along. Finally, just as I was setting the table for Shabbat with Dawn's sterling silver, I got the call from headquarters. No info, but at ten on Tuesday, I should be at the J. Edgar Hoover Building and ask for Carlos Ruiz of the Criminal Investigative Division.

Actually, I was a little wowed that they wanted my actual presence. Usually, in dealing with DC, it was text or teleconference. A double wow because the word was that the Crim Div had a tighter budget than Counterterrorism, so it was a biggish deal that they were flying me down.

Under ordinary circumstances, I would have recognized that an explanation to Josh was long overdue. But I guess I was upset. No, I was really angry that he'd been going off for panels and seminars without a peep that it was part of his having a grand strategy to move up to the court of appeals. (Well, for whatever reason, I hadn't peeped either, though unlike Josh's activities, my involvement with Pete hadn't been part of a game plan.)

In the past, when he wasn't leaving Eliza and me to bond, Josh and I relished the time after dinner, wallowing in normality: talking, reading quietly, watching a couple of episodes of some series, having our film festivals—courtroom dramas, espionage thrillers, musicals. We did deals, so for each of his Swedish films on the nature of reality, I got one classic rom-com. But that had been then. Now I mostly got Josh's charmer smile as he went to his study to work on his ascension to judicial heaven.

Anyway, it took nearly an hour at headquarters to make it up to the presence of Carlos Ruiz. He was deceptively cool looking, with clothes that actually fit as opposed to nearly all the men in the bureau who seemed to be following some unwritten requirement to buy their suits one size too large. His brown hair was longish, brushed back, and a tiny bit mussed up, and his brown eyes were supersize: there were handsome special agents, but Ruiz looked more MSNBC than FBI. But by the time the first few minutes were up, I could tell he was a by-the-book federal law enforcement type. He definitely had read my HR file and had spoken not only to my supervisors in Washington and New York but also to special agents I'd worked with.

At first he seemed to be taking my good reviews as a given, which surprised me. Not that I thought he'd view me as a nut job, but I'd assumed that he'd be more curious as to what about Pete Delaney had piqued my interest. But that minor mystery was solved within the hour, when someone came to take me down for a lie detector test and interview.

All special agents have to take the test, and in Counterterrorism—as in the Joint Terrorism Task Force—we were good for at least two a year. I was fine with it. It was just me and the usual nonjolly polygraph tech; this one needed orthodontia or had a lemon wedge stuck between her upper lip and gum. There was also a guy, jacket off and draped over the back of his wheel-chair. The sleeves of his starched white shirt were rolled up, or more exactly, folded crisply three times to under his elbow.

As the tech put on the blood pressure cuff and assorted skin sensors, he said, "We'll start with a series of the usual questions, just to get a good baseline, then I'll ask some others." The polygraph looked far more sophisticated than the ones I had experience with in New York, and the sensors didn't have wires but instead seemed to send readings via Bluetooth.

"Okay," I said.

Since there wasn't any *Hi, I'm Joe,* I realized, in the first minute or two while the equipment ran, it was an excellent opportunity for me to give them a baseline reading of myself in anxiety mode, so that there wouldn't be a huge disparity between me giving my name and saying where I lived and my getting unsettled by his inevitable questions about my feelings toward Pete Delaney. Having been involved in lots of polygraph tests before, both as a bureau employee and as a special agent with a witness or subject, I figured they'd inevitably get to wondering about me. *Is she an ex-lover trying to get even? Does she have some kind of obsession, maybe sexual, about this particular guy? Did she become a wack job after retiring and somehow focus on him?*

The guy in the wheelchair, who I assumed was a shrink from Quantico, looked tough-minded and was eying me as if I were a fruit fly in an experiment. They wouldn't have sent up someone who looked to be at a high level for just a routine interview with a contract employee. He looked pretty astute. Still, I was nervous about how he'd interpret my answers to questions eliciting responses to *wack job?* Despite all I'd discovered about Pete, maybe I'd tripped off the deep end after choosing to live a normal life and hadn't noticed.

So as Lemon Lady stuck the last of the electrodes to an area uncomfortably close to my armpit, I thought about stuff that would agitate me, like if I really loved Josh so much, how come I couldn't make up my mind whether or not to have a baby with him. I pictured myself running my usual route in Shorehaven, past lawn after lawn, down to the bay, and while it was aesthetically more pleasing than running in Manhattan or Washington or Queens, it was boring as shit and when I'd sounded Josh out about maybe moving to Brooklyn, he'd recoiled before saying something like: *Well, it's certainly something to think about after Eliza graduates because, listen, we've both agreed on the value of not throwing any more changes at her because she's made such an excellent adjustment. Blah, blah, blah.*

Then, as the shrink was asking, "Are both your parents still alive?" I made an effort to dismiss Josh from my mind and thought about me kicking the shit out of some guy in a tae kwon do exhibition, even though I've never studied tae kwon do, except for a elementary classes with Eliza. However, at that moment, mental kicking felt like a good way to get my blood pressure up a little. He crossed his arms over his chest. Whatever the wheelchair was about, he appeared powerful, with big muscles in his forearms and broad shoulders: the strength combined with his focus made me wonder if he was a Paralympic-type athlete.

Other than registering a little agitation at the start, just to avoid any suspicion that I was overly reactive later on, I had no need to beat the machine. The easiest way to deal with being connected to a lie detector was to tell the truth.

The shrink, who'd moved his wheelchair closer to me, was using a method of questioning developed by the CIA, where the testers give you a question designed to elicit potential deception. They then look at and listen to how you react in the next five seconds, which is the crucial time— before your brain can kick in and mediate what you say or do.

And after that first five seconds, they start looking for verbal and nonverbal clues, like if rather than give a direct answer, you respond: *What do you mean by that,* it tells them you're buying time to think. Once he began with the stimulative questions, I felt relieved. He'd clearly read my bullet-pointed report many times over, and an hour and a half later, when Lemon Lady was pulling off the electrodes with surprising gentleness, he gave me his first and only sign of humanity—a nod. I sensed it was a benevolent nod, but then he said, "My colleague will escort you to a holding area. Mr. Ruiz will meet you there in about an hour."

I wasn't delighted with his use of "about an hour." Sixty-one minutes? Two hundred forty minutes? On the way to the holding area, which turned out to have all the graciousness of a waiting room in Penn Station, I used the ladies' room. If I hadn't thought about hidden cameras, I would have run cold water over my wrists for a while, just for some cool relief.

I hadn't expected anyone at headquarters to leap up, based on my report, and say: *Yes, your suspicions were correct!* (Though I thought it was a superb combo of detail and clarity.) But I was irrationally shaken that they'd spent so much time checking to see if I was crazy.

It took about twenty minutes more in the waiting room to go from shaken to crabby. I was aware the bureau didn't serve lunch, so I reached into the hobo bag I was carrying (a Mom/Dad birthday gift) and ate one of the two Kind bars I'd bought that morning at the airport. Ever since a short trip to Yemen in 2006 to observe the debriefing of an allegedly repentant wife of a terrorist, when I ate a plate of grayish stuff a guy called goat and a woman called chicken, I liked to travel prepared. Eating food veined with a bluish-green line was problematic, though I recognized my duty to my country not to offend its (then) ally.

Time dragged on. I was rereading *Great Expectations*, which I kept on my phone, for maybe the fiftieth time. I was on the verge of having to pee again when a woman came to get me and take me to back to Carlos Ruiz. "You did well on the polygraph test," Ruiz said. Though he didn't actually smile, his expression seemed more benevolent.

"Thanks."

"At the beginning of the polygraph test, you

worked yourself up, didn't you? To soften any strong reaction if a tough question surfaced."

"I thought I was being subtle."

"No. The psychologist is one of our best and the equipment is better than it used to be." Ruiz smoothed his forehead with his thumb and middle finger. Especially with controlled people, I always like to watch what part of themselves they touch first. I interpreted his smoothing as a tender caress to the intellect he was proud of and prepared to use. "What was the reaction you didn't want us to see?"

No point in trying to game this guy, so I said, "It was about what made me think initially something was off about Pete Delaney. I had a strong sense that he was hiding something or at least keeping part of himself under wraps."

"Where's the problem in that?" he asked.

"It's that when I first realized the offness, I remember I shuddered, and I'm not the shuddering type. But it was because of the recognition that he was close to me. Living the most normal life possible in the suburbs but having to hide part of myself. My connection, my former employment, with the bureau. The legend that I graduated with a major in Middle Eastern studies and that I went directly into publishing. Hiding my job but also hiding an aspect of my personality."

"And that is . . . ?"

Since I was in total truth mode now, I said, "My aggressiveness. My need not just to see beneath surfaces, which is what empathetic people do, but also to seek out deceit, evil intent, bullshit. Find out how it is being expressed and why."

"You look for this in everyone you meet?" He spoke suavely, with cool and maybe a touch of irony. Or maybe he was a cold guy and I was just creating a character I liked better. "Do you?"

I gave one of those dumb snort laughs, which of course mortified me. It was the situation: maybe he was just trying to unsettle me because I really hadn't passed the polygraph test and he wanted to see what I was hiding. I told the truth, but there could be a false positive, even with the Bluetooth equipment. Or possibly he didn't think it was worthwhile to follow up on my report. But then why had they brought me down to Washington? Or maybe he just thought I was being frivolous: I tended toward those snort laughs when first conversing with handsome men. It was amazing that I didn't snort myself out of a relationship with Josh.

"No," I said. "I don't go around trying to look into the soul of everybody I meet. It's just that if some quality in a person strikes me as false or weird, then I have the need to figure it out."

"Your father's with the NYPD?"

"Retired detective. My mom's an actress. Both jobs train you to seek out motivation."

Ruiz waited, then waited some more. Finally I got bored with looking at him, as I often did with needlessly handsome men, and his desk was nothing to write home about as there were no books or papers on it. I started feeling around my teeth with my tongue to make sure there were no residual fragments of cashew or blueberry from the nutrition bar, and I'd gotten to my lower left canine when he cleared his throat.

"And we know who your husband is," he finally said.

"Right."

"I'll be running the investigation, but I'd like to keep you on for the time being." I nodded. "I have some thoughts about how to approach him, so let me run them by you."

"Sure."

"I'll use a cell phone that's linked to a phony name and identity. I'll call this guy, Frank, and leave a message."

"What's the name you're using?"

"Mike Costa. Why?"

"I'd give another fake name initially." This was the point where men who would rather not work with women exhaled with excessive patience before speaking. He did not. "He'd expect a potential client to try to hide his identity?" I would have preferred *his or her identity,* but not for me to quibble.

"Right, or at least any potential client who's

cautious and intelligent. Let him pull it out of you."

"Not a bad idea. I'm going to lowball him about payment, whatever amount he sets. I want to see how much of a pro this Frank is."

"Do you have your story set?"

"I'm having problems cutting my wife loose. I want a fast divorce and she's holding me up."

"Is there a reason she's holding you up, or is it to be difficult, pry more money out of you?"

"It's that she found out I have a girlfriend . . . who's pregnant. I want our baby to be legitimate."

"That's good," I said. "I like the detail, rather than just 'I hate my wife.'" I was about to add: *When do you think you'll do it?* But then he opened a drawer and handed me a headset. No mic, but at least he wanted me listening in. I put the headset on and said a small prayer of thanksgiving that he hadn't offered me earbuds shiny with someone's wax.

Ruiz hadn't closed the drawer, and as he picked up the receiver of his landline, he kept glancing down into it as he pressed a series of numbers. He waited a second, then put in a 1, then the area code and the number I'd gotten. My mouth went sticky and dry; my heart slammed against my rib cage. It seemed he wasn't going through the same thing, because when I looked over toward him on the second ring, he seemed in neutral gear, as if he were listening to a computerized voice offering a menu of choices.

After the fourth ring, we got voicemail: "This is Frank. If you want me to call back, leave your full name and phone number. I also need the name of whoever referred you. I'll get back to you within twenty-four hours." That was it. Well, I didn't expect: *Have a nice day.*

"Frank," Carlos Ruiz said, "my name is Ted Jamison. You can reach me at . . ." And then he gave a number that I was pretty sure was Houston. Actually, I did hear a little Texas in Ruiz's pronunciation. Maybe it had been there all the time and he was just ramping it up. "I got your number from, uh"—he sounded as nervous as I felt, but from his expression and posture, he still seemed in neutral—"a guy, you know, a friend of a friend. His name's Billy Gregson. Uh, I'll be waiting for your call."

He hung up. He breathed while I gave a major sigh of relief. "Did the voice sound like Pete Delaney?" he asked as he reached out for the headset he'd given me.

"No." I felt bummed and also bad that I had somehow let Ruiz down. If he was disappointed, he definitely didn't show it. "Maybe Pete was using some really sophisticated voice-changing equipment," I went on. "But even then, the accent wasn't the same. Pete sounds midwestern, that kind of default American accent you hear on TV where you don't really notice any accent. Frank sounded, I don't know, maybe a little Chicago, and I don't think I'm getting that just from the area code. When he said something like 'If you want me to call back,' the 'back' had that flat Chicago sound. Not that I am a dialogue expert, but I have a good ear. To me, it didn't sound like Pete."

"You're disappointed?" Ruiz asked.

"Yes."

"Get over it."

"I have."

"No. Hey, I didn't mean to be rude. Maybe it wasn't Pete. Maybe it was Pete flattening his *a*'s. Maybe he just hired some kind of service to record the message." I must have looked dubious because he added: "Small business owners with some kind of accent do it all the time. Someone with default English, like you call it, or a Chicago accent could make a living doing that kind of thing. What I want you to hear is his callback. I'll be a little nervous, evasive. Whatever it takes to keep him talking more than he usually would."

"Good. That sounds good. I guess I should go back to New York then?"

He nodded. "I'll record it, send you the audio over the usual channels. Just call my voicemail to let me know when you get home."

"If it's not Pete, will you still keep working on the case?" Not even a second later I shook my head realizing what a dumb question that was. It wasn't as if they'd let some guy doing murder for hire take a walk just because he wasn't Pete Delaney.

"Relax," he said, sounding on the borderline of kindness. "We're on it. You did a good job on this thing. Now it could be you're dead wrong about Pete, taking a gut feeling and running too far with it. But even though the boat guy couldn't ID him, you got an ID from that guy in the shooting range, where he was talking about shooting bear. So I put my money on your being on the right track, and even if it's not your Long Island guy, the investigation seems spot-on."

I stood and we were about to shake hands when his cell phone went *ting-ting,* high-pitched wind chime sounds. He yanked open his drawer, then tossed the headset to me. I got it on fast and nodded. He answered, "Hello." Then he waited, then shook his head. "Hello?" he said again. "This is Ted." Texas was back in Ruiz's voice.

"Frank," the caller said. "You have a situation you need help with." It was less a question than a statement.

"Kind of," Ruiz said.

"Don't shit me. I'm busy. I'm selective about what I take on."

"It's my wife," Ruiz said. He pushed a piece of paper toward me and handed me a pen. I wrote: "Can't tell. If Pete, using a voice changer.

Deeper, but cadence same. 'Selective' business resemb how he talks." He leaned over his desk, pulled the pen from my hand, and made a big question mark over "cadence." Then he went back to talking. "Listen, the marriage hasn't been good for years. The problem is, she thinks I have a girlfriend—"

As the caller was saying, "Cut to the chase," I took the pen back and scribbled: "intonation + rhythm of words."

"The actual fact is, I do have a girlfriend. More than a girlfriend. I am in love and she's pregnant."

"The girlfriend?"

"Yes."

"Which one do you want to get out of your life?"

"My wife," Ruiz said, sounding a little stunned that such a question had to be asked. For such an all-business guy, he was a good actor.

"Where do you live?" the caller asked.

"In the Houston area."

"This isn't some game. When I ask you a question, I need an answer right away. Let's do it again. Where do you live?"

"It's an area called West University. Technically West University Place."

"Address."

"Fifty-two Thirty-Four Williams Street." The caller didn't say anything, and Ruiz continued in a shaky voice: "That's my actual address. Look, you're not—"

"Stop right now. We haven't discussed my fee. I haven't checked you out. I need to get an idea of what would be the best possible outcome in your mind."

"You mean, I have to, I get to choose how—"

"Right now, all you're doing is pissing me off. You don't get to do anything until I call you back. And I'm not going to call you and say 'Ted.' Tell me your name."

A couple of seconds' wait, then Ruiz said: "Mike. Michael Costa."

"If you check out and if I'm interested, I'll call you back within forty-eight hours. I'll tell you my fee then. No haggling. I'm the best there is and you're going to get what you pay for. You will say yes or no. If it's yes we need to talk details of transferring payment. If it's no . . ." And then the caller hung up.

# 21

The flight back to New York, less than an hour, felt interminable. I was so worked up I felt flung out of a world in which my body could sense time. But whatever new universe I'd entered—adrenaline based rather than carbon based—overlapped with my old reality. My seatmate's elbow and a snack bag of pretzels that hovered on the edge of my peripheral vision felt alien.

It was about six thirty when I got home from the airport. I was greeted by barks of utter delight, which were soon drowned out by a mix of hysterical sobs and dry heaves from Eliza. That would have been enough to tie my guts into knots for several weeks, except I simultaneously saw the cause—bright-red hair. Not regular dyed-red hair, but a screaming cherry almost thick enough to measure with a ruler.

Then she cried out: "Can't you help me?"

I wasn't going to say: *What made you think this was a good idea?* Still, her staring at me with disbelief as if I were enjoying her humiliation made the notion tempting. We'd been through the great bangs uproar about six months earlier when she wound up with a pathetic inch of scraggly fringe on her forehead. I'd taken her to the hairdresser to have it fixed—or at least hidden—and before, during, and after displayed only sympathy.

So I pulled myself together as best I could. "What would you like me to do?"

"Take me to have it fixed!" Her voice rose to the kind of high-decibel screech that made me regret having ears.

"If you want to go to the hairdresser, I'll take you. You make the appointment. The colorist's name is Nell. And this time I think we should split the cost of whatever has to be done."

Her mouth opened as in one of the nightmare Munch paintings. "What kind of a mother are you?" she gasped.

"A mother who wants her daughter to take responsibility for her actions. I bailed you out on the bangs. Fine. I told you that back then: everyone's entitled to one free ride. I'm giving you a ride and a half."

I might have gone on about how the worst life lesson was teaching someone she could buy herself out of any mess, but Eliza yelled, "I hate you!" Though part of me wanted to laugh at the predictability—those three words that are screeched or muttered in every generation—I also felt on the verge of crying. Some of it was exhaustion after the day in Washington, from the polygraph test to hearing Frank's voice on the headphones. I was also sensing Eliza was using her remaining scintilla of restraint not to blast me with: *I bet my real mother would take me!*

Maybe that thought was mine, and I was unfair putting it on her. So I said, "We can google 'get hair dye out.'"

"All of a sudden it's 'we'?" She wrenched her phone from the back pocket of her shorts, overpriced shreds of denim that just covered her butt. She plopped onto a kitchen chair, her back to me. I tried to comfort myself by thinking we had fewer of these fights than most mothers and daughters.

I wasn't comforted. Granted, it had been a hell of a day of stress and heart-banging exhilaration followed by a predictable but awful wrangle with Eliza. But that wasn't all.

Resentment? Regret? I had opted for normality and gotten far better than I'd dreamed of. But the trade-off was giving up exciting, sometimes risky work and leaving the exploits to someone else. For family's sake.

Adventure for moms? The dads got that one.

I couldn't forget the Special Forces guys I met, both through my job and socially, when I was living in Washington. A surprising number—at least it was a surprise to me—were husbands and fathers. When they went off on a mission, neither they nor their wives or kids knew if they'd return with another medal or in a body bag.

Simultaneously, I had a news report replaying inside my head, TV coverage of women soldiers as they heaved their gear over their shoulders and said good-bye to their families when they were called up for Iraq. Their expressions showed pure anguish. Okay, maybe dads felt the same grief, but their faces stayed blank.

Forget the war itself and how stupid it was. I couldn't spot the pride in those moms knowing they were both representing and serving their country. Just unadulterated pain. Because how many of them honestly thought the day would come when they'd have to leave the home front to fight an asshole war in 120-degree heat?

It's not that I couldn't bear leaving Eliza because I was a mom now. I could go off to Europe or the Middle East to a book fair for a week, take a couple of long weekends with Wynne, even do four or five days off the map doing contract work for the bureau. But none of what I did now involved serious peril. I could expect satisfaction from my work but not the exuberance of a job well executed.

I had chosen a lovely life, but that meant a safer life than I was destined for. It wasn't a cultural thing: no girls allowed. Girls were now allowed. But I'd made a choice and, with it, cut myself off from that thing in me that craved action.

That night in bed, I got what my friends called

into a loop, racing round and round with anxieties. Thoughts: Was Frank/maybe Pete researching a Michael Costa from Texas at this very hour—and had the bureau established enough of a presence so that Frank would be convinced? And the detail Frank had dropped: "I need to get an idea of what would be the best possible outcome in your mind." Ruiz had blinked on that one, and not just because he was playing the role of Mike Costa. I blinked, too, because I'd always pictured Pete shooting. What else, after all that practice with guns and rifles? Was he prepared for anything? Poison? A car bomb? Disemboweling somebody with a sushi knife?

But by being in a loop you're traveling around in a circle or an ellipse. So up next was Eliza: was last month the high point of our line graph, and today the start of a precipitous plunge? And then Josh: how could I not have confided in him, the smartest person I knew? Okay, I didn't want him to say no to my investigation, but if he had? Would I have had to give in to all his perfectly cogent reasons to lay off? Of course not. But then what would happen to our marriage? Oh my God, I hadn't said anything to my parents about keeping quiet about the Pete business, and what if they mentioned something? I had to call them first thing in the morning.

Get out of the loop. A little before 2 a.m., I turned on my side facing away from Josh so I

404

could watch a movie on my phone, one of my favorites: *The Lives of Others*. Fortunately it was a German-language film, which let me keep it on mute and read the subtitles. Josh said I probably loved it so much because it was more like an American film in that it ended in redemption. I told him that yeah, other people's lives weren't miserable enough; you always pick movies that start with misery and end in despair. Was that better?

At some point he must have turned over because I felt the cool warmth of his body cradling me. His arm went around me. I loved that he wasn't hot and sticky during the night, just exuded a lovely June balminess the year round.

"You okay?" he asked.

"Fine," I said, then sighed. "I'm in a loop. I couldn't fall asleep, so I'm watching a movie."

He took my wrist and turned it slightly so he could see what was playing on my cell phone. "That's the one about the East German secret police?" he murmured.

"Yes. This is only the fifth or sixth time I've seen it."

"Good. A bunch of Germans kicking down doors should relax you." There was silence and I saw he was falling back to sleep already, but he added, "Need me for anything? To talk or . . ." He slipped his hand up the tank top I was wearing with pajama bottoms. Maybe his heart was in it, but the rest of him could only try to sustain wakefulness.

I rested my hand on top of his. "It's okay, sweetheart. Go back to sleep. I'm almost there anyway."

Frank called back Ruiz the next midafternoon. Moments later, Ruiz let me know about it, though he didn't want to give me any details over the phone: "Listen to it a few times," he said. "Better if I don't give you my reactions. Make your own judgments. Then we'll talk."

Within a minute I heard the high-pitched *plink* from my phone: an audio file had come in. It was a ringtone that reminded me of the finger cymbals used in belly dancing. It always made me smile, though this time my happy face didn't last long. Frank's first words were: "Do you want the job done?"

Maybe I was overthinking, but the "Do" at the beginning of the sentence made me bet the speaker was more conventional than not and older rather than young since he kept the "Do" at the start of the sentence and didn't use "Hey" or "So." Of course this had nothing to do with any formal training in sociolinguistics; it was just my gut.

There wasn't time for any kind of analysis, since after a second Ruiz was saying yes.

"It's a one-hundred-thousand-dollar flat fee." I heard someone exhale—no doubt Ruiz—and Frank added, "Not negotiable."

"Look, I can get my hands on fifty now and within a couple of weeks—"

"Good-bye."

Had I been hoping to arrange for a homicide, it would have been an unnerving good-bye. It sounded not only final but also annoyed. You don't want a pissed-off hit man having your number.

"Okay, okay," Ruiz-as-Costa said quickly. "I'll find a way to get it." Hearing only silence made him become more definite: "I'll get it."

Now it was Frank's turn to exhale. "I'll call you back in a couple of minutes," he said. Just switching to another phone, I guessed, since there wasn't time enough to move to a different location. I shook my head. This guy's sense of how to avoid detection was years behind the times. Well, good for us.

I timed the wait: a minute, fourteen seconds.

"Let's talk about the job itself," Frank said. "I don't do fake suicides. That's a given."

"Can I ask why not?" Costa asked. Ruiz-as-Costa sounded cautious, afraid of Frank's getting angry.

"A suicide guarantees an autopsy and a police investigation. Sounds simple but it brings a much greater shot of it being viewed as a murder, especially because too many amateurs go for it when they want to kill. They think a bottle of pills, a jump out the window, a bullet in the head:

efficient, minimal suffering, and how could the cops know? They know. I'll call you back."

A longer wait this time, maybe five minutes. Frank might have gone to another location, as if to avoid geolocation by moving out of range of a cell tower. But the callback business was also a performance to allow Costa to absorb the complexity of a hit man's job. It was a clever bit of salesmanship to make Frank seem like a master of his craft. Except he wasn't, at least not techwise.

"All right," Frank said. "Do you have any directives, any particular way you want this done?"

"Nothing too violent." I guessed Ruiz's character, Mike Costa, was showing his humane side.

"Got it," Frank said sourly. "But if it's better fast? Like she gets run over by a truck."

"I guess that's okay if you think that's for the best. Except I was kinda hoping you could say something like, 'This is from Mike with love.' Just so she knows right before."

"Let me think about it. Does she work?"

"My wife? Get off her butt?" Silence. "No, no. She doesn't work."

"Kids?"

"No. Why do you think I want to marry my—"

"Anyone working in the house?"

"A maid." No response. "Oh, she comes in five mornings a week. Eight till twelve."

"And . . . do Ivy's friends come over during the day?"

"You know her name?"

"It would seem so, wouldn't it? Now shut up and listen. Do you want to have this done by a professional or not?"

"Sure. Of course," Costa said. Ruiz was making Costa sound even more eager. He wanted desperately to please Frank. "Most days she meets her friends for lunch, shopping, whatever they do."

Again, a break for the wait, then callback routine. This time around Frank probed deeper into Ivy's schedule, which included twice-a-week manicures, which I thought was a nice touch. Frank also wanted to know whether Ivy would have discussed her husband's girlfriend with her friends ("Probably") and if she'd ever met the girlfriend ("One hundred percent no!").

"Pay attention now," Frank said. "I take pride in my work. I know what I'm doing and I plan. None of my clients, zero, have even gotten arrested. No one's going to think 'homicide' or 'the husband.' Only you can fuck this up. So your girlfriend? You can't marry her or move in for one and a half years after Ivy's death."

"What? You shitting me? Totally out of the question."

"Don't interrupt," Frank said. "You are not going to marry her for eighteen months. Don't try. You can adopt the kid when you get married so you'll be its father." I got an all-over shiver because that last was so reminiscent of my situation. "If you marry her sooner, you run the risk of exposing yourself. That could mean exposing you hired someone like me. I'll be having the marriage records checked, and not just around Houston. If you marry her, she'll be a widow. Got that?"

"Yes."

There was another wait and callback. Frank was now ready to discuss money. "You get your mail at home or at your office?"

"Office," Mike said. "But I have a rule. No one gets near my mail with a letter opener. I don't want anyone prying—"

Frank cut him off. "Give me the exact address. I want to make sure I have it right." After that business was done, he said, "You'll be getting an invoice from L&L Property Consultants next Tuesday. That will sound like a natural with what you do, subdividing and building."

So Frank had researched not only Mike's marital situation but also the entire legend Ruiz had created for the character Mike Costa. Seemingly, it held up. He bought the fiction of Mike being the owner of the Costa Group. It was meant to sound imposing, a cluster of construction companies, but it would be pretty clear it was only Mike at the head of each company. He built low-priced houses on parcels of land he'd subdivided on the cheap, then falsely advertised them as being an easy commute to Houston.

"L&L's invoice will come bearing the name of a post office box," Frank told him. "That's where you send your check. If it doesn't arrive by Friday, your wife might outlive you."

Money Laundering 101, simple but effective. Mike paid for an ostensibly legitimate service from a consulting firm for business advice. His check to L&L Property Consultants would go to a box (which would never again be used by Frank) and get cashed. Then the hundred thousand would wind up in an offshore account. Frank could get his hands on that money by ordering his offshore bank to wire the money to his own business account. Or he could go to the bank itself, in the British Virgin Islands, Argentina, or whatever offshore haven he'd chosen. There, he could pick up actual cash, though he'd need to find a way of smuggling it back into the United States.

"After that Friday when I have your payment," Frank went on, "the job will be done in anytime from five days to a month. Depends on a lot of factors. I decide after I do the necessary surveillance."

"You'll be watching her?"

"You're sounding almost too fucking dumb to do business with." For a second, I thought that Frank and Pete Delaney could not be the same man. Pete had nice manners. Held open doors for people, offered his snowblower services, ladled soup in the church kitchen, said "No thanks" when a waiter would ask if he wanted a double espresso. But then I recalled the keying of the Tesla and how he'd acted threatening to his wife at that dinner with the Grillos.

What the lunch group saw was Pete playing decent Delaney, suburban family guy. On the audio he was another character, a hit man, contemptuous of human frailty. Was that second character, who sounded like a sociopath, the real Pete Delaney? Or just another role in his repertoire?

"Sorry," Mike said. "Sorry. No, of course you have to check out her, uh, pattern." He waited for confirmation but didn't get any. "How about . . . Can you at least give me an idea of when?"

An irritable exhalation. Then Frank said: "The idea is that when it comes, it will be a surprise to you. In a way. Anyone who sees you will describe you as a guy genuinely shocked. Don't start acting, staggering around, and saying, 'Oh my God.' Just be natural. That's why it's also better that you don't know what method I'll be using to do the job. You'll be like: *'What?'*"

"Okay."

"Read me my box number again, where you're sending your check to." Mike read off the box info. "You won't hear from me again."

"Listen to me, *please,*" Mike said, sounding frantic. I wanted to praise Ruiz: *You are some*

412

*actor!* Then his voice grew smaller, weaker. "Has anyone ever changed their mind?"

"Two. But there are no refunds, so you might as well solve your problem." Someone swallowed, presumably Mike. Frank continued: "Once the check clears, you'll have three days to change your mind. After that, it's a go."

I listened to the audio three more times, and I still couldn't say for sure that it was Pete. He sounded completely different, but that was a given, even if he had gone with a relatively cheap voice-changing device. His delivery was flat, the voice of someone who never heard the word "lively." So his side of the conversation sounded mostly like the dullest person somehow engaged in a frightful business. But when he told Ruiz-as-Mike, 'You're sounding almost too fucking dumb to do business with,' there was not only contempt but also anger at his having to deal with such stupidity. It wasn't the anger per se that struck me, but the level of emotion that was so high, so non–Pete Delaney.

I didn't kick this around too long with Carlos Ruiz, since he wasn't a chatty kind of guy, but he did seem genuinely pleased that I thought his performance as Mike was stellar. "Five stars," I said. "You sounded like someone who likes to think of himself as a player, but that tough outer layer is really a thin cover for someone running scared. If Frank has any grasp of subtlety, and that's an open question, he'd see Mike as a guy pushed around by his wife. So his girlfriend probably pushes even harder."

"I don't get people like him," Ruiz said. "All swagger and no guts. Why couldn't he just tell the wife he wants a divorce, that he's getting a killer for a lawyer, and if he has to fight her until he hasn't got a dime left, he'll do it, just to get rid of her?"

All of a sudden he was getting chatty, so I went with it, agreeing that Mike Costa had inflated the wife from just an enraged and rejected woman into a monster who needed to be put down— by a specialist. After a few minutes of that, we switched to a discussion of the tech the bureau was using to locate Frank.

"He obviously thinks he's outsmarting any possible eavesdroppers or law enforcement by switching phones," Ruiz said.

"The more I think about it," I said, "the less competent he seems, at least about technology. Switching phones? Even doing some kind of a crazy dance between cell towers? He's years behind the times. For someone who's such a perfectionist—"

"And so full of pride at his own cleverness—"

"That too. Look, he sits in the same place at our Wednesday lunches so he's facing the lot where he parks. Always pays in cash. Talks about his packaging designs or that he has to go to such and such a place to see a client, but never anything about himself."

"His family?"

"Sure, he'll say what he has to, but they wind up sounding like the generic American family. He'll say a little something about them when the conversation turns to holiday plans, or that he gets his kids T-shirts in every airport he visits. But he keeps conversation about himself to a minimum. He reminded me of me after a few lunches. Like I have a few stories about how I got into scouting Arabic-language books, but they're tailored to satisfy any curiosity, which I admit isn't great. He's the same way: a couple of stories about how he went from a big ad agency to a one-man show and that's it."

"That was in 2008," Ruiz said. "Right?"

"Right. I think that was the beginning of what became a sideline for him. Hit man. Then it grew into his major source of income. But as far as tech goes, he seems stuck in 2009 or 2010."

"Definitely. Like he watched too many episodes of *24*. Also, think about this: If he's sitting there watching his car or saying he's flying somewhere, not driving, it's more a smoke screen for the people around him. If he really viewed himself as a potential target of law enforcement, wouldn't you think he'd try to find what tools we're using now?"

"He'd definitely try," I agreed. "I remember

seeing him constantly changing cell phones, and I thought he loved gadgets or was doing something minor: stupid drug deals, cheating on his wife."

"Well, that's assuming the guy we got is Pete. Whoever he is, he buys mobile phones like they were going out of style. By the way, none of them are registered to any one person. Some are stolen shit he could get from any dealer, others are from . . . wherever."

"The land of lost phones," I said. "So where was he when he made the calls?" Within a couple of seconds of his calling Ruiz-as-Mike, the bureau would have located him. Then its technology would grab him—with astounding equipment that could mimic a cell tower. Except the signal was far more powerful—and cell phones were programmed to reach out for the strongest signal. So no matter how many times "Frank" switched phones when talking to Ruiz, the bureau's experts in wireless technology could find and take over his phone, recording any conversation. Not exactly an ACLU pleaser. Their favorite equipment, called a DRT box or dirtbox, could even get through an encryption system used to keep conversations private.

"He was in Brooklyn, so that's not far from Long Island." Ruiz's own phone was so high tech that not only did his voice have amazing clarity, but I could hear him eating potato chips—probably lifting up the mic while he chewed. The sound lacked the hard crack of a Dorito or the Styrofoamy crunch of a Cheez Doodle.

"Where in Brooklyn?" I asked.

"In an area called Dumbo. Down Under—"

"The Manhattan Bridge. I've been there. Expensive now, very cool, right by the East River. Or was he in a vehicle?" I asked.

"On foot. And close enough to the water that he was able to toss the phones in, one after another."

"Shit." Once they got the IMSI, the international mobile subscriber identity of any phone, they could still have traced him, whether or not the phone was on.

"Definitely shit," Ruiz said. "Because it was cloudy enough that they couldn't zoom in and get any pictures." Dirtboxes flew in small planes or drones, seeking the phones they wanted and then taking them over. When I'd been on the Joint Terrorism Task Force, we'd used them far more than civil libertarians would like. On clearer nights, the aircraft also could zoom in and get video, often not good enough for facial recognition but sufficient for determining the height, approximate weight, and length of stride for any target. "Hey, at least we know he was in the New York–Long Island area. That could mean Pete Delaney."

"Or not."

"Or not," Ruiz agreed. "We've got more work to do."

# 22

By seven thirty the next morning, Josh was off to the courthouse and Eliza to school. I walked Lulu, but when I got back, all I could do was amble from room to room pointlessly, like an uninterested real estate broker before an open house. Sit? Read? Make a spreadsheet of all the books I'd read for work, with a column for those I'd recommended—oh, and another for those that had actually been translated and published? Impossible. I was total energy, no thought.

Outside the temperature was heading toward sweltering, in the high eighties, one of those mid-June days that jogged my memory of New York City summers when breathing became an aerobic activity. I went downstairs and emptied the dishwasher, but after that I felt so jumpy I couldn't even concentrate long enough to put the Rice Chex back into the pantry.

I changed into one of those allegedly sweat-wicking T-shirts, slipped my driver's license and car key into the back pockets of my shorts. My phone went into what little cleavage my sports bra allowed. In spite of the dog's glare of betrayal, I drove unaccompanied to a beach about a mile and a half away.

It was low tide, and a hard run on compacted sand might exhaust me into serenity. Occasionally a breeze floated off the tops of the lazy ripples of Long Island Sound, offering unnecessary cooling to the beachfront homes whose mammoth air-conditioning units drowned out gulls' cries. I passed new, shingled megahouses (one with a birdhouse replica of itself) and white midcentury multilevels with walls of darkly tinted glass. A few of the old stone or brick Gold Coast manors had survived the twenties and now gazed away from the new neighbors, toward Westchester. One of them might once have had a green light at the end of its dock.

My legs were aching after almost an hour's run on the sand, but at least the roiling energy that had been getting me nowhere had dissipated. I walked up the splintered stairs that led from the beach to a small parking area and leaned against the fender of my car near the driver's door, emptying the sand out of my sneakers. I still had that runner's high. Since there was no mirror around, I was glorying in thinking of myself as a sweaty, glistening goddess (golden with the tan I'd developed in the last fifty minutes) making my eyes shine sky blue.

Damn. I felt a sharp insect bite right at the small fleshy spot where my arm met my back—right near my bra strap—a potentially dangerous area because it could randomly pop out as a fat blob when I was wearing a sleeveless dress. I slapped right where the bee or bug had stung, hoping for instant retribution.

Except even before I could pull away my hand to check for a squished insect, I was smashed with a wave of dizziness. *Bee sting? I never knew I was . . .* My brain instructed my body to bend knees, had me crumple to the ground rather than allowing me to crash. I was reaching under the neckline of my shirt to pull my cell phone out of my bra, but then darkness came. I think I welcomed it because it was so much better than terror.

*Such an uncomfortable position,* I thought. Not exactly "thought": it was a physical realization, like during sleep, when you rise to consciousness just enough to switch from some contorted position back to repose. So I shifted. Except I couldn't shift. The dread I felt in that instant was so profound I dismissed it as a neural glitch. Again, I tried to move. Oh God.

I was so drugged that it took me too long to figure out that I'd be better off opening my eyes. That wasn't much of a help because, wherever I was, there seemed to be no light. For a crazy minute, it was a relief; because I had the worst headache ever, as if my brain had been inflated and was too big for my head. The pressure felt strong enough to crack my skull. Each breath brought a tidal wave of nausea. There was nothing I could see, though I definitely understood this was no longer a day at the beach. I sensed I was indoors, but I was still so dizzy and mentally mushy that I couldn't have testified to it under oath.

At that point I realized I was sitting up. Yes, hard floor, indoors. For a second the pressure in my head got even more painful and I thought I'd just lie down, close my eyes again. There was nothing to see anyway. That must have been the point when I comprehended I was tied up. My legs stretched out straight in front of me bound at the ankles and midshins. Pulling them apart was useless because they were tied with . . .

I was able to think a little. They were tied with something that had not even a millimeter of extra space, like handcuffs. When I tried to reach out and feel what was on my legs, I realized my wrists were joined behind my back behind some kind of a post. My palms were positioned facing each other, touching. Even though the post wasn't wide, my position put an awful strain on my shoulders and neck, my arms pulling back and forcing me into an unnaturally upright posture.

I had to fight whatever drug was in my system, try to be alert to what was going on. Unfortunately, my eyes—unable to make out anything in the darkness—wanted to close. Because what was the point of looking into blackness?

I stared and rotated my head. It couldn't move much because it was pressed against the post. A post, not a column, because I felt definite edges. I can't say the realization exhilarated me, but it clarified my mind because I realized I was capable of processing information. Still, moving my head made the pressure against my skull such torment. Surveillance was agonizing. I could force myself to move, but it brought any thinking to a screeching stop.

I called out: "Is anybody here?" No answer. Then I realized how stupid it was to have let my captor know I was awake. Maybe now he was lifting a weapon with an infrared sight or silently gathering whatever tools he was going to torture me with. I waited. My heart was pounding to the point where I thought, *Oh, I'm having a heart attack.* For a minute I panicked, but then I calmed down by telling myself: *Better than having my fingers cut off.* All right, not calmed down. But at least I grasped two things: I'd made a major mistake in calling out. On the other hand, tied up and surrounded by darkness and silence, I was pretty sure I was alone.

Not that I'd bet a pile on the latter, but it was that same instinct that made some protohuman ancestor deep in a cave at night reach for a club—or not: *There's a threatening animal in here. There's not a threatening animal in here.*

What I would have bet on was that the

threatening animal was Pete Delaney. Though not impossible, it would be incredibly hard for a random assassin, a.k.a. Frank, to trace the woman who'd been asking questions on Galveston Island back to me. He (or possibly she) would need to have incredible investigative skills and a database equal to that of the bureau.

Why would he leave me alone in this place, assuming it was Pete? To let me die of thirst or hunger? Because as my thinking improved, I was able to escape the excruciating pain in my head and check outside myself. It was horribly hot. When I'd gone running that morning, assuming it was still the same day, it was so hot and humid that my shirt and shorts fused with my skin. It was so much hotter here, and still humid, though I was so dehydrated my tongue glued itself to the roof of my mouth. I figured it had to be over one hundred degrees.

Logic, whatever good that was, told me that Pete wouldn't let me die without learning what I knew. There was the possibility that I'd told all under the influence of sodium pentothal or some other blab-inducing drug, though I doubted it. If he wasn't here, there would be a purpose behind it. For all I knew, Pete could be putting in an appearance at the soup kitchen, ladling out lentils.

But what if my being here had nothing to do with Pete and whatever weaponry or equipment was in that super-secure garage of his? What if that sharp *Dexter*-like sting I felt as I emptied out my sneaker was some date-rape drug administered by a serial killer? Ironic, they would say at my funeral—or memorial service if they never found the body—that she'd faced so many dodgy situations in her life but succumbed to that flesh-eating monster of a man.

*Stop it! Now!* Just as we learned mindfulness in training, we also learned diversion, that most useful skill. Think of something that itself commands your attention, demands concentration. Instead of inhaling for its own sake, I sniffed the hot air. I knew that with each breath, the sense of smell diminishes, so I breathed through my mouth for a minute. Then I tried again, and it was what I'd smelled the first time. Wood, sawed wood. Not a powerful odor, like a lumberyard's. Not old, finished wood, like the scent surrounding you when you sit in the main reading room of the New York Public Library. It was similar to some apartment that Wynne's carpenters were remodeling, where a day or two before, a round power saw had sliced through strips of ceiling molding.

Okay, one more time: I inhaled again and noticed that the air, while blisteringly hot, was not thick with sawdust. But as I was sniffing away, I was also trying to figure out what I was tied with. My wrists being bound tightly together with my hands palm to palm, I wasn't able to touch anything. But I pulled my elbows outward, and it seemed to me the binding was narrow. So, small chance of duct tape. Better chance of zip ties, because the binding felt like plastic against my skin.

However, they weren't those skinny little strips that thread through a kind of buckle made of the same material. If Pete (or Frank) went into a hardware store, he wouldn't say: *Oh give me that cheap bunch of zip ties that I can use for fastening some electric wires together.* No, he would find stronger, wider zip ties that could keep two weighty things tight together—including ankles, shins, wrists—and wouldn't give even under strain. Law enforcement often uses handcuffs and leg restraints made from zip ties because they're disposable, no worries about DNA or blood contamination like with metal handcuffs.

My eyes were getting used to the darkness. Not that I could see much at all, but it seemed I was in a big space. I looked down to see if I could verify my conclusion about zip ties from the binding on my ankles or shins, but it was darker near the floor, plus looking down gave me a nice combo of fierce pain in my forehead and gagging from a wave of nausea. And when I looked straight out I didn't see anything resembling another human being in the space. Had he just left me here to weaken? Would he come back in and try to get me to talk by waving an iced tea and a Mallomar in front of me when I was on the verge of madness?

I realized then that he wouldn't come back in: no, he would come *up*. It hit me that I had to be in an attic. What I could feel of the post behind me was that it was wood, one of those plywood floor-to-ceiling two-by-fours you see all the time on home reno shows after they say, "We've got to blow out these walls." And then they reconfigure part of the huge space as a downstairs bathroom. But then they put up drywall, paint it, and it's a room. Here, they'd left the wood beams alone. He must have secured my hands behind the two-by-four and then, separately, zip-tied my wrists together.

During training the bureau had us watch a video on how to break out of duct tape, handcuffs, and zip ties. Then we had to run through it all. Our instructor and two assistants walked around the room watching us as we taped our wrists with duct tape so they wouldn't get horribly abraded during the practice. I couldn't think of the exact technique, which involved slamming your wrists against—I thought—your lower back. There was something also with hips, but I realized I was still drugged and none of my recollections were distinct. The only thing that actually came through clearly was a phrase from another lecture, about anesthetics and soporifics—"loss of mental acuity."

That was it for a while; I have no idea how long. But I realized I'd fallen asleep only when my own snore/snort woke me. The sound startled me so much that I panicked, pulling at my wrists, trying to lift up my butt and get my legs to bend at the knees. If anything, the attic seemed darker than before. There was no longer a way I could survey the room and recognize I was in a large area.

I tried to deduce why I believed there was less light and then had a brilliant *aha!* moment when I realized it had gotten dark. Whatever sunlight had penetrated the attic (if that's what it really had been) was gone. Assuming I hadn't been drugged for months and it was still June, a few days before the summer solstice, it was now after nine at night.

Having made that calculation, my mind was detoxed enough to realize I was in a universe populated by more than me and Pete Delaney. How had I not thought immediately about Josh, Eliza? What were they doing? Okay, Eliza would text me one time or maybe two when I didn't show to pick her up at tennis clinic. Or was it her volunteer day at the animal shelter? When a text didn't get a response, she'd call my cell, but it would go to voicemail. Unless—God forbid, God forbid—Pete answered and said something horrifying to her. Or just answered with "Hello," and the idea of a man having my phone . . . *Stop!* Josh and I both encouraged her to think. So what would she do? She'd get a ride home with someone she knew or she'd call the local taxi service; she knew to do that. Maybe on the way home she'd call Josh. Court would probably be in session so she'd leave a message. Fine, good, then she'd call my parents. *Oh no!*

But maybe not the worst thing in the world because not only was her grandfather of three years a retired detective, but he was also a detective who knew what I was up to. By seven o'clock, they'd all be gathering at the house. Josh would have called Wynne by this time, and she would tell him that truly she hadn't a clue to where I was. Knowing her, I imagined she'd mull for an hour and come to realize that something was truly wrong. By eight she would call him and tell all about our time in Galveston. But by then, my father, for whom trouble was an old, familiar adversary, would have filled Josh in on Corie's electrifying adventure that everyone except you seemed to know about, Josh.

So before it got as dark as it was now, Josh—ex-assistant United States attorney for the Southern District of New York, former chief of its Criminal Division—would have called someone in the FBI and by now would have been connected with Carlos Ruiz. Josh would be rational and effective. Frightened, too. He loved me. Not just that: he found me challenging, exciting. But was there something deep in his soul that was already agonizing: *Oh shit, am I going to have to find a new wife again?*

Except for the couple of seconds when I wondered if Josh would marry anyone we knew, I was also thinking about death, real death, and whether it was like instant nothingness. Or was it going down a long corridor into a white light, like in *Six Feet Under*, and would there be a welcoming committee: Jane Austen, Zaynab Fawwaz, Gene Roddenberry, my aunt Gussie, and my dad's partner Mickey Soong. I'd want to get acclimated to being dead before I went over to Shakespeare and told him how much his work meant to me.

Then I felt guilty that I'd left out God (whose existence I sometimes doubted), except then I realized I was making a list of greeters because most of all I was terrified of the opposite of instant nothingness: of being dead and conscious in a box. I could deal with bugs, but the horror of worms and slugs actually on me—in me—was a different story. I never thought I could scream with my mouth closed, but I did.

*Change the subject!* I would never again see Sami. An old song, but not one of mine, came into my head. I remembered my mom playing a cassette of her favorites in the car, so I must have been pretty young. But there was a lyric: "But I always thought that I'd see you again." I was—what?—seven or eight. I'd sobbed.

Even as an eight-year-old I understood *too soon* and *finality*.

I had a brief, fervent thought of Bayezid II, the sultan of the Ottoman Empire, who sent his navy to evacuate imperiled Jews from Spain in 1492. This was definitely not the kind of thinking the lecturer at Quantico had drawled about. "Focus on one thang: solving the problem." Maybe I was stereotyping and he was really from Oregon.

The standard way of getting out of zip ties, when your hands were tied behind your back, was to lift your arms way back so your wrists were about at hip level and then slam them into your lower back. This could put about fifty pounds of pressure on the ties and presumably be enough to snap the ratchet, the belt-buckle-looking thing that held the gears that went up the center of the strap, like a ladder. However, the gears were angled so that they could be pulled only one way: made tighter, not looser. Clever if you didn't break your coccyx and had enough strength in your arms, but my bound wrists were tied against the wooden two-by-four, so I couldn't raise them up.

I tried to pull at my ankles but recognized that if Pete/Frank/serial-killer-whom-I-wasn't-going-to-think-about came in, he would immediately see I'd somehow smashed open the ratchet. I did know a few good leg grabs, but unless he strolled over and offered me his upper body so I could grab his neck between my thighs—blech!—and sever his spinal cord, that wasn't the way to go. I shook at the image of not being able to break his neck or choke him to death and getting stuck with his head poking out from just above my knees, his eyes bulging with hate.

My nausea was a little better, but the headache wasn't, though that could have been because I was dehydrated. In addition to having run for almost an hour early in what I assumed was the same day, I'd had nothing to drink, and I was sweating. Rivulets (which is how sweat was always described) were streaming down just about every part of my body. I knew I could manage without food or water for twenty-five hours, since I'd been fasting on Yom Kippur every year since I was twelve. But I'd lost so much fluid. I had no idea how much of my weakness was due to that, along with whatever drug I'd been injected with, plus bottled-up hysteria (impersonating grace under pressure).

Only half aware, I had begun sawing the edge of the zip tie on the corner of the post to get through the smooth, hard edge and get to the gears. I knew my chances of success were close to zero, but there was no other way to slip out of the ties that went around my wrists. If I could saw them off, I had a decent shot of working my way out of the zip tie that was holding both hands behind the post.

I didn't have much room to move them up and down because they were trussed up so tightly. The plastic was incredibly hard—so I'd practically have to saw each individual molecule. Moving my wrists up and down faster didn't do much because my energy was so sapped that in under a minute I got breathless. I stopped and counted slowly to ten, which at least gave me rapid rest.

That's when I felt something weird on my finger. Ring finger, left hand. My wedding ring and engagement ring were gone. *Motherfucker!* I thought. I was so angry that I started sawing against the post harder than ever in my two inches of maneuverability. Like a crazy person. It was one thing for Pete or Frank to be a professional killer and a sociopath. But to be a thief? Fucking outrageous! When I came home with the ring, my dad said, "Holy shit!" And my mom said, "Utterly magnificent!" She placed her hand on her chest in wonderment. Then she asked, "You do know to turn it around when you're on the subway, right?"

It was so silent in that space that if Pete were there he'd have to be aware of the sawing. But I sensed he wasn't, because he would respond in some way to that sound, even if it was only to assure himself that nothing I was doing was helping me. Then the fear of his being behind me returned, of him watching me either with night vision glasses—though there wasn't enough light for them to function properly—or with infrared goggles that relied on thermal imaging. But even if he was in front of me, behind me, somewhere else watching on an infrared detecting camera, I wasn't being stopped. So I kept doing it.

I'd no idea where I was. I doubted it was Shorehaven because it was beyond too close to home. It *was* home. On the other hand, even if Pete made a hundred thousand dollars per hit, he wouldn't have enough money to fly me some- place, because it would have to end with him killing the pilot and . . . No, because there'd still be a plane and maybe even a flight plan; this wasn't a CIA rendition. More likely Pete had dumped me in the trunk of his car and driven me . . . wherever. Somewhere isolated, obviously, since he'd have to get me out of the trunk and schlep me up one or two flights of stairs into an attic, drag me through the room, and do the zip tie business.

Not that I needed confirmation, but I strained my neck to lower my head to the general area of my bra, and of course my cell phone wasn't there. Because otherwise, even with it turned off, I could be geolocated.

Meanwhile I kept sawing against the post.

Twenty seconds on, ten off, because if someone came into the place or climbed stairs—assuming I actually was in an attic and not in some unfinished, near-windowless space—I wanted to be able to hear.

Was I making any progress? I tried turning my wrists and squeezing them even tighter together, hoping to feel a rough spot on the zip tie, but I wasn't able to feel anything. Still, after listening for signs of life during each ten-second pause and then going back to sawing, I thought I felt a tiny section where the top edge of the plastic strip fit more easily against the right angle of the wood post. Was I imagining an infinitesimal slit? Even if it wasn't imaginary, I recognized that at this rate, I could abrade the plastic by the time I was forty.

Call it foxhole faith, but I remembered reading an article years earlier about the "choose life" command in the Bible. When God said, "I have put before you life and death, blessing and curse, therefore choose life!"—it wasn't "No abortion, no suicide"—though those were possible interpretations. It was that every choice we make needed to be life affirming, since every choice had reverberations in the world.

It was right after 9/11 that I decided to join the bureau. My thinking may have been that for me, choosing life meant fighting those who would deny it. I had the language skills, the street and people smarts, and the combative nature to be part of the battle.

Now I had to save myself—not just to choose life for myself but also to rid the world of this scourge. Hopefully not as Terminator, but as agent for justice.

I sawed even harder, then stopped and listened more intently. I began sawing again but at six seconds I froze. Someone had entered the space.

# 23

I have to go to the bathroom," I told him.
He'd come in almost silently. I hadn't heard him as much as sensed movement of air, but it was enough. At "bathroom" his movement came to a stop so abrupt that it made a sound: a near-inaudible *clunk* of the soles of sneakers banging together. Surprise, maybe: *What, a request? No hysteria?* He didn't answer, so I repeated it. "I really have to go."

"Tough shit." Pete Delaney made no attempt to disguise his voice. Not good. If I had a balance sheet, this wasn't headed for the assets column. Clearly, he didn't see me as having a long-term relationship with him—or with anyone.

Harsh, but sociopaths aren't given to random acts of kindness. The bathroom business was not as dire as it might have been, because I'd already peed twice. That was as repulsive as it sounds. I understood that if I lived, I would be horribly chafed. But I hoped against hope that in letting me go to the bathroom, he might at least turn on a light or loosen the zip ties on my ankles and shins. I could see the space I was in. With luck, I could trip him, kick him, take him down.

"Speaking of tough shit," he went on, "did you

ever hear that people shit out of pure terror." He stopped for a few seconds as if expecting I would respond, *Really? Do they?* "Or as they're dying. Sometimes after, because the muscles relax before rigor mortis sets in."

Clearly, he planned not just to kill me but also to try to terrify me. He could have gone straight to the killing, except he needed to know what I knew.

And vice versa. I hadn't an inkling about what he really knew about me. Had he somehow found out I'd been with the bureau? That I had been trained not to show terror unless it was tactically advantageous? During a lecture at Quantico that preceded the demos and then practice, someone had raised her hand and asked: "But if you're in a really terrifying situation, you may not be rational enough to decide what's tactically advantageous." And the lecturer shrugged and said, "Okay, then you're dead."

Not yet. I decided for the time being that there was no purpose in my talking. If you were being held captive, you were supposed to humanize yourself, changing yourself from a thing—an enemy, an opponent of your abductor's beliefs, an adversary who would restrict his freedom— into a fellow human being. Form a relationship with your kidnapper. Except sociopaths like Pete aren't the relationship type.

So I had to rely on ordinary life. When you

know someone, you can read his or her silence: a need for quiet, inward seething, passive aggression, quelling an angry outburst. But if someone's a stranger or a vague acquaintance? It's hard to read the words unsaid. So I figured I had a small shot at unnerving him with silence.

Naturally I didn't expect him to get distraught. No doubt in this second career of his, he'd come across people who determinedly clammed up—though my guess was eventually nearly all of them talked. Still, I wasn't a total stranger to him. He knew that while I wasn't a chatterer, I could be congenial, friendly enough, curious about other people's lives, eager to talk about books and movies. Possibly, not getting anything from me might bother him because it wasn't my MO.

"I see," Pete said wearily. "The silent treatment. You know how long that will work? Until I lose my patience. And if you think you've ever felt pain before, you're in for an ugly surprise."

I thought about praying. Not a beseeching: *God, don't let him do it.* Just the traditional prayer, the Shema. Jews are supposed to recite it twice a day and at their deaths; it's a declaration of the oneness of God and what God expects of you.

That's the way people do it, go out how they lived. Christians have last rites or prayers. Muslims' final words are supposed to be: "There is no God but Allah." I had a nanosecond of

438

regret about never learning what Hindus did.

Except I was pretty sure you were supposed to say the Shema right at your death. What if I lasted for another day or two? Would I remember to do it then? So I said it pretty fast, just in case, figuring that if there was an omniscient God, God would understand I had to get back to the "choose life" business.

*Amen.* Then right away I began to wonder if there was anything I could do about the zip ties on my ankles, which were 99 percent likely to be in Pete's line of sight. Speaking of sight, I figured he must be wearing thermal-imaging goggles.

"Having fun yet?" he asked. "Thirsty?" Then came a sound I'd never considered as being unmistakable, but it was: *thhhp.* The opening of a cooler, the solid plastic kind with the lift-up top you use for water bottles and soda and beer cans for a blistering afternoon outdoors. Then quickly closed to keep the ice frozen because (not counting a person like me, on the way to dying of thirst) who the hell wants a warm root beer?

"Don't waste what's left of your energy trying to get me to tell you my life story," he said. "I know what I am. I'm not one of those who have to boast about it. If you're thinking you can distract me, you've got another thing coming."

He was good at what he did: a simple sip, not a slurp. Going about drinking as if it were the normal thing to do. A few seconds and then another sip. This would go on until the can was empty. A little later, more soda or beer, maybe along with a sandwich. Guaranteed not Kraft Singles American Cheese. Italian salami, I thought, or maybe liverwurst, so I couldn't miss the aroma—the possibility—of food.

There was no need to close my eyes, but that's what you do when you're concentrating. In my mind, I opened a packet of Excedrin with my teeth, popped two pills, and drank a long glass of cool water. Not ice cold because that could make my headache beyond unbearable. I imagined the Excedrin heading down my esophagus toward my stomach. I watched as it broke into small pieces, then into teeny flakes, then into minuscule dots that traveled through my bloodstream up toward my head. When the sound of Pete sipping broke through my meditation, I imagined him drinking carbonated kale juice. That didn't work so I changed it to cat piss.

I envisioned him studiously ignoring me, maybe imagining my anguish at the sound of liquid. Except for an instant, I heard a teeny voice. Since I was far from clarity, it took me a minute of: *Huh? Wha'?* to realize he was listening to something through earphones. Not music. Words, and I remembered him saying at lunch that when he took long trips in a car or a plane, he listened to audiobooks. Had he said history? Maybe a cheery bio of Torquemada.

This wasn't a plus, I knew, his passing time with a cold drink, an interesting book, watching me through goggles. My guess was that for jobs that required him to gain information, he had a pattern, and this was part of it. I needed to shake him out of his usual way of doing things.

Okay, so did I have any advantage over the other people he'd killed? Well, I assumed he most likely didn't know them. And even if he ever had to establish some sort of relationship or even rapport, it would be in the service of carrying out a job that would earn him a hundred thousand dollars, maybe more. Also, given the fact that he was likely a sociopath, rapport probably meant zilch.

No doubt I also meant zilch to him. But the difference was that I knew the Pete Delaney who lived on Long Island, designed cute purse-size packaging for tampons, and put gas in his snowblower in October so he wouldn't be caught by a freak early snowstorm.

So he needed me to answer his questions: *How did I know? Who else knew? What did they know?* But I had one other qualification. I was probably the one person who could appreciate the extraordinary range of his skills. Sure, he told me he didn't need to boast. Yet I felt he wouldn't mind a witness to his brilliance, even for a few moments. And who could better attest to that than the hunter who'd become his prey?

Okay, so I could wait till he finished chapter nineteen of his audiobook, but by then I'd be weaker than I was now, possibly dead. I remembered reading some memo when I was on the Joint Terrorism Task Force about how to handle being kidnapped. There was a bullet point about electrolytes and what happens when you didn't have enough of them. It discussed the downward incline, complete with graph, of how your strength ebbs and your intellect . . . One of the women on the task force whose cubicle was next to mine, Nadia, read that part aloud. She said: "If my intellect wasn't already shot to shit, I wouldn't be here." I'd laughed and that was all I could recollect about assessing my electrolytes.

I had to interrupt his program with an announcement: "Pete!"

It took a couple of minutes for him to respond, though almost immediately I saw a brief pinprick of light as—I guessed—he turned off his phone or headphones. The blink (though it didn't last as long as that) wasn't right up close. Though I was an abysmal judge of distance, it appeared to come from beyond the point where he could just reach out and touch me—at least ten feet, maybe more.

Still, he didn't say anything. Possibly my calling him Pete unsettled him, since I doubted his victims were on a first-name basis with him.

Finally he answered: "What?" I could have

been reading too much into it, but in spite of his attempt to sound indifferent, the final *t* in the word was emphasized, almost spit out, as if he were pissed.

No point in theatrics like: *You've made a terrible mistake!* I didn't have time enough and he wouldn't have the patience. Pete Delaney, Shorehaven's nice guy, was probably reluctant to risk the identity he'd built up, which included his family and a business as a packaging designer, unless he was 99 percent sure I was a serious threat. So I said: "What made you take notice of me?"

"What are you trying to do? Form some kind of bond so I won't be able to kill you?"

"No. I don't think that's possible."

Anybody with even one shred of humanity would be dying to ask: *Hey, why don't you think it's possible?* And I had no doubt that the shred was there. Not that he cared about my opinion: he cared how he was perceived. Could I somehow have picked up that he was soulless? Also, he was deeply concerned if there was anyone else who felt the same way or whether I'd shared my suspicions about him. It wasn't in his nature to ask directly: *Hey, why don't you believe forming a bond with me is possible?* So it would force him to find out indirectly.

Not that I actually thought all this out. I wasn't up to that. It was simply what I knew from life and training and reading. Like if you throw out an idea: *He is unlike others in that he is utterly unfeeling,* then people (even the subject himself) will need to know: *Huh? What makes you think so? How did you find out? He's married, has kids. Doesn't he have bonds with them?* People want more than an explanation when you tell them someone can be born without a conscience. They want the story. I'd read some article by a philosopher who said human beings are hardwired for narrative; she didn't make an exception for sociopaths.

Time to rephrase the question, more directly. I asked: "What made you view me as a threat?"

"You were different from the others. I saw that a few months after you joined the group. Remember? There was a gigantic crack of thunder during lunch. Everyone else either jumped or screamed. Someone said, 'What the fuck?'" I shrugged. "You don't remember it?" I shook my head this time, and since he didn't demand any more of an answer, I decided my goggles theory was correct. "It was incredibly loud, like a Magnum revolver," he added. "You know what that is?"

"A big gun?"

I thought I heard an impatient exhalation, but maybe I just thought a sigh of irritation belonged in the narrative. "There was another time," he went on. "Fire engines went by the restaurant, around that curve onto Shore Road, and suddenly turned on the sirens. They screamed. They're made to disturb people, to get attention. And I looked at you. I don't think you even blinked. At some point, I guess the next Wednesday, you were across the table and I asked you something in a little lower than normal voice, to check your hearing. You heard it. So I asked myself, what kind of person is so cool under fire?"

"I don't see how you could decide that. For all you know, I could have some sort of cognitive disability."

"I don't have time for this shit," he said. I wouldn't say he became highly emotional, but he did sound exceedingly cranky. I tried to think of a comeback, but before I could he said, "You know what you reminded me of? You reminded me of me. Not just cool under pressure. Cold. Like you've been trained. Or just experienced, at something. I remember one time I was talking about a design job in St. Louis, but I'm also checking you out every once in a while, just to see if you're reacting to anything I'm saying."

"Was I?"

"No, because you were basically doing the same thing I was. You were taking green peppers out of something you were eating but also checking me out. But barely looking at me. An amateur would really think you were more into the green peppers, but I knew. What's that old saying? Takes one to know one."

"Takes one what?" I asked.

"Shut up! Do you remember that big cockroach?"

"Yes," I said. "You're talking about the one that came out of the breadbasket at that first restaurant, right? After that, we changed to La Cuisine."

"Do you remember what you said? Everyone else was disgusted. A couple were practically hysterical. And you said . . ."

He waited for me to fill in the blank. "I don't remember," I told him. "Was it something sarcastic?"

"You said, 'I guess I'll have to pass on the sourdough.'" I could hear he was angry that I'd been so offhand, so snotty. Maybe it was that he hated snide women. But my guess was it was more about the roach—that he'd been afraid of it, but I hadn't. "You didn't even goddamn flinch," he said.

"I had a boyfriend who went to medical school in Miami," I explained. "He had a room in a house where they had palmetto bugs. They're like two inches long. And they flew. At first I was beyond freaked, but it cured me of all my bug fears."

"I never met a woman who was completely not afraid of bugs," he said.

"I'm sure there are women entomologists and—"

"Shut the fuck up!"

For a while there was silence. I figured he must have been upset because he lost control. After what seemed like a long time, I thought I heard the little voice from his audiobook again. I strained, and then, when I was sure that's what it was, I started sawing again, twenty seconds on, ten off. I was making some progress. When I slanted my hands toward the left, the right angle of the post where I'd been working seemed to fit into a notch in the zip tie that was more pronounced than it had been earlier. At the least, I'd cut through the rounded edge of the tie; I had no idea what they called it, but it was the plastic equivalent of a rolled hem of a scarf.

When I stopped sawing to rest, I didn't hear the audio anymore, so I stayed still. I didn't hear anything else, but I did pick up a scent that I guessed was one of those prewet wipes people use on camping trips or when changing a baby's diaper. In that second, I really wanted to kill him, put my hands around his cool neck and bang his head against the wall.

"I'm always on guard duty," Pete said suddenly. "Always watching, always listening." As I was wondering what, if anything, I should say to this, he kept going: "People don't realize it, but I keep an eye on everyone. Our garbage guy? There's not a day I don't walk out and give him a friendly hello, like with friends. Except I'm watching every bit of stuff in those cans, even the shredded papers in black bags, get into the back of that truck. Early on, I told him I was still a kid at heart and loved to see the blade shovel the trash against the moving wall in the back. Do I give a crap if he thinks I'm a kid, or just suspicious? I always get a smile and he gets a big fat tip at Christmas."

I knew where he was going. "Sounds like a workable arrangement," I said.

"So obviously, I saw your car—well, not your car—one day when I went out. The second I got back into the house, I grabbed my binoculars and bingo, managed to get the plate number. Checked one of my databases, found out it was a rental, and double bingo. A loaner car from North Coast Subaru. Called, pretended I was a cop. Car making a left turn from the right lane. Do I have to tell you the et cetera?"

"What databases do you use?" I asked.

"Ticktock. Your time's running out. Want to hear about my databases?"

"No."

"I keep my eyes open and my ears open. One day at lunch, before you got to the restaurant, Lucy and John were talking about you, how you'd only been living on Long Island for three years. And that was how long you'd been married, three years. Some people might have let that go, but not me."

He appeared to be waiting for a response. I asked: "So what did you do?"

"I'm a success because I'm a nonstop analyzer. You come across very ordinary. A wisecrack here or there, but mostly just a regular married lady—who happens to have nerves of steel. I'm the only one who would have picked up on that aspect. My guess is most people see you as okay, friendly, someone with a job that's a little unusual but other than that not important. You seem to like what you're doing but not love it. You don't seem under any serious pressure to grow your business."

"Given the economics of publishing—"

"If I don't ask you to say something, keep your fucking mouth shut. So at first I thought, 'Why would she be under pressure? She's got a rich husband.' Isn't just a stepmother but adopted his kid. Good move. Shrewd. Catch him, then make it hard for him to get out of the deal. But I told you I'm an analyzer. Does it make sense that this kind of woman would spend ten or twenty years reading books in Arabic? You see, Mrs. Judge Geller, your CV doesn't compute. You're more like someone who changed course in midstream." I was going by his rules so I said nothing. He must have needed a response because he said, "Go ahead. You can talk."

"I'm one of those . . . sort of geeks who like doing things that don't appeal to most people. I love reading Arabic-language literature, learning about all the diverse cultures in which the language is spoken."

"With nerves like steel. And later I thought like someone maybe trained in one of those terrorist camps. Maybe you were following me because you knew I suspected you of something." It was only my alleged nerves of steel that kept me from rolling my eyes, just in case he had some super-tech thermal imaging goggles that allowed him to make out facial expressions.

"A terrorist?" I said. "In Shorehaven?"

"You don't make your living from knowing French. You make it from *Arabic*. I figured, 'Maybe she is a sleeper, who in a week or a year they can say go and blow up the Empire State Building and you'll do it.' But believe it or not, I'm a fair guy." I heard him take another sip from his soda can, but it must have been unpleasantly warm, because he opened the cooler again. "A nice icy bottle of water," he said. "And don't you wish you could have some?" I didn't answer. "I said," he yelled, "don't you wish you could have some? When I ask you a question, you answer."

"Yes, I wish I could have some."

"That's better. You're not getting any, but you knew that. So I did some more detective work on you. You think I want a terrorist living in town? You see something, say something, and all that shit. You know what I did? I called the Queens

College alumni office. I asked Phoebe and Iris one day where you went to school because I thought you looked familiar, and one of them told me Queens College."

Of course I was listening intently, but the headache was worse and moving even a fraction of an inch made me feel my skull couldn't take any more pressure.

"Here's what I did. I called up the placement office and told them I needed to clear up some confusion, that I called earlier about a job applicant, Corie Geller, class of . . . I wasn't sure, but she was mid- to late thirties. They put me on to the alumni office, but they said no Corie Geller was there." Not loud glugs, but he was definitely having more water. "They said no one by that name, and I told her, the lady there, that we were trying to do due diligence since one of our trainees seemed to have deleted the applicant's maiden name and could they possibly check for someone named Corie. She was applying for a top-tier job in our company and we'd like to hire her ASAP. We pride ourselves on being a great company to work for. An engineering company."

Pete was on a roll, relishing his story, but he was wasting what was left of my time.

"The lady was very cooperative. It took her maybe a minute to say there was no Corie, but there was a Coral Schottland. Except we don't have a school of engineering. She majored in

Asian and Middle Eastern studies. Emphasis on Arabic literature. So what did I say? I said actually, we're not looking for an engineer, but we have an opening in Dubai in our human resources department and thought she'd be fine as an administrator. A real people person. How about that, Coral Schottland?"

"Good," I said. *Tell them what they need to hear:* "Inventive." Actually, okay but not great. C+ to B−.

Pete went on. "Arabic, Arabic. I had two choices. Terrorist or spook."

He stopped talking, so I considered that he was hoping for another word like *inventive.* "Spook as in spy?" I asked. "Like the CIA? No, but I have to give you credit. You're in the right zone." I tried to sound exhausted, as if I were fading fast. The role wasn't a stretch. "I was a translator for NSA. I spent nine and a half years of my life sitting in front of a computer."

"I'm warning you now, if you want your life shortened by, say, forty or fifty years, play it that way." Like he was going to let me live. We'd go back to our lives: I'd ask him to pass the Splenda at next Wednesday's lunch. "No one gets used to explosion noise sitting in front of a computer in Washington," he said. "A giant clap of thunder. Fire engines that all start their sirens right practically where you're sitting. No one sees a giant cockroach—" It hadn't even been an inch long.

"—and doesn't blink, just makes a snotty remark. But when Billy Gregson in Galveston described who attacked him, I knew for sure you weren't a terrorist. And I had to get to you before you got to me."

# 24

This was one of those good news/bad news scenarios. Good was that he had no clue if this was just some crazy hunt I was doing on my own or if I had colleagues or confidants.

The bad was that a day or two had passed. He had to get back home if he was going to kill me and resume his old life. Maybe his wife would keep silent that he'd been gone for twenty-four or forty-eight hours when *Newsday*'s front-page headline gasped MISSING or FOUND DEAD. Though, for all I knew, she could be his accomplice. Also, he probably hadn't emailed Iris that he'd be away. Not to show up for croque monsieur, not to mourn my loss and discuss how such a thing could happen to Corie (who admittedly did know Arabic, not that there's anything suspicious with that), was odd. Possibly fishy.

Nevertheless, if Pete felt I wouldn't talk, he might accept the risk—shoot/strangle/stab me sooner rather than later and return to the security of his old life, surrounded by family, his time taken up by working at his two businesses.

I must have stayed quiet too long, because I heard him get up. Who knew there were so many specific sounds? This was "man getting up from metal folding chair." Was this a prelude to my end or just his having pins and needles in the butt? I quickly said, "This isn't the silent treatment. I was just summoning up—"

"Oh, shut up." His voice was louder, harsher, though maybe it just came across that way because he was standing. "I'm not interested in your bullshit excuses. For the last time. Your only chance of leaving here alive is to tell me everything. I've been more than patient."

"Patient? Maybe that's how you see it, and maybe that's how it actually is. But from my point of view—"

"I don't want your fucking point of view."

"You're planning on killing me no matter what I say or don't say. I don't think you're necessarily thrilled about it, but it's a—"

"Shut up!"

"Cost of doing business. Very shortsighted, Pete, because this is the deal: We both have to get out of this. Because if I'm dead, you're dead."

I heard a forced chuckle: *Huh huh* and he went on: "Even if that were true, which it isn't, do you think it matters? Do you actually think I'm scared of death?"

Not only was I almost crazed with the heat, I was so soaked with sweat that I went through periods, like at that exact moment, when I began to shiver uncontrollably in spite of how hellish it was. "I have no idea what you think about death," I told him. "But we both have to get out of this alive."

"I'll get out," he told me. I was pretty sure I heard him sit down again. "I'll be fine. I always am. I'm not just a meticulous planner. I'm a great improviser."

"Even if you get out, it won't be for long."

My guess was that a hundred responses were in his head, and he couldn't decide on the one he wanted. Finally he made a reasonable choice. "What do you mean, not for long?"

"People know I'm looking into your case."

"Like who?" I said nothing. Let him be uncomfortable. "Do you think anyone's going to take you seriously?" he demanded.

"If I disappear? Oh, very seriously."

"Who? The judge? He already had one wife die on him. If you're missing or found dead, who's the first one you think they'll suspect?"

"You," I said. Interesting that the self-described great planner had said missing or found dead, as if his plan weren't finalized. One way or another, however, I understood I'd be dead the instant I proved useful—or useless.

"What do you mean, they'll suspect me first?" He sounded completely in control, just curious. "Why me?"

"Because I've discussed you, by name, with at least three of my former colleagues in the FBI."

I thought he gulped, but I couldn't have sworn to it. "We're still in touch. I'm one of those former special agents they call in to do contract work." Silence. "My Arabic. Other skills, too."

Finally, Pete said, "You're lying. You didn't have enough on me to take to anybody."

"I did. And it won't just be the bureau coming after you. My dad was a detective in the NYPD. So add him and some of his cop buddies also."

"If that wasn't so pathetic, it would be actually funny." But too many seconds had passed for his ridicule to be spontaneous. He had needed a moment to calculate an answer. "How could I believe you're in the FBI? Oh excuse me, retired but contracting for them."

"I might have a better story, but this one has the advantage of being true. You know in most cases, Pete, if you were to kill a person and run, the bureau might eventually stop looking for you in any active sense. Listen, cold cases happen. Well, they happen unless one of your victims, like Trevor Schwarz for instance, the music man on Galveston Island, came from a family that would keep the pressure and PR on.

"But forget about Trevor for a minute. If you kill a retired agent, especially someone who still has ties to the bureau, they'd never stop looking." Dubious. "And your life would be so tough." True. "You know how daunting it is just traveling under an alias these days. And you're not living in a movie. This is real life. It's much harder to disappear than it used to be. No way you can find yourself a cute little community in the middle of Kansas and start a new life, not with embedded microchips in credit cards and digital devices. And not with facial recognition, social media. Definitely not if you kill a Fed."

There was no response, and I couldn't hear any movement. Was he deep in thought or just staring at me through his goggles, wondering: *Could it be possible?*

I began counting, so I knew four minutes had passed when he finally said, "I'm going to the bathroom. There's an infrared monitor focused on you, so I'll be right here, so to speak."

I suppose I should have been grateful it wasn't a two-way setup. "Very high tech," I said. "Do you have a lot of equipment? Like if I were you—"

"Don't waste my time, you stupid bitch. Do you think I'm so dumb that I would brag about my gear?"

I heard sneakers on the wood floor, a door opening. But then there wasn't a sound, no footsteps, no nothing. I guessed he'd stopped moving, was still in the room. A moment later he spoke: "If you're so much smarter than me, how come you're the one trussed up and dying of thirst?"

That's when I finally heard footsteps going down a flight of stairs and the creak of a single floorboard. He was either standing at the foot of the stairs or headed to a bathroom.

How much time did I have? Wynne and I once agreed it was a scientific fact that most men not only pooped every single day at the same time but took far longer to do it than women. Unless he just had to pee, he would be gone for at least a few minutes. Maybe scanning the latest issue of *American Hunter*. Maybe checking out the handgrips on the length of wire he'd be using to garrote me.

I counted off thirty seconds after I could no longer hear him. Then I sawed like hell. He might have a monitor that would display the up-down movement of my arms over the same couple of inches, but hopefully not. Or he might discount it as a feeble attempt at exercise.

At the same time, I bent my knees. For the first time since I'd woken, I was able to pull them toward my body, though the stretching of my knees and quads was excruciating. I pressed my lips together as hard as I could to shut up the cries of pain that wanted to escape me. But I didn't have the luxury of leisure, so even though my leg shook to the point of vibrating and my bound-up calves and shins felt as if they were made of shattered glass, I set my bare feet flat on the floor. Then I did five butt lifts, each time rising higher and holding each lift longer than the last.

Except that effort took my energy away from the sawing. I realized I was making progress there, so that was what I'd concentrate on. I could even feel the corner of the wood post with the sides of my hands, where thumb met wrist—and the post was definitely heated up.

Okay, I figured it wasn't like rubbing two sticks together to start a fire; the wood used to build a house was probably required to be fire-retardant. So while I had a momentary fantasy of the zip ties themselves melting from a mini friction fire, I figured Home Depot or wherever wasn't going to sell a product often used to bind wires together with a label: WILL TURN TO MALODOROUS PUDDLE OF LIQUID PLASTIC WHEN HEATED.

By the time I heard the footsteps again, slower this time, I was feeling heartened. Yes, it was agony when I moved my legs, and I might be dying of thirst, but I wasn't dead yet. And I was making progress with the zip tie around my wrists. Halfway through? More? I couldn't tell, but I knew I was getting somewhere. But: assuming I could break out of this tie and wriggle my arms out of the second one that was holding both arms to the post, it wouldn't do much good if Pete, when he resumed his seat, was cradling a rifle with a night vision scope. As Mom would say, "Hmm. Something that needs mulling over."

His slow movement up the stairs was for a

reason I soon found out. He was carrying some sort of food. It was probably something microwaved, one of those multiethnic meals kids love and parents gag from—Chick'n Chunx with cheddar pizza triangles. Though I couldn't see anything, I could almost picture an animated aroma wave coming toward me. The food stank, brought back my nausea, and also made me wildly hungry.

"Hope you don't mind if I have a bite," Pete said. His chewing was disgusting, a gross-out sound that could clear a restaurant. Having seen/heard him eat nearly every Wednesday for years, I understood this was psychological warfare and not ineffective.

"I just want to let you know that I'm going to move a little," I lied. "I'll hardly shift my position at all. My right leg is numb. It will be only a fraction of an inch."

"Do whatever you want. But if you move much more than that, the last thing you'll smell is your hair frying as you get electrocuted." That sentence came off so matter-of-factly. I guessed it could be called a gift, his not appearing sadistic. Pete's indifference was scarier than cruelty.

"If I die, you die," I told him. "Because accounts of what you've done will come out. You may think you've never left a print or strand of DNA, but they'll be at your house, grabbing your hairbrush, toothbrush, your favorite box of cereal, your leather shoes, the toilet seat you lift. They'll be heading into that garage of yours— no matter how locked or alarmed you think it is." God, how I wished I could see his face. I'd have bet anything that there was no lack of emotion now. But in the dark there was no way of telling whether it was closer to fear or rage. So I just went on: "They will send out a bulletin; states will be going through unsolved crimes that they've classified as possible murders for hire. They'll be matching up any random skin cell under a victim's fingernail. Oh, and they'll probably waive federal charges—kidnapping and homicide—"

He cut me off. "Homicide is not a federal crime."

"I thought you were a great planner. You should have done some legal research. The murder-for-hire statute, Pete. If a defendant uses interstate commerce facilities, blah, blah to kill another person, it becomes a federal offense. Most likely they'd wind up extraditing you to a state like Texas that has the death penalty and highly unpleasant prisons." No response from him, not even: *Shut up.* "I'm sure you care for your family. You're not just using them for cover. Do you want them to go through that?"

"No. I really don't care about any of them." And sure enough, he was using that flat voice— no suppression of emotion because there was none to suppress. But I gave it a shot. "Wouldn't you miss your kids?"

"No. Truthfully? Kids are more trouble than they're worth."

"And your wife?"

"She's . . . a little different. I've got to admit I admire how she keeps everything going, leaves me alone. And she's a first-class housewife, a good cook. You hate to lose somebody like that. But I can't say I'd actually *miss* her. Except that there aren't many women like her around these days." He started chewing again and while he was preoccupied with his meal, I faked sobbing softly so I could work the post without him hearing, putting all the strength I had into the zip tie. Finally I heard him set down the remains of his culinary delight on the floor. "I can tell," he said. "You think I'm the classic sociopath with no feelings. You're waiting for me to boast, because a sociopath needs to have others recognize his cleverness. Are you positive that's what I am? Because you'd be wrong, you know. How about a practical, cold-blooded business-man?"

"It's a business?" I asked.

"I perform a service. Sometimes individuals feel the need to get rid of an impediment. They're happy to pay the big bucks for it to be accomplished in an efficient manner, leaving them completely out of it." He cleared his throat.

"Aren't you going to say, 'But you're talking about a human life'?"

"No."

"Maybe you're the sociopath," he said. When I didn't answer he went on: "If I have one regret it's that it'll be next to impossible starting a new packaging design business. I never realized how much I enjoyed it until those fuckers fired me and I had to go out on my own. And that turned out much better than working in an ad agency. Except it wasn't a decent living, though obviously I found a way to supplement my income."

"Did you just think: 'A hit man is a good second job even though there are no health care benefits'?"

"It was a lucky coincidence. Since I was a kid, I was beyond what they called a crack shot. The men wanted to go hunting with me, just to watch me with a rifle." I thought it was telling that he didn't mention his father, though I didn't know what it told. "Ten years old and I was hitting whitetail deer, feral pigs. Practically between the eyes," Pete continued. "They got zilch, I got the bag limit. Never gave a crap about birds. Quail? Give me a break."

"So you just changed your quarry?"

"You know, you're so dumb you could never pass an FBI IQ test, not that I'm saying that's a high standard. You don't just decide that you're going to help people solve their problems and then put an ad in *Soldier of Fortune*."

I waited, but he'd stopped reminiscing. "So how did you find your way into a new field?" I asked.

"You think by buying time, getting me to talk, you're going to postpone the inevitable?" I didn't respond. "Okay, since you're so curious . . . A lucky coincidence. A year after I got canned, some guy I knew, not too well, said his friend was having an issue with his father-in-law who he worked for. His friend was afraid the old man was being pressured to alter his will and leave the business to his son, who was useless. Kind of implied his friend was in the market for help. I was just about to say, 'I don't know anybody like that,' when I thought, 'Someone's going to get big bucks for the job.' So I told him I'd heard about a guy, a couple of years ago, but didn't know his name. I'd check. One thing led to another. I went from being three months behind on my mortgage to . . . now? Over a mil per year, nice and safe offshore. Don't think it's easy money. I'm painstaking about my work. Not greedy."

"The guy who originally approached you about his friend? Did you kill him, too, so there was no link to you?"

"Very good. Maybe you could pass their IQ test. Sure I got rid of him. Not by shooting. Once you establish an MO, you're as good as caught. I figured versatility is the key. Think about what the client wants. Not just wants, needs. That's true in packaging, too."

His talk ended and I heard the sound of the cooler opening again. Not a can this time, but a bottle being opened by an old-fashioned bottle opener. The cap must have flipped up because I heard its small metallic sound as it fell to the floor. I imagined him picking it up, just because he was so orderly and careful: *Hmm, must pick this up so I don't trip on it and also take it with me so there is not a trace of physical evidence.*

After a couple of minutes, I thought I smelled beer. Once I caught a faint sucking sound, as if he were taking a big, cold swallow. I waited until I heard him putting down the bottle. When I started speaking, I decided to make my voice sound weak, but it did that on its own. He didn't hear me. So I spoke in my new normal, which sounded not only faint, but distressingly feeble. "How many days have I been here?"

"Time flies when you're having fun, doesn't it? I happened to run into you at the end of Wyatt's Beach Road two days ago. After I got you here you were unconscious for so long I thought you were just going to die. What a waste of a good plan. So now let's just get to it, all right? No more bureau stories, no more interstate shit. You need to get real."

"That's as real as I can get."

"You better rethink that. I'm going to lose patience and just walk the hell out and leave you here. Maybe shoot you in the head, but I'm not sure I want to put you out of your misery. So you better goddamn speak up."

"Where are we?"

"Where you'll never be found. Well, eventually you will. We're in a spec house in a development, a gated community. They have to finish the other houses before they get back to work here. Do you know how they'll find you if you aren't more cooperative? From the stench when you're decomposing. Or maybe when your fluids start dripping through the floorboards."

"What do you want to know?" I asked, as loud as I could.

"Better. Much better if you cooperate. Do you know what I have here? A straw. I'll give you a bottle of water with a straw, hold it for you, as soon as you tell me who you told about me." I tried to swallow, but that didn't work so well and I gagged, which either was music to his ears or went unheard. "Here's the deal. You name names, and I give you eight ounces of Poland Spring. I have some in my cooler, but there is one bottle out if you prefer it at room temperature."

"One sip so I can talk."

"Cut the shit. Water is a reward, not an incentive."

"FBI."

"I don't want to hear that." I knew he was angry. His voice was flat but the words came out fast.

I pictured myself from Pete's point of view: As I worked at sawing the zip tie by moving my wrists up and down, he might notice my elbows jutting out and then withdrawing, over and over. Even if it was the tiniest motion, sooner or later he'd pick it up. I alternated sobbing and coughing to cover any noise. Slowly, I elongated my torso. I worried that he'd think it weird that a captive had such self-assured posture, but it was a small risk I had to take, because stretching out my body made the bend of my arms less noticeable. I also discovered I got more power just sawing downward.

"I know you don't want to hear it. But I was a special agent, first in Washington, then New York. The Joint Terrorism Task Force. I worked with the NYPD, ATF, CIA, DEA . . ."

"You're wasting your strength," he said. "You think I'm going to sit around here and listen to your bullshit? Wait till you die of thirst?"

"Why don't you just kill me now?"

I assumed I just thought that. But—scary—I must have said it out loud because he replied: "I only kill for money."

That's when it happened. I knew I was making progress, but suddenly the zip tie around my wrists split. I said a fast *Thank you,* though it might have been *Thanks,* which I hoped I didn't say—it was too breezy for God, who never struck me as the jaunty type. Anyway, though it came as a surprise to me, almost a shock, I was sure that Pete had heard something: a ripping sound, maybe, or a pop as the last millimeter of plastic tore apart.

*Talk!* I ordered myself. I still was tied to the post by the zip tie higher on my forearm. I needed time. I couldn't saw it because that would take forever and require time and strength I didn't have. I'd have to wriggle out without making any kind of shimmying movement that would alert him to something going on back there.

"Of course," Pete went on, "I would have to kill for self-preservation. For example, if you don't give me anything to go on, I'll have to assume you told your judge. I think with him, I'd do it when he comes out of the courthouse at the end of the day, on the way to his car."

Somewhere I picked up the notion that when people are watching you, they tend to look at the right side of your body, most people being right-handed. Was that true? I had no idea, but I started twisting my left arm back and forth trying to lift it while using my right to keep the zip tie from riding up; all the while, I kept my back as straight as I could and my shoulders as rigid as I could. Hopefully, from the front, he might not notice any movement.

Pete kept talking. "I thought he was supposed to be rich. The first wife. I think I once heard family money. His. But what kind of rich guy drives an Audi S4? See, I told you I prepare. Anyway, if I do it at court, the cops will assume it has something to do with one of his cases." The FBI would investigate the murder of a federal judge, but I thought it best not to mention the bureau again.

All along, I had convinced myself that getting my arms out of the zip tie that held them behind the post would be comparatively easy, since, like the rest of my body, they must be covered in sweat. Also, my arms were tapered, so the more I lifted, the looser the tie would be. The sweat did make the twisting a little easier, but I could feel that just to get leverage to lift up a fraction of an inch, I was scraping off layers of skin. Pulling my arm against the edge of the zip tie was like skinning myself with a Parmesan grater.

Pete sounded thoughtful: "Maybe someone he sentenced got out recently and wants revenge. Like a gang member. Or someone in the Russian mafia or a Latin American drug cartel. I'll do a little more research, check out the cases he's been on, and maybe that will give me some ideas." If I started begging, Pete would be gratified as it would be a sign that my supply of bravado was all gone. Since he was on a roll, I kept quiet. "What does the mob like?" he reflected. "Long gun, flamethrower, radioactive poison? Who knows?"

It took me far too long to realize what was coming next. But clarity had disappeared from my skill set. I could steel myself to listen to him talk about killing Josh because I'd told enough people about Pete Delaney. Once it got out that I was missing or dead, he'd be the prime suspect and Josh would be surrounded by US marshals, part of whose job was to guard federal judges.

Pete would talk about Eliza next. Of course she would have protection, too, and she'd be taken to a safe place. She wouldn't be abandoned— except by me, of course. How many mothers can a kid lose? If I had really considered her, truly loved her enough, would I have been so consumed by the chase? Still, whatever my guilt, my selfishness, my not sticking to the vow I'd made to myself—*I am choosing a normal life*— the very idea of Pete even saying her name was beyond desecration.

"Forget the Russians." He was still on Josh. "The Latin Americans go for torture. Cutting off a man's balls is just a preliminary."

Actually, that was inaccurate, but I was past offering him my credentials, including knowledge gained through working terrorist cases in the Tri-Border Area. Like eyeballs before testicles. But in that second, with one hideous scrape (that felt as if it took off a broad swath of skin from the top of my forearm down to my knuckles), I pulled my left arm out of the zip tie. Instinctively, my right hand grabbed the tie before it could fall to the floor. I felt behind the post and picked up the other tie that had strapped my wrists together.

"Poor Judge Josh," Pete said. "He lost one wife, then another, and if that wasn't enough—"

My screaming cut him off. This was no braying, as in: *I can't take it anymore.* My howl rose in pitch and volume until it was a shriek that nearly drowned out Pete's loud: "Shut up! No one can hear you." He boomed: "Cut it out or I'll slit your fucking throat!" But only someone with acute hearing could have made out his words through my clamor.

"Get it away! Get it away!"

"Shut up! You're having a goddamn hallucination."

"No! I swear, it's real. I felt it. Oh God!" The noise I was making was so primal that—whatever else was going on—I got frightened. What started out as a scream became one of those mind-body loops, so when the awful sounds from my throat and chest hit my ears and punched into my brain, I grew more petrified and screeched even louder. "Get it away!"

"You're hysterical! Look, I'm sick of this." He got up and stomped toward me. What I knew were sneakers from when he went down the stairs now sounded as heavy as military boots. They were moving so fast I realized he must be wearing goggles. I hadn't even considered him using superexpensive thermal military binoculars, but fortunately reality matched my mental image.

Then, at last, after another couple of steps, I could sense more than see a hole in the darkness: his shape. Maybe an arm's length in front of me. "When I say shut up, I mean it!"

Was he keeping his distance because there was some sort of perimeter barrier? Strobes, sirens, explosives? I got my answer—no barrier—when he stepped toward me again, grabbed a fistful of my shirt near my neck, and started to shake me, banging my head against the post. I took a deep breath and kept screaming.

"What? What is it? Shut up!"

"I'm not sure." My voice surprised me—not hoarse from the screaming. "I thought it was a mouse—"

"Oh for chrissakes!"

"But there was weight to it," I yelled, the way you would at someone not paying attention to danger. "I felt it twice. It could have been a rat!" He released my shirt and took a step back, which was when I added: "Maybe it was some sort of horrible, giant bug, I don't know! I've never felt anything like it. It was hairy and so disgusting and—"

Pete stepped from foot to foot, still practically next to me. It was as if he couldn't bear having both feet on the floor at once. Now or never.

I grabbed his leg and leaned in to head-butt his balls, but I missed. He had the advantage of sight, but instead of grabbing my hair he went for my neck. It was hard for him to get a choking grip because I was so sweaty and also because he had only one leg to stand on. He tried to free his other leg from my grasp, but I held on tight.

He slid his hand toward my throat. Quickly, I moved my chin sideways, then lowered my head and bit through his hand. Blech! The dentist is terrible enough, but at least there you're not spitting out someone else's blood. Now he was the one screaming, and I raised the leg I still had hold of as high as I could, as if pulling on a wishbone.

Except I was still on the floor, legs tied, so in fact I was pushing up on a wishbone. But both my mind and my body recalled what my dad's crazy Israeli friend, the guy who taught krav maga to the NYPD SWAT teams, had croaked at least four times per class: "Use your body as a weapon." His raspy voice and accent were still in my head. Even though I knew my two tied-together legs were one, I couldn't help trying to pull my feet toward me to stand. A total no-go. Even if I had been able to get up, I'd be as effective as someone in a sack race.

So I rammed all the weight in my torso against the leg Pete was standing on while twisting the one I was holding. That knee, which normally would have been facing up, was now twisting toward the floor. He roared in rage, and I could feel him leaning forward, trying to grab on to the post for balance. I knew he'd fall any second, so while I had the chance, I made a fist, my middle finger higher than the others, and punched him twice in the area where I figured his balls were. (Not that I expected him to be wearing them as earrings, but that was how dark it was.) The second hit connected, and he went down fast, with a loud grunt. Then he hit the floor hard. From his piercing scream, I figured he might have broken something.

Still, he was both strong and resilient, and he also had the advantage of being able to see me. Suddenly I felt him, so he must have rolled over and, facing up, must be trying to grab me around the arms in a wrestling hold. I screamed in his ear, as loud as I had when I was doing my mouse–rat–giant hairy cockroach routine, which took care of both his arms since his hands automatically reached up to cup his ear; they brushed the side of my face on the way, but he didn't notice.

I couldn't give him time to recover. This wasn't a match and it wasn't a tournament. I was fighting for my life. Yet, despite years of on-and-off training, I had an overwhelming desire to escape him, roll away, get the hell out. I was surprised by how hard it was to fight the compulsion to get away.

The fight isn't finished until your opponent is finished. He was close enough to feel, and I found his head. I grabbed both his ears as if they were handles and twisted his head. Fast, I retracted my left hand. With my right, I slammed the side of his head onto the floor. *Whomp,* at the temple. That's where the skull is weakest.

And he was out, probably for a while, probably with a concussion. There was a shot that he could wind up with a massive brain hemorrhage and die. Not that I caught my breath and relaxed, but I took a few seconds. Then I pulled off his goggles. The rubber eye guards and the straps were soaked. Revolting beyond words, like putting on some stranger's soiled underwear, and so sweaty I had a struggle to get them on. Plus my wrists had been tied so long and so tight I could barely move my fingers, so the repulsive task took triple the time it normally would have taken.

The only thing that kept me from a gagging fit was looking at where I was through his thermal goggles, so I could see everything visible within the infrared spectrum. I'd been right in thinking it was an attic—huge, unfinished. Since nearly everything gives off some kind of heat I could make out the floorboards. I could even see the metallic nails that reflected the infrared heat around them.

And of course I could see Pete. He was unconscious, his body slack. Nevertheless, I wanted to
crawl away as fast as I could, as if he were some
evil movie character who you assume is a goner
but then pops up and suddenly an entire audience
is screaming. The goggles were good, though not
state-of-the-art from what I'd read. The images
were black and white, not the familiar green of
night vision goggles or scopes that rely on light
rather than heat, and not the new thermals with
gradations of color.

I had to take the time to search him for any kind
of a weapon. Naturally, I was hoping for a knife
so I could cut the ties on my legs, but his pockets
were empty except for car keys. It looked like
one of those rental car key rings that wouldn't
open, and the two keys had no notches, which I
could have used for cutting: they were long and
flat, with rectangular heads that had the usual
little buttons to lock the car, unlock it, and open
the trunk.

It occurred to me it didn't say Jeep, and the
trunk icon looked more trunk-like than SUV-like.
I realized then that I must have been transported
to wherever I was in a car trunk. That sickened
me so much that I began to sob—huge, gulping
inhalations. But then I stopped because I was
afraid of rousing Pete. Also, I realized there was
an upside to being drugged to unconsciousness.
For me, awareness of being inside a car trunk

would have been a one-way ticket to psychosis. Anyway, I stuck the car keys into my bra.

The two zip ties that had held me to the post were on the floor. I picked up the one I'd sawed through. Its edges were so rough they almost cut my thumb when I felt them. I did think: *I bet this could slit his throat,* even though I simultaneously knew that was off-limits: bureau regs, the Ten Commandments. So I took the other zip tie, the one that held my forearms behind the posts and that I'd managed to slip out of. Like the one I'd sawed off, it was basically a belt, not the zip tie handcuffs law enforcement used with a loop for each wrist.

Though my hands weren't working very well, I'd at least had a manicure three or four days earlier, and my thumbnail was still in peak shape. I was able to release the plastic thingy down far enough to enlarge the belt. My legs were still bound together and I wasn't going to waste time doing a military crawl around Pete. So I managed to flop over him, grab his hands, and slip them into the zip tie belt. All I had to do then was pull it tight. I got up on my knees and yanked it with all the strength I had. Then I flopped off and rotated to check out where Pete had been sitting.

With the goggles on, I could see his setup across the room: a metal folding chair; a cooler chest that must have been filled with icy soda cans and beer bottles. He was using the chest as his table. On top of it was a cell phone with small headphones plugged in and a cardboard microwave plate that must have held the glop he ate.

But it was a long way off. I did a slow visual check of each floorboard looking for wires, transmitters, anything that might explode or set off an alarm if I somehow managed to get free. I went with the assumption any equipment I found in that attic was meant for him—or me—not to signal a confederate. I was as sure as I could be that he was working alone.

I started reaching down my legs, trying to open the zip tie around my calves and shins. And then Pete spoke: fury broke through his semiconsciousness as he slurred, "You took my goggles!"

# 25

Admittedly, Pete Delaney didn't sound in fine fettle, but he was alert enough to be ferocious. No time to get rid of the zip ties on my legs. My arms weren't strong enough to drag the rest of my body: a combo of muscle atrophy from being shackled to the post and shooting pains in my right hand and wrist from punching Pete Delaney in the balls and slamming his head to the floor.

I stiffened myself into a log and rolled across the attic. It hurt a lot more than when I used to do it as a little kid to amuse myself as stupid toy commercials played during *Teenage Mutant Ninja Turtles*. Not only did having breasts make rolling harder, I was no longer traveling on the cushioning of my mom's beloved Chinese rug. Also, each time I revolved onto my stomach, I had to lift my head and strain my neck so as not to dislodge the thermal goggles. The farther I rolled, the less immediate the threat of Pete's groans and yowls seemed. But then I heard him groan out: "You have no idea what's waiting for you downstairs." At least he needed to take a breath to get himself through the sentence.

Assuming I got downstairs, what would I find?

Nothing? An IED like those used against forces in Iraq and Afghanistan?

Finally I made it to the cooler. I took his phone, which was lying on top, pulled out the head-phones, and tossed them. I had to readjust his car keys so there was room to stuff in the phone. As for the cooler, he'd have to take it with him. Pete probably knew that any object brought to a crime scene could pick up something there—a random blade of grass, a small stone, even tree pollen. Later, all those traces could be ID'd as coming from the area where the crime was committed. So he'd get rid of his snacks and their containers along with his shoes, clothes, and devices. Possibly even his weapon.

I leaned on the cooler to pull myself into a sitting position, then lifted the top off. I had to have some water. There were three water bottles inside, but my hands were so limp that I couldn't open any of them. I grabbed a can of soda and took a tiny sip. Then, slowly, another and one more before setting it aside, though not without being unsettled by a twinge of regret: too bad I didn't slit his throat so I could have the leisure to down the whole can, even though it was putrid, overcarbonated fruit punch. I turned back to check Pete. He was still lying on his side, but every few seconds he grunted as though making an effort to either speak again or move.

Just before getting to the cooler and the chair,

I'd noticed a great, illuminated rectangle to my right. Whether it was a result of two days of sensory deprivation or some quality of the thermal image, it had burned my eyes. I squeezed them shut. When I opened them again, I realized the rectangle was a window that was almost completely covered with black cloth. I turned my head away for a second. When I looked back, I could make out a wide piece of tape. So a deliberate attempt to keep me in the dark. Why hadn't he simply taped my eyes closed? My only guess was that based on his experience with cruelty, allowing me my vision kept me trying to see outward rather than turning inward; maybe psychologically that was more effective in getting into a dialogue with me.

I reached into the cooler and took out cans and bottles and gel ice packs. I hurled a few overhand in his direction, but my throwing arm was undependable at best—as my teammates on the Forest Hills High School softball team had been aware—and now it was feeble. I rolled the rest of the cans and bottles as hard as I could. I wasn't necessarily trying to hit him, I was only trying to make his path toward the door more difficult to navigate in the blackness. I did stick one soda can into my panties, hoping that the stretch fabric would be benevolent about my putting on a few between navel and pubes.

I turned the cooler onto its side, then back-handed the lid a foot or two toward Pete: Use whatever you have to impede your opponent. With that in mind, I lay down flat on my back and grabbed the leg of the metal folding chair. Using my tied-together legs to propel myself to the door—and glancing backward every few seconds so I wouldn't do something stellar like clunking my head on a wall—I dragged it along with me.

When I got to the door, I used the chair to help me stand and also for balance. Quietly, I turned the knob. Once the opening was what I judged to be the width of my hips, I got back down on the floor in a sitting position and shimmied, one hip at a time, out the door.

I was at the top of the long staircase. Thankfully, it was not one of those pulldown things that lead to attics, with rough wood plank steps. These were actual stairs. I must have sat there for a minute, trying to figure out what to do next, but at that point my body took over to save me the effort of thinking. I twisted around so I was facing the attic and, as quietly as I could, set the chair on its side as yet another barrier. I think I debated whether to try closing the door with my fingertips, but I must have decided that even though keeping it open meant Pete could hear me—as I'd heard his sneakers on the stairs—I needed to hear if he became mobile in any way.

I decided to slide down the stairs on my butt,

cautiously though, since I was in such bad shape. On the second step, I paused and lifted the goggles. There was barely enough light to see that the stairs ended in a small hall. Reluctantly, I put them back on because I could see the ties on my legs more clearly that way. I lifted up my feet so they were on the second step, not far from my butt, where I could examine my bound ankles. Again, I stuck my fingernail into the locking mechanism of the zip tie. I pressed down and pulled it open. Much easier this time.

I took a deep if tremulous breath, then another. The second zip tie around my shins and calves was much tighter than it felt. Also, the little gizmo that could open it was behind me, and even though I could feel for it, my fingernail—reinforced with two coats of Apricot Sunrise plus a top and bottom coat—failed me this time. I crossed my ankles hoping to compress the muscle of the leg on top so that the area under the zip tie would be smaller. Nothing, no progress at all, not even one second of hope. Pete must have pulled the zip tie so hard that it squeezed and puckered my flesh—and I had relatively little flesh, just calf muscles the size and density of lacrosse balls. So stair by stair, I got to the bottom by using my butt.

That minor effort knocked me out. I reached into my panties and took out the soda. Cola, but a store brand. Not that I was overly picky, but if you're making a hundred thousand dollars per murder, you could go for Coke. Anyway, I drank more than half of it slowly. While I wouldn't call it nectar of the gods, it made me feel better. I reached down to try to open the tie again, except I heard something way in the back of the attic. At first it was muted, like someone giving a couple of sweeps with a broom. Was he turning over? Trying to move? He did know the layout of the space. I waited for another muted, brushing sound—but what came next wasn't muted.

Two deep, loud grunts followed by a scream of pain. Then one more sweep. Could Pete be dragging himself across the floor in the dark? How could he? I'd tied his wrists behind his back really tight. And when he'd fallen, I'd been positive he'd at least done major harm to his knee, and probably broken it, to say nothing of his head.

Before another sweep sound came or another gut-grinding wail, I dumped the rest of the crappy cola onto the floor at the bottom of the stairs next to my feet and turned the can on its side so Pete might trip on it. What else should I do?

It took me a little too long to clear my head enough to be able to analyze the situation— after which I had no new ideas. So I rolled along the short hall. Then a right-angle turn and a longer hall with, blessedly, daylight seeping in from some of the rooms. I realized there would be no long roll to the front door, as this was a traditional, two-story house. I was on the bedroom level.

I maneuvered myself into a sitting position, then went butt-feet, butt-feet, kind of like a caterpillar creep, until my back was braced against the hallway wall. Lowering my head to try to see the zip tie fastener behind my ankles didn't work since I could hardly bend my back after two days tied to that post. The thingy I had to depress with my fingernail wasn't visible. I should have realized that before I tried, but not only was I dull witted, I was also frightened by the noises upstairs. Worse than any haunted house because these were real: Pete Delaney dragging himself, groaning, screaming not only in pain now but also in a violent shriek of wrath that bordered on hysteria. Then came a soft, high-pitched wheeze of fear—but that was me.

Wherever he was in the attic, he wasn't directly above me. Still, I sensed he was making progress. I tried to picture how he could have gotten as far as he had with only one operative limb. Only then did it occur to me that his arms might have been long enough so that he could stretch them down so they formed a U behind him. With that, he could work his butt and legs over the bottom of the U so that his hands could be in front of him. Could he do this with a badly disabled (maybe smashed-up) leg? Why not, if his life depended on it?

After that, I was clueless as to what he was planning, but his shrieks were coming closer together now. Whatever he had in mind, he was picking up speed, bearing the pain. From where I was, down on the second floor, it was almost impossible to locate where in the attic the sweepy noise of his movement was coming from. But I had to assume he was headed for the door.

By now I was a zip tie expert and should have been able to run my fingertip over the fastener and feel the little gizmo to push down. Should have but couldn't. Again I tried to cross my ankles and press my right calf against my left shin to ease things up. Maybe I could get it moving by using the pads of my thumbs, like when you manage to pull on a pair of unreasonably small tights falsely advertised as "medium," you have to get out of them by working them down over your hips, quarter inch by quarter inch.

I couldn't get anywhere, yet I realized that if I used all the strength in my arms, I could push the zip tie down, though the rough edge of its plastic could conceivably slice off more than a couple of layers of skin because it was so tight. The tie's diameter was narrower than my legs', especially where my calves bulged out. Pain was endurable, but I couldn't cut off part of my flesh. Nevertheless, taking a piece from my leg as if it were a stick of butter was the only solution, intriguing in theory. But when I tried, I couldn't do it. Naturally I started beating myself up about being spineless, but on the other hand I tried to get some perspective by telling myself that butter can't bleed to death.

*Haul ass,* I ordered myself. Wynne and I started saying that in middle school, thinking it made us sound sophisticated, a couple of seventh-grade dames who'd been around the block more than once. But I was so tired, and for just a couple of minutes before I hauled ass I wanted to shut my eyes. They hurt from the combination of the bright light of the second floor after all that time in the attic and being so dehydrated that my tear ducts had nothing left to give.

But Pete's screams seemed to be getting louder, which was an excellent motivator. I started rolling again, this time along the polyurethaned wood floor of the hallway toward a wide, curving staircase: A realtor would call this a major selling feature, pointing to the potential buyers' toddler, a kid with a dirty finger exploring the wonders of her nostril, and saying: *Picture little Bethany descending on her wedding day.*

Just then, I heard a great bang, and then an awful, high-pitched howl. I couldn't see it, but I could picture it: Pete jumping down that first step from the attic, heading toward the second floor. He'd be putting all his weight on the banister.

The amazing thing was that he'd gotten upright.

I could be wrong, I told myself. It could be just some weird bang, him falling over the chair I'd laid down to block the doorway. That could be, because the silence that followed lasted so long. I was so mesmerized by the quiet that I almost had to shake myself awake to start rolling again. Only a couple of revolutions later the second big bang came and a slightly more modulated scream, which was when I knew I should have trusted my gut. This was Pete, on his way to me.

Could a dry mouth get even drier? Because I really wanted to scream for help, so someone could hear me ten miles away, though for all I knew he could have driven me to the middle of nowhere. One of my dad's favorite sayings was: "God helps those who help themselves," though he meant that as an approach to life rather than a statement of fact or a theological pronouncement. He had been a detective in Homicide and Sex Crimes too long and seen too much slaughter to believe it was always possible to help oneself or even that God could or would come to the aid of self-helpers. Anyway, how much fucking more could I help myself?

Then Pete made it down yet another step, and with such a hideous thud that I felt its reverberations through the floor. Not much of a scream but a sonorous "Oooh, oooh" from deep within him. I rolled a few more times until I

489

was almost at the top of the grand staircase. As I turned from side to stomach, his car keys and phone dug into my breastbone. That's when I realized that what I had there wasn't just evidence and wasn't just a way of taking away his means to escape.

I pulled out the phone, deliberately not looking to see if there was any earwax on it. You can make an emergency 911 call even if the phone is locked. As the operator answered, Pete went back to screaming as he hopped down to the next step. I knew there was a special two-digit code a law enforcement officer was supposed to use if calling a 911 center out of her jurisdiction. But they'd probably changed it four times since I'd left, and anyway I couldn't remember it. So I said (and didn't have to fake the urgency): "Officer down!" I prayed that whatever call center I'd reached had enhanced 911 so it could geolocate me. Without disconnecting, I stuffed the phone back into its place beside the car keys.

There were a lot of steps coming down from the attic. When I was bumping down them, they had seemed countless, like those in a Mayan temple. So how could Pete, with a concussion and probably a broken knee, expect to catch up with me? Also, he knew now I could fight, though he may have decided my downing him was pure chance, not skill. Was he actually coming after me or simply trying to escape? Did he realize I'd taken his car keys?

His progress was slow but resolute. Actually, considering that even if he'd managed to get his wrists from behind him to in front, in a normal guy they'd be wobbling and swaying under the weight of his body. But he was actually going faster than he should have been, because he was so fit. I ruefully recalled Iris describing Pete in his wet T-shirt and how ripped he was. Then I remembered a lecture at Quantico about thinking like your opponent: You know what you're doing, but is that enough when you could be in peril? Heck no. So you got to ask yourself, *What's in his head? How does he figure he's gonna get you?*

Maybe Pete had escaped the zip tie. Not the way I did on my wrists, because he hadn't had time. I truly doubted he'd been able to wriggle out of it, because I'd pulled it incredibly tight.

That's when I discovered I'd put my thumbs and index fingers on the tie still binding my own legs. I was recognizing the likelihood of Pete having a knife somewhere in that giant length and width of attic. I could easily have missed it. Yet even in the blackness, he knew the turf well enough to find it. And once he had it, he could figure out how to hold the hilt: maneuver it so the blade stuck out from under his arm, sit on it so the blade rose up at a forty-five-degree angle, and cut the zip tie. If you're beyond desperate and have one good leg, two strong arms, and the ability to endure the torment his screams suggested, you could get far in life.

If I was going to get far, I had to make a move. I edged myself over right beside the banister on top of the staircase that led to the first floor. At the same time, I pushed down on the edge of the plastic tight around my lower legs and pulled up my right leg with all the force I could muster. The awful part of it was that at first nothing happened—except agony and bleeding. That was never a great duo, but I had to keep at it.

Keep at it and not make any noise that would give away to Pete that I was still on the second floor. Finally, I counted to ten and with one horrific slice along the side of my right leg, I was free. I looked down only because I needed to check if I was merely bleeding or gushing and needed to make a tourniquet. Just bleeding from a long strip on the side of my leg that was a couple of inches wide. So I could keep my shirt on. There wasn't time to throw up.

I was next to the first baluster, not a plain spindle but squared off at the bottom and then rounder and thinner as it rose up. I went hand over hand, pulling myself up, then leaned on the curved, fancied-up top of the beginning of the banister. Each of my legs went through its own trauma, trembling and nearly collapsing as if controlled by a separate brain. My arms weren't exactly at their peak, but as I took the first step down, I knew they would have to be doing most of the work. By the third step, I could have kicked myself, if that were a possibility, for not simply going down slowly on my butt. Still, butt-sliding made some noise, and with Pete still on the attic stairs, periodically screaming his head off, I could be quieter going step-by-step.

Also, I couldn't keep rolling once I got to the bottom, because I might not be able to find something to brace myself on to open the front door and get away. So I had to get my legs to work. My goal was to get as far away from the house as I could with as much speed as I could muster. That took walking.

I rested for a few seconds after each step I took. My knees kept banging together because my ankles and shins, tied together so long, kept trying to fuse with each other, while my thighs just wanted to get a move on.

There wasn't any clever trick I could think of to walk when your legs are so floppy. When I got down to the next to last step, I sat and yanked on the baluster hoping to discover shoddy construction. The baluster would come loose and—voilà—I'd have a hiking stick/weapon. Of course that didn't work, so I pulled myself up again and started walking.

The grand staircase, naturally, ended in a grand hallway about half the size of my parents' apartment. A ridiculous space that would doubt-less wind up with no furniture but a giant round table in the middle—a humongous bowl filled with expensive flowers on top, and little Bethany's boogers underneath.

I began to cross the hallway. My arms were stretched out for balance, and for an instant I remembered, as a kid, walking similarly—lurching from one foot to the other—imitating Frankenstein's creature. I started criticizing myself again for not rolling, but then changed my mind when I imagined the infection in my skinless leg that could come from the dirt of hundreds of construction boots that had clomped around. The floor was composed of giant squares that looked like that gray-veined white marble they always wind up choosing for countertops on home renovation shows after rejecting twenty less boring alternatives.

I was nearly at the door, panting a little from the exertion but enjoying the freezing cold floor under my feet after so much time in that oven of an attic. Just then I realized Pete hadn't screamed for a while.

I turned to check out what was behind me. My blood had made a meandering trail on the floor, but the good news was that the closer I got to the door, the less bleeding there was. I discovered the bad news when I looked up. Pete Delaney was at the top of the staircase. Speaking of blood, one side of his face—where I'd smacked his head to the floor—was covered with blood, already darkening into a mask that resembled a negative of the Phantom of the Opera mask, not that he was singing. He was mostly prone on the wood floor up there, though partway between stomach and side, presumably to keep pressure off his bad leg.

Well, there was actually badder news. The knife I'd worried about? Not in view. The pistol I hadn't even considered? Aimed right at me.

I don't know how many times I'd heard the question: *You know that incredible sinking feeling?* But whatever sank took a fraction of a second to do so. During that time I must have made some calculations. One, that he was a great shot. The people at two gun ranges were seriously wowed by him. I even got a mental image of what his target paper would look like: six feet long with all the bullet holes in a two-by-two square. Second, that he'd just made an enormous physical effort getting downstairs from the attic and propelling himself along the wood floor with a seriously damaged leg and a head injury. Still, someone so adept with guns and rifles could operate almost completely on instinct, especially when pumping gallons of adrenaline.

But three was the kicker. There had been no knife, and no, he hadn't nibbled through the zip tie. His wrists were still bound together. True, his hands were now in front of him, arms stretched out, in position to fire. He'd even managed to rotate his wrists slightly so that his left hand, the support hand, looked as if it was doing its job, providing about 70 percent of the strength of his grip, allowing his right-hand trigger finger to be relaxed enough to get off an accurate shot.

My calculation was something like: *Oh shit. Well, at least I've got a metaphoric shot at getting the fuck out of here.*

After the fraction of the second all of that took, I turned my back on Pete Delaney.

"Turn around!" he called out. I took another step, which brought me within inches of the door. "Listen to me. I'm not threatening. Since you know about Galveston you know what kind of a shot I am."

I grasped the doorknob, a big, brass handful. I wanted him to think I had my hand on the door, ready to try my luck, but I didn't want him to feel I was about to run. Still, I was shaking and when I tried turning it, as imperceptibly as I could, nothing happened.

"I have a proposition for you." When I didn't respond, he said, "It's not only for you, obviously. It's for the benefit of both of us." Early on, at the Wednesday lunches, I'd always thought of him as having a flat personality. But now there was something in his voice that sounded reasonable. I even detected a bit of warmth, as in:

*Hey kid, we've been through so much together.*

"What is it?" I asked.

"Turn around and talk to me. We can both get out of this alive."

I took a deep breath, exhaled it slowly, and then took another. I even moved my foot back, the way you would if you were about to pivot in order to speak to someone behind you. Then I brought my left hand up to meet the right one on the brass knob and turned it as hard as I could. It opened, and just as I dived over the threshold and hit the ground, the first shot struck the edge of the door, right where my spine had been a millisecond earlier.

At some point I got up and started zigzagging away as fast as I could, my legs much steadier now. I couldn't figure out whether someone in Pete's position could see downstairs and out the windows. I guessed that if he could see me, he could kill me. The whole point of being a hunter is bringing down not just a coyote hanging at a watering hole but also a fleet-of-foot buck.

On the other hand, all I'd seen was the pistol in his hands, which probably wasn't effective over more than a twenty-yard distance. And since my mental image of twenty yards was fuzzy to the point of invisibility, I just kept running or, more accurately, rapidly shambling.

Finally I felt sure I'd run enough. Well, semisure, but I couldn't go farther at that speed.

I slowed to more of a hobble and began to look around. It was a curved street with unpainted houses, some of a grand size, like the one I'd been in, others more cottage-like. The street was paved, but what would be lawns were just brown dirt, and all the driveways were empty except for the occasional dumpster. Lifeless, except for the place I'd escaped.

Where the hell were the cops? What emergency call center would pass off "Officer down" as a prank? Could Pete have taken me to some boondock with a two-person police force that didn't have geolocation equipment? I found myself standing in one place because my legs wouldn't move anymore; all they could do was support me, and probably not for much longer. The same seemed true of my mind. But I warned myself that Pete was not a quitter and that even if it took him hours, he would find me if I stayed where I was.

I closed my eyes for a minute just to con-centrate on sound. It seemed that way behind the houses across the street from where I'd been, there was a *shhh* sound that came and went with some frequency. I strained, because I didn't want to stagger in that direction and find it was wind blowing through newly planted trees. Except it wasn't windy. It was traffic: a well-traveled road, a parkway—a place where cars didn't have to stop.

Only then did I think, *Was that operator still hanging on?* I took out the phone and, as I was putting it to my ear, I heard sirens. They weren't very far away and they were headed toward me. Out loud, I said, "Thank you, God." Very loud in fact, which I started thinking was dumb since if there was an omniscient or concerned deity, it wouldn't be God with a hearing loss. Except then I realized I was shouting over the noise of the sirens. They had arrived.

Three squad cars circled me, two officers in each. They exited with weapons drawn. I fell to the ground more than sat, put up my hands, and said, "No officer down. Me."

One of them came closer. "What's your name?" she asked, actually pretty mildly for a cop. A state trooper? They were all wearing Stetsons instead of peaked caps. Gray uniforms.

"Corie—"

"Corie Geller?" she asked.

"Yes." She squatted beside me. "Call FBI Washington," I said. "Ruiz. Please. Sorry I didn't say please." She holstered her weapon. "My husband. Can you—"

"Sure," she said and called to the others: "It's Corie!" Two of the others came and squatted on either side of her. "Don't worry. We know the numbers to call." She had dark brown skin and lots of short braids coming out the sides of her hat. Her name tag said Carolyn Morris. She peered at my leg and called out to another officer to call for an ambulance and to get water. "What happened?" she asked. "Is there anyone else—"

"Oh my God," I said. "Yes, armed. Pistol. Expert shot." I closed my eyes. That's all I wanted to do. When I opened them I felt as though I'd fallen asleep and just woken, but the three troopers were still kneeling beside me. "His left leg is probably broken," I continued. "I think at the knee."

"How did that happen?" she asked.

"He'd tied me to a post in the attic, but I was able to saw off one of the zip ties and slip the other one. I got him to come over."

"He wasn't near you?"

"Way on the other side of the attic. It was so dark in there, but he had thermal imaging goggles so he could see me." She made a small gesture with her hand as in: *Keep talking.* "I grabbed one of his legs and twisted it so he was off balance. He fell." I pointed to the house and was surprised. It seemed so much closer than I'd thought. "He brought me here in a car or some other vehicle. He may have put it in the garage." I reached down into my bra and handed her the keys. The three of them glanced at each other and then back to me.

The trooper on the left, whose belly appeared to be resting comfortably on his thighs, said, "Bet you got some story to tell."

I tried to smile and he smiled back, but all I could think of to say was: "Sorry I smell."

"Don't worry. You're still in the minor leagues."

A bottle of water appeared and Carolyn Morris handed it to the guy I was talking to, then stood and stepped back, talking into the mouthpiece of a headset I hadn't noticed.

One of the other troopers was standing guard, and I assumed the other two were headed toward the house. "Listen," I told the guy with the belly, who'd moved closer to me. "I know you people know your business, but I hope the people going to that house can defend—"

"She's calling in a SWAT team," said Robert J. Anello, whose name tag I could now see. He opened the bottle of water and kept his hand on it while I brought it up to my mouth. "Do I have to tell you: 'Sip, wait, sip'?"

"Probably," I said.

Anello seemed intuitive, like my dad, guiding my drinking, keeping my head up just long enough before I got that choky feeling. Each time, right when I was about to hold up my hand to signal I needed to pause between sips, he somehow knew to take the bottle away. He also supported me so my body was at a slight slant and so I couldn't turn into any position that could bring the damaged part of my leg in contact with the pavement.

The third of the original group around me, whom I now thought of as the dearest of colleagues (though I didn't know number three's name), strode over to one of the cars, an SUV, and got a packaged Mylar blanket from the back. It was only then that I realized I'd missed the huge New York State seal on the car doors, surrounded by the words New York State Police.

The trooper opened the blanket and gently eased it under my messed-up leg. "The best for our visitors in this county," he said.

"What county?" I asked.

"Westchester," he said. I was about to turn to check his name tag, when I heard another siren. An ambulance careened around the curve of the road and slammed on its brakes: a noisy, dramatic, but adept entrance as the rear of the vehicle wound up no more than a foot from me. The sight of it brought both relief and regret, because I really had an image of me being there—with a kindly cop to hold my head up a little higher—so I could watch the SWAT team descend on the house. On the other hand, I was starting to get desperate for some heavy-duty pain medication.

Trooper Carolyn—whose last name I'd temporarily forgotten—came over and said: "Your family will meet you at the hospital."

I knew they'd have to check me out, but I wanted to get home and see Lulu, lie on my side and put my arm around her, have her lick my nose—her way of saying *Sleep tight.* When I woke up, my parents would be there, my mom would stroke my forehead, and we'd all have pizza in the bedroom.

Wasn't normality what I'd always yearned for?

I heard another siren and as the EMTs were shifting me onto a gurney, I turned, stunned that a SWAT team would blare out its presence. Except it was another ambulance.

"Another ambulance?" I asked.

"It was a couple of blocks away," she said. "They just like to make noise whenever they have the chance."

"What about the SWAT team?"

"They got here about ten minutes ago. It's over."

"Over?" I said. "You got him?"

"No," she said. "You got him."

# 26

I woke up in the Westchester division of New York–Presbyterian Hospital, with a many-tubed IV in my arm and bandages around my wrists and arms. Eliza immediately began telling me how I talked in my sleep during the twelve hours I was out. Nearly all of what I said—except the occasional "No!"—sounded like slowed-down audio. Neither she nor Josh could under-stand anything, other than "pastrami sandwich," though that was in response to her question: "Momby, is there anything we can do for you?"

She did an imitation of my unintelligible sleep talk, "Waaah, maaaah, goobla . . ." and so forth, until Josh told her: "Give her time to wake up." My mom beamed at me—*Welcome back to the land of the living!*—then started to weep, real crying that started with a whoop inhaled and got exhaled as copious tears and mucus.

My dad kissed my cheek and said, "You got our attention, kiddo." His line came across as some-thing he'd worked out beforehand, just jokey enough so he wouldn't sob like my mother. He tried squatting into a catcher's stance; I was surprised he could still do that, though it's a gift a surprising number of cops seem to have. But the hospital bed was too high, so he stood and bent over. Tenderly, he brushed my hair off my forehead, though that was cover for his murmur: "Pete—prison hospital at Bellevue. Shattered knee, hairline fracture of skull." He patted my fingers. "Good work."

I smiled at all of them and made it broad enough so I wouldn't have to look directly at Josh and see his *How could you not have told me?* expression—anger, hurt, or something even worse. The four of them were lined up on the side of my bed that didn't have the IV pole. But with a high school football maneuver I'd never seen before, Josh led with his shoulder and got them to stand back so he could be closest to me.

"Are you in pain?" he asked.

I was so overcome by seeing them all that I had to think about his question for a minute. "Weak. Exhausted, actually. Like having three flus. My leg hurts." I looked down the bed. The sheet was held up by a tentlike support, so I couldn't see my legs. "Is everything okay down there?" I was a little unsettled by the possibility that what I was feeling was the phantom pain that comes after amputation, though not majorly nervous, so I assumed they'd given me a sedative.

"It will be fine," he said. "Possibility of a skin graft, but they'll decide that tomorrow." He took my hand gently and held it. "Corie, look at me." He was wearing a Henley T and I realized I'd been talking to his clavicle. This was Josh at his wildest, wearing a collarless shirt.

"I'm so sorry," I whispered. Then I finally looked at him and started crying.

"I was terrified," he said. "No note, nothing. The cops found your car down by the beach." He cried, too, or at least his eyes were crying, though he didn't seem to realize it.

"Did you think I, like, did a Virginia Woolf?"

"You? No, of course not. Anyway, the water's not warm enough for you until August." He reached for a tissue on the nightstand and handed it to me. "It was so outside your behavior. I called your parents. They were nervous after Eliza's call, so I wanted to calm them, except I couldn't think of anything calming to say. Your dad filled me in on what you'd been doing."

Behind him, my parents and Eliza were leaning in, not trying very hard to hide their frustration at not being able to hear our conversation.

"Were you angry?" I managed to say.

"What do you think?" I hadn't known until that moment that he could yell in a whisper. "Why couldn't you confide in me? You let your parents and Wynne in on it."

"It just never came up, and by the time I knew I really had to talk to you, it was too late."

Josh turned to Eliza and my parents: "We need a few minutes together. Could you come back in five?" They started to go, but he called after my mother: "Margo, you have the pastrami sandwich in your bag. Don't worry, I'll just let her have a bite or two."

In case he might weaken, my mom added: "Don't overdo it. They said when she got up, she could only have Jell-O or applesauce."

The sandwich was in a bag, then wrapped in aluminum foil, then in deli paper. By the time he got it open, they were out of the room. Unfortunately, he was able to pick up the thread of our conversation. "Why did it become too late for you to tell me?"

"Because I was afraid you'd try to stop me. I knew . . . I felt . . . that I was really onto something and I didn't want you telling me to let the cops or the bureau handle it." He started shaking his head, but I kept going. "You would say if Pete really was what I thought, it wasn't something I should be handling because it was too dangerous. Like what if Eliza lost another mother?"

I suppose that last sentence would have been better left unsaid since Josh responded, "And me? I'd just say, 'Easy come, easy go'? What the hell were you thinking? That we have some Victorian marriage and I could forbid you to do what you want? Besides. I always loved how brave you are."

I was in an odd state. Maybe drugs, maybe post-traumatic weirdness. Part of me was frightened that Josh was going to say: *Too bad this marriage didn't work out.* But the other part was more: *Que será será* and wondered if he'd consider it horribly rude if I took a bite of the sandwich.

"Sometimes you're intimidating," I told him.

"In what way?"

"You do what you want, always steer the conversation to substance. You take over dinner and don't seem to get that some people aren't perpetually seeking meaningful conversation. And then you go off to your study. Or New Orleans."

"You never told me I shouldn't go off to my study." I tried to remember if this was actually true. When he continued, he acted slightly chastised: "And you and Eliza were bonding so well that I felt I could pull back a little."

"But by the end of our first year, 'a little' got to be a lot. And Josh, don't give me the business of how you got so caught up in thinking about jurisprudence that you had no concept of time."

"I understand how you could feel that way."

"You sound like a defendant trying to avoid pleading guilty."

He smiled, less in acknowledgment than in relief that I was able to put up a fight. "Whatever. But it was so gratifying, the way you two took to each other. And also, not to be the sole parent and not to have to watch *High School Musical* for the fourth time. There was an adult in the house who actually liked *High School Musical*."

"That's condescending."

Josh was shaking his head before I even finished the sentence. "No, it's an aesthetic preference. I respect it."

"Fine, then I respect that your aesthetic sensibility leans toward a choral reading of *The Anatomy of Melancholy*." Either that shut him up or he chose to be quiet for a moment.

"You lied to me," he said. "That was hard to take."

"I lied to you? When?"

"When you said you were going to Galveston to keep Wynne company, have a fun friends weekend."

"Oh. Right. Of course. Josh, I'm sorry I lied."

Then he asked me if I wanted him to hold the sandwich for me. I nodded my head and took a bite. The pastrami was still a little warm, and it was the best thing I'd ever tasted. I was savoring it when Josh continued: "I don't get how you're intimidated by me, someone who loves you so much, but you're not intimidated by a multiple murderer."

I hate talking through food, so I put up my finger for him to wait a minute, at which point my parents and Eliza walked through the door. Quickly, I spoke through the mouthful, pursing my lips to hide the rye bread–pastrami mush and said, "I love you, too."

Late that afternoon, after my parents left, Josh

went out and bought me a new phone while Eliza gave me a shampoo in a hospital basin. By evening, whatever pleasant medication they'd sedated me with had worn off, so I was coherent enough to call and leave a message for Carlos Ruiz. He called back about ten minutes later to say he would fly up and come to the hospital first thing in the morning. The doctors said I was okay to be debriefed for fifteen or twenty minutes at a time, as long as I got a break in between.

"How are you holding up?" he asked.

"Pretty well," I said. I was able to hold up because Josh and Eliza were in the room with me. They insisted on spending the night on those leatherette reclining chairs that probably had diphtheria dribble near the top, but I scored a couple of pillowcases from a pleasant nurse so they could lay their heads on something theoretically clean. "Did Pete say anything?" I asked Ruiz.

"Nothing to write home about except that he was outraged. Said you lured him there, then attacked him."

"Lured him there for what?" I asked. "Sex or just to beat the crap out of him?" I looked toward Eliza and was about to mouth *Joke,* but she was already grinning.

"Sex, but then you snapped."

"Happens to me all the time," I told him.

"Must be satisfying, the sound of a skull

cracking. So Pete did a few minutes on you duping him. Then he said he wanted a lawyer and shut up. I'll see you tomorrow. I'll call early, before I leave, just to make sure it's okay."

Carlos Ruiz was at the hospital at eleven the next morning, which worked out nicely since the doctors working on me decided I did need a skin graft on my leg as a late afternoon activity. He bought me a box of French macarons from Washington, a big cocoa-colored box prettily tied with a peach ribbon. Seeing that my wrists and arms were bandaged, he set it down on the hospital tray table with some finesse, not the discomfited *plop* with which some men hand over tastefully wrapped gifts to women, as if relieved to be rid of the worry of estrogen exposure from a satin ribbon. He did add, "We were scared shitless the whole time you were gone."

"So was I, but I had the advantage of being drugged for a couple of days, including the road trip, which was probably in the trunk of a car. I never saw or heard him coming. Just a bee sting"—I pointed to where I'd felt it—"and then I blacked out. I remember falling, but not hitting the ground. Thank God I missed being stuffed into the trunk of a car."

"Yeah, I'd be nuts. Probably try to chew my way through the steel. But the thing was, once we knew you were gone, we were ninety-nine-point-nine percent sure Pete had grabbed you.

But before we knew you'd been taken, your local police found your car down at a beach in the afternoon, assumed you were gone for a run. Once your husband called, they went back. No you, no car keys, but they had the sense to hold it as a crime scene until we came."

"Tire marks nearby?" I asked.

"Yes, but none from a Jeep."

I told him how the car keys Pete was carrying looked as if they were from a rental, two keys on an unopenable key ring.

"Right. He rented a car out in Suffolk County somewhere. Cutchogue."

"How did you know it was Cutchogue?"

"I like to get out more than one sentence at a time," Ruiz said.

"I was just prompting you, so you wouldn't leave anything out."

"Right. Thank you. He used a stolen Discover card the owner hadn't discovered was stolen yet. Same with the driver's license. So he drove it back to Shorehaven, snatched you, and took you up to Westchester that night. He didn't worry about CCTV or anything, because his disguise was good. Baseball cap, frizzy hair, snake tattoo growing up his neck. But we didn't get that until yesterday. From those car keys you got, we traced the car to the rental place, got footage from their security camera. Weird thing is, he looks almost exactly the same as the guy whose license was stolen: thirty-two years old. Incredible resemblance."

"Packaging design," I said.

"You bet. Then, after he got you into the attic and tied up, he must have realized you weren't waking up anytime soon. Or more likely, he'd planned it all out and drove that first car back down to the Bronx, set it on fire. We're doing the lab work, though it's doubtful there'll be any traces of you left in the trunk."

"Which fortunately I was out of."

"Christ, I didn't think of that. Sorry. Not a great thing to hear. You want me to get a nurse, maybe get something to calm you down?"

"No thanks. Let's change the subject fast. How did he get back to Westchester?"

"He had another rented car parked a couple of blocks away. That's the one he drove back up and that we found in the garage of the house, with the keys that belonged to it behind the driver's visor. He held on to the keys of the first car. At first we couldn't figure it out, but it makes sense with your theory that he planned to get rid of everything associated with the crime. Even if he set the first car on fire, the keys wouldn't be destroyed. We're sure he has a methodical way of disposing of stuff. Oh, sorry I said that."

"No problem," I said. "Though I'd appreciate it if you could change the subject again."

"Sure. Tell me what happened in the attic. Anything you talked about, any phone conversations you might have overheard."

"No phone conversations. But when he was with me, once I was awake, he was trying to find out if anyone else knew. I was afraid he would want to kill me if he thought of me as just a neighborhood nut out to blackmail him, so I wanted to make sure he believed I'd spoken to other people. But when I told him the FBI knew about him and that I was a former special agent, he dismissed it. Said I was making up a story, that all I did was read books."

I went through everything I could recall about what Pete and I had said to each other. About my getting out of the first zip tie by sawing it.

Ruiz had a lot of questions about the details, and I wound up adding particulars as they floated up to awareness, like Pete's trip to the bathroom, his bringing back a gross microwaved meal. I gave him the little I knew about how Pete turned his skill with firearms into a business. Finally Ruiz said that I looked like I'd had enough, and we'd talk again once I was out of the hospital. He poured me a cup of water but didn't get up to leave.

"I'm not supposed to eat before surgery," I told him, "but let's have a macaron." I opened the box and pushed it toward him. Without too much indecision, he chose a mint green one, and I took a pink hoping for raspberry, which it was. I took only a small bite, so I wouldn't aspirate an entire cookie during surgery, and wrapped the rest in a tissue. "Excellent! Thanks so much for bringing them."

"Here is what we think happened," Ruiz said. "We went to his house. His wife said he was on a business trip to Detroit, and there was his Jeep, right in the driveway."

"Just curious: did you get a warrant?" I asked.

"Curiously, we did." I started to apologize, but he waved it away. "A couple of hours after your husband called. For premises, vehicles. Including that garage. Your dad said you mentioned something to him about it being alarmed to some crazy extent. Interestingly, all we found were some long guns in lockers—high-quality padlocks, so kids couldn't get to them. Also a biometric gun safe. Nothing in it, no residue as far as the tech could tell on visual examination, so chances are he keeps his handguns wrapped in something other than cloth. Or whatever he keeps in there. Superneat setup he's got. In my life, I've never seen a garage that clean, that organized, even where guys set it up as a woodworking shop. Bottom line, all the weapons he had there could legitimately be used for hunting. He's also got a lot of hunting gear. We didn't find explosives or bomb-making paraphernalia. Not in the garage, not in the house. Nothing potentially lethal in the house either, except the usual cleaning products and stuff like that."

I thought that through, then said: "My guess is that he uses the garage to store whatever he needs for an upcoming job, but then gets rid of everything. Definitely the weapon he uses. Writes it off as a cost of doing business. So there's never anything there that can be connected to a crime that's already been committed."

I couldn't get out of bed for two days after the skin graft and then had to stay another three to make sure the graft took. Painful and tedious, though after three days I gave up on painkillers because whatever stuff they were giving me in those little drip bags was so sublime it made me think about taking up permanent residence in the hospital.

Josh and Wynne took turns spending the night in my room, which was helpful. When I woke from a nightmare or just got up bleating with fear from unknown causes, they pulled me out of the danger zone fast and, right afterward, comforted me.

My parents, who were staying at the house to oversee Eliza, visited every day; my mom brought cellophane bags of organic dates and apricots (aware that prunes lacked subtlety), which I knew meant she was worried I'd get constipated but was reluctant to mention it, as a thirty-eight-year-old child might find that sort of silent suggestion intrusive. My dad confessed that he and three of his buddies had alternated twelve-hour shifts staking out Pete's house the whole time I was missing, intending to grab him if he came home.

My in-laws came on the fourth day, with my mother-in-law making a valorous attempt to be upbeat, which meant smiling as she entered and exited. My father-in-law called me Dawn only once.

I was supposed to take it easy after I got home. Limited physical activity. Lulu lounged on my good leg. An overly chatty special agent came to the house to return my wedding and engagement rings that Pete had taken. The weather was as beautiful as June can get in New York, which was exquisite—sky the purest blue with some thin, abstract expressionist streaks of the whitest clouds and twenty different shades of green leaves set against it. I moved from the porch to the backyard. An air conditioner hummed now and then, a plane on its way from LaGuardia droned overhead, and Lulu would bark at the occasional rabbit hopping across the lawn, though at no time getting up from her sprawl.

I read a fascinating photo essay on Cairene prostitutes in the twenties and thirties and thought it would make a fabulous coffee table book—the sepia photos were exquisitely detailed, and the essay had much to say about paid ladies versus wives, both Muslim and Christian. I was having trouble figuring whose coffee table it would go on, a necessity before I could try to convince the agents I was scouting for to work to get it published. I set my iPad down on the grass and took a nap.

Ruiz called every day with questions and updates, though the updates were pretty much the same: Pete Delaney wasn't talking and his lawyer was insisting I was the attacker and Pete was my victim. I talked this over not only with Ruiz but also with Josh. Both told me what I already knew, that it was a joke of a defense; there was so much evidence proving he was my kidnapper and very nearly my murderer.

Still, when you've spent a fair of time being fixated on someone—as I had been with Pete—then having his lawyer portray you as a crazed woman with a sexual obsession and a vendetta against the man who rejected you is not laughable.

The bureau was making some progress in tying Pete to the Trevor Schwarz killing. Aaron Meadows, the boat rental guy, was now able to pick Pete's picture out from a bunch of photos—which were presumably better than the photo of Pete I'd showed him in Galveston—of middle-aged white guys in the bureau's Houston office. Two days later, they flew him to New York. They presented him with a lineup in the Metropolitan Correctional Center—four guys in wheelchairs. He identified Pete as the one who had been talking about renting a boat from him on the day Trevor Schwarz was killed. At the same time, Houston techs found contact DNA belonging to Pete in Aaron's office at the marina. Pete had used one of a bunch of pens in a can to sign the boat rental contract.

They were also moving along on two other unsolved homicides that the police departments in St. Louis and Sacramento believed might be murders for hire and that occurred on days when Pete told Iris by text that he'd be out of town, so there was digital evidence from her cell phone. Now the bureau was going through the long but necessary reinvestigation of those two killings.

Wynne came over a couple of times that week bearing gifts, from tinted sunblock lip gloss to what must have been an insanely expensive pair of sneakers in a strawberry design; she knew they'd would make me want to leap up and twerk. That wouldn't be for a couple of weeks, because the wound from the donor site—my thigh—was still sore and I was supposed to take it easy.

"The plastic surgeon said I'll always have scars," I told Wynne. "She said she could put something on them, sheets of plasma, silicone. Something I can't remember. That would make the scars look better, but they are still going to be *repulsivo*. Can you see me on a beach in those beige-orange tights under a high cut? If I wear a two-piece, I'll have to roll down the tights, and then it will look like some bizarre fat-dissolving procedure gone wrong."

"Own it," Wynne said. "You got them doing a job for the Federal Bureau of Investigation. To be able to say that? Sublime." That day it was pouring, but by now it had subsided to a fine drizzle, the type free spirits like to walk in. We were on the porch, me on a couch, Wynne in a Dawn-upholstered rocking chair so she wouldn't have to look at it.

"I'd like to see how fast you would own it," I told her. "People will stare into my eyes constantly when they talk to me because they're afraid of looking at my leg, which will make me so uncomfortable that I'll become a recluse."

"Then wear a burqa on the beach," Wynne said. "What's the other long one that's more like a coat?"

"You mean the abaya?" I closed my eyes for a minute. I inhaled a wonderful scent, not suburban country as much as Queens, a combo of mesh from the porch's screens and the ozone that seems to rise from the sidewalk after a hard rain, not that we had a sidewalk.

"That, or I'll tell you what's infinitely better. How about a lamba? It's a sarong women still

520

wear in Madagascar. I did a shoot there when I was still at *Vogue*. We all bought armfuls of them."

She smiled at the memory and also because she was in love again. Visiting me at the hospital, she'd met a doctor in the elevator, an infectious disease specialist, half Jewish, half African American. She admired his white piqué shirt and asked where he'd bought it. He said at Barneys, and they'd taken the elevator to the cafeteria, had fruit salad, and talked. They'd already gone out twice.

"Lambas are charming, and you'd adore them because they come in all sorts of prints on this side of garish, though of course you'd cross over to the other side."

"I wonder if deep down, Josh is going to want to switch sides of the bed, so he can always approach me from the left and not have to look at my right leg. He'd never say it. But trust me, he could come up with some way to make it happen. He's pretty inventive." She did our fourth-grade *Har-har-har.* "I had a garter belt and black stockings thought. That would cover up the scars. But wouldn't that get old fast?"

"You're getting old fast," she said, "which means I am, too."

"Do you ever wonder about the state of your ovaries?" I asked.

"You mean with all those senescent eggs, and

521

that even if I wanted a child, which I'm dubious about, it might be too late?"

"That's what I mean."

"No," Wynne said. "I never think about it."

"You know what I never thought about?" She nodded at me to go ahead but first smoothed her ponytail with one hand and then the other, which meant she was ready to give complete attention. "I never thought I could die," I told her. "I mean, how many people of our age think, *Oh shit, it could come tomorrow.* Not normal death: I mean die by going after Pete. Not that it was a game for me. It was a case. But even though he was a killer, it didn't occur to me that he presented a danger to me."

"I can understand that," Wynne said.

"You can?"

"Sure. He killed for money. He has the emotional range of a sock, or at least that's how it seemed to you and probably most other people. But you were suspicious of him because he reminded you of you."

"True."

"Hiding an aspect of yourself: in your case, that you'd worked on counterterrorism. You were supposed to keep that quiet. But also that you were trained, that you could fight. What you didn't consider is that, along with the fact that part of his life was also not for public consumption, his mind might work like yours. And that somehow he focused on you because he realized you were after him."

"I've been worried about my judgment for the past few days."

She thought for an instant I was being light-hearted but then saw I wasn't. "Tell me what you mean," she said.

"My failure to assess that Pete might be as smart as I am and figure me out. But also, my judgment about my whole life. I got what I always dreamed of. Josh is so intelligent and good-looking and decent. I did want to get married, but I always thought I would settle for a very nice man, someone interesting, someone who enjoyed reading, theater, but he'd have bunions and want me to keep kosher. But Josh is so special."

"Don't forget rich," Wynne said softly, as if she expected a drone with a microphone to come flying over the porch. "Not incredibly wealthy, like some of my clients, but third-generation family money? Sooo good."

"Rich is good," I said just as quietly. "But where are our values?"

"I think my values are as decent as anybody else's," she said. "Though I myself may be a little more superficial than most." She gave a wry grin. "Anyway, you were saying Josh is so special."

"And so is Eliza, though not in the same way. She's special because she's totally genuine and loving. Just an excellent person."

"Right, but she's not fully formed yet. I can't see her turning rotten, but on the other hand, she might not stay the way she is. She might blossom in ways you can't imagine."

"So why aren't I more satisfied?" I asked.

"Because your work doesn't grip you. Patriotism means something to you. So does adventure. Literature? I'm not so sure. And how can you be satisfied stepping into another woman's house and life? Other than your relationships with Eliza and getting Lulu, you haven't created your own bio. Hey, I could be wrong. Who the hell is satisfied anyway?"

"Josh is. He's just like that. He'd be satisfied with me or without me," I told her.

"Corie, Josh's wife dropped dead. All she ever wanted to do besides buying unappealing furniture was to make him happy. Well, maybe deep down she wasn't satisfied but ascribed it to perimenopause or the unfinished basement. But she's dead. Suddenly Josh had to be a single parent, leave his partnership in a high-powered law firm, and drop his exciting cases, because he couldn't put Eliza in his attaché case while he flew to Tokyo for two weeks. How come you think he's content? He did the honorable thing, which is a lot more than most guys would do. He took a lesser job . . . lesser for him. Granted, he's not on an assembly line, and it's prestigious and probably challenging. But Josh is a star and he's doing work he's trained for but not cut out for. I think that's what most of his substance crap is about. He's trying to merge with his work so he's not conflicted. The one thing in his life that changed for the better was you."

# 27

Visitors to the Metropolitan Correctional Center, the federal jail in lower Manhattan, got their hands stamped in blue. (Not that I had become totally self-involved, but I noted the tone was just a little lighter than my eyes.) After the visit, you stuck your hand under a scanner and were free to leave.

I must have appeared slightly edgy or about to pass out as we got off the elevator to go into the Visitors' Center, because Ruiz said, "The stamp doesn't fade. It'll take a couple of days to wash off totally. You'll get out of here." For a guy who had the sleek-haired, square-chinned gravitas of a cable news anchor, he didn't act at all like a smooth dude. I had a becoming-my-mother moment and suppressed the urge to tell him how intuitive he was. Sweet, too, for a guy with too much starch in his white shirts.

"I know," I told him. "There were some weeks I wound up coming over here almost every day."

"Of course. I forgot."

"But thanks for saying something, because I think I have a slight anticonfinement PTSD thing going."

Okay, not so slight. I couldn't close the door

completely when I went to the bathroom, and my first night home from the hospital, Josh turned over and caught me wide awake with the lamp on, bookless. He held me but also suggested a night-light. The next day I bought one, scallop shaped and wide, like the shell Venus stands on in the Botticelli painting. The illumination it gave off was tawdry pink, which comforted me with its fuck-you flamboyance. Still, I was waking up four or five times during the night, panicked for a few seconds until I recognized that the pink light meant I was not in the attic.

Ruiz and I walked through the long, narrow reception, which had a guard desk, a couple of vending machines, and chairs for inmates. One of the guards recognized me and said, "Hey, how you been?" as though I'd only been away on vacation for a couple of weeks.

"Great," I said. "Good seeing you!" I smiled at him, though by the end of the smile I'd spotted Pete Delaney in the room directly behind him.

It was easy because each of the individual visitors' rooms arrayed behind the guard desk had a glass door. Pete's lawyer, a woman in a light gray suit—jacket and skirt—sat beside him so they both were behind a table, facing the door. He was in a wheelchair, she on one of those ugly Bureau of Prisons chairs with curved metal backs and dark-red, fake-leather seats: the cheapest kind of fake that split and exuded blobs of rubbery padding. She was soundlessly reading something on her iPad. One of those white Apple pencils was gripped between her teeth, making her mouth look like a grimace.

Seeing Pete was not at all a surprise since inmates were never allowed to have their backs toward the door. Still, it was heartening that when he spotted Ruiz and me heading toward the room, he quickly put down the paper coffee cup he was drinking from and set his manacled hands on his lap. His smashed-up knee was in some kind of black cast resting on a board that rose from the wheelchair. His good leg was zip-tied at the ankle to a rod just above the chair's footrest.

Ruiz shook hands with his lawyer. "Amanda Gates," she told us. Her hair was gray and black, and so spiked with gel that she could have been wearing a porcupine on her head, though it coordinated nicely with her gray suit. "Can I assume you're Corie Geller?"

"Yes," I said as I took my seat. I nodded politely but didn't offer to shake her hand, though I caught her examining the lacerations around my wrists and arms. Fortunately, they still looked repulsive enough after a week and a half that I'd picked out a short-sleeve cotton sweater for the meeting to show them off. Ruiz and I had already arranged that he'd be across from Pete. Still, there we were, Pete and me, two Long Islanders (each with an escort) across a table from each other, though admittedly it wasn't a Wednesday and the MCC didn't offer the occasional salade aveyronnaise as a special.

"Our position remains the same," Gates said. "Whatever Ms. Geller did or did not suspect Mr. Delaney of, the fact remains that she lured him up to Westchester, promising sexual favors." She paused for an instant, maybe in the hope that I would go the "You've got to be kidding" route, but I said nothing, so she kept going.

"And then she suddenly and brutally attacked him. My client sustained severe injuries. I repeat, severe. We maintain that—"

Other than wearing an inmate's uniform rather than his usual bland shirt and loose pants, Pete didn't look any different from the man who'd attended Wednesday lunch group meetings. His hair was comb marked and precisely parted, his thin line of lips was pale enough to match his complexion, and he calmly looked from his lawyer to Ruiz to me, giving each of us a few seconds of his remote gaze.

"So you've said several times," Ruiz told her. "But solely in the matter of Ms. Geller, who at the time of the kidnapping and assault was employed by the Federal Bureau of Investigation as a contract worker, Delaney is facing federal charges. Many, many counts, but we can save the details. Just as a matter of interest, we have one vehicle he rented along with the keys to the other one. They go nicely with surveillance footage of him"—he made air quotes—" 'in costume' at each of the car rental dealers. In one of the bedrooms of the house we found a wig and a baseball cap like the ones in the footage. His fingerprints and DNA were all over them. We also found Mr. Delaney's right thumb and index finger prints on the undercarriage of the car he burned in the Bronx." Gates opened her mouth, but Ruiz kept talking. "Maybe he ran through the last of his disposable gloves and thought, 'What the hell.' You'll see it all in the discovery material. But right now the plan is not to charge him federally. As of today, the powers that be want to send him to Galveston County, Texas, where he can be charged for murder one under state law."

"As of today, that seems little more than wishful thinking," Gates said. Though her suit was severe, she was wearing an incredibly frilly white shirt with its own ruffled scarf, as if she dreamed of becoming Ruth Bader Ginsburg.

"Again, on the Texas homicide, we have considerable physical evidence along with an eyewitness who identified Delaney not only from photographs but also in a lineup." I noticed Ruiz never looked once at Pete, as if Pete were already well on his way to being a dead man. I'd seen that technique, naturally, but I'd never watched it played out so artfully. "We also have testimony from the man whom he negotiated the hit with. Oh, and information on the bank that transferred money to Delaney's offshore account. All of which pretty much boils down to lethal injection."

"You're FBI," the lawyer said. "While I certainly mean no disrespect, we can wait to discuss these matters with the US attorney."

"Like he's a stranger to us?" Ruiz said. "He wants what we want."

"Justice," Pete said suddenly, with the short *huh* of a cynical chuckle. The three of us looked at him. "Right, Corie?" he asked me.

At first I said nothing, but after that silence I knew what my lines were. I'd run them with Ruiz and an assistant US attorney several times the day before. We had no idea whether having me in the room would upset Pete or not touch him at all: his psyche was beyond us. But my take on it was that while my presence could rile him up (since few men like to recollect getting punched in the nuts and then beaten up by a woman) it could also be—comforting wasn't quite the word. Familiar. I was a little slice of his safe life, part of the Wednesday group. We'd heard that his wife had visited him only twice since he'd been transferred to the MCC from Bellevue, the first time for twenty minutes, the second for ten.

"If you'd rather not go to Texas, enjoy prison comforts there for a year or two, and then go

531

out with that"—Ruiz mimicked pushing down the plunger of a syringe—"you may want to think about the possibility of life in a federal penitentiary."

Gates slammed both hands on the desk in protest of the syringe business, but Pete spoke first. "What kind of deal would I have to make to get some kind of federal sentence?" he asked

"Let me handle this, Mr. Delaney," Amanda Gates warned her client. I didn't like her. She was tough, pissy, but ineffective.

"Pete," I said. "I know how meticulous you are. Of course we will want any records you have, a list of all the people you've killed, disappeared, maimed, whatever—"

"I suggest you shut up," Gates told me. She reached up and straightened a couple of the spikes of her hair.

"And of course the names of the people who hired you to commit the murders. You will have to testify at every single case that we or the locals bring to trial. You'll also have to provide bank and financial records of the money they paid you as well as any recordings you made."

Pete drew back as if I'd accused him of taking three pats out of the butter dish at La Cuisine Délicieuse and leaving none for me. "Do you honestly believe I would record anything of that sort . . . if I was involved in that kind of thing?" he demanded.

Gates turned to him and boomed, "If you want me to continue representing you, I strongly suggest you shut your mouth now."

Before she could boom even louder in my direction, I said to Pete: "Yeah, you'd make recordings. For insurance. And what if you got arthritis in your trigger finger? Packaging design and blackmail. Not as stimulating as doing hits, but still, if you feel you need a second career . . ."

As we had prearranged, Ruiz put his left hand on the table. That meant my part had been played.

I sat in my office, my feet, in socks, propped on the desk, and read the same sentence from a Tunisian police procedural over and over. My mind set up a roadblock to the words I was trying to read. I was distracted, too, which didn't help: the branches of the nearest tree—an oak, I was almost sure—were scratching at the window, just irregularly enough to make my muscles tense as I waited for the next scratch. I half expected it would be louder, wild and harsh, like animal claws. I glanced up and gasped at a figure at the door. I exhaled audibly as Josh moved into the light of an overwrought brass floor lamp.

"Please, don't do that to me," I said, shaking my head. "I don't think I'm done with being unglued."

"I'm sorry," he replied. "I should have been more careful." He took the novel off my lap and sat on the edge of the desk, fiddling mindlessly with the book's jacket. "How is work going?"

I plopped my feet onto the floor and rubbed my eyes. "It's not going at all, really. I can't focus. The only reason I'm sitting near the computer is that I couldn't take the recliner anymore. I have no idea what I'm going to do."

"You'll get back into the swing." His voice was filled with confidence, but then, when was he ever in doubt? He flipped through the pages without really looking at them, which was just as well. He couldn't read Arabic.

"I wish I could be sure I'll be swinging again." Josh looked as if he was about to say something, so I waited a bit. He still seemed to hesitate. Finally, I asked, "What's up?"

"I called Roger," he said, and I could tell I was supposed to know who Roger was.

"Roger?"

"Roger Ackler. You met him. Remember the night we went out to that Greek fish place on Forty-Eighth Street with those judges from Utah?"

I nodded, though my only memory was of being surprised at how much the judge seated next to me had to say about trout, and did I know sea trout was a freshwater fish. "Not ocean fish, like we're eating here." He chuckled mightily at his observation, as did I, several rounds of ha-ha-ha-ha, though I had no idea what was funny. The guy was still on cutthroat trout when the waiter asked if we wanted dessert.

"Roger was the one you sat next to."

"Right. The trout man."

"He's the one who was behind the offer to hear the case in New Orleans." Josh looked up at me, hitting me with the full brilliance of those jade eyes. We hadn't talked about New Orleans since I escaped Pete.

"Okay?" I said, inviting him to say more.

"I turned him down. You need me here."

"Yes," I said. I almost added: *I'm a little afraid to be alone.* But I held back. I didn't know if I wanted to hide that much dependence on him or if by admitting to having that fear, I'd repulse him. He liked my alleged bravery, so he'd wind up buying me a rottweiler, escaping to New Orleans, and then returning with a jumbo jar of seafood boil spice and a three-carat sapphire ring.

"I didn't turn it down because you're still a little shaky." He gave me the trademarked Joshua Geller crooked smile. "I want to do this, be here for you. I'm still young—at least as far as federal judges go. The court of appeals isn't going anywhere."

"Are you sure?" I asked.

"When am I not?" he said, smiling. "Actually? After I called him, I felt relieved."

I took the book, put it on the desk, then took his

hand, weaving our fingers together. "Thank you," I murmured. "And Josh, while we're at it?"

"Hmmm?" *Oh God,* I thought. *He thinks I'm going to say I want three children and four fur coats or vice versa, and it would make him so happy.*

"It's all right with you if I redecorate this room? Even if I get rid of the wallpaper and some of the things that belonged to Dawn?" I'd taken the stand she used for free weights as a bookshelf and couldn't wait to put a rug on her shiny maple gym floor. I gestured widely around the office. "I was thinking. I'd really like to go to work in a place that's more me. I feel funny even saying that, because until you, I lived in apartments where my main concern was whether I could fit an extra chair in my bedroom, not whether my office would fit into some grand aesthetic plan."

"You shouldn't feel funny. It always surprised me you didn't want to make more changes." *Like move,* I was tempted to say, but of course didn't. How can you say that to a guy who just gave up a huge gig in New Orleans? Josh paused, looking around the room. "It's funny," he said. "When I go through the house, I don't even think, 'Oh, Dawn chose this or that.' It's all of a piece. I don't notice anything."

"That's sort of what I was feeling. But these last couple of weeks . . . I want to come in here, see a room that's mine, to notice and value everything that's in it. I don't want to walk around the house not seeing it." I wasn't sure if I was making sense but at least Josh nodded. "Wynne will be ecstatic," he added.

"Until I say, 'I love those blue-and-white Dutch tiles.' And then she'll try not to look sad for me and my congenital lack of taste. Trust me, it will wind up in a major brawl."

"But you're used to that," he said, glancing at my still-bandaged leg.

"What did John Paul Jones say?" Josh knew and seemed ready with the quote. Possibly he was smarter, but he wasn't faster. I told him: " 'I have not yet begun to fight!' "

What had it been, three weeks since I'd been to a Wednesday lunch? Four, tops. Still, when I got to La Cuisine Délicieuse, it seemed both familiar and strange to me, like some restaurant I'd gone to with my parents when I was a kid but hadn't seen since.

Four bistro tables were set outside for summer, two on either side of the door, though I'd seen that for at least two years. Patrons sat there and sipped café crème or apéritifs and watched life go by on Main Street with the same detached curiosity as they would had it been Boulevard Saint-Michel.

Inside looked different, too, and I asked Darby Penn, the photo retoucher, if they'd changed anything. "They repainted the ceiling," he said. "There was a huge leak, but instead of the old sky color with the white cloud blobs . . ." He looked up and so did I. The ceiling was now darkish green, and he said that the only name he could come up for the color was French Bistro Ceiling Green. "Never saw that particular shade anyplace else except in bistros," he said.

"You say that like a guy who's been to a lot of bistros," I said. He nodded and seemed pleased with my observation.

"Do you speak any French?" he asked.

"I've picked up just enough to manage if I exist only in the present tense."

John Grillo, the landscape drainage expert, was next to the last to come in, followed by Lucy Winters, the data miner. Once the waiter took our drink orders—Diet Cokes, Perrier, and iced tea— Iris Kubel pulled her chair an inch closer to the table.

"I know you've been away," she said to me. Her hair was shorter and she was wearing tortoiseshell combs on either side. It gave her the look of a late 1940s starlet, the wholesome girl.

"Right. Cairo for genre fiction symposium. Mysteries, thrillers, science fiction, some romance. I was kind of dreading the whole thing, but it turned out great. And I figured since I was in the neighborhood, I went to Israel for a week. And then I visited the girl, woman, whose family

I stayed with in Jordan one summer during college. Fabulous trip!" Then I added, in case Iris had come to the backyard to replenish the herbs in my pots and spotted me: "I was home last week, but I didn't come because I was so jet-lagged. Beyond incoherent."

None of that was true. Other than going to Shakespeare in the Park with Josh and having dinner out a few times—once with Wynne, once with my parents—I did nothing beyond visit an FBI-approved shrink twice a week, a guy who specialized in post-traumatic stress disorder. Naturally his office was so far west in Manhattan that it practically hung on the New Jersey Palisades, but the bureau wanted its employees and contractors going only to psychologists and psychiatrists who had security clearance.

I asked the doctor how bad I was, since to me a few nightmares here and there, plus losing my appetite when I saw food even though I was hungry, seemed understandable, not a disorder. Admittedly, I hadn't told him about the door business, including bathrooms.

He said I didn't seem that bad. "But aren't you seeing some barriers you'd like to kick out of the way?" I liked that phrase better than "issues you need to deal with," though Ruiz might have noted my interest in martial arts on whatever form he sent in. The shrink was turning out to be helpful, though I had trouble looking at him because he had a voluminous toothbrush mustache. It seemed to move independently of his upper lip, and I was disturbed at not being able to comprehend the mechanics of it.

"How was Cairo?" Marcalynn Schechter the speechwriter asked. Unlike Iris's, her hair had gotten longer and wasn't as sprayed. She was looking less like Alice in Wonderland and more like a star of Republican adult movies.

"Cairoish," I said. "Beautiful, dirty, crowded, exciting. And an oppressive military presence." It was a description anyone who watched PBS might have given.

"I guess you might have heard about—" Iris began.

Phoebe, the eBay queen, cut her off: "Pete Delaney! Did you? Hear about it? He's what they call a contract killer!"

"Hit man," Lucy said.

"I heard," I told them. We all shook our heads in disbelief. Pete was going to plead guilty to federal charges and go off to a maximum security prison in Pennsylvania. Along with Ruiz and my New York supervisor on the task force, I decided not to disclose my role either with the bureau or in Pete's capture. That way, my years in counterterrorism could remain secret. Also, if I kept my name out of the Pete Delaney matter, no neighbor had to worry that I might punch him in the nuts at the drop of a hat.

"My wife knew his wife fairly well," John Grillo was saying. "And liked her. The thing of it was, Pete and I might not have been friends, but we were on good terms. I mean, I'm not Mr. Congeniality, but I can get along with almost everyone. Except there was something about Pete that made me keep my distance. It's like he had no real interest in other people." Across the table, Phoebe leaned forward. Her lips were pursed so forcefully that her normal age lines deepened so they looked like spokes on a wheel. It was taking big-time mouth muscles for her to stay silent. "My wife basically told me she suspected from the way Jenny seemed scared of him that he could be abusive to her," John explained. "But neither of us ever got the idea that he was into something like murder for money. A hit man? I didn't even know he went hunting."

"Maybe because being a New Yorker, he'd think you might have some qualms about it or something?" Iris asked.

"No," John said. "Because I go hunting every fall. I was thinking back and I'm almost sure I talked about it in front of him. But not one word. Not a clue."

"Do you think his wife had any sense about what he was doing?"

John chewed half his bottom lip for a moment, then shook his head. "You know, Peggy and I

541

talked about it when we heard. Well, once we got over the shock. She said, 'If you put Pete and crime in the same sentence, you'd think tax evasion—at worst.' Even if he was terrible to his wife, she was a good person. She would have gone to the police. I don't see her knowing her husband was a killer."

"I've got to admit, I never picked up on anything about him," Darby said. "He was more quiet than not, but not abnormal. He was a guy with a lot of talent. Thoughtful, too. We have an old crabapple tree that was starting to go on tilt. I thought I'd have to pay a tree company to stake it. Anyway, one day Pete brings over his two brothers-in-law and we staked the tree ourselves. I kind of took him aside and asked if I could, you know, offer them something and he said, 'No way. Wouldn't you do it for me?' That was such a nice way to handle it. And I wasn't even friendly with him. I basically just knew him from lunch on Wednesdays."

I asked them if they knew if his wife and children were still around town. Iris said no, that she'd called and offered to visit, but they were moving. When I asked where, the consensus seemed to be somewhere near the South Shore of Nassau County—Rockville Centre, Oceanside.

"I've got to admit I was never a fan. He was kind of odd, but even now I can't tell you what exactly it was. But anyway, his next-door neighbor goes to my church," Iris chimed in. "She said they once had what turned out to be a raccoon family living in their attic. Could not get her husband to go up there and look. Can you imagine the mess? The noise?"

The word "attic" had never been a favorite, but it was at least among sixty or seventy thousand on my neutral list. Now, however, it was loaded. Swallowing? Didn't work. I decided not to order quiche. Fruit and cheese and pass on the cheese. Maybe move the fruit around on a plate.

"Anyway," Iris continued, "I think they did know that Pete went hunting sometimes because they said something about did he know anyone who would be willing to shoot the raccoons because trapping them, like with an exterminator, was close to a thousand dollars! They were hoping that he would offer to do it but felt funny asking him directly. And Pete said, 'Sorry. It's against the law to kill raccoons. I'll be glad to set a have-a-heart trap and take it away once the critters are in there. No problem. I'll check it for you so you don't have to go all the way up there.' Does that not sound like Mr. Nice Guy?" Phoebe was now shaking her head, but it was a private act. Was it what the lunch people were saying, or what was being left unsaid?

"And the soup kitchen," I added.

"That's right," John said. "And he wasn't even a Lutheran."

"There was something a little weird about him," Phoebe finally said. "A lot weird, as a matter of fact. I saw something in Great Neck that I'll never forget!" Darby raised his eyes Godward, as if praying for a lightning bolt, and Lucy stretched toward the breadbasket seeking sustenance. "I was just walking toward Jildor—the shoe place—and I see a Jeep about to park, but . . . !" She placed her right hand over her heart and raised her left to signal, *Let me get my breath.* "A Tesla snuck in and took his space. Sooo aggressive. Right? But then the Jeep guy got out of his car, and it was Pete Delaney! Well, the next thing I knew, he's getting out of his car. He goes over to hers and calls out: 'You're a C-word!' Loud like you wouldn't believe!"

Phoebe definitely had their attention. "But that's just the beginning." Interestingly, no one appeared discouraged. She glanced at me and I gave her a nod that told her she was doing the right thing by telling her story to the group. "And he gouged a deep line from the back of the car all the way to the front. THE ENTIRE SIDE! He must have pressed so hard because it looked like he dented the metal."

"What guy our age would do something like that?" John demanded. "It's so adolescent."

"It's so insane," Marcalynn corrected him.

Phoebe went on. "Wait. I'm not finished. Then he put the key in his other hand and he very casually turned around and did it again, lower down on the door!"

"Jesus!" Darby said, shaking his head.

"Call me crazy, call me dumb," Phoebe said. Everyone kept a straight face. "But it was like he pasted on a personality of a neighborly guy, but it really wasn't him."

"What did you think was underneath?" I asked. I noticed I was rubbing my right wrist and reached for my iced tea. I forgot I couldn't swallow and took a few sips.

"That's the thing. I didn't think he was a terrible person who killed people for God knows how much money. And not somebody who's like broiling inside and could blow up any second. When he keyed the car, he didn't seem angry. Like he was doing something—a necessary job. What struck me is that whatever he was underneath, it wasn't anything."

Everyone seemed to be waiting for Phoebe to continue, but I understood she had finished her analysis. So did Iris, who was nodding. "I think Phoebe's onto something. When I think back, the one thing I really never felt with him was comfortable." She glanced at me, and when I didn't speak, she added: "More like he never cared, even when we were talking together, whether I was there or not. If I'd have disappeared in the middle of a sentence, I doubt if he would've even scratched his head. And maybe that was true with everyone he dealt with." She waved one of her beautifully manicured fingers at the waiter, then hesitated. "It is okay if we order?" she asked the group.

We all said sure, and I wound up asking for mushroom quiche. Then I said: "I had that same feeling as Iris. Not as specific, but just that something wasn't right. Little things like wanting the same chair all the time. Not because he was a creature of habit, which I can understand, but because he seemed fixated on his car. Okay, that's one thing. But there was always a different phone. Always cash, never a credit card. Lots of little nothings can add up. Zero plus zero plus zero equals a big zero. Or it can be one big something."

"He didn't always murder people by shooting," Lucy said. "You should read BuzzFeed. They say that in Atlanta, someone wanted her hus- band—"

Darby put his hands into a T, the time-out sign, and put them right in front of Lucy's face. "Lucy, at the risk of being rude, what you're going to say doesn't go with poached salmon."

"Oh. Sorry. I'll tell the rest of you later." Phoebe and Iris shook their heads. "Well, if anyone wants to know, I'm going to get Gorilla Glue after lunch at the hardware store, so you can keep me company. Meanwhile . . ."

"Meanwhile," Iris told the Wednesday group, "let's all of us get back to normal."

"Absolutely," I agreed. "All of us."

Except maybe me.

# Acknowledgments

Help!
Well, I asked for it and received it. My thanks to the following generous and patient individuals who answered all sorts of questions (though when their facts didn't fit with my fiction, I went with the story). Molly Abramowitz, Nathan Abramowitz, Gini Alhadeff, Bobby Asher, Janice Asher, Cindy Cohen, George Hiltzik, Judith Kelman, Maureen Kennedy, William M. Klein, Fran Lebowitz, Ken Lipper, Mary Shannon Little, Angela Mancini, Megan O'Donnell, B. Aviva Preminger, Robert M. Radick, Monique Sharon, Laura Weinberg, Susan Zises, and Jay Zises.

The following bighearted folks made donations to Long Island charities by bidding to have a character named after them in this novel: John Grillo, Rhonda Jaffee, Jillian King, Iris Kubel, and Marcie Schechter (who asked that I use the name Marcalynn Schechter). I hope they enjoy their other selves. Ginny Glasser, I am looking forward to another tea party and good conversation. And Toni Weiner, sorry I put your name in the wrong folder; you will be in the sequel to *Takes One to Know One*.

I am a woman of several hats and many baseball

caps, and all of them are off to my new publisher, Grove Atlantic, and its imprint, the Atlantic Monthly Press. Their insight, energy, hard work, and courtesy have wowed me. Morgan Entrekin, publisher and editor, enjoyed my novel so much that he bought it—and then told me how to make it better. All his suggestions were superb. I also want to thank Ian Dreiblatt, Chad Felix, Gretchen Mergenthaler, Deb Seager, Sara Vitale, Julia Berner-Tobin, and Brenna McDuffie.

My assistant Ronnie Gavarian has (as always) been a great help.

I am so grateful to my agent, Richard Pine. Besides being savvy (and a great reader!), he is honorable, loyal, and hardworking. I couldn't ask for better.

My children are now adults, benevolent, intelligent, and great readers. Happily, they married people who share these attributes. I want to thank them individually. My son Andy Abramowitz not only answered all my questions about business and corporate law but offered a paean to spreadsheets that delighted me so much I took it, exaggerated it, and put it in the book. My daughter-in-law Leslie Stern made terrific suggestions about what to cut, but also what ought to be added. She was and is a truly creative editor. My good-natured and brilliant son-in-law Vincent Picciuto answered all my questions on consciousness and mental states.

In this book, my daughter Elizabeth Picciuto gets her own paragraph. Not only did she read the novel and give me invaluable ideas for rewriting, she comprehended the structure of the book far better than I. She took in more than the narrative. She got the big picture. Also, Elizabeth understood connections between characters that often I only grasped intuitively. (Her years of teaching philosophy made her a stellar explainer!). My daughter was the greatest asset a writer can have, an honest cheerleader.

And finally, my love and gratitude to my husband, Elkan Abramowitz. Decades ago, when I left my job as an editor at *Seventeen* magazine to stay home and raise our children, his gift to me was an electric typewriter. He supported me at the beginning and has never stopped. Besides being my go-to guy on criminal justice, he is a great cross-examiner of my characters. He also loves reading—a most desirable attribute.

So let me repeat what I have written in the Acknowledgments of every one of my books: Elkan Abramowitz is the best person in the world. It's still true.

| Books are produced in the United States using U.S.-based materials | Books are printed using a revolutionary new process called THINKtech™ that lowers energy usage by 70% and increases overall quality | Books are durable and flexible because of Smyth-sewing | Paper is sourced using environmentally responsible foresting methods and the paper is acid-free |

**Center Point Large Print**
600 Brooks Road / PO Box 1
Thorndike, ME 04986-0001 USA

**(207) 568-3717**

**US & Canada:**
**1 800 929-9108**
**www.centerpointlargeprint.com**